THE
HARSH CRY
OF THE
HERON

RIVERHEAD BOOKS

a member of Penguin Group (USA) Inc.

New York · 2006

THE
HARSH CRY
OF THE
HERON

LIAN HEARN

The Last Tale of the Otori

RIVERHEAD BOOKS
Published by the Penguin Group
Penguin Group (USA) Inc., 375 Hudson Street, New York, New York 10014, USA • Penguin
Group (Canada), 90 Eglinton Avenue East, Suite 700, Toronto, Ontario M4P 2Y3, Canada
(a division of Pearson Penguin Canada Inc.) • Penguin Books Ltd, 80 Strand, London WC2R 0RL,
England • Penguin Ireland, 25 St Stephen's Green, Dublin 2, Ireland (a division of Penguin Books Ltd)
• Penguin Group (Australia), 250 Camberwell Road, Camberwell, Victoria 3124, Australia
(a division of Pearson Australia Group Pty Ltd) • Penguin Books India Pvt Ltd, 11 Community Centre,
Panchsheel Park, New Delhi–110 017, India • Penguin Group (NZ), Cnr Airborne and Rosedale
Roads, Albany, Auckland 1310, New Zealand (a division of Pearson New Zealand Ltd) •
Penguin Books (South Africa) (Pty) Ltd, 24 Sturdee Avenue, Rosebank,
Johannesburg 2196, South Africa

Penguin Books Ltd, Registered Offices:
80 Strand, London WC2R 0RL, England

The author gratefully acknowledges permission to quote from *The Tale of the Heike,* translated by
Helen Craig McCullough. Used by permission of Stanford University Press. Copyright © 1994
by the Board of Trustees of the Leland Stanford Jr. University.

Library of Congress Cataloging-in-Publication Data
Hearn, Lian.
The harsh cry of the heron / by Lian Hearn.
p.   cm.—(Tales of the Otori ; bk. 4)
ISBN 1-59448-923-8
I. Title.
PR9619.3.H3725H37   2006   2006049364
823'.914—dc22

Printed in the United States of America
1   3   5   7   9   10   8   6   4   2

BOOK DESIGN BY CLAIRE VACCARO
CLAN SYMBOL ART BY JACKIE AHER

For J

THE HARSH CRY
OF THE HERON

MAIN CHARACTERS

Otori Takeo: ruler of the Three Countries

Otori Kaede: his wife

Shigeko: their eldest daughter, heir to Maruyama

Maya:

Miki: their twin daughters

Arai Zenko: head of the Arai clan, lord of Kumamoto

Arai Hana: his wife, Kaede's sister

Sunaomi:

Chikara: their sons

Muto Kenji: head of the Muto family and the Tribe

Muto Shizuka: Kenji's niece and successor, mother to Zenko and Taku

Muto Taku: Takeo's spymaster

Sada: a member of the Tribe; Maya's companion
Mai: Sada's sister
Yuki (Yusetsu): Kenji's daughter, Hisao's mother
Muto Yasu: a merchant
Imai Bunta: Shizuka's informant

Dr. Ishida: Shizuka's husband, Takeo's physician

Sugita Hiroshi: senior retainer of Maruyama

Miyoshi Kahei: Takeo's commander in chief, lord of Yamagata
Miyoshi Gemba: Kahei's brother

Sonoda Mitsuru: lord of Inuyama
Ai: his wife, Kaede's sister

Matsuda Shingen: Abbot of the temple at Terayama
Kubo Makoto (later Eikan): his successor, Takeo's closest friend

Minoru: Takeo's scribe

Kuroda Junpei:
                    Takeo's bodyguards
Kuroda Shinsaku:

Terada Fumio: explorer and sea captain

Lord Kono: a nobleman, son of Lord Fujiwara
Saga Hideki: the Emperor's general, lord of the Eastern Isles

Don João: a foreign merchant

Don Carlo: a foreign priest
Madaren: their interpreter

Kikuta Akio: head of the Kikuta family
Kikuta Hisao: his son
Kikuta Gosaburo: Akio's uncle

Horses

Tenba: a black horse given by Shigeko to Takeo

The two sons of Raku, both gray mane with black tail
Ryume: Taku's horse
Keri: Hiroshi's horse

Ashige: Shigeko's gray horse

The sound of the Gion Shoja bells echoes
the impermanence of all things.
The color of the sala flowers reveals the truth
that the prosperous must decline.
The proud do not endure, they are like a dream
on a spring night;
The mighty fall at last, they are
as dust before the wind.

THE TALE OF THE HEIKE
translated by Helen Craig McCullough

THE
HARSH CRY
OF THE
HERON

ome quickly! Father and Mother are fighting!"

Otori Takeo heard his daughter's voice clearly as she called to her sisters from within the residence at Inuyama castle, in the same way he heard all the mingled sounds of the castle and the town beyond. Yet he ignored them, as he ignored the song of the boards of the nightingale floor beneath his feet, concentrating only on his opponent: his wife, Kaede.

They were fighting with wooden poles. He was taller, but she was naturally left-handed and hence as strong with either hand, whereas his right hand had been crippled by a knife cut many years ago and he had had to learn to use his left; nor was this the only injury to slow him.

It was the last day of the year, bitterly cold, the sky pale gray, the winter sun feeble. Often in winter they practiced this way: It warmed the body and kept the joints flexible, and Kaede liked her daughters to see how a woman might fight like a man.

The girls came running. With the new year the eldest, Shigeko, would turn fifteen, the two younger ones thirteen. The boards sang under Shigeko's tread, but the twins stepped lightly in the way of the Tribe. They had run across the nightingale floor since they were infants, and had learned almost unconsciously how to keep it silent.

Kaede's head was covered with a red silk scarf wound around her face, so Takeo could see only her eyes. They were filled with the energy of the fight, and her movements were swift and strong. It was hard to believe she was the mother of three children—she still moved with the strength and freedom of a girl. Her attack made him all too aware of his age and his physical weaknesses. The jar of Kaede's blow on his pole set his hand aching.

"I concede," he said.

"Mother won!" the girls crowed.

Shigeko ran to her mother with a towel. "For the victor," she said, bowing and offering the towel in both hands.

"We must be thankful we are at peace," Kaede said, smiling and wiping her face. "Your father has learned the skills of diplomacy and no longer needs to fight for his life!"

"At least I am warm now!" Takeo said, beckoning to one of the guards, who had been watching from the garden, to take the poles.

"Let us fight you, Father!" Miki, the younger of the twins, pleaded. She went to the edge of the veranda and held her hands out to the man. He was careful not to look at her or touch her as he handed over the pole.

Takeo noticed his reluctance. Even grown men, hardened soldiers, were afraid of the twins—even, he thought with sorrow, their own mother.

"Let me see what Shigeko has learned," he said. "You may each have one bout with her."

For several years his oldest daughter had spent the greater part of the year at Terayama, where under the supervision of the old abbot, Matsuda Shingen, who had been Takeo's teacher, she studied the Way of the Houou. She had arrived at Inuyama the day before, to celebrate the New Year with her family, and her own coming of age. Takeo watched her now as she took the pole he had used and made sure Miki had the lighter one. Physically she was very like her mother, with the same slenderness and apparent fragility, but she had a character all her own, practical, good-humored, and steadfast. The Way of the Houou was rigorous in its discipline, and her teachers made no allowances for her age or sex, yet she accepted the teaching and training, the long days of silence and solitude, with wholehearted eagerness. She had gone to Terayama by her own choice, for the Way of the

Houou was a way of peace, and from childhood she had shared in her father's vision of a peaceful land where violence was never allowed to spread.

Her method of fighting was quite different from the way he had been taught, and he loved to watch her, appreciating how the traditional moves of attack had been turned into self-defense, with the aim of disarming the opponent without hurting him.

"No cheating," Shigeko said to Miki, for the twins had all their father's Tribe skills—even more, he suspected. Now they were turning thirteen these skills were developing rapidly, and though they were forbidden to use them in everyday life, sometimes the temptation to tease their teachers and outwit their servants became too great.

"Why can't I show Father what I have learned?" Miki said, for she had also recently returned from training—in the Tribe village with the Muto family. Her sister Maya would return there after the celebrations. It was rare these days for the whole family to be together—the children's different education, the parents' need to give equal attention to all of the Three Countries meant constant travel and frequent separations. The demands of government were increasing—negotiations with the foreigners; exploration and trade; the maintenance and development of weaponry; the supervision of local districts who organized their own administration; agricultural experiments; the import of foreign craftsmen and new technologies; the tribunals that heard complaints and grievances. Takeo and Kaede shared these burdens equally, she dealing mainly with the West, he with the Middle Country, and both of them jointly with the East, where Kaede's sister Ai and her husband, Sonoda Mitsuru, held the former Tohan domain, including the castle at Inuyama where the family were staying for the winter.

Miki was half a head shorter than her sister, but very strong and quick; Shigeko seemed hardly to move at all in comparison, yet the younger girl could not get past her guard, and within moments Miki had lost her pole. It seemed to fly from her fingers, and as it soared upward Shigeko caught it effortlessly.

"You cheated!" Miki gasped.

"Lord Gemba taught me how to do that," Shigeko said proudly.

The other twin, Maya, tried next with the same effect.

Shigeko said, her cheeks flushed, "Father, let me fight you!"

"Very well," he agreed, for he was impressed by what she had learned and curious to see how it would stand up against the strength of a trained warrior.

He attacked her quickly, with no holding back, and the first bout took her by surprise. His pole touched her chest; he restrained the thrust so it would not hurt her.

"A sword would have killed you," he said.

"Again," she replied calmly, and this time she was ready for him; she moved with effortless speed, evaded two blows and came at his right side where the hand was weaker, gave a little, enough to unsettle his balance, and then twisted her whole body. His pole slipped to the ground.

He heard the twins, and the guards, gasp.

"Well done," he said.

"You weren't really trying," Shigeko said, disappointed.

"Indeed I was trying. Just as much as the first time. Of course, I was already tired out by your mother, as well as being old and unfit!"

"No," Maya cried. "Shigeko beat you fairly!"

"But it is like cheating," Miki said seriously. "How do you do it?"

Shigeko smiled, shaking her head. "It's something you do with thought, and spirit and hand, all together. It took me months to get it. I can't just show you."

"You did very well," Kaede said. "I am proud of you." Her voice was full of love and admiration, as it usually was for her oldest daughter.

The twins glanced at each other.

They are jealous, Takeo thought. *They know she does not have the same strength of feeling for them.* And he felt the familiar rush of protectiveness toward his younger daughters. He always seemed to be trying to keep them from harm—ever since the hour of their birth, when Chiyo had wanted to take the second one, Miki, away and let her die. This was the usual practice with twins in those days, and probably still was in most of the country, for the birth of twins was considered unnatural for human beings, making them seem more like an animal, a cat or a dog.

"It seems cruel to you, Lord Takeo," Chiyo had warned him. "But it is better to act now than to bear the disgrace and ill-fortune that, as the father of twins, people will believe you to be subject to."

"How will people ever give up their superstitions and cruelty unless we show them?" he replied with anger, for in the way of those born into the Hidden he valued the life of a child above all else, and he could not believe that sparing a child's life would be the cause of disapproval or bad luck.

He had been surprised subsequently by the strength of the superstition. Kaede herself was not untouched by it, and her attitude to her younger daughters reflected her uneasy ambivalence. She preferred them to live apart, and most of the year they did, one or the other of them usually with the Tribe; and she had not wanted them both to be present at their older sister's coming of age, fearing that their appearance would bring bad luck to Shigeko. But Shigeko, who was as protective of the twins as her father, had insisted that they both be there. Takeo was glad of it, never happier than when the whole family was together, close to him. He gazed on them all with fondness, and realized the feeling was being taken over by something more passionate: the desire to lie down with his wife and feel her skin against his. The fight with poles had awakened memories of when he had first fallen in love with her, the first time they had sparred against each other in Tsuwano when he was seventeen and she fifteen. It was in Inuyama, almost in this very spot, that they had first lain together, driven by a passion born of desperation and grief. The former residence, Iida Sadamu's castle, had burned when Inuyama fell, but Arai Daiichi had rebuilt it in a similar fashion, and now it was one of the famous Four Cities of the Three Countries.

"The girls should rest before tonight," he said, for there would be lengthy ceremonies at the shrines at midnight, followed by the New Year Feast. They would not go to bed until the Hour of the Tiger. "I will also lie down for a while."

"I will have braziers sent to the room," Kaede said, "and join you in a little while."

THE LIGHT HAD faded by the time she came to him, and the early winter dusk had set in. Despite the braziers, glowing with charcoal, her breath was a cloud of white in the freezing air. She had bathed, and the fragrance of rice bran and aloes from the water clung to her skin. Beneath the quilted winter robe her flesh was warm. He undid her sash and slipped his hands inside the garment, drawing her close to him. Then he loosened the scarf that covered her head and pulled it off, running his hand over the short silky pelt.

"Don't," she said. "It is so ugly." He knew that she had never gotten over the loss of her beautiful long hair, or the scars on the white nape of her neck, that marred the beauty that had once been the subject of legends and superstition, but he did not see the disfigurement, only the increased vulnerability that in his eyes made her more lovely.

"I like it. It is like an actor's. It makes you look like both man and woman, both adult and child."

"Then you must bare your scars to me too." She drew off the silk glove that he habitually wore on his right hand, and brought the stumps of the fingers to her lips. "I hurt you earlier?"

"Not really. Just the residual pain—any blow jars the joints and sets them aching." He added in a low voice, "I am aching now, but for another reason."

"That ache I can heal," she whispered, pulling him to her, opening up to him, taking him inside her, meeting his urgency with her own and then melting with tenderness, loving the familiarity of his skin, his hair, his smell, and the strangeness that each separate act of love brought newly with it.

"You always heal me," he said afterward. "You make me whole."

She lay in his arms, her head on his shoulder. She let her gaze drift around the room. Lamps shone from iron holders, but beyond the shutters the sky was dark.

"Perhaps we have made a son," she said, unable to hide the longing in her voice.

"I hope we have not!" Takeo exclaimed. "Twice my children have nearly cost you your life. We have no need of a son," he went on more lightly. "We have three daughters."

"I once said the same to my father," Kaede confessed. "I believed I should be the equal of any boy."

"Shigeko certainly is," Takeo said. "She will inherit the Three Countries, and her children after her."

"Her children! She seems still a child herself, yet she is nearly old enough to be betrothed. Who will we ever find for her to marry?"

"There is no hurry. She is a prize, a jewel almost beyond price. We will not give her away cheaply."

Kaede returned to her earlier subject as though it gnawed at her. "I long to give you a son."

"Despite your own inheritance and Lady Maruyama's example! You still speak like the daughter of a warrior family."

The dark, the quietness around them led her to voice her concerns further. "Sometimes I think that the twin girls closed my womb. I think that if they had not been born, sons would have come to me."

"You listen to superstitious old women too much!"

"You are probably right. But what will happen to our younger daughters? They can hardly inherit, should anything befall Shigeko, Heaven forbid it. And whom will they marry? No nobleman's or warrior's family will risk accepting a twin, especially one tainted—forgive me—with the blood of the Tribe and those skills so close to sorcery."

Takeo could not deny that the same thought often troubled him, but he tried to put it from him. The girls were still so young—who knew what fate had in store for them?

After a moment Kaede said quietly, "But maybe we are already too old. Everyone wonders why you do not take a second wife, or a concubine, to have more children with."

"I want only one wife," he said seriously. "Whatever emotions I have pretended, whatever roles I have assumed, my love for you is unassumed and true—I will never lie with anyone but you. I have told you, I made a vow to Kannon in Ohama. I have not broken it in sixteen years. I am not going to break it now."

"I think I would die of jealousy," Kaede admitted. "But my feelings are unimportant compared to the needs of the country."

"I believe for us to be united in love is the foundation of our good government. I will never do anything to undermine that," he replied. He pulled her close to him again, running his hands gently over her scarred neck, feeling the hardened ribs of tissue left by the flames. "As long as we are united, our country will remain peaceful and strong."

Kaede spoke half-sleepily. "Do you remember when we parted at Terayama? You gazed into my eyes and I fell asleep. I have never told you this before. I dreamed of the White Goddess: She spoke to me. *Be patient,* she said: *He will come for you.* And again at the Sacred Caves I heard her voice saying the same words. It was the only thing that sustained me during my captivity at Lord Fujiwara's. I learned patience there. I had to learn how to wait, how to do nothing, so he had no excuse to take my life. And afterward, when he was dead, the only place I could think of to go was back to the caves, back to the goddess. If you had not come, I would have stayed there in her service for the rest of my life. And you came: I saw you, so thin, the poison still in you, your beautiful hand ruined. I will never forget that moment: your hand on my neck, the snow falling, the harsh cry of the heron . . ."

"I don't deserve your love," Takeo whispered. "It is the greatest blessing of my life, and I cannot live without you. You know, my life has also been guided by a prophecy . . ."

"You told me. And we have seen it all fulfilled: the Five Battles, Earth's intervention—"

I will tell her the rest now, Takeo thought. *I will tell her why I do not want sons, for the blind seer told me only my son could bring death to me. I will tell her about Yuki, and the child she had, my son, now sixteen years old.*

But he could not bring himself to cause his wife pain. What was the purpose of raking over the past? The Five Battles had entered into the mythology of the Otori, though he was aware that he himself had chosen how to count those battles—they could have been six, or four, or three. Words could be altered and manipulated to mean almost anything. If a prophecy was believed, it often came true. He would not utter the words, in case by so doing he breathed life into them.

He saw that Kaede was nearly asleep. It was warm under the quilts, though the air on his face was freezing. In a little while he must arise, bathe, dress in formal clothes, and prepare himself for the ceremonies that would welcome the New Year. It would be a long night. His limbs began to relax, and he, too, slept.

ll three of Lord Otori's daughters loved the approach to the temple at Inuyama, for it was lined with statues of white dogs, interspersed with stone lanterns where on the nights of the great festivals hundreds of lamps burned, sending flickering lights over the dogs and making them seem alive. The air was cold enough to numb their faces, fingers, and toes, and was filled with smoke and the smell of incense and fresh-cut pine.

Worshippers making the first holy visit of the New Year thronged on the steep steps that led upward to the temple, and from above the great bell was tolling, sending shivers down Shigeko's spine. Her mother was a few paces in front of her, walking next to Muto Shizuka, her favorite companion. Shizuka's husband, Dr. Ishida, was away on one of his trips to the mainland. He was not expected back until spring. Shigeko was glad Shizuka would spend the winter with them, for she was one of the few people the twins respected and heeded; and, Shigeko thought, she in her turn genuinely cared for them and understood them.

The twins walked with Shigeko, one on each side. Every now and then someone in the crowd around them would stare at them before moving away out of reach lest they jostle against them; but mostly, in the half-light, they went unnoticed.

She knew guards accompanied them both in front and behind, and that Shizuka's son, Taku, was in attendance on her father as he performed the ceremonies at the main temple. She was not in the least afraid. She knew Shizuka and her mother were armed with short swords, and she herself had hidden within her robe a very useful stick that Lord Miyoshi Gemba, one of her teachers at Terayama, had shown her how to use to disable a man without killing him. She half-hoped she would have the chance to try it out, but it did not seem likely that they would be attacked in the heart of Inuyama.

Yet there was something about the night and the darkness that put her on her guard: Hadn't her teachers told her frequently that a warrior must always be prepared, so that death, whether one's opponent's or one's own, could be avoided through anticipation?

They came to the main hall of the temple, where she could see her father's figure, dwarfed by the high roof and the huge statues of the lords of Heaven, the guardians of the next world. It was hard to believe the formal person seated so gravely before the altar was the same man she had fought that afternoon on the nightingale floor. She felt a wave of love and reverence for him.

After making their offerings and prayers before the Enlightened One, the women went away to the left and climbed a little higher up the mountain to the temple of Kannon the all-merciful. Here the guards remained outside the gate, for only women were allowed inside the courtyard. Kaede went alone to the feet of the goddess and bowed to the ground before her.

There was a moment of silence as they all followed her example, but as Shigeko knelt on the lowest wooden step before the gleaming statue, Miki touched her older sister on the sleeve. "Shigeko," she whispered. "What's that man doing in here?"

"Where is *here*?"

Miki pointed to the end of the veranda, where a young woman was walking toward them, apparently carrying some gift: She knelt before Kaede and held out the tray.

"Don't touch it!" Shigeko called. "Miki, how many men?"

"Two," Miki cried. "And they have knives!"

In that moment Shigeko saw them. They came out of the air, leaping toward them. She screamed another warning and drew out the stick.

"They are going to kill Mother!" Miki shrieked.

But Kaede was already alerted by Shigeko's first cry. Her sword was in her hand. The girl threw the tray in her face as she pulled out her own weapon, but Shizuka had leaped to Kaede's side, also armed, deflected the first thrust, sent the weapon flying through the air, and turned to face the men. Kaede seized the woman and threw her to the ground, pinioning her.

"Maya, inside the mouth," Shizuka called. "Don't let her take poison."

The woman thrashed and kicked, but Maya and Kaede forced her mouth open and Maya slipped her fingers inside, locating the poison pellet and extracting it.

Shizuka's next blow had cut one of the men, and his blood was streaming over the steps and floor. Shigeko hit the other on the side of the neck, where Gemba had showed her, and as he reeled thrust the stick up between his legs, into his private parts. He doubled up, vomiting from the pain.

"Don't kill them," Shigeko cried to Shizuka, but the wounded man had fled out into the crowd. The guards caught up with him but could not save him from the enraged mob.

Shigeko was not so much shocked by the attack as astonished by its clumsiness, its failure. She had thought assassins would be more deadly, but when the guards came into the courtyard to bind the two survivors with ropes and lead them away, she saw their faces in the lantern light.

"They are young! Not much older than I am!"

The girl's eyes met hers. She would never forget the look of hatred. It was the first time Shigeko had fought seriously against people who wanted her dead. She realized how close she had come to killing, and was both relieved and grateful that she had not taken the life of these two young people, so near to her in age.

hey are Gosaburo's children," Takeo said as soon as he set eyes on them. "I last saw them when they were infants, in Matsue." Their names were written in the genealogies of the Kikuta family, added to the records of the Tribe that Shigeru had gathered before his death. The boy was the second son, Yuzu, the girl Ume. The dead man, Kunio, was the oldest, one of the lads Takeo had trained with.

It was the first day of the year. The prisoners had been brought into his presence in one of the guardrooms within the lowest level of Inuyama castle. They were on their knees before him, their faces pale with cold but impassive. They were tied firmly, arms behind their backs, but he could see that though they were probably hungry and thirsty, they had not been ill treated. Now he had to decide what to do with them.

His initial outrage at the attack on his family had been tempered by the hope that the situation might be turned to his advantage in some way, that this newest failure, after so many others, might finally persuade the Kikuta family, who had sentenced him to death years before, to give up, to make some kind of peace.

I had grown complacent about them, he thought. *I believed myself immune from their attacks: I had not reckoned on them striking at me through my family.*

A new fear seized him as he remembered his words to Kaede the previous day. He did not think he could survive her death, her loss; nor could the country.

"Have they told you anything?" he asked Muto Taku. Taku, now in his twenty-sixth year, was the younger son of Muto Shizuka. His father had been the great warlord, Takeo's ally and rival Arai Daiichi. Taku's older brother, Zenko, had inherited his father's lands in the West, and Takeo would have rewarded Taku in a similar fashion; but the younger man declined, saying he had no desire for land and honors. He preferred to work with his mother's uncle, Kenji, in controlling the network of spies and informants that Takeo had established through the Tribe. He had accepted a political marriage with a Tohan girl, whom he was fond of and who had already given him a son and a daughter. People tended to underestimate him, which suited him. He took after the Muto family in build and looks and the Arai in courage and boldness, and generally seemed to find life an amusing and agreeable experience.

He smiled now as he replied. "Nothing. They refuse to talk. I'm only surprised they're still alive—you know how the Kikuta kill themselves by biting off their tongues! Of course, I have not tried all that hard to persuade them."

"I don't have to remind you that torture is forbidden in the Three Countries."

"Of course not. But does that apply even to the Kikuta?"

"It applies to everyone," Takeo said mildly. "They are guilty of attempted murder and will be executed for that eventually. In the meantime they must not be ill treated. We will see how much their father wants them back."

"Where did they come from?" Sonoda Mitsuru inquired. He was married to Kaede's sister Ai, and though his family, the Akita, had been Arai retainers, he had been persuaded to swear allegiance to the Otori in the general reconciliation after the earthquake. In return, he and Ai had been given the domain of Inuyama. "Where will you find this Gosaburo?"

"In the mountains beyond the Eastern border, I imagine," Taku told him, and Takeo saw the girl's eyes change shape slightly.

Sonoda said, "Then no negotiations will be possible for a while, for the first snow is expected within the week."

"In spring we will write to their father," Takeo replied. "It will do Gosaburo no harm to agonize over his children's fate. It might make him more eager to save them. In the meantime, keep their identity secret and do not allow contact with anyone but yourselves."

He addressed Taku. "Your uncle is in the city, is he not?"

"Yes; he would have joined us at the temple for the New Year celebrations, but his health is not good, and the cold night air brings on coughing spasms."

"I will call on him tomorrow. He is at the old house?"

Taku nodded. "He likes the smell of the brewery. He says the air there is easier to breathe."

"I imagine the wine helps too," Takeo replied.

"**IT IS THE** only pleasure left to me," Muto Kenji said, filling Takeo's cup and then passing the flask to him. "Ishida tells me I should drink less, that alcohol is bad for the lung disease, but . . . it cheers me up and helps me sleep."

Takeo poured the clear, viscous wine into his old teacher's cup. "Ishida tells me to drink less too," he admitted as they both drank deeply. "But for me it dulls the joint pain. And Ishida himself hardly follows his own advice, so why should we?"

"We are two old men," Kenji said, laughing. "Who would have thought, seeing you trying to kill me seventeen years ago in this house, that we would be sitting here comparing ailments?"

"Be thankful we have both survived so far!" Takeo replied. He looked around at the finely built house with its high ceilings, cedar pillars, and cypress-wood verandas and shutters. It was full of memories. "This room is a good deal more comfortable than those wretched closets I was confined in!"

Kenji laughed again. "Only because you kept behaving like some wild animal! The Muto family have always liked luxury. And now the years of peace, the demand for our products have made us very wealthy, thanks to you, my dear Lord Otori." He raised his cup to Takeo; they both drank again, then refilled each other's vessels.

"I suppose I'll be sorry to leave it all. I doubt I'll see another New Year," Kenji admitted. "But you—you know people say you are immortal!"

Takeo laughed. "No one is immortal. Death waits for me as it does for everyone. It is not yet my time."

Kenji was one of the few people who knew everything that Takeo had been told in prophecy, including the part he kept secret: that he was safe from death except at the hands of his own son. All the other predictions had come true, after a fashion: Five Battles had brought peace to the Three Countries, and Takeo ruled from sea to sea. The devastating earthquake that put an end to the last battle and wiped out Arai Daiichi's army could be described as delivering Heaven's desire. And no one so far had been able to kill Takeo, making this last one seem ever more probable.

Takeo shared many secrets with Kenji, who had been his teacher in Hagi, instructing him in the ways of the Tribe. It had been with Kenji's help that Takeo had penetrated Hagi's castle and avenged Shigeru's death. Kenji was a shrewd, cunning man with no sentimentality but more sense of honor than was usual among the Tribe. He had no illusions about human nature and saw the worst in people, discerning behind their noble and high-minded words their self-interest, vanity, folly, and greed. This made him an able envoy and negotiator, and Takeo had come to rely on him. Kenji had no desires of his own beyond his perennial fondness for wine and the women of the pleasure districts. He did not seem to care for possessions, wealth, or status. He had dedicated his life to Takeo and sworn to serve him; he had a particular affection for Lady Otori, whom he admired; great fondness for his own niece, Shizuka; and a certain respect for her son, Taku, the spymaster; but since his daughter's death he had been estranged from his wife, Seiko, who had died herself a few years earlier, and had no close bonds of either love or hatred with anyone else.

Since the death of Arai and the Otori lords sixteen years before, Kenji had worked with slow, intelligent patience toward Takeo's goal: to draw all sources and means of violence into the hands of the government, to curb the power of individual warriors and the lawlessness of bandit groups. It was Kenji who knew of the existence of the old secret societies that Takeo had been unaware of—Loyalty to the Heron, Rage of the White Tiger, Narrow Paths of the Snake—that farmers and villagers had formed among themselves during the years of anarchy. These they now used and built on so the people ruled their own affairs at village level and chose their own leaders to represent them and plead their grievances in provincial tribunals.

The tribunals were administered by the warrior class; their less-military-minded sons, and sometimes daughters, were sent to the great schools in Hagi, Yamagata, and Inuyama to study the ethics of service, accounting and economics, history, and the classics. When they returned to their provinces to take up their posts, they received status and a reasonable income. They were directly answerable to the elders of each clan, for whom the head of the clan was held responsible; these heads met frequently with Takeo and Kaede to discuss policy, set tax rates, and maintain the training and equipment of soldiers. Each had to supply a number of their best men to the central band, half army, half police force, who dealt with bandits and other criminals.

Kenji took to all this administration with skill, saying it was not unlike the ancient hierarchy of the Tribe—and indeed many of the Tribe's networks now came under Takeo's rule, but there were three essential differences: The use of torture was banned, and the crimes of assassination and taking bribes were made punishable by death. This last proved the hardest to enforce among the Tribe, and with their usual cunning they found ways to circumvent it, but they did not dare deal in large sums of money or flaunt their wealth, and as Takeo's determination to eradicate corruption became harder and more clearly understood even this small-scale bribery dwindled. Another practice took its place, since men are only human: that of exchanging gifts of beauty and taste, of hidden value, which in turn led to the encouragement of craftsmen and artists, who flocked to the Three

Countries not only from the Eight Islands but from the countries of the mainland, Silla, Shin, and Tenjiku.

After the earthquake ended the civil war in the Three Countries, the heads of the surviving families and clans met in Inuyama and accepted Otori Takeo as their leader and overlord. All blood feuds against him or against each other were declared over, and there were many moving scenes as warriors were reconciled to each other after decades of enmity. But both Takeo and Kenji knew that warriors were born to fight—the problem was, against whom were they now to fight? And if they were not fighting, how were they to be kept occupied?

Some maintained the borders on the East, but there was little action and their main enemy was boredom; some accompanied Terada Fumio and Dr. Ishida on their voyages of exploration, protecting the merchants' ships at sea and their shops and godowns in distant ports; some pursued the challenges Takeo established in swordsmanship and archery, competing in single combat with each other; and some were chosen to follow the supreme path of combat: the mastery of self, the Way of the Houou.

Based at the temple at Terayama, the spiritual center of the Three Countries, and led by the ancient abbot, Matsuda Shingen, and Kubo Makoto, this was a mountain sect, an esoteric religion whose discipline and teachings could be followed only by men—and women—of great physical and mental strength. The talents of the Tribe were innate—the powerful vision and hearing, invisibility, the use of the second self—but most men had within them untapped abilities, and the discovery and refinement of these were the work of the sect, who called themselves the Way of the Houou after the sacred bird that dwelt deep in the forests around Terayama.

The first vow these chosen warriors had to make was to kill no living thing, neither mosquito nor moth nor man, even to defend their own life. Kenji thought it madness, recalling all too clearly the many times he had thrust knife into artery or heart, had twisted the garrote, had slipped poison into a cup or bowl or even into an open sleeping mouth. How many? He had lost count. He did not feel remorse for those he had dispatched into the next life—all men had to die sooner or later—but he recognized the courage it took to face the world unarmed, and saw that the decision not to kill might be far harder than the decision to kill. He was not immune to the peace and spiritual strength of Terayama. Lately his greatest pleasure was to accompany Takeo there and spend time with Matsuda and Makoto.

The end of his own life, he knew, was approaching. He was old; his health and strength were deteriorating—for months now he had been troubled by a weakness in the lungs and frequently spat blood.

So Takeo had tamed both Tribe and warriors: Only the Kikuta resisted him, not only attempting to assassinate him but also making frequent attacks from across the borders, seeking alliances with dissatisfied warriors, committing random murders in the hope of destabilizing the community, spreading unfounded rumors.

Takeo spoke again, more seriously. "This latest attack has alarmed me more than any other, because it was against my family, not myself. If my wife or my children were to die, it would destroy me, and the Three Countries."

"I imagine that is the Kikuta's aim," Kenji said mildly.

"Will they ever give up?"

"Akio never will. His hatred of you will end only in his death—or yours. He has devoted his entire adult life to it, after all." Kenji's face became still and his lips twisted into a bitter expression. He drank again. "But Gosaburo is a merchant, and pragmatic by nature. He must resent losing the house in Matsue and his trade, and he will dread losing his children— one son dead, the other two in your hands. We may be able to put some pressure on him."

"That was what I thought. We will keep the two survivors until spring, and then see if their father is prepared to negotiate."

"We'll probably be able to extract some useful information from them in the meantime," Kenji grunted.

Takeo looked up at him over the rim of the cup.

"All right, all right, forget I said it," the old man grumbled. "But you're a fool not to use the same methods your enemies use." He shook his head.

"I'll wager you're still saving moths from candles too. That softness has never been eradicated."

Takeo smiled slightly but did not otherwise react. It was hard to grow out of what he had once been taught as a child. His upbringing among the Hidden had made him deeply reluctant to take human life. But from the age of sixteen he had been led by fate into the way of the warrior. He had become the heir to a great clan and was now leader of the Three Countries; he had had to learn the way of the sword. Moreover, the Tribe, Kenji himself, had taught him to kill in many different ways and had tried to extinguish his natural compassion. In his struggle to avenge Shigeru's death and unite the Three Countries in peace he had committed countless acts of violence, many of which he deeply regretted, before he had learned to bring ruthlessness and compassion into balance, before the wealth and stability of the countries and the rule of law gave desirable alternatives to the blind power conflicts of the clans.

"I'd like to see the boy again," Kenji said abruptly. "It might be my last chance." He looked at Takeo closely. "Have you come to any decision about him?"

Takeo shook his head. "Only to make no decision. What can I do? Presumably the Muto family—you yourself—would like to have him back?"

"Of course. But Akio told my wife, who was in contact with him before her death, that he would kill the boy himself rather than give him up, either to the Muto or to you."

"Poor lad. What kind of an upbringing can he have had!" Takeo exclaimed.

"Well, the way the Tribe raise their children is harsh at the best of times," Kenji replied.

"Does he know I am his father?"

"That's one of the things I can find out."

"You are not well enough for such a mission," Takeo said reluctantly, for he could think of no one else to send.

Kenji grinned. "My ill health is another reason why I should go. If I'm not going to see the year out anyway, you may as well get some use out of me! And besides, I want to see my grandson before I die. I'll go when the thaw comes."

Wine, regrets, and memories had filled Takeo with emotion. He reached out and embraced his old teacher.

"Now, now!" Kenji said, patting him on the shoulder. "You know how I hate displays of sentiment. Come and see me often through the winter. We will still have a few good drinking bouts together."

he boy, Hisao, now sixteen years old, looked like his dead grandmother. He did not resemble the man he believed to be his father, Kikuta Akio, nor his true father, whom he had never seen. He had none of the physical traits of either the Muto family of his mother or the Kikuta—and, it was becoming increasingly obvious, none of their magical talents, either. His hearing was no more acute than that of anyone of his age; he could neither use invisibility nor perceive it. His training since childhood had made him physically strong and agile, but he could not leap and fly like his father, and the only way he put people to sleep was through sheer boredom in his company, for he rarely talked, and when he did it was in a slow, stumbling fashion, with no spark of wit or originality.

Akio was the Master of the Kikuta, the greatest family of the Tribe, who had retained the skills and talents that once all men had possessed. Now even among the Tribe those skills seemed to be disappearing. Hisao had been aware since early childhood of the disappointment he had caused his father—he had felt all his life the careful scrutiny of his every action, the hopes, the anger, and always, in the end, the punishment.

For the Tribe raised their children in the harshest possible way, training them in complete obedience, in endurance of extremes of hunger, thirst, heat, cold, and pain, eradicating any signs of human feeling, of sympathy and compassion. Akio was hardest on his own son, Hisao, his only child, never in public showing him any understanding or affection, treating him with a cruelty that surprised even his own relatives. But Akio was the Master of the family, successor to his uncle, Kotaro, who had been murdered in Hagi by Otori Takeo and Muto Kenji at the time when the Muto family had broken all the ancient bonds of the Tribe, had betrayed their own kin and become servants of the Otori. And as Master, Akio could act as he chose; no one could criticize or disobey him.

Akio had grown into a bitter and unpredictable man, eaten up by the grief and losses of his life, the blame for all of which lay with Otori Takeo, now the ruler of the Three Countries. It was Otori Takeo's fault that the Tribe had split, that the legendary and beloved Kotaro had died, and the great wrestler Hajime and many others, and that the Kikuta were persecuted to the extent that most of them had left the Three Countries and moved north, leaving behind their lucrative businesses and money-lending activities to be taken over by the Muto, who actually paid tax like any ordinary merchant and contributed to the wealth that made the Three Countries a prosperous and cheerful state where there was little work for spies, apart from those Takeo himself employed, or assassins.

Kikuta children slept with their feet toward the West, and greeted each other with the words "Is Otori dead yet?" replying, "Not yet, but it will soon be done."

It was said that Akio had loved his wife, Muto Yuki, desperately, and that her death, as well as Kotaro's, was the cause of all his bitterness. It was assumed that she had died of fever after childbirth—fathers often unfairly blamed the child for the loss of a beloved wife, though this was the only weaker human emotion Akio ever displayed. It seemed to Hisao that he had always known the truth: His mother had died because she had been given poison. He could see the scene clearly, as though he had witnessed it with his own unfocused baby eyes. The woman's despair and anger, her grief at leaving her child; the man's implacable command as he brought about the death of the only woman he had ever loved; her defiance as she gulped down the pellets of aconite; the uncontrollable wave of regret, shrieking, and sobbing, for she was only twenty years old and leaving her life long before she was ready; the shuddering pains that racked her; the man's grim satisfaction that revenge was partially completed; his embracing of his own pain, and the dark pleasure it gave him, the beginning of his descent into evil.

Hisao felt that he had grown up knowing these things; yet he had forgotten how he had learned them. Had he dreamed them, or had someone told him? He remembered his mother more clearly than should have been possible—he had been only days old when she died—and was aware of a presence at the edge of his conscious mind that he connected with her. Often he felt she wanted something from him, but he was afraid of listening to her demands, for that would mean opening himself up to the world of the dead. Between the ghost's anger and his own reluctance, his head seemed to split apart in pain.

So he knew his mother's fury and his father's pain, and it made him both hate Akio and pity him, and the pity made it all easier to bear: not only the abuse and punishment of the day, but the tears and caresses of the night, the dark things that happened between them that he half-dreaded, half-welcomed, for then was the only time anyone embraced him or seemed to need him.

Hisao told no one of how the dead woman called to him, so no one knew of this one Tribe gift that he had inherited, one that had lain dormant for many generations since the days of the ancient shamans who passed between the worlds, mediating between the living and the dead. Then, such a gift would have been nurtured and honed and its possessor feared and respected, but Hisao was generally despised and looked down upon. He did not know how to tune his gift; the visions from the world of the dead were hazy and hard to understand. He did not know the esoteric imagery used to communicate with the dead, or their secret language—there was none living who could teach him.

He only knew the ghost was his mother, and she had been murdered.

He liked making things, and he was fond of animals, though he learned to keep this secret, for once he had allowed himself to pet a cat only to see his father cut the yowling, scratching creature's throat before his eyes. The cat's spirit also seemed to enmesh him in its world from time to time, and the frenzied yowling would grow in intensity in his ears until he could not believe no one else could hear it. When the other worlds opened to include him, it made his head ache terribly, and one side of his vision would darken. The only thing that stilled the pain and noise, and distracted him from the cat, the woman, was making things with his hands. He fashioned water wheels and deer scarers from bamboo in the same way as his unknown great-grandfather, as though the knowledge had been passed down in his blood. He could carve animals from wood so lifelike it seemed they had been captured by magic, and he was fascinated by all aspects of forging: the making of iron and steel, swords, knives, and tools.

The Kikuta family had many skills in forging weapons, especially the secret ones of the Tribe—throwing knives of various shapes, needles, tiny daggers, and so on—but they did not know how to make the weapon called a firearm that the Otori used and so jealously guarded. The family were in fact divided over its desirability, some claiming that it took all the skill and pleasure out of assassination, that it would not last, that traditional methods were more reliable; others that without it the Kikuta family would decline and disappear, for even invisibility was no protection against a bullet, and that the Kikuta, like all those who desired to overthrow the Otori, had to match them weapon for weapon.

But all their efforts to obtain firearms had failed. The Otori confined their use to one small body of men: Every firearm in the country was accounted for. If one was lost, its owner paid with his life. They were rarely used in battle: only once, with devastating effect, against an attempt by barbarians to set up a trading post with the help of former pirates on one of the small islands off the southern coast. Since that time, all barbarians were searched on arrival, their weapons confiscated and they themselves confined to the trading port of Hofu. But the reports of the carnage had proved as effective as the weapons themselves: All their enemies, including the Kikuta, treated the Otori with increased respect and left them temporarily in peace while making secret efforts to gain firearms themselves by theft, treachery, or their own invention.

The Otori weapons were long and cumbersome: quite impractical for the secret assassination methods on which the Kikuta prided themselves. They could not be concealed or drawn and used rapidly; rain rendered them useless. Hisao listened to his father and the older men talking about these things, and imagined a small, light weapon, as powerful as a firearm, that could be carried within the breast of a garment and would make no sound, a weapon that even Otori Takeo would be powerless against.

Every year some young man who thought himself invincible, or an older one who wanted to end his life with honor, set out for one or another of the cities of the Three Countries, lay in wait on the road for Otori Takeo or crept stealthily at night into the residence or castle where he slept, hoping to be the one who would end the life of the murderous traitor and avenge Kikuta Kotaro and all the other members of the Tribe put to death by the Otori. They never returned. The news came months later of their capture, so-called trial before Otori's tribunals, and execution— for assassination attempted or achieved was one of the few crimes, along with other forms of murder, taking bribes, and losing or selling firearms, punishable now by death.

At times Otori was reported wounded and their hopes rose, but he always recovered, even from poison, as he had recovered from Kotaro's poisoned blade, until even the Kikuta began to believe that he was immortal, as the common people said, and Akio's hatred and bitterness grew, and his love of cruelty increased. He began to look more widely for ways to destroy Otori, to try to make alliance with Takeo's other enemies, to strike at him through his wife or his children. But this, too, proved almost impossible. The treacherous Muto family had split the Tribe and sworn loyalty to the Otori, taking the lesser families, Imai, Kuroda, and Kudo, with them. Since the Tribe families intermarried, many of the traitors also had Kikuta blood, among them Muto Shizuka and her sons, Taku and Zenko. Taku, like his mother and his great-uncle, had many talents, headed Otori's spy network, and kept constant guard over his family. Zenko, less talented, was allied to Otori through marriage: they were brothers-in-law.

Recently Akio's cousin Gosaburo's two sons had been sent with their sister to Inuyama, where the Otori family had celebrated the New Year. They had mingled among the crowds at the shrine and had attempted to stab Lady Otori and her daughters in front of the goddess herself. What had followed was unclear, but it appeared the women had defended themselves with unexpected fierceness. One of the young men, Gosaburo's eldest son, was wounded and then beaten to death by the crowd. The others were captured and taken to Inuyama castle. No one knew if they were dead or alive.

The loss of three young people, so closely related to the Master, was a terrible blow. As the snow melted with the approach of spring, opening the roads once more, no news came of them, and the Kikuta feared they were dead. They began to make arrangements for funeral rites to be held, mourning all the more that there were no bodies to burn and no ashes.

One afternoon, when the trees were shining with the green and silver of their new leaves and the flooded fields were alive with cranes and herons and the croaking of frogs, Hisao was working alone in a small terraced field, deep in the mountain. During the long winter nights he had been brooding on an idea that had occurred to him the previous year, when he had seen the crops—beans and pumpkins—in this field wither and die. The fields below were watered from a fast flowing stream, but this one was viable only in years of great rainfall. Yet in all other ways it held promise, facing south, sheltered from the strongest winds. He wanted to make the water flow uphill, using a water wheel in the stream's channel to turn a series of smaller wheels that would raise buckets. He had spent the winter making the buckets and the ropes; the buckets were fashioned from the lightest bamboo and the ropes strengthened with iron-vine that would make them rigid enough to carry the buckets uphill yet much lighter and easier to use than metal rods or bars.

He was concentrating deeply on the task, working in his patient, unhurried way, when the frogs suddenly fell silent, making him look around. He could see no one, yet he knew there was someone there, using invisibility in the manner of the Tribe.

He thought it was one of the children, come with some message, and called out, "Who's there?"

The air shimmered in the way that always made him feel slightly sick, and a man of indeterminate age and unremarkable looks stood before him. Hisao's hand went immediately to his knife, for he was certain he had never seen the man before, but he had no chance to use it. The man's outline rippled as he vanished. Hisao felt the invisible fingers close over his wrist and an immediate paralysis in his muscles as his hand opened and the knife fell.

"I'm not going to hurt you," the stranger said, and spoke his name in a way that made Hisao believe him, and his mother's world washed over the edge of his; he felt her joy and pain and the first intimation of his headache and half-vision.

"Who are you?" he whispered, knowing at once that this man was someone his mother had known.

"Can you see me?" the man replied.

"No. I can't use invisibility, or perceive it."

"But you heard me approach?"

"Only from the frogs. I listen to them. But I cannot hear from afar. I don't know anyone who can do that among the Kikuta now."

He heard his own voice say these things and marveled that he who was normally so reticent should speak so freely to a stranger.

The man came back into sight, his face barely a hand's breadth from Hisao's, his eyes intent and searching.

"You don't look like anyone I know," he said. "And you have no Tribe skills?"

Hisao nodded, then looked away across the valley.

"But you are Kikuta Hisao, Akio's son?"

"Yes, and my mother's name was Muto Yuki."

The man's face changed slightly, and he felt his mother's response of regret and pity.

"I thought so. In that case, I am your grandfather, Muto Kenji."

Hisao absorbed this information in silence. His head ached more fiercely: Muto Kenji was a traitor, hated by the Kikuta almost as much as

Otori Takeo, but his mother's presence was swamping him and he could feel her voice calling, "Father!"

"What is it?" Kenji said.

"Nothing. My head hurts sometimes. I'm used to it. Why have you come here? You will be killed. I should kill you, but you say you are my grandfather, and anyway I am not very good at it." He glanced down at his construction. "I would rather make things."

HOW STRANGE, the old man was thinking. *He has no skills, either from his father or his mother.* Both disappointment and relief swept through him. *Who does he take after? Not the Kikuta, or the Muto, or the Otori. He must be like Takeo's mother, the woman who died the day Shigeru saved Takeo's life, with that dark skin and broad features.*

Kenji looked with pity at the boy in front of him, knowing how hard a Tribe childhood was, especially on those of little talent. Hisao obviously had some skills; the contraption was both inventive and adroitly executed, and there was something else about him, some fleeting look in his eyes that suggested he saw other things. What did he see? And the headaches—what did they indicate? He looked a healthy young man, a little shorter than Kenji himself, but strong, with a mostly unblemished skin and thick, glossy hair not unlike Takeo's.

"Let's go and find Akio," Kenji said. "I have certain things to say to him."

He did not bother dissembling his features as he followed the boy down the mountain path toward the village. He knew he would be recognized—who else could have gotten this far, evading the guards on the pass, moving unseen and unheard through the forest?—and anyway Akio needed to know who he was, that he came from Takeo with an offer of truce.

The walk left him breathless, and when he paused on the edge of the flooded fields to cough he tasted the salt blood in his throat. He was hotter than he should be, though the air was still warm, the light turning golden as the sun descended in the west. The dikes between the fields were brightly colored with wildflowers, vetch, buttercups, and daisies, and the light filtered through the new green leaves of the trees. The air was full of the music of spring, of birds, frogs, and cicadas.

If it is to be the last day of my life, it could not be more beautiful, the old man thought with a kind of gratitude, and felt with his tongue for the capsule of aconite tucked neatly into the space left by a missing molar.

He had not known of this particular place before Hisao's birth, sixteen years before—and then it had taken him five years to find it—but since then he had visited it from time to time, unknown to any of its inhabitants, and had also had reports on Hisao from Taku, his great-nephew. It was like most of the Tribe villages, hidden in a valley like a narrow fold in the mountain range, almost inaccessible, guarded and fortified in many different ways. He had been surprised on his first visit by the number of inhabitants, well over two hundred, and had subsequently found out that the Kikuta family had been retreating here ever since Takeo began his persecution of them in the West. As he had uncovered their hiding places within the Three Countries, they had gone north, making this isolated village their headquarters, beyond the reach of Takeo's warriors, though not of his spies.

HISAO DID NOT speak to anyone as they walked between the low wooden houses, and though several dogs bounded eagerly toward him he did not stop to pat them. By the time they reached the largest building, a small crowd had formed behind them; Kenji could hear the whispering and knew he had been recognized.

The house was far more comfortable and luxurious than the dwellings around it, with a veranda of cypress boards and strong pillars of cedar. Like the shrine, which he could just see in the distance, its roof was made of thin shingles, with a gentle curve as pleasing as that of any warrior's country mansion. Stepping out of his sandals, Hisao went up onto the veranda and called into the interior. "Father! We have a visitor!"

Within moments a young woman appeared, bringing water to wash the visitor's feet. The crowd behind Kenji fell silent. As he stepped inside the house, he thought he heard a sound like a sudden intake of air, as though all those gathered outside had gasped as one. His chest ached sharply and he felt the urge to cough. How weak his body had become! Once he could demand anything from it. He remembered with regret all the skills he had had; they were a shadow of what they had been. He longed to leave his body behind like a husk and move into the next world, the next life, whatever lay beyond. If he could somehow save the boy . . . but who can save anyone from the journey that fate maps out at birth?

All these thoughts flashed through his mind as he settled himself on the matted floor and waited for Akio. The room was dim; he could barely make out the scroll that hung on the wall to his right. The same young woman came with a bowl of tea. Hisao had disappeared, but he could hear him talking quietly in the back of the house. A smell of sesame oil floated from the kitchen and he heard the quick sizzling of food in the pan. Then there came the tread of feet; the interior door slid open and Kikuta Akio stepped into the room, followed by two older men, one somewhat plump and soft-looking whom Kenji knew to be Gosaburo the merchant from Matsue, Kotaro's younger brother, Akio's uncle. The other he thought must be Imai Kazuo, who he had been told had gone against the Imai family to stay with the Kikuta, his wife's relatives. All these men, he knew, had sought his life for years.

Now they tried to hide their astonishment at his appearance among them. They sat at the other end of the room, facing him, studying him. No one bowed or exchanged greetings. Kenji said nothing.

Finally Akio said, "Put your weapons in front of you."

"I have no weapons," Kenji replied. "I have come on a mission of peace."

Gosaburo gave a sharp laugh of disbelief. The other two men smiled, but without mirth.

"Yes, like the wolf in winter," Akio said. "Kazuo will search you."

Kazuo approached him warily and with a certain embarrassment. "Forgive me, Master," he mumbled. Kenji allowed the man to feel his clothes with the long deft fingers that could slip a man's weapon from his breast without him noticing a thing.

"He speaks the truth. He is unarmed."

"Why have you come here?" Akio exclaimed. "I can't believe you are so tired of life!"

Kenji gazed at him. For years he had dreamed of confronting this man who had been married to his daughter and deeply implicated in her death. Akio was approaching forty; his face was furrowed, his hair graying. Yet the muscles were still iron hard beneath his robe; age had neither softened nor gentled him.

"I come with a message from Lord Otori," Kenji said calmly.

"We do not call him Lord Otori here. He is known as Otori the Dog. He can send no message that we will ever listen to!"

"I am afraid one of your sons died," Kenji addressed Gosaburo. "The oldest, Kunio. But the other lives, and your daughter too."

Gosaburo swallowed. "Let him speak," he said to Akio.

"We will never make deals with the Dog," Akio replied.

"Yet even to send a messenger suggests a weakness," Gosaburo pleaded. "He is appealing to us. We should at least hear what Muto has to say. We may learn from it." He leaned forward slightly and questioned Kenji. "My daughter? She was not hurt?"

"No, she is well." *But my daughter has been dead for sixteen years.*

"She has not been tortured?"

"You must know torture is banned in the Three Countries. Your children will face the tribunal for attempted assassination, for which the punishment is death, but they have not been tortured. You must have heard that Lord Otori has a compassionate nature."

"This is another of the Dog's lies," Akio scoffed. "Leave us, uncle. Your grief weakens you. I will speak with Muto alone."

"The young people will remain alive if you agree to a truce," Kenji replied swiftly, before Gosaburo could get to his feet.

"Akio!" Gosaburo begged his nephew, tears beginning to burst from his eyes.

"Leave us!" Akio also stood, enraged, pushing the old man toward the door, bundling him out of the room.

"Truly," he said as he sat down again. "This old fool is useless to us! Now he has lost his shop and his business, he does nothing but mope all day. Let Otori kill the children, and I'll kill the father—we will be rid of a nuisance and a weakling."

"Akio," Kenji said. "I speak to you as one Master to another, in the way that affairs of the Tribe have always been settled. Let us talk clearly with each other. Listen to what I have to say. Then make your decision on what is best for the Kikuta family and the Tribe, not on your own hatred and rage, for these will destroy them and you. Let us remember the history of the Tribe, how we have survived since ancient times. We have always worked with great warlords—let us not work against Otori. Because what he is doing in the Three Countries is good—it is approved by the people, farmers and warriors. His society is working—it is stable; it flourishes; people are content; no one starves to death and no one is tortured. Give up your blood feud against him. In return the Kikuta will be pardoned and the Tribe will be united again. We will all benefit."

His voice had taken on a mesmeric lilting quality that stilled the room and silenced those outside. Kenji was aware that Hisao had returned and was kneeling just beyond the door. When he stopped speaking, he summoned up his will and let the waves from it flow out into the room. He felt calm descend over them all. He sat with his eyes half-closed.

"You old sorcerer." Akio broke the silence with a shout of rage. "You old fox. You can't trap me with your stories and your lies. You say the Dog's work is good! People are content! When have these things ever concerned the Tribe? You have gone as soft as Gosaburo. What's happening to all you old men? Is the Tribe decaying from the inside? If only Kotaro had lived! But the Dog killed him—he killed the head of his family, to whom his life was already forfeit. You were witness to it—you heard the vow he made in Inuyama. He broke that oath. He deserved to die for it. But he murdered

Kotaro, the Master of his family, instead—with your help. He is beyond any pardon or any truce. He must die!"

"I will not argue with you about the rights or wrongs of his action," Kenji replied. "He did what seemed best at the time, and surely his life has been better lived as one of the Otori rather than as Kikuta. But all that is past. I could appeal to you to give up your campaign against him so the Kikuta can return to the Three Countries—Gosaburo can have his business back!—and enjoy life as we all do now, but these simple pleasures apparently mean nothing to you. I will only say to you, give up—you will never succeed in killing him."

"All men can die," Akio replied.

"But he will not die at *your* hands," Kenji said. "However much you desire it, I can assure you of that."

Akio was gazing at him with narrowed eyes. "Your life is also forfeit to the Kikuta. Your betrayal of the Tribe must also be punished."

"I am preserving my family and the Tribe. It is you who will destroy it. I came here without weapons as an envoy; I will return in the same way and take your regrettable message back to Lord Otori."

Such was the power he commanded that Akio allowed him to stand and walk from the room. As he passed Hisao still kneeling outside, Kenji said, turning back, "This is the son? He has no Tribe skills, I believe. Let him accompany me to the gate. Come, Hisao." He spoke back into the shadows. "You know where to find us if you change your mind."

Well, he thought as he stepped from the veranda and the crowd parted to allow him through, *it seems I am to live a little longer after all!* For once he was in the open and beyond Akio's gaze he knew he could go invisible and disappear into the countryside. But was there any chance of taking the boy with him?

Akio's rejection of the offer of a truce did not surprise him. But he was glad Gosaburo and the others had heard it. Apart from the main house, the village looked impoverished. Life would be hard here, especially during the bitter winter. Many of the inhabitants must hanker, like Gosaburo, after the comforts of life in Matsue and Inuyama. Akio's leadership, he felt, was based less on respect than on fear; it was quite possible that the other members of the Kikuta family would oppose his decision, especially if it meant the lives of the hostages would be spared.

As Hisao came up from behind and walked beside him, Kenji was aware of some other presence that occupied half of the boy's sight and mind. He was frowning, and from time to time he raised his hand to his left temple and pressed it with his fingertips.

"Is your head hurting?"

"Mmm." He nodded without speaking.

They were halfway down the street. If they could make it to the edge of the fields, and run along the dike to the bamboo groves . . .

"Hisao," Kenji whispered. "I want you to come back to Inuyama with me. Meet me where we met before. Will you do that?"

"I cannot leave here! I cannot leave my father!" Then he gave a sharp exclamation of pain, and stumbled.

Just another fifty paces. Kenji did not dare turn round, but he could hear no one following him. He continued to walk calmly, unhurriedly, but Hisao was lagging behind.

When Kenji turned to encourage him, he saw the crowd still staring after him, and then suddenly pushing between them, Akio, followed by Kazuo—both had drawn knives.

"Hisao, meet me," he said, and slid into invisibility, but even as his shape disappeared Hisao caught at his arm and cried, "Take me with you! They'll never let me! But she wants me to go with you!"

Maybe it was because he was invisible and between the worlds, maybe it was the intensity of the boy's emotion, but in that moment he saw what Hisao saw . . .

His daughter, Yuki. Sixteen years dead . . .

And realized with astonishment what the boy was.

A ghostmaster.

He had never encountered one; he knew of them only from the chronicles of the Tribe. Hisao himself did not know, nor did Akio. Akio must never know.

No wonder the lad had headaches. He wanted to laugh. He wanted to cry.

Kenji could still feel Hisao's grip on his arm as he looked into his daughter's spirit face, seeing her as he did in his memories, as child, adolescent, young woman, all her energy and life present but attenuated and faint. He saw her lips move and heard her say, "Father," though she had not called him that since she was ten years old.

She bewitched him now as she had then.

"Yuki," he said helplessly, and let visibility return.

IT PROVED EASY for Akio and Kazuo to seize him. None of his talents in invisibility or using the second self could save him from them.

"He knows how to get at Otori," Akio declared. "We will extract it from him, and then Hisao must kill him."

But the old man had already bitten into the poison and ingested it; the same ingredients that his daughter had been forced to swallow. He died in the same way, in agony, full of regrets that his mission had failed and that he was leaving his grandson behind. In his last moments he prayed that he might be allowed to stay with his daughter's spirit, that Hisao would use his powers to keep him. *What a powerful ghost I might be,* he thought, and the idea made him laugh, as did the realization that life with all its pain and joy was over. But he had walked his path to its end, his work in this world was completed, and he died by his own choice. His spirit was freed to move into the eternal cycle of birth, death, and rebirth.

·5·

inter in Inuyama was long and severe, though it brought many pleasures of its own—during the time spent inside Kaede read poetry and old tales aloud to her daughters, and Takeo spent long hours overseeing the records of administration with Sonoda, and for relaxation studied painting with an artist of the black-ink style and drank with Kenji in the evenings. The girls were occupied with studying and training, and there were the diversions of the Bean Festival, a noisy and cheerful occasion in which demons were driven out of doors into the snow and good luck welcomed in, and Shigeko's coming of age, for the New Year had seen her turn fifteen. The celebration was not lavish, for in the tenth month she was to receive the domain of Maruyama, which was inherited through the female line and had passed to her mother, Kaede, after the death of Maruyama Naomi.

It seemed that Shigeko would eventually be the ruler of the Three Countries, and her parents agreed that she should take over the Maruyama lands this year, now that she was an adult, establishing herself there as a ruler in her own right and learning firsthand the principles of government. The ceremony in Maruyama would be both solemn and splendid, confirming an ancient tradition and, Takeo hoped, establishing a new precedent; that women might inherit land and property and run their households or become heads of villages, equally with their brothers.

The cold weather and the confinement indoors sometimes frayed nerves and weakened health, but at even the bleakest time the days were lengthening as the sun returned, and in the bitterest cold the plum trees put out their fragile white blossom.

Takeo could never forget, however, that while his closest family was shielded from cold and boredom through the long winter months, other relatives of his, two young people not much older than his daughters, were held in captivity deep within Inuyama castle. They were far better treated than they had expected to be, but they were prisoners, and faced death unless the Kikuta accepted the offer of a truce.

After the snows melted and Kenji had departed on his mission, Kaede and her daughters left with Shizuka for Hagi. Takeo had noticed his wife's growing discomfort with the twins and thought Shizuka might take one of them, Maya perhaps, to the hidden Muto village Kagemura for a few weeks. He himself delayed leaving Inuyama, hoping to hear from Kenji within the month, but when the new moon of the fourth month came and there was still no news, he set out somewhat reluctantly for Hofu, leaving instructions with Taku to bring any message to him there.

Throughout his rule he had journeyed in this way, dividing the year between the cities of the Three Countries, sometimes traveling with all the splendor expected of a great lord, sometimes taking on one of the many disguises he had learned in the Tribe, mingling with ordinary people and learning from their own mouths their opinions, their joys and grievances. He had never forgotten the words that Otori Shigeru had spoken once to him: *It is because the Emperor is so weak that warlords like Iida flourish.* The Emperor ruled in name over the entire country of the Eight Islands, but in practice the various parts took care of their own affairs—the Three Countries had suffered conflict for years as warlords strove for lands and power, but Takeo and Kaede had brought peace and maintained it by constant attention to every aspect of the land and the lives of its people.

He could see the effects of this now as he rode toward the West, accompanied by retainers, two trusted bodyguards from the Tribe—the cousins Kuroda Junpei and Shinsaku, known always as Jun and Shin—and his scribe. Throughout the journey he noticed all the signs of a peaceful and well-governed country: healthy children, prosperous villages, few beggars, and no bandits. He had his own anxieties—for Kenji, for his wife and daughters—but he was reassured by all he saw. His aim was to make the country so secure that a girl child could rule it, and when he arrived in Hofu he was able to reflect with pride and satisfaction that this was what the Three Countries had become.

He had not foreseen what awaited him in the port city, nor had he suspected that by the end of his stay there his confidence would be shaken and his rule threatened.

IT SEEMED THAT as soon as he arrived in any one of the cities of the Three Countries delegations appeared at the gates of the castle or palace where he was staying, seeking audiences, asking for favors, requiring decisions that only he could make. Some of these could in fact be passed on to the local officials, but occasionally complaints were made against these officials themselves, and then impartial arbitrators had to be supplied from among his retinue. This spring in Hofu there were three or four of these cases, more than Takeo would have liked, and it made him question the fairness of the local administration; furthermore, two farmers had complained that their sons had been forcibly conscripted, and a merchant divulged that soldiers had been commandeering large amounts of charcoal, wood, sulphur, and niter. *Zenko is building up forces and weapons*, he thought. *I must speak to him about it.*

He made arrangements to send messengers to Kumamoto. The next day, however, Arai Zenko, who had been given his father's former lands in the West and also controlled Hofu, came himself from Kumamoto, ostensibly to welcome Lord Otori but, as it soon became obvious, with other motives. His wife, Shirakawa Hana, the youngest sister of Takeo's wife, Kaede, came with him. Hana was very like her older sister, even held by some to be more beautiful than Kaede in her youth, before the earthquake

and the fire. Takeo neither liked nor trusted her. In the difficult year following the birth of the twins, when Hana turned fourteen, she had fancied
herself in love with her sister's husband, and had constantly sought to seduce him into taking her as second wife or concubine, she did not care
which. Hana was more of a temptation than Takeo cared to admit, looking just like Kaede when he first fell in love with her, before her beauty was
marred, and offering herself at a time when his wife's ill health kept him
from her. His steady refusal to take her seriously had wounded and humil-
iated her; his wish to marry her to Zenko had outraged her. But he had
insisted—it seemed to deal with two problems at once, and they had been
married when Zenko was eighteen and Hana sixteen. Zenko was more
than happy—the alliance was a great honor to him; Hana was not only
beautiful, she quickly produced three sons, all healthy children, and furthermore, though she never professed to be in love with him, she was interested in him and ambitious for him. Her infatuation with Takeo soon
melted away, to be replaced by a rancor against him and jealousy of her sister, and a deep desire that she and her husband should take their place.

Takeo was aware of this desire—his sister-in-law revealed more of herself than she thought, and besides, like everyone, the Arai often forgot how
acute his hearing was. It was no longer as sharp as when he was seventeen,
but it was still good enough to overhear conversations that others thought
secret, to be aware of everything around him, of where each person of the
household was, of the activities of the men in the guardroom and stables,
of who visited whom at night and for what purpose. He had also acquired
a watchfulness that enabled him to read the intentions of others in their
stance and the movements of their body, to the extent that people said he
could see clearly into men's hidden hearts.

Now he studied Hana as she bowed deeply before him, her hair
spilling to the floor, parting slightly to reveal the perfect white of her nape.
She moved with an easy grace, despite being the mother of three children—
you would not think her more than eighteen years, but she was the same
age as Zenko's younger brother, Taku—twenty-six.

Her husband, at twenty-eight, looked very like his father: large, power-fully built, with great strength, an expert with both the bow and the sword. At twelve he had seen his father die, shot by a firearm before his eyes, only the third person in the Three Countries to die in that manner. The other two had been bandits, and Zenko had witnessed their death too. Arai had died in the same moment when he had broken his oath of alliance with Takeo. Takeo knew these things taken together had produced a deep re-sentment in the young boy, which had turned over the years to hatred.

Neither husband nor wife gave any sign of their malevolence. Indeed, their welcomes and inquiries after his health and that of his family were ef-fusive. Takeo replied equally cordially, masking the fact that he was in more pain than usual from the damp weather and repressing the desire to remove the silk glove that covered his right hand to massage the scar where his fin-gers used to be.

"You should not have gone to so much trouble," he said. "I will only be in Hofu for a day or two."

"Oh, but Lord Takeo must stay longer." Hana spoke, as she often did, before her husband. "You must stay until the rains are over. You cannot travel in this weather."

"I have traveled in worse," Takeo said, smiling.

"It is no trouble at all," Zenko said. "It is our greatest pleasure to be able to spend time with our brother-in-law."

"Well, there are one or two things we need to discuss," Takeo replied, deciding to take the blunt approach. "There can be no need, surely, of in-creased numbers of men under arms, and I'd like to know more about what you are forging."

His directness, coming as it did right after the courtesies, startled them. He smiled again. They must surely know little escaped his notice throughout the Three Countries.

"There is always a need for weapons," Zenko said. "Glaives, spears and so on."

"How many men can you muster? Five thousand at the most. Our records show them all fully equipped. If their weapons have been lost or damaged, it is their responsibility to replace them at their own expense. The domain's finances can be better employed."

"From Kumamoto and the southern districts, yes, five thousand. But there are many untrained men of fighting age in other Seishuu domains. It seemed an ideal opportunity to give them training and weapons, even if they return to their fields for the harvest."

"The Seishuu families answer to Maruyama now," Takeo replied mildly. "What does Sugita Hiroshi think of your plans?"

Hiroshi and Zenko disliked each other. Takeo knew Hiroshi had harbored a boyish desire to marry Hana himself, had formed an illusory picture of her based on his devotion to Kaede, and had been disappointed when the Arai marriage was arranged, though he never spoke of it. But the two young men had never liked each other since they first met so many years ago in the turbulent period of civil war. Hiroshi and Taku, Zenko's younger brother, were close friends despite their differences, far closer than the two Arai brothers, who had grown cold to each other over the years, though again they never spoke of it, masking the distance between them with a feigned and mutually beneficial conviviality usually fueled by wine.

"I have not had the opportunity to speak to Sugita," Zenko admitted.

"Well, we will discuss it with him. We will all meet in Maruyama in the tenth month and review military requirements in the West then."

"We face threats from the barbarians," Zenko said. "The West lies open to them—the Seishuu have never had to face attack from the sea before. We are totally unprepared."

"The foreigners seek trade above all," Takeo replied. "They are far from home; their vessels are small. They learned their lesson in the attack on Mijima; they will deal with us through diplomacy now. Our best defense against them is to trade peacefully with them."

"Yet they boast when they talk of their king's great armies," Hana said. "One hundred thousand men at arms. Fifty thousand horses. One of their horses is bigger than two of ours, they say, and all their foot soldiers carry firearms."

"These are, as you say, boasts," Takeo observed. "I daresay Terada Fumio makes similar claims about our superiority in the islands of the South and ports of Tenjiku and Shin." He saw Zenko's expression darken at the mention of Fumio's name, and recalled that it had been Fumio who had killed Zenko's father, shooting him in the chest at the moment the earth shook and Arai's army was destroyed. He sighed inwardly, wondering if it was ever possible to wipe the desire for revenge from a man's heart, knowing that Fumio may have held the weapon but Zenko put the blame on him.

Zenko said, "There, too, the barbarians use trade as an excuse to get a foothold in a country. Then they weaken it from within with their religion, and attack from without with superior weapons. They will turn us all into their slaves."

Zenko could be right, Takeo thought. The foreigners were mainly confined to Hofu, and Zenko saw more of them than any other of his warriors. Which in itself was dangerous—even though he called them barbarians, Zenko was impressed by their weapons and ships. If they should join together in the West . . .

"You know I respect your opinions on these matters," he replied. "We will increase our surveillance of the foreigners. If there is any need to conscript more men, I will inform you. And niter must only be bought directly by the clan."

He gazed at Zenko as the younger man bowed reluctantly, a line of color at his neck the only sign of his resentment at the rebuke. Takeo was thinking of the time when he had held Zenko across his horse's neck, the knife at his throat. If he had used it then, he would have no doubt saved himself many troubles. But Zenko had been a child of twelve years; Takeo had never killed a child and prayed he never would. *Zenko is part of my fate,* he thought. *I must handle him carefully. What more can I do to flatter him and tame him?*

Hana spoke in her gentle honeyed voice. "We would do nothing without consulting Lord Otori. We have only the interests of you and your family and the welfare of the Three Countries at heart. Your family are all well, I trust? My oldest sister, your beautiful daughters?"

"I thank you; they are all well."

"It is a great sorrow to me to have no daughters," Hana went on, her eyes demurely lowered. "We have only sons, as Lord Otori knows."

Where is she going with this? Takeo wondered.

Zenko had less subtlety than his wife and spoke more bluntly.

"Lord Otori must long for a son."

Ah! Takeo thought, and said, "Since a third of our country is already inherited through the female line, it does not present a problem to me. Our oldest daughter will be the eventual ruler of the Three Countries."

"But you should know the joy of having boys in the household," Hana exclaimed. "Let us give you one of ours."

"We would like you to adopt one of our sons," Zenko said, direct and affable.

"It would honor us and bring us joy beyond words," Hana murmured.

"You are extremely generous and thoughtful," Takeo replied. The truth was he did not want sons. He was relieved Kaede had had no more children and hoped she would not conceive again. The prophecy that he would die at the hands of his own child did not frighten him, but it saddened him deeply. He prayed at that moment, as he often did, that his death would be like that of Shigeru, not like that of the other Otori lord, Masahiro, whose throat had been cut with a fishing knife by his illegitimate son; and that he would be spared until his work was finished and his daughter old enough to rule his country. He wondered what truly lay behind Zenko and Hana's offer. He did not want to insult them by rejecting it outright. Indeed, it had much to recommend it. It would be entirely appropriate to adopt his wife's nephew; he could even perhaps betroth the child to one of his daughters one day.

"Please do us the honor of receiving our two oldest boys," Hana said, and when he nodded in assent, she rose and moved toward the door, with her gliding walk so like Kaede's. She returned with the children—they were aged eight and six, dressed in formal robes, silenced by the solemnity of the gathering. They both wore their hair long in front.

"The oldest is Sunaomi, the younger Chikara," Hana said as the boys bowed to the ground before their uncle.

"Yes, I remember," Takeo said. He had not seen them for at least three years, and had never seen Hana's youngest child, born the previous year and presumably now in the care of his nurse. They were fine-looking children—the older one resembled the Shirakawa sisters, with the same long limbs and slender bone structure. The younger one was rounder and stockier, more like his father. He wondered if either of them had inherited any of the Muto Tribe skills from their grandmother, Shizuka. He would ask Taku or Shizuka. It would be pleasant, he mused, for Shizuka, too, to have a grandson to bring up along with his own daughters, to whom she was like a second mother, both companion and teacher.

"Sit up, boys," he said. "Let your uncle see your faces."

He was taken with the older boy, who looked so like Kaede. He was only seven years younger than Shigeko, five years younger than Maya and Miki—not an impossible age difference in marriage. He questioned them about their studies, their progress with sword and bow, their ponies, and was pleased with the intelligence and clarity of their replies. Whatever their parents' secret ambitions and hidden motives might be, the boys had been well brought up.

"You are very generous," he said again. "I will discuss it with my wife."

"The children will join us for the evening meal," Hana said. "You may get to know them better then. Of course, though he is nothing out of the ordinary, Sunaomi is already a great favorite with my older sister."

Takeo remembered now that he had heard Kaede praise the boy for his intelligence and quickness. He knew that she envied Hana and regretted never having a son. Adopting her nephew might be a compensation, but if Sunaomi became his son . . .

He put this line of thought from him. He must follow what seemed the best policy—he must not allow himself to be influenced by a prophecy that might never come true.

Hana left with the children, and Zenko said, "I can only repeat what an honor it would be if you were to adopt Sunaomi—or Chikara—you must choose."

"We will discuss it again in the tenth month."

"May I make one more request?"

When Takeo nodded, Zenko went on. "I don't want to cause offense by bringing up the past, but—you remember Lord Fujiwara?"

"Of course," Takeo replied, holding down his surprise and anger. Lord Fujiwara was the nobleman who had abducted his wife, and had brought about his heaviest defeat. He had died in the great earthquake, but Takeo had never forgiven him, hating even to hear his name spoken. Kaede had sworn to him that this spurious husband had never lain with her, yet there had been some strange bond between them. Fujiwara had intrigued and flattered her; she had entered into a pact with him and had told him the most intimate secrets of Takeo's love for her. He had supported her household with money and food and given her many gifts. He had married her with the permission of the Emperor himself. Fujiwara had tried to take Kaede into death with him—she had narrowly escaped being burned alive when her hair burst into flames, causing the scars, the loss of her beauty.

"His son is in Hofu and seeks an audience with you."

Takeo said nothing, reluctant to admit that he did not know it.

"He goes under his mother's name, Kono. He came by boat a few days ago, hoping to meet you. We have been in correspondence over his father's estate. My father was, as you know, on very good terms with his father—forgive me for reminding you of those unpleasant times—and Lord Kono approached me about matters of rent and taxes."

"I was under the impression the estate had been joined to Shirakawa."

"But legally Shirakawa was also Lord Fujiwara's, after his marriage, and so is now his son's. For Shirakawa is male-inherited. If it is not Kono's to claim, it should pass to the next male heir."

"Your oldest son, Sunaomi," Takeo said.

Zenko bowed his head without speaking.

"It is sixteen years since his father's death. Why does he suddenly appear now?" Takeo questioned.

"Time passes swiftly in the capital," Zenko said. "In the divine presence of the Emperor."

Or perhaps some scheming person, you or your wife—almost certainly your wife—seeing how Kono could be used to put more pressure on me, wrote to him, Takeo thought, concealing his fury.

The rain strengthened on the roof, and the smell of wet earth floated in from the garden.

"He may come and see me tomorrow," he said finally.

"Yes. It is a wise decision," Zenko replied. "It is too wet to travel, anyway."

THIS MEETING ADDED to Takeo's unease, reminding him of how closely the Arai needed to be watched; how easily their ambitions could lead the Three Countries back into civil war. The evening passed pleasantly enough—he drank sufficient wine to mask the pain temporarily, and the boys were lively and entertaining. They had recently met two of the foreigners in the same room and were full of excitement about the encounter—how Sunaomi had spoken to them in their own language, which he had been studying with his mother; how they had looked like goblins with their long noses and bushy beards, one red-haired, the other black, but Chikara had not been afraid at all. They called to the servants to bring in one of the chairs that had been fashioned for the foreigners from an exotic wood, teak, transported from the great trading port known as Fragrant Harbor in the holds of the Terada treasure ships that also brought jasper bowls, lapis lazuli, tiger skins, ivory, and jade to the cities of the Three Countries.

"So uncomfortable," Sunaomi said, demonstrating.

"Like the Emperor's throne, though," Hana said, laughing.

"But they did not eat with their hands!" Chikara said, disappointed. "I wanted to see that."

"They are learning good manners from our people," Hana told him. "They are making great efforts, just as Lord João makes efforts to learn our language."

Takeo could not prevent a slight shiver at the sound of the name, so like that of the outcaste Jo-An, whose death had been the most regretted act of his life, whose words and appearance often came to him in dreams. The foreigners held beliefs similar to the Hidden and prayed to the Secret God, yet they did so openly, often causing great distress and embarrassment to others. They displayed the secret sign, the cross, on prayer beads worn around their necks on the breast of their strange uncomfortable-looking clothes. Even on the hottest days they wore tight-fitting garments with high collars and boots, and they had an unnatural horror of bathing.

The persecution of the Hidden was supposedly a thing of the past, though it was impossible to remove people's prejudices by law. Jo-An himself had become something of a deity, sometimes confused with one or other of the manifestations of the Enlightened One—his help was invoked in matters of conscription and other work-related levies and duties; he was worshipped by the very poor, the destitute, and the homeless in a way that would horrify him as heresy. Few knew who he had been or remembered the details of his life, but his name had become attached to the laws that governed taxation and conscription. No landowner was permitted to take more than thirty parts in a hundred from any resource, be it rice, beans, or oil, and military service was not demanded of farmers' sons, though a certain amount of public work was, to drain land, build dikes and bridges, and excavate canals. Mining was also a source of conscription; the work was so hard and dangerous few volunteered for it; but all forms of conscription were rotated through districts and age groups so no one bore an unfair burden, and various levels of compensation were set in place for death or accident. These were known as the Jo-An Laws.

The foreigners were eager to talk about their religion, and Takeo had cautiously arranged meetings with Makoto and other religious leaders, but these had ended in the usual way, with both sides convinced of the truth of their own position, wondering privately how anyone could believe the nonsense their opponents did. The beliefs of the foreigners, Takeo thought, came from the same source as those of the Hidden but had accrued centuries of superstition and distortion. He himself had been raised in the tradition of the Hidden but had abandoned all the teachings of his childhood and viewed all religions with a certain amount of suspicion and skepticism, particularly the foreigners' brand, for it seemed to him to be linked with their greed for wealth, status, and power.

The one belief that occupied his thoughts greatly—that it is forbidden to kill—did not appear to be shared by them, as they came fully armed with long thin swords, daggers, cutlasses, and of course firearms, though they took pains to conceal these just as the Otori hid the fact that they already possessed them. Takeo had been taught as a child that it was a sin to take life, even to defend yourself, yet now he ruled in a land of warriors, the legitimacy of his rule based on conquest in battle and control by force. He had lost count of how many he himself had killed or had had executed. The Three Countries were at peace now—the terrible slaughter of the years of war lay far in the past. Takeo and Kaede held in their own hands all resources for the violence necessary for defense or punishment of criminals—they held their warriors in check and gave men outlets for ambition and aggression. And many warriors now followed the lead of Makoto, putting aside their bows and their swords, taking the vow never to kill again.

One day I will do the same, Takeo thought. *But not yet. Not yet.*

He drew his attention back to the gathering, seeing Zenko and Hana at their best, with their children, and made a silent vow to solve whatever problems arose without bloodshed.

he pain returned in the early hours of the morning, waking him with its insistency. He called to the maid to bring tea, the warmth from the bowl momentarily soothing his crippled hand. It was still raining, the air inside the residence stifling and humid. Sleep was impossible. He sent the maid to wake his scribe and the appropriate official and bring lamps, and when the men came sat outside on the veranda with them and examined such records of Shirakawa and Fujiwara as existed in the center of the administrative district and port, discussing details and questioning discrepancies until the sky began to pale and the first tentative birdsong sounded from the garden. He had always had a good memory, strongly visual and retentive; with training over the years it had become prodigious. Since the fight with Kotaro, when he lost two fingers from his right hand, he dictated much to scribes, and this also increased the power of memory. And like his adopted father, Shigeru, he had come to love and respect records—the way everything could be noted and retained; the way they supported and corrected memory.

This particular young man accompanied him most of the time lately; one of the many boys orphaned by the earthquake, he had found refuge at Terayama and had been educated there; his quick intelligence and skill with the brush had been recognized, as well as his diligence—he was one of those who study by the light of fireflies and the reflection of snow, as the saying goes—and he had eventually been chosen by Makoto to go to Hagi and join Lord Otori's household.

He was of a silent nature, and did not care for alcohol, seeming on the surface to have rather a dull personality, yet he possessed a fine vein of sarcastic wit when alone with Takeo, was not impressed by anyone or anything, treated everyone with the same considerate deference, noting all their weaknesses and vanities with clarity and a certain detached compassion. His name was Minoru, which amused Takeo because he had carried that name for a brief time in what seemed now like another life.

His writing was swift and beautiful.

Both estates had been severely damaged by the earthquake, the country mansions destroyed by fire. Shirakawa had been rebuilt and his other sister-in-law, Ai, frequently visited for long periods of the year with her daughters. Her husband, Sonoda Mitsuru occasionally accompanied her, but his duties kept him mostly in Inuyama. Ai was practical and hardworking and had profited from her sister's example. Shirakawa had recovered from the mismanagement and neglect of their father and was flourishing, giving high returns in rice, mulberries, persimmons, silk, and paper. Fujiwara's estate had been administered by Shirakawa; fundamentally it was richer and it was also now showing a fair profit. Takeo felt a certain reluctance to hand it back to Fujiwara's son, even if he was the legal owner. As it was now, its profitability fed back into the economy of the Three Countries. He suspected Kono would want to take what he could, exploit the land for all it was worth, and spend the results in the capital.

When it was fully light, he bathed and had a barber pluck and trim his hair and beard. He ate a little rice and soup and then dressed in formal clothes for the meeting with Fujiwara's son, finding little pleasure in the soft feel of the silk and the restrained elegance of the patterns—the pale mauve wisteria blossom on the deep purple background of the under robe and the more abstract weave of the outer.

The servant placed a small black hat on his head, and Takeo took the sword, Jato, from the elaborate carved stand where it had rested all night and hung it from his sash, thinking of all the disguises he had seen it in, starting with the shabby black sharkskin that had wrapped its hilt when, in Shigeru's hand, it had saved his life. Now both hilt and scabbard were richly decorated and Jato had not tasted blood for many years. He wondered if he would ever unsheath the blade again in battle, and how he would manage with his damaged right hand.

He crossed the garden from the east wing to the main hall of the mansion. The rain had stopped, but the garden was drenched and the wisteria flowers hung heavy with moisture, their fragrance mingling with that of the wet grass, the tang of salt from the port, and all the rich smells of the town. Beyond the walls he could hear the thud of shutters as the town awoke, and the distant cries of the morning street sellers.

Servants glided noiselessly before him, sliding open the doors, their feet soft on the gleaming floors. Minoru, who had gone to eat his own breakfast and dress, joined him silently, bowing deeply and then following a few paces behind him. A servant at his side carried the lacquered writing desk, paper, brushes, inkstone, and water.

Zenko was already in the main hall, dressed formally like Takeo but more richly, gold thread gleaming at collar and sash. Takeo nodded to him, acknowledging his bow, and handed Jato to Minoru, who placed the sword carefully in an even more ornately carved stand to the side. Zenko's sword already rested in a similar stand. Takeo then sat at the head of the room, glancing round at the decorations, the screens, wondering how it would look to Kono after the Emperor's court. The residence was not as large or as imposing as those in Hagi or Inuyama, and he regretted he was not receiving the nobleman there. *He will get the wrong impression of us: He will think we are unrefined and unsophisticated. Is it best that he should think so?*

Zenko spoke briefly about the previous night. Takeo expressed his approval of the boys and praised them. Minoru prepared the ink at the small writing table and then sat back on his heels, eyes cast down as if he were meditating. Rain began to fall softly.

A short time later they heard the sounds that heralded a visitor, the barking of dogs and the heavy tread of palanquin bearers. Zenko rose and went to the veranda. Takeo heard him greet their guest, and then Kono stepped into the room.

There was the slightest moment of awkwardness when it was apparent neither of them considered they should be the first to bow; Kono raised his eyebrows in a minute movement and then bowed, but with a kind of mannered affectation that drained the gesture of any respect. Takeo waited for the space of a breath, and then returned the greeting.

"Lord Kono," he said quietly. "You do me a great honor."

As Kono sat up, Takeo studied his face. He had never seen the man's father, but that had not prevented Fujiwara from haunting his dreams. Now he gave his old enemy his son's face, the high forehead, the sculpted mouth, not knowing that Kono did indeed resemble his father in some ways, though by no means in all.

"Lord Otori does me the honor," Kono replied, and though the words were gracious Takeo knew that the intention was not. He saw at once that there was little chance of frank discussions. The meeting would be difficult and tense, and he would need to be astute, skillful, and forceful. He tried to compose himself, fighting tiredness and pain.

They began by talking about the estate, Zenko explaining what he knew of its condition, Kono expressing a desire to visit it for himself, a request which Takeo granted without argument, for he felt that Kono had little real interest in it and no intention of ever living there; that his claim on the land could probably be dealt with quite simply by recognizing him as the absent landlord and remitting a certain amount to him in the capital—not the full taxation but a percentage of it. The estate was an excuse for Kono's visit, a perfectly plausible one. Kono had come with some other motive, but after over an hour had passed and they were still discussing rice yields and labor requirements Takeo began to wonder if he was ever going to hear what it was. However, shortly afterward a guard appeared at the door with a message for Lord Arai. Zenko made profuse apologies and said he would be forced to leave them for a while but would join them for the midday meal.

His departure left them in silence. Minoru finished noting what had been said thus far and laid down his brush.

Kono said, "I have to speak of a somewhat delicate matter. It may be best if I talk to Lord Otori alone."

Takeo raised his eyebrows and replied, "My scribe will remain." He gestured to the rest of the attendants to leave the room.

When they had gone, Kono did not speak for a while. When he did, his voice was warmer and his manner less artificial.

"I want Lord Otori to know that I am merely an envoy. I have no animosity toward you. I know little of the history of our two families—the unfortunate situation with Lady Shirakawa—but my father's actions often distressed my mother while she was alive and myself. I cannot believe that he was entirely without fault."

Without fault? Takeo thought. *All the fault lay with him: my wife's suffering and disfigurement, the murder of Amano Tenzo, the senseless slaying of my first horse, Raku, all those who died at the battle of Kusahara and in the retreat.* He said nothing.

Kono went on, "Lord Otori's fame has spread throughout the Eight Islands. The Emperor himself has heard of it. His Divine Majesty and his Court admire the way you have brought peace to the Three Countries."

"I am flattered by their interest."

"It is unfortunate that all your great achievements never received imperial sanction." Kono smiled with seeming kindness and understanding. "And that they stem from the illegal death—I won't go so far as to call it murder—of the Emperor's recognized representative in the Three Countries, Arai Daiichi."

"Lord Arai died, like your father, in the Great Earthquake."

"I believe Lord Arai was shot by one of your followers, the pirate Terada Fumio, already a criminal. The earthquake resulted from the horror of Heaven at such a treacherous act against an overlord—that is what is believed in the capital. There were other unexplained deaths that concerned the Emperor at the time—Lord Shirakawa, for instance, possibly at the hands of one Kondo Koichi, who was in your service, and who was also implicated in my father's death."

Takeo replied, "Kondo died years ago. This is all past history. In the Three Countries it is believed that Heaven took a hand in punishing my grandfather's brothers and Arai for their evil deeds and betrayals. Arai had just attacked my unarmed men. If there was any sort of treachery, it was his." *Earth delivered what Heaven desired.*

"Well, his son, Lord Zenko, was an eyewitness, and a man of his probity will tell the truth," Kono said blandly. "My unpleasant duty is to inform Lord Otori that, since you have never sought the Emperor's permission or endorsement, have never sent tax or tribute to the capital, your rule is illegal and you are requested to abdicate. Your life will be spared if you retire in exile to some isolated island for the remainder of your days. The ancestral sword of the Otori must be returned to the Emperor."

"It is beyond my comprehension that you dare to bring such a message," Takeo replied, masking his shock and fury. "It is under my rule that the Three Countries have become peaceful and prosperous. I have no intention of abdicating until my daughter is old enough to inherit from me. I am willing to enter into treaties with the Emperor, and anyone else who approaches me peacefully; I have three daughters for whom I am prepared to make political marriages. But I will not be intimidated by threats."

"No one really thought you would be," Kono murmured, his expression unreadable.

Takeo demanded, "Why have you come suddenly now? Where was the Emperor's interest years ago, when Iida Sadamu was pillaging the Three Countries and murdering its people? Did Iida act with a divine sanction?"

He saw Minoru make a very slight movement with his head, and tried to rein in his temper. Of course Kono hoped to enrage him, hoped to bring him into an open statement of defiance, which would be construed as further rebellion.

Zenko and Hana are behind this, he thought. *Yet there must be another reason why they—and the Emperor—dare to move against me now. What weakness are they exploiting? What additional strengths do they now think they possess?*

"I intend no disrespect to the Emperor," he said carefully. "But he is revered throughout the Eight Islands for his pursuit of peace. Surely he will not go to war against his own people?"

Surely he cannot raise an army against me?

"Lord Otori cannot have heard the latest news," Kono said with an air of sorrow. "The Emperor has appointed a new general—the descendant of one of the oldest families in the East, lord of many countries and leader of tens of thousands of men. The Emperor seeks peace above all things, but he cannot condone criminal activity, and now he has a strong right arm with which to enforce punishment and justice."

The words, so softly spoken, had all the sting of insult, and Takeo felt a wave of heat. It seemed almost unendurable to be considered a criminal—his Otori blood rebelled against it. Yet for many years he had settled challenges and disputes by shrewd negotiation and diplomacy. He did not believe these methods would fail him now. He let the words and the insult wash over him while he regained his self-mastery, and started considering what his response would be.

So they have a new warlord. Why have I not heard of him? Where is Taku when I need him? Where is Kenji?

The extra arms and men Arai had been preparing—could they be in support of this new threat? The arms—what if they *were* firearms? What if they were already on their way to the East?

"You are here as the guest of my vassal, Arai Zenko," he said finally. "And therefore as my guest. I think you should extend your stay in the West, visit your late father's estate, and return with Lord Arai to Kumamoto. I will send for you when I have decided how to reply to the Emperor, where I will go if I am to abdicate, and how best to preserve peace."

"I repeat, I am only an envoy," Kono said, and bowed with apparent sincerity.

Zenko returned and the midday meal was prepared; lavish and delicious as it was, Takeo hardly tasted it. The conversation was light and courteous; he attempted to contribute to it.

When they had eaten, Kono was escorted by Zenko to the guest apartment. Jun and Shin had been waiting outside on the veranda. They rose and followed Takeo silently as he returned to his own rooms.

"Lord Kono is not to leave this house," he said to them. "Jun, set guards at the gates. Shin, take instructions at once to the port. Lord Kono will stay in the West until I give written permission for him to return to Miyako. The same applies to Lady Arai and her sons."

The cousins exchanged a glance but made no comment beyond "Certainly, Lord Otori."

"Minoru," Takeo said to the scribe, "go with Shin to the port and find out details of all embarking vessels, particularly those bound for Akashi."

"I understand," Minoru replied. "I will be back as soon as possible."

Takeo settled himself on the veranda and listened to the mood of the house change as his instructions were carried out—the tread of the guards' feet, Jun's fierce, insistent commands, the nervous scurry of maids and their whispered comments, one exclamation of surprise from Zenko, Hana's murmured advice. When Jun returned, Takeo told him to stay outside his rooms and let no one disturb him. He then retired within, and went through Minoru's account of the meeting with Kono while he waited for his scribe to return.

The characters leaped from the page at him, stern and graphic in Minoru's near perfect hand. *Exile, criminal, illegal, treachery.*

He fought to control the rage that these insults provoked, aware of Jun barely three strides away from him. He had only to speak one order, and they would all be dead—Kono, Zenko, Hana, the children . . . their blood would wash out the humiliation that he could feel staining his bones, corroding his vital organs. Then he would attack the Emperor and his general before the summer was over, drive them back to Miyako, lay waste the capital. Only then would his rage be assuaged.

He closed his eyes, seeing the patterns of the screens etched into his eyelids, and breathed out deeply, remembering another warlord who had killed to wipe out insults and had come to love killing for its own sake, saw how easy it would be to take that path and become like Iida Sadamu.

He consciously put the insults from him and thrust the humiliation aside, telling himself his rule was ordained and blessed by Heaven—he saw this in the presence of the houou, in the contentment of his people. He came to the decision again that he would avoid bloodshed and war as long as possible, and that he would do nothing without consulting Kaede and his other advisers.

This resolution was tested almost immediately, when Minoru returned from the harbor officials' record room.

"Lord Otori's suspicions were correct," he said. "It looks as though a ship left for Akashi on last night's tide, but its cargo examination certificate had not been completed. Shin persuaded the harbor master to investigate immediately."

Takeo narrowed his eyes, but made no comment.

"Lord Otori must not concern himself," Minoru said to reassure him. "Shin hardly had to be violent at all. The men responsible were identified—the customs official who allowed the ship to leave and the merchant who handled the freight. They are being held, awaiting your decision on their fate." He lowered his voice. "Neither of them has admitted to the nature of the cargo."

"We have to suspect the worst," Takeo replied. "Why else avoid the inspection procedures? But do not speak of it openly. We must try to recover them before they reach Akashi."

Minoru smiled slightly. "I have some good news for you too. Terada Fumio's ship is waiting to dock. They will be in Hofu at the high tide this evening."

"He has come at just the right time," Takeo exclaimed, his spirits lifting immediately. Fumio was one of his oldest friends, and, with his father, supervised the fleet of ships with which the Otori carried out trade and defended their coastline. He had been away for months with Dr. Ishida, on one of their frequent voyages of trade and exploration.

"Tell Shin to take a message that he may expect a visit tonight. No need to make it explicit. Fumio will understand."

He was deeply relieved on several counts. Fumio would have up-to-date news of the Emperor; if he could leave at once he had a good chance of catching up with the illegal shipment; and Ishida would have medicine, something to relieve the insistent pain.

"And now I must speak to my brother-in-law. Please ask Lord Zenko to come here at once."

He was glad to have the excuse of the customs officials to rebuke his brother-in-law. Zenko expressed his profound apologies and promised to arrange the executions himself, assuring Takeo that it was an isolated occurrence, an instance of human greed, nothing more sinister.

"I hope you are right," Takeo replied. "I want you to assure me of your complete loyalty to me—you owe me your life; you are married to my wife's sister; your mother is my cousin and one of my oldest friends. You hold Kumamoto and all your lands through my will and my permission. Yesterday you offered me one of your sons. I accept your offer. Indeed I will take both of them; when I leave for Hagi they will accompany me. From now on they will live with my family and be brought up as my sons. I will adopt Sunaomi, if you remain loyal to me. His life and his brother's will be forfeit at the slightest sign of disloyalty. The question of marriage will be decided later. Your wife may join her sons in Hagi if she desires, but I am sure you will want her to remain with you."

Takeo watched his brother-in-law's face closely during this speech. Zenko did not look at him. His eyes flickered slightly and he spoke too quickly in reply.

"Lord Takeo must know that I am completely loyal to him. What did Kono say to you that prompted this? Has he spoken of affairs in the East?"

Don't pretend you don't know! Takeo was tempted to challenge him directly, but decided it was not yet the time.

"We will disregard what he said—it is of no importance. Now, in front of these witnesses, swear your fealty to me."

Zenko did so, prostrating himself, but Takeo remembered how his father, Arai Daiichi, had sworn an alliance with him only to betray him, and in the extreme moment had chosen power over the life of his sons.

The son will be the same, he thought. *I should order him now to take his own life.* But he shrank from such an act, for all the sorrow it would cause to his own family. *Better to keep trying to tame him, rather than kill him. But how much simpler it would be if he were dead.*

He put the thought from him, committing himself once again to the more complex and difficult path, away from the deceptive simplicities of assassination or suicide. Once Zenko had finished his prostrations, all faithfully recorded by Minoru, Takeo retired to his own apartments, saying he would dine alone and retire early since he intended to leave for Hagi in the morning. He was longing to be in the place he regarded above all others as his home, to lie with his wife and open his heart to her, to see his daughters. He told Zenko the two boys must be ready to travel with him.

It had been raining on and off all day, but now the sky was clearing, a soft wind from the south dispersing the heavy clouds. The sun set in a pink and golden glow that made the many green hues of the garden luminous. It would be fine in the morning, a good day for traveling, and fine also for the evening activities he had in mind.

He bathed and dressed in a light cotton robe as if preparing for sleep, ate lightly but drank no wine, and then dismissed all the servants, telling them he was not to be disturbed till morning. Then he composed himself, cross-legged on the matting, eyes closed and first finger and thumb pressed together as if deep in meditation. He set his ears to listen to the sounds of the mansion.

Every sound came to him—the quiet conversation of the guards at the gate, the kitchen maids chatting as they scoured the dishes and put them away, the dogs barking, music from the drinking places around the port, the endless murmur of the sea, the rustle of leaves and owls hooting from the mountain.

He heard Zenko and Hana discuss the arrangements for the following day, but their conversation was innocuous, as though they had remembered he might be listening. In the dangerous game they had initiated, they could not risk him overhearing their strategy, especially if he was to hold their sons. A short time later they met Kono for the evening meal, but they were equally circumspect—he learned nothing more than the current hairstyles and fashions at court, Kono's passion for poetry and drama, and the noble sports of kickball and dog hunting.

The conversation grew more animated—like his father, Zenko loved wine. Takeo stood and changed his clothes, putting on a faded unremarkable robe such as a merchant might wear. As he went past Jun and Shin, seated as they always were outside his door, Jun raised his eyebrows; Takeo shook his head slightly. He did not want anyone to know he had left the mansion. He slipped into straw sandals at the garden steps, took on invisibility, and walked through the still-open gates. The dogs followed him with their eyes, but the guards did not notice him. *Be thankful you do not guard the gates of Miyako*, he said silently to the dogs. *For they would shoot you full of arrows for sport.*

At a dark corner not far from the port, he stepped into the shadow invisible and stepped out in his guise of a merchant hurrying late from some assignment in the town, eager to ease his weariness with a few drinks and the company of friends. The air smelled of salt, drying fish, and seaweed on racks on the shore, grilled fish and octopus from the eating places. Lanterns lit the narrow streets and lamps glowed orange from behind the screens.

At the dockside, wooden ships rubbed against each other, creaking in the swell of the tide, the water lapping at their hulls, their stubby masts dark against the starry sky. In the distance he could just make out the islands of the Encircled Sea; behind their jagged profile was the faint sheen of moonrise.

A brazier burned beside the mooring ropes of one large vessel, and Takeo, using the town dialect, called to the men who squatted near it, roasting pieces of dried abalone and sharing a flask of wine. "Did Terada come on this ship?"

"He did," one replied. "He is eating at the Umedaya."

"Did you hope to see the kirin?" the other added. "Lord Terada has hidden it somewhere safe until he can show it to our ruler, Lord Otori."

"The kirin?" Takeo was astonished. A kirin was a mythical beast, part dragon, part horse, part lion. He thought it existed only in legends. What could Terada and Ishida have found on the mainland?

"It's supposed to be secret," the first man rebuked his friend. "And you keep blabbing to everyone!"

"But a kirin!" the other replied. "What a miracle to have one alive! And doesn't it prove Lord Otori is just and wise above all others? First the houou, the sacred bird, returns to the Three Countries, and now a kirin has appeared!" He took another swig of wine and then offered the flask to Takeo.

"Drink to the kirin and to Lord Otori!"

"Well, thank you," Takeo said, smiling. "I hope I may see it one day."

"Not before Lord Otori has set eyes on it!"

He was still smiling as he walked away, the rough liquor lifting his spirits as much as the goodwill of the men.

When I hear nothing but criticism of Lord Otori—then I will abdicate, he told himself. *But not before then, not for ten emperors and their generals.*

· *7* ·

he Umedaya was an eating house between the port and the main district of the town, one of many low wooden buildings that faced onto the river, flanked by willow trees. Lanterns hung from the veranda posts and from the flat boats moored in front of it that carried bales of rice and millet and other farm produce from the inland to the sea. Many customers sat outside enjoying the change in the weather and the beauty of the moon, now above the mountain peaks, reflected in silver fragments in the flow of the tide.

"Welcome! Welcome!" the servants called as Takeo parted the shop curtains to step inside; he mentioned Terada's name and was shown toward a corner of the inner veranda where Fumio was busily gulping stewed fish while talking loudly. Dr. Ishida sat with him, eating as heartily, listening with a half-smile on his face. Several of Fumio's men, some of whom Takeo recognized, were with him.

Standing unnoticed in the shadows, Takeo studied his old friend for a few moments while the maids hurried to and fro past him with trays of food and flasks of wine. Fumio looked as robust as ever, with his plump cheeks and fine mustache, though he appeared to have a new scar across one temple. Ishida looked older, more gaunt, his skin yellowish.

He was glad to see both of them and stepped up onto the seating area. One of the former pirates immediately leaped to his feet to bar his way, thinking him some merchant of no importance, but after a moment of baffled surprise Fumio rose, pushed his man to one side, whispering "It is Lord Otori!" and embraced Takeo.

"Even though I was expecting you, I did not recognize you!" he exclaimed. "It is uncanny—I never get used to it."

Dr. Ishida was smiling broadly. "Lord Otori!" He called to the maid to bring more wine, and Takeo sat down next to Fumio, opposite the doctor, who was peering at him in the dim light.

"Some trouble?" Ishida said after they had toasted each other.

"A few things I need to talk about," Takeo replied. Fumio made a gesture with his head, and his men took themselves off to another table.

"I have a present for you," he said to Takeo. "It will distract you from your troubles. See if you can guess what it is! It is greater than any of your heart's desires!"

"There is one thing I desire above all others," Takeo replied. "And that is to see a kirin before I die."

"Ah. They told you. The worthless scum. I'll tear their tongues out!"

"They told a poor, insignificant merchant," Takeo said, laughing. "I must forbid you to punish them. Anyway, I hardly believed them. Can it be true?"

"Yes and no," Ishida said. "Of course, it is not really a kirin—a kirin is a mythical creature and this is a real animal. But it is a most extraordinary beast, and more like a kirin than anything else that I have ever seen under Heaven."

"Ishida is in love with it," Fumio said. "He spends hours in its company. He is worse than you and that old horse of yours, what was its name?"

"Shun," Takeo said. Shun had died of old age the previous year; there would never be another horse like him.

"You can't ride this creature, but maybe it will replace Shun in your affections," Fumio said.

"I long to see it. Where is it now?"

"In the temple, Daifukuji; they have found a quiet garden for it, with a high wall. We will show you tomorrow. Now you have ruined our surprise, you may as well tell us your troubles."

Fumio poured more wine.

"What do you know about the Emperor's new general?" Takeo said.

"If you had asked me a week ago, I would have said, 'Nothing,' for we have been six months away, but we came back by way of Akashi, and the free city is abuzz with talk of him. His name is Saga Hideki, nicknamed the Dog Catcher."

"The Dog Catcher?"

"He loves dog hunting, and excels at it, they say. He is a master of the horse and bow, and a brilliant strategist. He dominates the Eastern Isles, has the ambition, they say, of conquering all the Eight Islands, and recently received the Emperor's appointment to fight His Divine Majesty's battles and destroy his enemies in order to achieve that end."

"It seems I am among his enemies," Takeo said. "Lord Fujiwara's son, Kono, called on me today to inform me. Apparently the Emperor will be sending me a request to abdicate, and if I refuse, he will send his Dog Catcher against me."

Ishida's face had paled at the mention of Fujiwara's name. "Troubles indeed," he muttered.

"That was not mentioned in Akashi," Fumio said. "It has not yet been made public."

"Was there any indication that firearms are being traded in Akashi?"

"No, on the contrary; several merchants approached me, asking about weapons and niter, hoping to get around the Otori prohibition. I must warn you, they were offering huge sums of money. If the Emperor's general is preparing war against you, he is probably attempting to buy arms—for that money, sooner or later someone is going to supply them."

"I'm afraid they are already on their way," Takeo said, and told Fumio about his suspicions of Zenko.

"They have less than a day's start," Fumio said, draining his glass and getting to his feet. "We can intercept them. I wanted to see your face when I showed you the kirin, but Ishida will tell me about it. Keep Lord Kono in the West until I return. While they cannot match the firearm, they will not provoke you into battle. But once they have it—they have more resources, iron ore and smiths, and more men than we do. The wind is westerly—we'll catch the tide if we leave now." He called to the men, and they also rose, cramming the last of the food into their mouths, draining the wine cups, bidding the maids a reluctant farewell. Takeo gave them the name of the boat.

Fumio departed so swiftly they hardly had time to say good-bye.

Takeo was left with Ishida. "Fumio has not changed," he said, amused by his friend's immediate action.

"He is always the same," Ishida replied. "Like a whirlwind, never still." The doctor poured more wine and drank deeply. "He is a stimulating traveling companion, but exhausting."

They spoke of the voyage, and Takeo gave news of his family, in whom Ishida always took the keenest interest, for he had been married for fifteen years to Muto Shizuka.

"Your pain has increased?" the doctor said. "It shows in your face."

"Yes, the damp weather aggravates it—sometimes I feel there must be a residue of poison that flares up. Often the wound seems inflamed beneath the scar. It makes my whole body ache."

"I will look at it, in private," Ishida said.

"Can you come back with me now?"

"I have quite a supply of root from Shin, and a new soporific made from poppies. Luckily, I decided to bring them with me," Ishida remarked, taking up a cloth bundle and a small wooden chest. "I had intended to leave these on the ship. They would be halfway to Akashi by now and little use to you."

A bleak tone had come into Ishida's voice. Takeo thought he might say more, but after a moment of uncomfortable silence the doctor seemed to regain his self-control; he gathered up his things and said cheerfully, "And then I must go and check on the kirin. I will sleep at Daifukuji tonight. The kirin is used to me and even attached to me—I do not want it to fret."

Takeo had been aware for a little while of a discordant sound from within the eating house, a man speaking in the foreigners' language and a woman's voice translating. The woman's voice interested him, for the accent held a tone of the East in it, though she spoke in a local dialect, and there was something about her intonation that was familiar to him.

As they went through the inside room he recognized the foreigner, the one called Don João. He was sure he had never seen the woman kneeling beside him, yet there was something . . .

While he was pondering who she might be, the man spotted Ishida and called out to him. Ishida was a great favorite with the foreigners and spent many hours in their company, exchanging medical knowledge, information on treatment and herbs, and comparing their customs and language.

Don João had met Takeo several times, but always in formal circumstances, and he did not appear to recognize him now. The foreigner was delighted to see the doctor and would have liked him to sit and chat, but Ishida pleaded the needs of a patient. The woman, who might have been twenty-five or so years old, glanced at Takeo, but he kept his face turned away from her. She translated Ishida's words—she seemed quite fluent in the foreign tongue—and turned her gaze toward Takeo again; she seemed to be studying him closely, as though she thought she might know him in the same way as he thought he knew her.

She raised her hands to her mouth; the sleeve fell back and revealed the skin of her forearm, smooth and dark, so like his own, so like his mother's.

The shock was overwhelming, stripping his self-control, turning him into a scared, persecuted boy. The woman gasped and said, "Tomasu?"

Her eyes filled with tears. She was shaking with emotion. He remembered a little girl crying in the same way over a dead bird, a lost toy. He had imagined her lifeless over the years, lying next to her dead mother and her older sister—she had their calm, broad features, and she had his skin. He spoke her name aloud for the first time in over sixteen years:

"Madaren!"

It drove everything else from his mind—the threat from the East, Fumio's mission to retrieve the smuggled firearms, Kono, even the pain, even the kirin. He could only stare at the sister he had imagined dead; his life seemed to melt and fade away. All that existed in his memory was his childhood, his family.

Ishida said, "Lord, are you all right? You are unwell." He said quickly to Madaren, "Tell Don João I will meet him tomorrow. Send word to me at Daifukuji."

"I will come there tomorrow," she said, her eyes fixed on Takeo's face.

He regained his self-control and said, "We cannot speak now. I will come to Daifukuji; wait for me there."

"May he bless and keep you," she said, using the prayer the Hidden use in parting. Even though it was at his command that the Hidden were now free to worship openly, it still shocked him to see revealed what had once been secret, just as the cross Don João wore on his breast seemed a flagrant display.

"You are more unwell than I thought!" Ishida exclaimed when they were outside. "Shall I send for a palanquin?"

"No, of course not!" Takeo breathed in deeply. "It was just the closeness of the air. And drinking too much wine, too fast."

"And you received some terrible shock. Did you know that woman?"

"From a long time ago. I did not know she translated for the foreigners."

"I've seen her before, but not recently—I have been away for months." The town was growing quieter, the lights being extinguished one by one, the last shutter being closed. As they crossed the wooden bridge outside the Umedaya and took one of the narrow streets that led toward the mansion, Ishida remarked, "She did not recognize you as Lord Otori, but as someone else."

"As I said, I knew her a long time ago, before I became Otori."

Takeo was still half-stunned by the meeting—and more than half-inclined to doubt what he had seen. How could it be her? How could she have survived the massacre in which his family had been destroyed and his village burned? Doubtless she was not only an interpreter—he had seen that in Don João's hands and eyes. The foreigners frequented brothels like any other men, but the women were mostly reluctant to sleep with them—

only the lowest-class prostitutes went with them. His skin crawled as he thought of what her life must have been.

Yet she had called him by name. And he had recognized her.

At the last house before the mansion gates, Takeo drew Ishida into the shadows. "Wait here for a short while. I must go inside unobserved. I will send word to the guards to admit you."

The gates were already closed, but he tucked the long hem of his robe up into his sash and scaled the wall lightly enough, though the jolt of landing on the far side sent the pain throbbing again. Taking on invisibility, he slipped through the silent garden, past Jun and Shin to his room. He changed back into his night robes and called for lamps and tea, sending Jun to tell the guards to let Ishida in.

The doctor arrived—they exchanged delighted greetings as if they had not seen each other for six months. The maid poured tea and brought more hot water, then Takeo dismissed her. He drew off the silk glove that covered the crippled hand and Ishida moved the lamp closer so he could see. He pressed the scar tissue gently with the tips of his fingers and flexed the remaining digits. The growth of scar tissue had clawed the hand slightly.

"Can you still write with this hand?"

"After a fashion. I support it with the left." He showed Ishida. "I believe I could still fight with the sword, but I have not had reason to for many years."

"It does seem inflamed," Ishida said finally. "I will try the needles tomorrow, to open up the meridians. In the meantime, this will help you sleep."

As he prepared the tea, he said in a low voice, "I often did this for your wife. I am afraid to meet Kono; just the mention of his father's name, the knowledge that the son lies somewhere in this mansion, has stirred up many memories. I wonder if he has grown like his father."

"I never laid eyes on Fujiwara."

"You were fortunate. I did his bidding, obeying him in everything, for most of my life. I knew he was a cruel man, but he always treated me with kindness, encouraged me in my studies and my travels, allowed me access to his great collections of books and other treasures. I turned my eyes away from his darker pleasures. I never believed his cruelty would fall on me."

He stopped abruptly and poured the boiling water onto the dried herbs. A faint smell of summer grass rose from them, fragrant and soothing.

"My wife has told me a little of that time," Takeo said quietly.

"Only the earthquake saved us. I have never experienced such terror in my life, though I have faced many dangers—storms at sea, shipwreck, pirates and savages. I had already thrown myself at his feet and begged to be allowed to kill myself. He pretended to consent, playing with my fears. Sometimes I dream about it; it is something I will never recover from— absolute evil in the person of a man."

He paused, lost in memories. "My dog was howling," he said very quietly. "I could hear my dog howling. He always warned me of earthquakes like that. I found myself wondering if anyone would look after him."

Ishida took up the bowl and handed it to Takeo. "I am profoundly sorry for the part I played in your wife's imprisonment."

"It is all long past," Takeo said, taking the bowl and draining it gratefully.

"But if the son is anything like the father, he will only do you ill. Be on your guard."

"You are drugging me and warning me in the same breath," Takeo said. "Maybe I should put up with the pain—at least it keeps me awake."

"I should stay here with you . . ."

"No. The kirin needs you. My own men are here to guard me. For the time being I am in no danger."

He walked through the garden with Ishida as far as the gate, feeling the deep relief as the pain began to dull. He did not lie awake long—just long enough to tally the amazing events of the day—Kono, the Emperor's displeasure, the Dog Catcher, the kirin. And his sister—what was he going to do about Madaren, a foreigner's woman, one of the Hidden, sister to Lord Otori?

· 8 ·

he sight of her older brother, whom she had believed dead, was no less of a shock to the woman who had once been called Madaren, a common name among the Hidden. For many years after the massacre Madaren had been called by the name given to her by the woman to whom the Tohan soldier had sold her. He was one of the men who had taken part in the rape and murder of her mother and sister, but Madaren had no direct memory of that; she remembered only the summer rain, the smell of the horse's sweat when her cheek pressed against its neck, the weight of the man's hand holding her still, a hand that seemed larger and heavier than her whole body. Everything smelled of smoke and mud and she knew she would never be clean again. At the start of the fire and the horses and the swords she had screamed out for her father, for Tomasu, as she had called earlier that year when she had fallen into the swollen stream and been trapped on the slippery rocks, and Tomasu had heard her from the fields and come running to pull her out, scolding her and comforting her.

But Tomasu had not heard her this time; nor had her father, already dead; no one had heard her and no one had ever come to her aid again.

Many children, not only among the Hidden, suffered in a similar way when Iida Sadamu ruled in his black-walled castle at Inuyama; nor did the situation change after Inuyama fell to Arai. Some lived to grow up, and Madaren was one of them, one of the large number of young women who serviced the needs of the warrior class, becoming maids, kitchen servants, or women of the pleasure houses. They had no families and therefore no protection; Madaren worked for the woman who bought her, the lowest of the servants, the one who rose first in the morning before even the roosters were awake and could not lie down to sleep until the last customers had gone home. She thought exhaustion and hunger had dulled her to everything around her, but when she became a woman and briefly desirable in the way young girls usually do, she realized she had been learning all the time from the older girls, observing them and listening to them, and had become wise without knowing it in their favorite—indeed their only— subject: the men who visited them.

The pleasure house was possibly the meanest in Inuyama, set far from the castle in one of the narrow streets that ran between the main avenues, where tiny houses rebuilt after the fire clustered together like a wasp's nest, each clinging onto the next. But all men have their desires, even porters, laborers, and night soil collectors, and among these are as many who can be made fools for love as in any other class. So Madaren learned; at the same time she learned that women who are ruled by love are the least powerful beings in the city, more dominated even than dogs, as easily discarded as unwanted kittens, and she used this knowledge shrewdly. She went with men that the other girls shunned, and took advantage of their gratitude. She extracted gifts from them, or sometimes stole, and finally allowed a failing merchant to take her with him to Hofu, leaving the house in the early morning before dawn and meeting him at the misty dockside. They boarded a ship carrying cedar wood from the forests of the East, and the smell reminded her of Mino, her birthplace, and she suddenly recalled her family and the strange half-wild boy who had been her brother, who infuriated and enchanted their mother. Tears filled her eyes as she crouched beneath the lumber planks, and when her lover turned to embrace her she pushed him away. He was easily cowed, and no more successful in Hofu than he had been in Inuyama. He bored and infuriated her, and eventually she went back to her early life, joining a pleasure house a little higher in class than her first one.

Then the foreigners came with their beards, their strange smell, and their large frames—and other parts. Madaren saw some power in them that might be exploited and volunteered to sleep with them. She chose the one called Don João, though he always thought he had chosen her—the foreigners were both sentimental and ashamed when it came to matters of the body's needs. They wanted to feel special to one woman, even when they bought her. They paid well in silver; Madaren was able to explain to the owner of the house that Don João wanted her only, and soon she did not have to sleep with anyone else.

At first their only language was that of the body—his lust, her ability to satisfy it. The foreigners had an interpreter, a fisherman who had been plucked out of the water by one of their kind after a shipwreck and taken back to their base in the Southern Islands, for they themselves came from a land far away in the west—you could sail for a year with the wind behind you and still not reach it. The fisherman had learned their language. He sometimes accompanied them to the pleasure house; it was obvious from his speech that he was uneducated and low-born, yet his association with the foreigners gave him status and power. They depended on him completely. He was their entry into the complex new world they had discovered and from which they hoped to gain wealth and glory, and they believed everything he told them, even when he was making it up.

I could have something of that power, for he is no better than I, Madaren thought, and she began to try to understand Don João, and encouraged him to teach her. The language was hard, full of difficult sounds and put together back to front—everything had a gender, she could not imagine the reason, but a door was female, and so was rain; the floor and the sun were male— but it intrigued her; and when she spoke in the new language to Don João she felt as if she were turning into another person.

As she became more fluent—Don João never mastered more than a few words of her language—they spoke of deeper things. He had a wife and children back in Porutogaru, about whom he wept when he had been drinking. Madaren discounted them, not believing he would ever see them again. They were so remote she could not imagine their life. And he spoke of his faith and his God—Deus—and his words and the cross he wore round his neck awakened childhood memories of her family's faith and the rituals of the Hidden.

He was eager to speak of Deus, and told her of priests of his religion who longed to convert other nations to their faith. This surprised Madaren. She remembered little of the beliefs of the Hidden, only the need for utter secrecy and an echo of the prayers and rituals that her family shared with their small community. The new lord of the Three Countries, Otori Takeo, had decreed that people could worship freely and believe whatever they chose to believe, and old prejudices were slowly giving way. Indeed, many were interested in the foreigners' religion and even willing to try it if it increased trade and wealth for everyone. There were rumors that Lord Otori himself had once been one of the Hidden, and that the former ruler of the Maruyama domain, Maruyama Naomi, had also held their beliefs, but Madaren did not think either was very likely—for had not Lord Otori slain his great uncles in revenge? Did not Lady Maruyama throw herself into the river at Inuyama with her daughter? The one thing everyone knew about the Hidden was that their god, the Secret One, forbade them to take life, neither their own nor anyone else's.

It was on this point that the Secret One and Deus seemed to differ, for Don João told her that his countrymen were both believers and great warriors—if she understood him properly, for she knew that she often understood every word yet did not quite grasp the meaning. Was it *both* or *neither, always* or *never, already* or *not yet?* He was always armed, with a long thin blade, its helm curved and guarded, inlaid with gold and mother-of-pearl, and he boasted that he had had cause to use this sword many times. He was surprised that torture was forbidden in the Three Countries, and told her how it was used in his country and on the natives of the Southern Islands to punish, to extract information, and to save souls. This last she found hard to understand, though it interested her that the soul should be female and she wondered if all souls were like wives to the male Deus.

"When the priest comes you must be baptized," Don João told her, and when she understood the concept she remembered what her mother used to say: *born by water,* and she told him her water name.

"Madalena!" he repeated, astonished, and made the sign of the cross in the air in front of him. He was fiercely interested in the Hidden, and wanted to meet more of them; she caught this interest and they began to meet with believers in the shared meal of the Hidden. Don João asked many questions and Madaren translated them, and the answers. She met people who had known of her village and heard of the massacre so long ago in Mino; they thought her escape a miracle, and declared she had been spared by the Secret One for some special purpose. Madaren took up the lost faith of her childhood with fervor, and began to wait for her mission to be revealed to her.

And then Tomasu was sent to her, and she knew it had something to do with him.

The foreigners understood very little of manners and politeness, and Don João expected Madaren to accompany him everywhere he went, especially as he came to depend on her for translating. With the single-minded determination with which she had escaped from Inuyama and learned the foreign tongue, she studied the unfamiliar surroundings, always kneeling humbly a little behind the foreigners and their interlocutors, speaking quietly and clearly, and embellishing her translation if it did not seem courteous enough. She often found herself in merchants' houses, aware of the disdainful and suspicious glances from their wives and daughters, and sometimes even in higher places, recently even to Lord Arai's mansion. It amazed her to see herself, one day in the same room as Lord Arai Zenko, and the next in some inn like the Umedaya. She had been right in her instincts—she had learned the foreigners' language and it had given her access to some of their power and freedom. And some of that power she used over them—they needed her and began to rely on her.

She had seen Dr. Ishida several times, and had acted as interpreter in long discussions. Ishida sometimes brought texts and read them for Madaren to translate, for she could not read or write; Don João also read to her from the holy book and she recognized fragments of phrases from childhood prayers and blessings.

That night Don João had spotted Ishida and called to him, hoping to talk with him, but Ishida had pleaded the demands of a patient. Madaren had guessed he meant his companion and had looked at the other man, noting the crippled hand and the furrows between the eyes. She had not recognized him immediately, but her heart had seemed to stop and then it started hammering, as though her skin had known his and had known at once they had been made by the same mother.

She had hardly been able to sleep, had found the foreigner's body next to hers unbearably hot, and had crept away before daybreak to walk by the river beneath the willows. The moon had traversed the sky and now hung in the west, swollen and watery. The tide was low and crabs scuttled on the mudflats, their shadows like clutching hands. Madaren did not want to tell Don João where she was going—she did not want to have to think in his language or have to worry about him. She went through the dark streets to the house where she used to work, woke the maid, washed and dressed there, then sat quietly drinking tea until the morning was fully light.

As she walked toward Daifukuji she was seized by misgivings—it had not been Tomasu; she had been mistaken, had dreamed the whole thing. He would not come; he had obviously risen in the world; he was a merchant now—albeit not apparently a very successful one—who would want nothing to do with her. He had not come to her help—he had been alive all this time and had not sought her out. She walked slowly, oblivious to the bustle of the river around her as the tide swept in, bringing the beached boats back to life.

Daifukuji faced the sea—its red gates could be seen from far across the waves, welcoming sailors and traders home and reminding them to give thanks to Ebisu, the sea god, for protecting them on their voyages. Madaren looked at its carvings and statues with dislike, for she had come to believe like Don João that such things were hateful to the Secret God and equal to devil worship. She wondered why her brother should have chosen such a place to meet, feared that he was no longer a believer, slid her hand inside her robe to touch the cross Don João had given her, and realized that this must be her mission—to save Tomasu.

She hovered just inside the gate, waiting for him, partly uneasy at the sound of chanting and bells from within, partly, despite herself, charmed and lulled by the beauty of the garden. Irises fringed the pools, and the first summer azaleas were bursting into vermilion flower. The sun grew hotter and the shade of the garden drew her in. She walked toward the back of the main hall. On her right stood several ancient cedars, each girdled with gleaming straw ropes, and just beyond them was a white-walled enclosure around a garden of much smaller trees, cherries she thought, though the blossom was long fallen, replaced by green foliage. A small crowd of men, mainly monks with shaved heads and subdued colored robes, stood outside the wall, staring upward. Madaren followed their gaze and saw what they were looking at: another strange carving, she thought at first, a depiction of some avatar or demon—and then it blinked its long-lashed eyes, flapped its patterned ears, and ran its dark gray tongue over its soft fawn nose. It turned its horned head and looked benignly down at its admirers. It was a living creature, yet what creature ever had a neck so long that it could look over a wall higher than the tallest man?

It was the kirin.

As she gazed at the extraordinary animal, her tiredness and the confusion of her thoughts suddenly made her feel as if she were in a dream. There was a bustle of activity from the main gate of the temple, and she heard a man's voice call excitedly, "Lord Otori is here!" She felt the shock of the dream as she sank to her knees and looked at the ruler of the Three Countries as he came into the garden, surrounded by a retinue of warriors. He was dressed in formal summer robes of cream and gold, with a small black hat on his head, but she saw the damaged hand in the silk glove, and recognized the face, and realized it was Tomasu, her brother.

· *9* ·

akeo was aware of his sister kneeling humbly in the shade at the side of the garden, but he took no notice of her. If she stayed, he would speak to her in private; if she left and disappeared again from his life, whatever his personal feelings of sadness and regret, he would not look for her. It would be better, probably, simpler, if she were to disappear. It would be easy enough to arrange it—he considered the idea briefly but put it from him. He would deal with her justly, as he would Zenko and Kono—by negotiation, according to the law he himself had established.

As if in confirmation of Heaven's approval, the gate to the walled garden opened and the kirin appeared. Ishida held it by a red silken cord attached to a collar beaded with pearls. Ishida's head came barely to its withers, but it followed him in a manner that was both confident and dignified. Its coat was a pale chestnut color, broken into cream-outlined patterns the size and shape of a man's palm.

It smelled water and stretched its long neck toward the pool. Ishida allowed it to approach, and it spread its legs sideways so it could bend to drink.

The small crowd of monks and warriors laughed in delight, for it looked as if the marvelous animal had bowed to Lord Otori.

Takeo was no less delighted with it. When he approached it, it allowed him to stroke its soft and amazingly patterned coat. It seemed quite un-afraid, though it preferred to stay close to Ishida.

"Is it male or female?" he inquired.

"Female, I believe," Ishida replied. "It does not have any external male parts, and it is more gentle and trusting than I would expect a male animal of this size to be. But it is still very young. Maybe it will show some changes as it grows older, and then we will be sure."

"Wherever did you find it?"

"In the south of Tenjiku. But it came from another island, farther west still; sailors talk about a huge continent where animals like this graze in vast herds, along with elephants of both land and river, huge golden lions, and rose-pink birds. The men are twice our size and as black as lacquer in color, and can bend iron in their bare hands."

"And how did you acquire it? Surely such a creature is beyond price?"

"It was offered to me, as a sort of payment," Ishida replied. "I was able to perform some small service for the local prince. I thought immediately of Lady Shigeko, and how much she would like it, so I accepted it and made arrangements for it to accompany us home."

Takeo smiled, thinking of his daughter's skill with horses and love for all animals.

"Was it not hard to keep it alive? What does it eat?"

"Luckily the voyage home was calm, and the kirin is placid and easy to please. It eats leaves from the trees in its own land, apparently, but it is happy to accept grass, fresh or dried, and other palatable greenstuff."

"Would it be able to walk to Hagi?"

"Perhaps we should transport it around the coast by ship. It can walk for miles without getting tired, but I do not think it can go over moun-tains."

When they had finished admiring the kirin, Ishida took it back to the enclosure, and then went with Takeo to the temple, where a short cere-mony was performed and prayers made for the health of the kirin and of Lord Otori. Takeo lit incense and candles and knelt before the statue of the god; he carried out all the necessary religious practices expected of him with reverence and respect. All sects and beliefs were permitted in the Three Countries as long as they did not threaten the social order, and while Takeo himself did not believe in any one god, he recognized the need of humans for a spiritual ground to their existence, and indeed shared that need himself.

After the ceremonies, in which the Enlightened One, the great teacher, and Ebisu, the sea god, were both honored and thanked, tea was brought with sweets of bean paste, and Takeo, Ishida, and the Abbot of the temple spent a merry time exchanging stories and composing poems full of puns about the kirin.

A little before midday Takeo rose to his feet, said he would sit alone in the garden for a while, and walked along the side of the main hall to the smaller one behind it. The woman still knelt patiently in the same spot. He made a slight movement with his hand as he went past, indicating that she should follow.

The building faced east—its southern side was bathed in sunlight, but on the veranda, in the deep shade of the curved roof, the air was still cool. Two young monks were engaged in cleaning the statues and sweeping the floor; they retreated without a word. Takeo sat on the edge of the veranda; the wood was weathered silver-gray and still warm from the sun. He heard Madaren's hesitant tread on the pebbles of the path, heard her rapid, shallow breathing. In the garden, sparrows were chirping and doves murmured in the cedars. She dropped to her knees again, hiding her face.

"There is no need to be afraid," he said.

"It is not fear," she replied after a moment. "I . . . don't understand. Perhaps I have made a stupid mistake. But Lord Otori is speaking alone with me, which would never happen unless what I believe is true."

"We recognized each other last night," Takeo said. "I am indeed your brother. But it is many years since anyone has called me Tomasu."

She looked directly at him; he did not meet her gaze, but turned his eyes away toward the deep shade of the grove of trees and the distant wall where the kirin's head swayed above the tiles like a child's toy.

He realized his calmness seemed like indifference to her, and he was aware of a kind of rage smoldering within her. Her voice when she spoke was almost accusing.

"For sixteen years I have heard ballads and stories made up about you. You seemed like some remote and legendary hero—how can you be Tomasu from Mino? What happened to you while I was sold from one pleasure house to another?"

"I was rescued by Lord Otori Shigeru—he adopted me as his heir and desired me to marry Shirakawa Kaede, the heir to Maruyama."

It was the barest outline of the extraordinary, turbulent journey that had led him to be the most powerful man in the Three Countries.

Madaren said with bitterness, "I saw you kneel before the golden statue. And I know from the tales I hear that you have taken life."

Takeo made the smallest movement of assent with his head. He was wondering what she would demand from him, what he could do for her—what, if anything, would heal her broken life.

"I suppose our mother and sister . . ." he said with pain.

"Both dead. I do not even know where their bodies lie."

"I am sorry for everything you must have suffered." He realized even as he spoke that his tone was stilted, the words inadequate. The gulf between them was too huge. There was no way that they could approach each other. If they had still shared the same faith they might have prayed together, but now the childhood beliefs that once united them formed a barrier that could not be overcome. The knowledge filled him with distress and pity.

"If you have need of anything, you may approach the town authorities," he said. "I will make sure you are looked after. But I cannot make our relationship public knowledge, and I must ask you not to speak of it to anyone."

He saw he had hurt her, and felt the twist of pity again, yet he knew he could not allow her any more place in his life than this: to be under his protection.

"Tomasu," she said. "You are my older brother. We have obligations toward each other. You are the only family I have. I am aunt to your children. And I have a spiritual duty to you too. I care for your soul. I cannot watch you go to hell!"

He got to his feet and walked away from her. "There is no hell," he replied over his shoulder. "Other than that which men make on earth. Do not attempt to approach me again."

nd the disciples of the Enlightened One saw that the tigers and their cubs were starving," Shigeko said in her most pious voice, "and with no thought for their own lives they threw themselves over the precipice and were cashed to death on the rocks below. Then the tigers could eat them."

It was a warm afternoon in early summer, and the girls had been told to study quietly inside until the heat lessened. For a while they had diligently practiced writing, Shigeko demonstrating her elegant flowing hand, and then the strident drone of the cicadas and the shimmering air had made them lazy and sleepy. They had been out early, before sunrise while the day was still cool, and little by little their limbs relaxed from the formal pose they sat in to write. Shigeko had been easily persuaded to unroll the scroll of animal pictures and then to tell stories.

But it seemed even the best stories had to have a moral. Shigeko said with solemnity, "That's the example we should follow; we should give our own lives to be used for the benefit of all sentient beings."

Maya and Miki exchanged glances. They loved their older sister unreservedly, but lately she had become a little too fond of preaching to them.

"Personally, I would rather be one of the tigers," Maya said.

"And eat the dead disciples!" her twin sister agreed.

"Someone has to be the sentient beings," Maya argued, seeing Shigeko frown.

Her eyes gleamed with a secret knowledge, as they often did these days. She had just returned from several weeks in Kagemura, the hidden Muto village, where her innate Tribe skills had been trained and honed. Next it would be Miki's turn. The twin girls spent little time in each other's company; they did not fully understand the reason why, but knew it was connected with their mother's feelings toward them. She did not like to see them together. Their identical look repulsed her. Shigeko, on the other hand, had always been fascinated by them, always took their side and protected them, even when she could not tell them apart.

They did not like the separations, but they had become accustomed to them. Shizuka consoled them, telling them it would make the psychic bond between them strong. And so it did. If Maya fell sick, Miki came down with a fever. Sometimes they met in dreams; they were hardly able to discern between what happened in that other world and what happened in the real world.

The world of the Otori had many compensations—Shigeko, the horses, the beautiful surroundings that their mother created everywhere she lived—but both of them preferred the mysterious life of the Tribe.

The best times were when their father came in secret to the Tribe village, sometimes bringing one of them and taking the other back with him. For a few days they would be together—they could show him what they had learned and the new skills that had begun to appear. And he, who in the world of the Otori was usually distant and formal, in the Muto world became a different person, a teacher like Kenji or Taku, treating them with the same irresistible blend of strong discipline, impossibly high expectations, and constant affection. They bathed together in the hot springs and splashed around him, as sleek as otter cubs, tracing the scars on his skin that mapped his life, never tiring of hearing the story of each one, starting with the terrible fight in which he had lost two fingers from his right hand to the Kikuta master Kotaro.

At the name Kikuta, both girls unconsciously touched the tips of their fingers to the deep crease that crossed their palm, marking them like their father, like Taku, as Kikuta.

It was a symbol of the narrow line they walked between the worlds. Secretive by nature, they had taken eagerly to deception and pretense. They knew their mother disapproved of their Tribe skills, and that the warrior class in general believed them to be sorcery. They had learned early that what might be proudly displayed in the Muto village was to be kept hidden in the palaces of Hagi or Yamagata, but sometimes the temptation to outwit their teachers, tease their sister, or punish someone who crossed them was too great.

"You are like me when I was a child," Shizuka had said when Maya had hidden inside a bamboo basket for half a day without moving, or when Miki had climbed into the rafters as lithe and swift as a wild monkey, invisible against the thatch. Shizuka was rarely angry. "Enjoy these games," she'd said. "Nothing will ever be as exciting."

"You are so lucky, Shizuka. You were there at the fall of Inuyama! You fought with Father in the war!"

"Now Father says there will be no more war in the Three Countries; we will never get to fight properly."

"We pray there will not be," Shigeko had said. The twins had groaned together.

"Pray like your sister that you will never know real war," Shizuka warned them.

Maya returned to this theme now, for war interested her even more than tigers. "If there is to be no war, why do Father and Mother insist on us learning fighting skills?" she asked, for all three girls, like all children of the warrior class, learned the ways of bow and horse and sword, taught by Shizuka and by Sugita Hiroshi or the other great warriors of the Three Countries.

"Lord Hiroshi says preparing for war is the best defense against it," Shigeko replied.

"Lord Hiroshi," Miki whispered, elbowing Maya. Both twins giggled.

The color rose in Shigeko's face. "What?" she demanded.

"You are always telling us what Lord Hiroshi says, and then you blush."

"I was not aware of it," Shigeko said, covering her embarrassment with formal speech. "Anyway, it has no particular significance. Hiroshi is one of our instructors—and a very wise one. It is natural I should have learned his maxims."

"Lord Miyoshi Gemba is one of your instructors," Miki said. "But you rarely quote what he says."

"And he does not make you turn red!" Maya added.

"I think you could do considerably better at writing, sisters. You obviously need much more practice. Take up the brush!" Shigeko unrolled another scroll and began to dictate from it. It was one of the ancient chronicles of the Three Countries, full of difficult names and obscure events. Shigeko had had to learn all this history, and the twins would have to as well. They might as well start now. It would punish them for teasing her about Hiroshi and, she hoped, dissuade them from mentioning the subject again. She resolved to be more careful, not to allow herself the foolish pleasure of saying his name, not to gaze at him all the time, and above all not to blush. Luckily he was not in Hagi at present, having returned to Maruyama to oversee the bringing in of the harvest and the preparations for the coming ceremony in which the domain would become hers.

He wrote often, for he was the senior retainer and her parents expected her to know every detail about her land. The letters were of course formal, but she liked looking at his hand, a warrior's writing style, bold and well-formed, and he included information that she knew was for her, about people who were special to her for some reason, and above all about horses. He described each foal born and how they were developing, and how the colts he and Shigeko had broken in together were progressing. They discussed bloodlines and breeding, looking always for a larger, stronger horse—the Maruyama horses were already a hand higher than they had been twenty years ago, when Hiroshi was a child.

She missed him and longed to see him again. She could not remember a time when she did not love him—he had been like a brother to her, living in the Otori household, regarded as a son of the family. He had taught her to ride, to use the bow and to fight with the sword; he had also instructed her in the art of war, strategy, and tactics, as well as the art of government. She wished above all that he might become her husband, but did not think it would ever be possible. He might be her most valuable adviser, even her most treasured friend, but nothing more. She had overheard enough discussions about her marriage to be aware of that, and as she had now turned fifteen she knew plans would soon be made for a betrothal, some match that would strengthen her family's position and underpin her father's desire for peace.

All these thoughts ran through her mind as she read slowly and carefully from the scroll. The twins' hands were aching and their eyes itching by the time she had finished. Neither of them dared make any further comment, and Shigeko relented of her sternness. She corrected their work with kindness, made them practice the characters they had misstroked only a few dozen times, and then, since the sun was descending toward the sea and the air was a little cooler, suggested a walk before the evening's training.

The twins, chastened by the severity of their punishment, agreed docilely.

"We will go to the shrine," Shigeko announced, cheering her sisters immensely, for the shrine was sacred to the river god and to horses.

"Can we go by the weir?" Maya pleaded.

"Certainly not," Shigeko replied. "The weir is only used by urchins, not by the daughters of Lord Otori. We will walk to the stone bridge. Call Shizuka and ask her to come with us. And I suppose we had better take some men."

"We don't need men."

"Can we take our swords?" Maya and Miki spoke at once.

"For a visit to the shrine, in the center of Hagi? We will not need swords."

"Remember the attack at Inuyama!" Miki reminded her.

"A warrior should always be prepared," Maya said in a passable mimicry of Hiroshi.

"Maybe you need a little more writing practice," Shigeko said, looking as if she would sit down again.

"Let it be as you say, older sister," Miki said quickly. "Men, no swords."

SHIGEKO DELIBERATED FOR a few moments over the perennial question of the palanquin: whether to insist on the girls being carried in obscurity or to allow them to walk. None of them cared for the palanquin, for its uncomfortable motion and confinement, but it was more suitable to be so transported, and she knew their mother did not like the twin girls to be seen together in public. On the other hand, this was Hagi, their hometown, less formal and austere than Inuyama, and her restless sisters might be calmed and tired after walking. Tomorrow Shizuka would take Miki to the Muto village, Kagemura, and Shigeko would be left with Maya to wonder at the new skills and secret knowledge she had acquired, to console her in her loneliness, and to help her learn all that Miki had learned while she was away. Shigeko herself needed to walk, to be distracted for a few moments by the vibrant life of the city, its narrow streets and tiny shops filled with a variety of produce and craft—the first of the summer fruit, apricots and plums, young sweet beans and green vegetables, eels lashing in buckets, crabs and small silver fish thrown onto hot grills to sizzle, die, and be eaten in an instant. And then the makers of lacquer and pottery, of paper and silk clothes. Behind the broad main avenue that led from the castle gates to the stone bridge lay a whole delightful world that the girls were rarely allowed to visit.

Two guards walked ahead of them and two behind; a maidservant brought a small bamboo basket filled with flasks of wine and other offerings, including carrots for the shrine horses. Shizuka was beside Maya, and Miki accompanied Shigeko. They all wore wooden clogs and light cotton summer robes. Shigeko held a sunshade, for her skin was as white as her mother's and she feared the sun, but the twins had the golden-colored skin of their father, and anyway could not be bothered with protecting it.

The tide was ebbing as they came to the stone bridge, and the river smelled of salt and mud. The bridge had been destroyed in the Great

Earthquake, people said in punishment of Arai Daichi's treachery, for he had turned on his Otori allies right alongside the stone carved with the words THE OTORI CLAN WELCOMES THE JUST AND THE LOYAL. LET THE UNJUST AND THE DISLOYAL BEWARE.

"And look what happened to him!" Maya said in satisfaction as they stood before the stone for a few moments, making an offering of wine, thanking the river god for protecting the Otori and remembering the death of the stonemason who had been walled up alive long ago within the parapet of the bridge. His skeleton had been found in the river and had been buried again during the rebuilding of the bridge, beneath the stone, which had also been retrieved from the river. Shizuka often told the girls this story, and that of his daughter, Akane, and sometimes they visited the shrine at the volcano's crater where Akane's tragic death was commemorated and her spirit invoked by unhappy lovers, men and women.

"Shizuka must grieve for Lord Arai, though," Shigeko said quietly as they left the bridge. For a moment the twins walked side by side; passersby dropped to their knees as Shigeko went past, but from the twins they averted their faces.

"I grieved for the love that was once between us," Shizuka replied. "And for my sons, who saw their father die before their eyes. But Arai had already made me an enemy, and had ordered my death. His own death was no more than a just end to the way he chose to live."

"You know so much about those times!" Shigeko exclaimed.

"Yes, probably more than anyone," Shizuka admitted. "As I grow older, all that is past becomes clearer in my mind. Ishida and I have been recording all my memories—your father requested it."

"And you knew Lord Shigeru?"

"For whom you are named. Yes, I knew him closely. We confided in each other for years and trusted each other with our lives."

"He must have been a good man."

"I have never met another like him."

"Was he a better man than my father?"

"Shigeko! I cannot judge your father!"

"Why not? You are his cousin. You know him better than most people."

"Takeo is very like Shigeru—he is a great man and a great leader."

"But . . . ?"

"All men have flaws," Shizuka said. "Your father tries to master his, but his nature is divided in a way that Shigeru's was not."

Shigeko shivered suddenly, though the air was still warm. "Don't say any more! I'm sorry I asked you."

"What's wrong? Did you have a premonition?"

"I have them all the time," Shigeko replied quietly. "I know how many people seek my father's death." She gestured at the twins, now waiting at the gate to the shrine. "Our family is divided in the same manner—we are the reflection of his nature. What will happen to my sisters in the future? What will their place be in the world?" She shivered again, and made an effort to change the subject.

"Has your husband returned from his latest voyage?"

"He is expected any day; he may already be in Hofu. I have not heard."

"Father was in Hofu! Maybe they met there. Maybe they will return together." Shigeko turned and gazed back toward the bay. "Tomorrow we will climb the hill and see if their ship is in sight."

They entered the shrine enclosure, passing beneath the huge gate, whose architrave was carved with mythical animals and birds, houou, kirin, and shishi. The shrine was enfolded in greenery. Huge willow trees lined the riverbank; on the other three sides grew live oak and cedars, the last elements of the primeval forest that had once covered the land from mountain to river. The clamor of the city faded into stillness, broken only by birdsong. The slanting western light lit up the dust between the massive trunks in rays of gold.

A white horse in an elaborately carved stable neighed greedily on seeing them, and the twins went to offer carrots to the sacred beast, patting its plump neck and fussing over it.

An elderly man appeared from behind the main hall. He was the priest, and had been dedicated to the service of the river god as a young boy after his oldest brother drowned at the fish weir. His name was Hiroki. He was the third son of Mori Yusuke, the horsebreaker to the Otori. His older brother, Kiyoshige, had been Lord Shigeru's closest friend, and had died at Yaegahara.

Hiroki was smiling as he approached them. He shared in the city's unanimous approval of Shigeko, and had a particular bond with her through their love of horses. He had maintained his family's tradition, taking care of the Otori horses after his father went to the end of the world in search of the swift horses of the steppes. Yusuke himself never returned, but he sent back a stallion that became the sire of Raku and Shun, who were both broken in and trained by Takeshi, Shigeru's younger brother, before his death.

"Welcome, lady!" Like many people, he ignored the twins as though their existence was too shameful to acknowledge. The girls withdrew a little under the shade of the trees, watching the priest carefully with their opaque eyes. Shigeko saw they were angry. Miki in particular had a fiery temper, which she had not yet learned to bring under control. Maya's temper was colder but more implacable.

After they had exchanged courtesies and Shigeko had presented the offerings, Hiroki pulled on the bell rope to waken the spirit, and Shigeko made her usual prayer for the protection of the horses, seeing herself as an intermediary between the physical world and the spiritual for beings who had no speech and therefore no prayers.

A half-grown cat came scampering along the veranda, chasing a fallen leaf. Hiroki caught it up in his arms, caressing its head and ears. It began to purr throatily. Its eyes were huge and amber, its pupils slitted against the bright sun, its pale rust-colored fur splashed by patches of black and ginger.

"You have a new friend," Shigeko exclaimed.

"Yes, he came to seek shelter one wet night and has stayed ever since. He is a good companion, the horses like him, and he terrifies the mice into silence."

Shigeko had never seen a more handsome cat; the contrasts in its coloring were striking. She saw the old man had grown fond of the animal, and she was glad for him. His family were all dead—he had lived through the defeat of the Otori at Yaegahara and the destruction of the city in the earthquake. His only interests now were his service of the river god and his care of the horses.

The cat allowed itself to be patted for a moment, then struggled until Hiroki put it down. It dashed away, tail high.

"There's a storm coming," Hiroki said, chuckling. "He feels the weather in his fur."

Maya had picked up a twig. She bent down and scratched the leaves with it. The cat went still, its eyes intent.

"Let's go and see the horses," Shigeko said. "Come with me, Shizuka."

Miki ran after them, but Maya remained crouched in the shade, enticing the cat to come closer. The maid waited patiently on the veranda.

One corner of the small field had been fenced with bamboo, and a black colt was confined within it. The ground was worn and rutted where the horse had been pacing, and when it saw them, it neighed shrilly and reared. The two other young horses called in reply. They were nervous and skittish. Both had recent bite marks on neck and flank.

A boy was filling the colt's water bucket. "He kicks it over on purpose," he grumbled. One of his arms bore the signs of teeth-marks and bruising.

"Did he bite you?" Shigeko asked.

The boy nodded. "He's kicked me too." He showed another dark purple bruise on his calf.

"I don't know what to do with him," Hiroki said. "He has always been difficult: now he has become dangerous."

"He's beautiful," Shigeko said, admiring the long legs and muscled back, the fine-shaped head and large eyes.

"Yes, he's fine looking, and tall—the tallest horse we have. But his temperament is so intractable, I don't know if he'll ever be broken, or if we should breed from him."

"He looks ready to breed!" Shizuka remarked, and they all laughed, for the horse was showing all the signs of an eager stallion.

"I'm afraid putting him with the mares will make him worse," Hiroki said.

Shigeko moved closer to the colt. It rolled its eyes and put its ears back.

"Be careful," Hiroki warned, and at that moment the horse tried to bite her.

The horse boy smacked it as Shigeko drew back out of reach of the horse's teeth. She studied the animal for a few moments without saying anything.

"Confining him must make him worse," she said. "Move the other young ones and let him have this field to himself. How would it be if you brought a couple of old, barren mares—would they calm him down and teach him manners?"

"It's a good idea; I'll try it," the old man said, and told the boy to take the other two horses to the farther meadows. "We'll bring the mares in a day or two. He'll appreciate company more if he's lonely!"

"I will come every day and see if he can be gentled," Shigeko said, thinking she would write to Hiroshi and ask his advice. *Maybe Hiroshi will even come and help me break him in . . .*

Shigeko was smiling to herself as they returned to the shrine.

Maya was sitting on the veranda next to the maid, eyes cast down in a semblance of docility. The cat lay limp in the dirt, a small bundle of fur, all its beauty and vitality faded.

The old man cried out, and went hurrying, stumbling, toward it. He picked it up and held it close. It moved slightly, but did not waken.

Shizuka went at once to Maya. "What have you done?"

"Nothing," she replied. "It looked at me, and then it fell asleep."

"Wake up, Mikkan," the old man implored in vain. "Wake up!"

Shizuka was gazing in alarm at the cat. With a visible effort to control her reaction, she said quietly, "It will not waken. Not for a long time, if ever."

"What is it?" Shigeko said. "What did she do to it?"

"I didn't do anything," Maya said again, but her eyes, when she looked up, were hard and bright, almost excited, and when she looked at the old man, who had begun to weep quietly, her mouth twisted scornfully.

Then Shigeko realized and said, feeling sick, "It's one of those secret skills, isn't it? Something she learned while she was away? Some horrible sorcery!"

"Let's not talk about it here," Shizuka murmured, for the shrine servants had gathered round and were staring open-mouthed, fingering their amulets and invoking the protection of the river spirit. "We must go back. Maya must be punished. But it may be too late."

"Too late for what?" Shigeko demanded.

"I will tell you later. I only half-understand these Kikuta skills. I wish your father were here."

SHIGEKO LONGED EVEN more for her father to come home as she faced her mother's anger. It was late on the same day; Shizuka had taken the twins away to inflict some kind of punishment on Maya, and they had been sent to separate rooms to sleep. Thunder rolled in the distance, and now from where she knelt, head bowed before her mother, she could see the glimmer on the gold-embossed walls as lightning flashed far out at sea. The cat's weather prediction had been correct.

Kaede said, "You should not have taken them there together! You know I do not want them seen in public together."

"Forgive me, Mother," Shigeko whispered. She was not accustomed to her mother's disapproval, and it hurt her deeply. Yet she was concerned for the twins, too, and felt her mother was unjust to them. "It had been a hot day; they had studied hard. They needed an outing."

"They may play in the garden here," Kaede replied. "Maya must be sent away again."

"It is the last summer we will all spend together in Hagi," Shigeko pleaded. "Let her stay at least until Father comes home."

"Miki is manageable, but Maya is growing beyond control," Kaede exclaimed. "And no punishment seems to touch her. Separation from her twin, you, and her father may be the best way of curbing her will. It would also give us some peace during the summer!"

"Mother . . . ?" Shigeko began, but then could not continue.

"I know you think I am hard on them both," Kaede said after a moment of silence. She approached her daughter, and raised her head so she could see her face. Then she drew her close and caressed the long, silky hair.

"How beautiful your hair is! Just like mine used to be!"

"They wish you could love them," Shigeko dared to say, feeling her mother's anger abate. "They believe you hate them because they are not boys."

"I do not hate them," Kaede said. "I am ashamed of them. It is a terrible thing to have twins, like a curse. I feel it was a punishment of some kind, a warning from Heaven. And when incidents like this one with the cat occur, they frighten me. Often I think it would be better if they had died at birth, like most twins. Your father would not hear of it. He allowed them to live. But now I ask myself: For what purpose? They are Lord Otori's daughters; they cannot go off and live with the Tribe. They will soon be of marriageable age—who among the warrior class will ever marry them? Who would take a sorceress for a wife? If their skills were disclosed, they might even be put to death for them."

Shigeko felt her mother trembling.

"I do love them," Kaede whispered. "But sometimes they cause me so much pain and fear that I wish they were dead. And I have always longed for a son; I can't pretend I have not. The question of whom you will marry also torments me. I used to consider it the greatest blessing of my life that I loved your father and was able to marry him. But I have come to see that it was not without cost. I acted foolishly and selfishly in many ways. I went against everything I had been taught from childhood, that I had been expected and advised to do, and will probably pay for it for the rest of my life. I would not wish you to make the same mistakes, especially because, as we have no sons and you will inherit, the choice of your husband has become a political matter."

"I have often heard Father say he is happy that a girl—I—will inherit your realm."

"So he always claims. It is to spare my feelings. All men want sons."

Yet Father does not seem to, Shigeko thought. But her mother's words, their hint of regret, and the seriousness of her tone, remained in her heart.

ews of Muto Kenji's death took some weeks to reach Inuyama. The Kikuta were divided between the desire to keep it secret as long as possible while they tried to rescue the hostages, and the temptation to boast about it to show Otori that beyond the Three Countries he was powerless.

During Takeo and Kaede's rule, roads throughout the Three Countries had been improved, and messages were carried swiftly between the great cities. But across the Eastern border, where the High Cloud Range formed a natural barrier, lay miles of wild country almost all the way to the free city of Akashi, the port that formed the gateway to the Emperor's capital of Miyako. The rumors of Muto Kenji's death were heard in Akashi around the beginning of the fourth month, and from there the news traveled to Inuyama by way of a merchant who traded in the free city and often passed on information from the East to Muto Taku.

Even though he had expected it, Taku was both saddened and angered by his uncle's death, feeling the old man should have passed away peacefully in his own home, fearing that the approach would seem like weakness to the Kikuta and would only encourage them further, and praying that Kenji's death had been swift and not without some meaning.

He felt he himself should break the news to Takeo, and Sonoda and Ai agreed that he should leave at once for Hofu, where Takeo had gone for reasons of government while Kaede and their children had returned to Hagi for the summer.

A decision on the fate of the hostages also had to be formally delivered by either Takeo or Kaede. They would be executed now, presumably, but it had to be done according to the law and not seen as an act of revenge. Taku himself had inherited Kenji's cynicism and was not averse to committing acts of revenge, but he respected Takeo's insistence on justice—or at least the appearance of justice. Kenji's death also affected the Tribe, as he had been its head for well over twenty years—someone would have to be chosen from the Muto family to succeed him. Taku's older brother, Zenko, was the closest male relative, for Kenji had had no children apart from his daughter, Yuki, yet Zenko had taken his father's name, had no Tribe skills, and was now a warrior of the highest rank, head of the Arai clan and lord of Kumamoto.

Which left Taku himself, in many ways the obvious heir, highly talented in invisibility and the use of the second self, trained by Kenji, trusted by Takeo. It was another reason to travel now through the Three Countries, to meet with the Tribe families, confirm their loyalty and support, and discuss who should be the new Master.

Furthermore, he was restless—he had been in Inuyama all winter. His wife was pleasant, his children amused him, but domestic life bored him; he bade his family farewell with no regrets, and despite the sad nature of his mission set out the following day with a sense of mingled relief and anticipation, riding the horse Takeo had given him when he was still a child—it was the son of Raku, to whom many horse shrines were now dedicated, and had the same pale gray coat and coal black mane and tail, the coloring most highly prized in the Three Countries. Taku had named him Ryume.

Ryume himself had fathered many colts, and was now old and venerable, yet Taku had never had a horse he liked as much as this one that he had broken in himself and that had grown up with him.

It was not a good time to travel, the spring rains having just commenced, but the news could not be delayed, and no one could take it but himself. He rode fast, despite the bad weather, hoping to catch Takeo before he left Hofu.

THE ARRIVAL OF the kirin and encounter with his sister had prevented Takeo from leaving for Hagi immediately as he wished. His nephews, Sunaomi and Chikara, were prepared for the journey, but a heavy storm delayed their departure for a further two days. Thus he was still in Hofu when Muto Taku came from Inuyama to his older brother's house, asking to be admitted to Lord Otori's presence immediately. It was obvious that Taku was the bearer of bad news. He arrived alone, late in the evening when the light had almost faded, weary and travel-stained, yet would not bathe or eat until he had spoken to Takeo.

There were no details, only the grim fact that Muto Kenji was dead. There was no corpse to weep over, no stone to mark the grave—the hardest of deaths to mourn, distant and unseen. Takeo's grief was intense, made worse by his sense of despair. Yet he felt unable to give way to it in Zenko's house, and unable to confide in Taku as completely as he would have liked. He resolved to leave the next morning for Hagi, and to ride fast. His main desire was to see Kaede, to be with her, to find comfort with her. Yet his other concerns would not stand aside and wait while he dealt with grief. He had to keep at least one of Zenko's sons with him; he would take Sunaomi—the boy would have to ride as fast as he did—and send the younger boy with Ishida and the kirin, by boat, as soon as the weather cleared. Taku could take care of that. And Kono? Perhaps Taku could also stay in the West and keep an eye on him. How soon would he hear from Fumio? Had he managed to intercept the smuggled firearms? And if he had not, how long would it take Takeo's enemies to match him in weaponry?

Memories of his teacher and of the past assailed him. He mourned not only the loss of Kenji but all its associations. Kenji had been among Shigeru's closest friends—one more link had been broken.

Then there was the question of the hostages in Inuyama. They must now be put to death, yet it must be done legally, and he or a member of his family should be present. He would have to write to Ai's husband, Sonoda, send the order to him, and Ai would have to stand in for Kaede, something his tender-hearted sister-in-law would flinch from.

He spent most of the night awake in the company of grief, and at first light called for Minoru and dictated the letter to Sonoda and Ai, but before affixing his seal he spoke again to Taku.

"I find myself more than usually reluctant to order the deaths of these young people. Can we turn to any alternative?"

"They were involved in an assassination attempt on your own family," Taku replied. "You yourself established the laws and the penalties. What would you do with them? To pardon them and set them free would seem like weakness, and long imprisonment is crueler than swift death."

"But will their deaths prevent future attacks? Will they not simply enrage the Kikuta further against me and my family?"

"Akio's feud against you is already absolute. He will never relent while you remain alive," Taku replied, and then added, "But the deaths will remove two more assassins, and sooner or later they will run out of those willing or competent. You must outlive them."

"You sound like Kenji," Takeo said. "As realistic and pragmatic as he always was. I suppose you will take over the leadership of the family now?"

"I will discuss it with my mother. And my brother, of course, for form's sake. Zenko has few Tribe skills, and carries our father's name, but he is still my senior in age."

Takeo raised his eyebrows slightly. He had preferred to leave the handling of Tribe matters to Kenji and Taku, trusting Kenji completely. He was uneasy at the idea of Zenko sharing in some of their secrets.

"Your brother has approached me with the proposition to adopt one of his sons," he said, allowing a note of surprise to enter his voice, which he knew Taku would not miss. "Sunaomi will accompany me to Hagi. I'll leave within the hour. But there are many things we must discuss first. Let's walk in the garden."

"Lord Otori," Minoru reminded him, "will you finish this letter first?"

"No, bring it with us. I will discuss the matter further with my wife before I come to a decision. We will send it from Hagi."

The early light was gray, the morning damp and humid, with more rain threatening. The journey would be wet and uncomfortable. Takeo could already anticipate how the ache in his old injuries would be made worse by the days on horseback. He was aware that Zenko was probably watching him, resenting his closeness to Taku, knowing he would be confiding in his brother. The reminder that Zenko was also Muto by birth, and related, like Taku, to the Kikuta, had put him on his guard. He hoped it was true that Zenko's Tribe skills were negligible, and spoke quietly, telling Taku briefly about Lord Kono's message, as well as the smuggled weapons.

Taku absorbed all this information in silence; his only comment was, "Your trust in my brother has been eroded, I imagine."

"He has renewed his oaths to me, but we all know oaths mean nothing in the face of ambition and the lust for power. Your brother has always blamed me for your father's death—and now it seems the Emperor and his court do too. I do not trust either your brother or his wife, but while their sons are in my care I think their ambitions can be contained. They must be contained—the alternatives are that we fall again into civil war or I must order your brother to take his own life. I will avoid this for as long as I can. But I must ask you to be more than usually discreet, and to disclose nothing that might advantage him."

Taku's habitual expression of amused cynicism had darkened.

"I would kill him myself if he were to betray you," he said.

"No!" Takeo replied swiftly. "That brother should kill brother is unthinkable. Those days of blood feuds are over. Your brother, like everyone else—including yourself, my dear Taku—must be contained by law." He paused for a moment and then said quietly, "But tell me: Did Kenji ever speak to you about the prophecy that was given to me, that I am safe from death, except at the hands of my son?"

"Yes, after one of the attempts on your life, he remarked that the prophecy might be true after all—he was not usually credulous about prophecies and signs. He told me then what had been spoken about you.

He said it partly to explain your constant fearlessness, and why the threat of attack did not paralyze you or make you ferociously cruel, as it would most men."

"I am not credulous either," Takeo replied, smiling ruefully. "And sometimes I believe in the truth of the words, and sometimes I don't. It has suited me to believe because it has given me time to achieve everything I wanted, without living in fear. However, the boy is sixteen years old now, easily old enough, in the Tribe, to take life. So now I find myself trapped—can I cease to believe when it no longer suits me?"

"It would be easy enough to get rid of the boy," Taku offered.

"Taku, you have learned nothing from all my efforts! Those days of secret assassination are over. I could not take your brother's life when my knife was at his throat in the heat of battle. I could never order the death of my own son."

After a moment Takeo went on, "Who else knows of this prophecy?"

"On the occasion Kenji told me, Dr. Ishida was present. He had been treating the wound, and trying to control the fever. Kenji spoke as much to reassure him that you might not be at the point of death, for Ishida had given up all hope."

"Zenko does not know?"

"He knows of the existence of your son—he was in the Muto village when news came of Yuki's death. Everyone talked about little else for weeks. But I don't think Kenji spoke of the prophecy on any other occasion save the one I have just told you about."

"Then let it remain a secret between us," Takeo said.

The younger man nodded. "I will stay here with them, as you suggest," he said. "Watch closely, make sure Chikara leaves with Ishida, and maybe discover more of his parents' true intentions."

As they parted, Taku said, "Just one more thought. If you do adopt Sunaomi, and he becomes your son . . ."

"That is when I definitely choose not to believe!" Takeo replied, assuming a lightness he did not feel.

akeo set out around the Hour of the Snake; the rain held off, but toward evening it began to fall heavily. Sunaomi was quiet, eager to behave correctly and with courage yet clearly apprehensive about leaving his parents and family. Two of Zenko's retainers came with him to take care of him, while Takeo was accompanied by Jun and Shin, as well as a band of about twenty warriors and Minoru. They stayed the first night in a small village, where several inns had been established in these years of prosperity now that merchants and their goods traveled frequently between Hofu and Hagi. The road was kept in good repair, graveled or paved for its entire length; each small town was guarded, and travel had become safe and swift. Despite the rain, they came to the confluence of the rivers on the evening of the third day, and were met by Miyoshi Kahei, who had already been alerted by messengers that Lord Otori was traveling north.

Kahei had been rewarded for his loyalty to Takeo with the city of Yamagata and the lands that surrounded it, the luxuriant forest that made up the heart of the Middle Country and the rich farmland on either side of the river. Yamagata had been ceded to the Tohan after the Otori defeat at Yaegahara, and its return to the Middle Country had been an occasion of prolonged and ecstatic celebration. The Miyoshi were one of the greatest hereditary families of the Otori clan, and Kahei was a popular and effective ruler. He was also an inspired military leader, an expert in strategy and tactics who, Takeo thought, secretly regretted the years of peace and longed for some new conflict to test the validity of his theories and the strength and skill of his men. His brother, Gemba, had more sympathy for Takeo's desire to put an end to violence, and had become a disciple of Kubo Makoto and a follower of the Way of the Houou.

"You will go to Terayama?" Kahei questioned after they exchanged greetings and were riding side by side northward, toward the city.

"I have not yet decided," Takeo replied. "It is not that I don't deeply desire to, but I do not want to delay getting to Hagi."

"Shall I send word to the temple, and they will come to the castle?"

He could see no way of avoiding one or the other without offending his oldest friends. However, Kahei had several lively children who did not seem much in awe of their powerful father, and that evening, as Sunaomi opened up in the affectionate teasing atmosphere, Takeo thought suddenly that it would do the boy no harm to visit the most sacred place of the Otori, see the graves of Shigeru, Takeshi, and Ichiro, and meet Makoto and the other warriors of great spiritual maturity who made the temple their center and home. Sunaomi seemed both intelligent and sensitive—the Way of the Houou might be the correct discipline for him, as it had proved to be for Takeo's daughter Shigeko. He felt an unexpected spark of interest—how wonderful it would be to have a son to raise and educate in this way; the strength of the emotion surprised him. Arrangements were made to leave early the next morning. Minoru was to remain at Yamagata to oversee administrative details and prepare such records of evidence as might be necessary for the current tribunals.

The rain had turned to mist and the face of the earth was shrouded in gray; above the mountains the sky was leaden, and swathes of pearl-white cloud drifted like banners on the slopes. The cedars, their trunks streaked by the rain, dripped moisture. The horses' tread was dulled by the sodden ground. They rode in silence; Takeo was in no less pain than he had anticipated, and his mind was occupied with memories of his first visit to the temple and those who had ridden with him so long ago. He recalled in particular Muto Kenji, the most recent name to be written in the ledgers of the dead. Kenji, who on that journey had pretended to be a foolish old man, fond of wine and painting, who that night had embraced Takeo. *I must be getting fond of you. I don't want to lose you.* Kenji, who had both betrayed him and saved his life, who had vowed to protect him while he lived, and who had kept that vow despite all appearances to the contrary. He felt an aching sense of loneliness, for Kenji's death had left a gap in his life that would never be filled, and he felt freshly vulnerable, as vulnerable as he had first felt after the fight with Kikuta Kotaro that had left him crippled. Kenji had taught him to defend himself with the left hand dominant, had supported and advised him in the early years of establishing his control over the Three Countries, had split the Tribe for his sake and brought four of the five families under his control, all but the Kikuta, and had maintained the network of spies that kept him and his realm secure.

His thoughts then turned to Kenji's only surviving descendant, his grandson, held by the Kikuta.

My son, he thought, with the familiar mixture of regret, longing, and anger. *He has never known his father or his grandfather. He will never say the necessary prayers for his ancestors. There is no one else to honor Kenji's memory. What if I were to try to recover him?*

But that would mean revealing the boy's existence to his wife, his daughters, to the whole country. The secret had lain hidden for so long he did not know how he could speak of it. If only the Kikuta would be prepared to negotiate in some way, to make some concession. Kenji had thought they might be; he had chosen to approach Akio, and now he was dead, and two more young people would die as a result. Like Taku, Takeo wondered how many assassins the Kikuta had left, but unlike Taku the idea that their number must be dwindling did not lift his spirits.

The path was narrow, and the small group—Sunaomi and his two retainers, Takeo's two guards from the Tribe and another three Otori warriors, and two of Kahei's men—rode in single file. But after they left the horses at the lodging place at the foot of the holy mountain, Takeo called to Sunaomi to walk beside him, telling him a little of the history of the temple, of the Otori heroes who were buried there, of the houou, the sacred bird that nested in the deep groves behind the temple, and of the warriors who dedicated themselves to the Way of the Houou.

"We may send you here, when you are older; my own daughter comes here every winter and has done so since she was nine years old."

"I will do whatever my uncle desires for me," the boy replied. "I wish I might see a houou with my own eyes!"

"We will get up early in the morning and go to the grove before we return to Yamagata. You will almost certainly see one, for there are many of them now."

"Chikara gets to travel with the kirin," Sunaomi exclaimed, "and I get to see the houou! That's fair. But, uncle, what do you have to learn to follow the Way of the Houou?"

"The people we are coming to meet will tell you—monks like Kuba Makoto; warriors like Miyoshi Gemba. The main teaching is to renounce violence."

Sunaomi looked disappointed. "So I won't learn the way of the bow and the sword? That is what my father teaches us, and what he wants us to excel at."

"You will continue at training with the sons of warriors in Hagi, or in Inuyama when we reside there. But the Way of the Houou demands greater self-mastery than any other, and greater strength, physical and mental. You may not be suited for it."

He saw a light come into the boy's eyes. "I hope I will be," Sunaomi said, half-aloud.

"My oldest daughter will tell you more about it when we get to Hagi."

Takeo could hardly bear to speak the name of the town, so great was his longing to be there and to be with Kaede. However, he hid these feelings, in the same way as all day he had masked pain and grief. At the temple gates they were greeted with surprise and pleasure, and a monk was sent to apprise the Abbot, Matsuda Shingen, and Makoto of their arrival. They were escorted to the visitors' residence. Leaving Sunaomi and the men there, Takeo went straight through the garden, past the fish pools where the red and golden carp milled and splashed, to the sacred grove behind the temple, up against the steep rise of the mountain, where the Otori lords were buried.

The mist was heavier here, shrouding the gray lanterns and tombstones, which were darkened by moisture and speckled with green and white lichen. Moss, deeper green, covered their bases. A new straw rope gleamed around Shigeru's grave, and a small crowd of pilgrims stood with bowed heads before it, praying to the man who had become a hero and an avatar, the spirit of the Middle Country and the Otori clan.

They were mostly farmers, Takeo thought, possibly a merchant or two from Yamagata among them. When they saw him approach, they knew him at once from the crest on his robes, from the black-gloved hand. They dropped to the ground, but he greeted them and told them to get up, then asked them to leave him alone by the grave. He himself knelt, gazing on the offerings placed there, a handful of scarlet flowers, rice cakes, flasks of wine.

The past lay all around him, with all its painful memories and its demands. He owed his life to Shigeru; and he had lived it according to the will of the dead. His face was wet from the mist and from tears.

There was a movement behind him, and he turned to see Makoto walking toward him, carrying a lamp in one hand and a small incense holder in the other. He knelt and placed both before the grave. The gray smoke rose slowly, heavily, mingling with the mist, scenting the air. The lamp burned steadily, all the brighter for the dullness of the day.

For a long time they did not speak. Then a bell rang out from the temple courtyard, and Makoto said, "Come and eat. You must be hungry. It is so good to see you."

They both rose to their feet and studied each other. They had first met in this very place, seventeen years earlier, had taken an instant liking to each other, and had been lovers briefly in the way of passionate young men. Makoto had fought alongside Takeo in the battles of Asagawa and Kusahara and for many years had been his closest friend. Now with his usual swift understanding, he said, "What has happened?"

"I will tell you quickly. Muto Kenji is dead. He went to try to negotiate with the Kikuta and did not return. I am going to Hagi to break the news to my family. We will return to Yamagata tomorrow."

"I am very sorry for this loss. Kenji had been a loyal friend for many years. Of course you will want to be with Lady Otori at a time like this. But must you leave so soon? Forgive me, but you look terrible. Stay for a few days here and recover your strength."

Takeo smiled, tempted by the idea, envying Makoto his appearance of perfect physical and spiritual health. He was now in his mid-thirties, but his face was unlined and calm; his eyes were filled with warmth and amusement. His whole demeanor exuded serenity and self-mastery. Takeo knew his other old friend, Miyoshi Gemba, would look the same, as would all the followers of the Way. He felt a certain regret that the path he had been called to walk on was so different. As always when he visited Terayama, he fantasized about retreating there, devoting himself to painting and designing gardens like the great artist Sesshu; he would donate Jato, the sword he always bore though he had not fought with it for years, to the temple, and give up the life of warrior and ruler. He would forswear killing, abdicate the power of life and death that he held over every person in the land, unburden himself from the agonizing decisions this power entailed.

The familiar sounds of the temple and the mountain enveloped him. Consciously he opened the gate of his hearing and let the noise wash over him, the distant splash of the waterfall, the murmur of prayers from the main hall, Sunaomi's voice from the guests' residence, kites mewing from the tops of the trees. Two sparrows alighted on a branch, their gray feathers made distinct by the dull light and the dark foliage. He saw how he would paint them.

But there was no one else to take on his role—it was not possible simply to walk away from it.

"I am fine," he said. "I drink too much, but that eases the pain. Ishida gave me some new draught, but it dulls me—I won't use it often. We will stay one night here—I wanted Arai's son to see the temple and meet you. He is to live with my family. I may send him here in a year or two."

Makoto raised his eyebrows. "Zenko is causing problems?"

"Even more than usual. And there have been developments in the East that I must tell you about. I need to plan my response very carefully. Perhaps I should even travel to Miyako. We will talk about it later. How is Lord Matsuda? I am hoping for his advice too."

"He is still with us," Makoto replied. "He hardly eats, hardly even appears to sleep. He seems already half in the next world. But his mind is as clear as ever, maybe even clearer, like a mountain lake."

"I wish mine were," Takeo said, as they turned to walk back to the temple. "But it is more like one of those fish ponds—tens of ideas and problems mill and thrash around in it, each fighting for my attention."

"You should try to still your mind each day," Makoto observed.

"The only meditation skills I have are those of the Tribe—and their purpose is somewhat different!"

"Yet I have often observed that the skills innate in you, and other members of the Tribe, are not so unlike those that we have acquired through self-discipline and self-knowledge."

Takeo did not agree—he had never seen Makoto or his disciples use invisibility, for example, or the second self. He felt Makoto saw his skepticism, and regretted it.

"I don't have any time for it, and besides I have had little training or teaching in those ways. And I don't know if it would help anyway. I am involved in government . . . at least, if not, at present, in war."

Makoto smiled. "We pray for you here all the time."

"I suppose it makes a difference! Maybe it is your prayers that have maintained peace for nearly fifteen years."

"I am sure it is," Makoto replied serenely. "Not just empty prayers or meaningless chanting, but the spiritual balance we hold here. I use the word 'hold' to indicate the muscle and strength it requires; the strength of the archer to bend the bow or of the beams in the bell tower to support the weight of the bell."

"I suppose I believe you. I see the difference in those warriors who follow your teaching—their self-discipline, their compassion. But how will this help me deal with the Emperor and his new general, who are about to order me to go into exile?"

"When you have told me everything, we will advise you," Makoto promised. "First we will eat, and then you must rest."

TAKEO DID NOT think he would sleep, but after they had eaten the frugal midday meal of mountain vegetables, a little rice, and soup, it began to rain heavily again. The light became dim, greenish, and suddenly the idea of lying down seemed irresistible. Makoto took Sunaomi to meet some of the young students; Jun and Shin sat outside, drank tea, and conversed quietly.

Takeo slept, the pain receding as if dissolved by the steady drum of rain on the roof as much as the spiritual calm that had enveloped him. He dreamed of nothing, and awoke with a renewed sense of clarity and purpose. He bathed in the hot spring, remembering how he had soaked in this same pool in the snow when he had fled to Terayama all those years ago. When he had dressed again, he stepped onto the veranda just as Makoto and Sunaomi returned.

The boy had been touched by something, Takeo realized. His face was alight and his eyes were shining.

"Lord Miyoshi told me how he lived in the mountain, alone, for five years! The bears fed him, and on freezing nights curled up against him to keep him warm!"

"Gemba is here?" Takeo questioned Makoto.

"He returned while you were sleeping. He knew you were here."

"But how did he know?" Sunaomi demanded.

"Lord Miyoshi knows these things," Makoto replied, laughing.

"Did the bears tell him?"

"Very likely! Lord Otori, let us go and see the Abbot now."

Leaving Sunaomi with the Arai retainers, Takeo walked with Makoto past the refectory, where the youngest monks were clearing away the bowls from the evening meal, across the stream that had been diverted to flow past the kitchens, and into the courtyard in front of the main hall. From within this hall, hundreds of lamps and candles glowed around the golden statue of the Enlightened One, and Takeo was aware of the silent figures who sat in meditation within. They followed the boardwalk across another branch of the stream into the hall that held the Sesshu paintings, and looked out onto the garden. The rain had lessened, but night was falling and the rocks in the garden were no more than dark shadows, barely discernible. A sweet fragrance of blossom and wet earth pervaded the hall. The waterfall was louder here. On the far side of the main branch of the stream, which raced along one edge of the garden and away down the mountain, stood the women's guest house where Takeo and Kaede had spent their wedding night. It was empty; no lights shone from it.

Matsuda was already in the hall, leaning against thick cushions, which were propped up against two silent, unmoving monks. He had appeared old when Takeo had first met him; now he seemed to have passed beyond the confining borders of age, even of life, and to have entered a world of pure spirit.

Takeo knelt and bowed to the ground before him. Matsuda was the only person in the Three Countries whom he would so honor.

"Come closer," Matsuda said. "Let me look at you. Let me touch you."

The affection in his voice moved Takeo deeply. He felt his eyes grow hot as the old man leaned forward and clasped his hands. Matsuda's eyes searched his face; embarrassed by the threatening tears, Takeo did not return his gaze but looked beyond him to where the incomparable paintings stood.

Time has not moved for them, he thought. *The horse, the cranes—they are still as they were, and so many who looked on them with me are dead, flown away like the sparrows.* For one screen was empty, the legend being that the painted birds were so lifelike they took wing.

"So the Emperor is concerned with you," Matsuda said.

"Fujiwara's son, Kono, came ostensibly to visit his father's estate but in reality to inform me that I have incurred the Emperor's displeasure—am a criminal, in fact; I am to abdicate and go into exile."

"I am not surprised the capital is alarmed by you." Matsuda chuckled. "I am only surprised it has taken them so long to start threatening you."

"I believe there are two reasons. One is that the Emperor has a new general who has already brought much of the East under his control and must now fancy himself strong enough to provoke us. The other is that Arai Zenko has been in touch with Kono—again ostensibly concerning the estate. I suspect Zenko has been suggesting himself as my successor."

He felt the anger begin to simmer again, and knew at once that Matsuda and Makoto saw it. At the same time, he was aware of another person in the hall sitting in the shadows behind Matsuda. This man leaned forward now, and Takeo realized it was Miyoshi Gemba. They were almost the same age, yet like Makoto, Gemba did not seem to have been marked by the passage of time. He had a smooth, rounded look to him, relaxed yet powerful—not unlike a bear, in fact.

Something happened to the light. The lamps flickered and a bright flame leaped before Takeo's eyes. It hovered for an instant, then shot like a falling star out into the dark garden. He heard the hiss as the rain extinguished it.

His anger vanished in the same moment.

"Gemba," he said. "I am glad to see you! But have you been spending your time here learning magic tricks?"

"The Emperor and his court are very superstitious," Gemba replied. "They have many soothsayers, astrologists, and magicians. If I accompany you, you may be assured we will be able to match them in their tricks."

"So I should go to Miyako?"

"Yes," Matsuda said. "You must confront them in person. You will win the Emperor over to your side."

"I will need more than Gemba's tricks to persuade him. He is raising an army against me. I am afraid the only sensible response is with force."

"There will be some contest of a small nature in Miyako," Gemba said. "Which is why I must come with you. Your daughter should also come."

"Shigeko? No, it is too dangerous."

"The Emperor must see her and give her his blessing and approval if she is to become your successor—as she must."

Like Gemba, Matsuda spoke these words with complete certainty.

"We will not discuss this?" Takeo questioned. "We will not consider all the alternatives, and reach a rational conclusion?"

"We can discuss it if you like," Matsuda said. "But I have reached the age where long discussions tire me out. I can see the end we will reach eventually. Let's go straight to it."

"I must also seek my wife's opinion and advice," Takeo said. "As well as that of my senior retainers, and my own general, Kahei."

"Kahei will always favor war," Gemba said. "Such is his nature. But you must avoid outright warfare, especially if the warriors from the East have firearms."

Takeo felt a prickle of unease around his scalp and neck. "Do you know that they have?"

"No, I am just assuming they soon will have."

"Again it is Zenko who has betrayed me."

"Takeo, my old friend, if you introduce any new invention, be it weapon or whatever, if it is effective its secret will be stolen. This is the nature of men."

"So I should not have allowed the development of the firearm?" It was something he often regretted.

"Once you had been introduced to it, it was inevitable that you would develop it in your quest for power and control. Just as it is inevitable that your enemies will use it in their struggle to overthrow you."

"Then I must have more and better firearms than they do! I should attack them first, take them by surprise, before they can arm themselves."

"That would be one strategy," Matsuda observed.

"Certainly what my brother, Kahei, would advise," Gemba added.

"Makoto," Takeo said. "You are very silent. What are your thoughts?"

"You know I cannot advise you to go to war."

"So you will not advise me at all? You will sit here and chant and play tricks with fire, while everything I have worked to achieve is destroyed?" He heard the tone of his voice and fell silent, half-ashamed of his own irritation and half-alarmed that Gemba might dissolve it in flame again.

There was no showy trick this time, but the profound silence that followed had an equally powerful effect. Takeo felt the combined calm and clarity of the three minds and knew that these men supported him completely but would make the utmost effort to prevent him from acting rashly or dangerously. Many of those around him flattered him and deferred to him. These men would never do either, and he trusted them.

"If I am to go to Miyako, should I go immediately? In the autumn, when the weather is better?"

"Next year, perhaps, when the snows melt," Matsuda said. "You do not need to be in a hurry."

"That gives them nine months or more to raise an army!"

"It also gives you nine months to prepare for your visit," Makoto said. "I believe you should go with the greatest splendor, taking the most brilliant gifts."

"It also allows your daughter time to prepare herself," Gemba said.

"She turned fifteen this year," Takeo said. "She is old enough to be betrothed."

The thought disturbed him—to him she was still a child. And who would he ever find suitable to marry her?

"That may also be to your advantage," Makoto murmured.

"In the meantime she must perfect her horse riding, using the bow," Gemba declared.

"She will have no chance to display those skills in the capital," Takeo replied.

"We will see," Gemba said, and smiled in his enigmatic way. "Don't worry," he added, as if noticing Takeo's renewed irritation. "I will come with you, and no harm will befall her."

And then he said with sudden astuteness, "The daughters that you have deserve your attention more than the sons you do not have."

It felt like a rebuke, and it stung, for he took pride in the fact that his daughters had had all the education and training of boys, Shigeko in the way of the warrior, the twins in the skills of the Tribe. He pressed his lips firmly together and bowed again before Matsuda. The old man gestured to him to come closer and wrapped his frail arms around him. He did not speak, but Takeo knew suddenly that Matsuda was saying farewell to him, that this would be their last meeting. He drew back a little so he could look into the old priest's eyes. *Matsuda is the only person I can look in the face,* he thought. *The only person who does not succumb to the Kikuta sleep.*

As if reading his thoughts, Matsuda said, "I leave behind not one but two worthy—more than worthy—successors. Don't waste your time grieving for me. You know everything you need to know. Just try to remember it."

His tone held the same mixture of affection and exasperation that he had used when teaching Takeo the use of the sword. Again Takeo had to blink back tears.

As Makoto accompanied him to the guest house, the monk said quietly, "Do you remember how you went alone to Oshima, to the pirates' lair? Miyako cannot be more dangerous than that!"

"I was a young man then, and fearless. I did not believe anyone could kill me. Now I am old, crippled, and I fear far more—not for my own life in particular, but for my children and my wife, and for my land and people, that I will die leaving them unprotected."

"That is why it is best to delay your response—send flattering messages, gifts and promises. You know, you have always been impetuous; everything you do is done in haste."

"That is because I know my life is short. I have so little time to achieve what I have to."

HE FELL ASLEEP thinking about this sense of urgency that had driven him most of his life, and dreamed that he was in Yamagata, the night he had climbed into the castle and put an end to the suffering of the tortured

Hidden. In his dream he moved again with the infinite patience of the Tribe, through a night that seemed endless. Kenji had taught him how to make time slow down or speed up at will. He saw in his dream how the world altered according to his perception, and he woke with the feeling that some mystery had just eluded him, but also with a kind of elation, and miraculously still free from pain.

It was barely light. He could hear no sound of rain, just birds beginning to call, and the drip of the eaves. Sunaomi sat upright on his mattress, staring at him.

"Uncle? You're awake? Can we go and see the houou?"

The Arai retainers had stayed awake outside all night, though Takeo had assured them Sunaomi was in no danger. Now they leaped to their feet, helped their young lord put his sandals on, and followed him as Takeo led him to the main gate. This had been unbarred at dawn and was deserted—the guards had gone to eat breakfast. Passing through it, they turned to their right and took the narrow track that led along the outer walls of the temple grounds and up the steep slope of the mountain.

The ground was rough and stony, often slippery from the rain. After a while, one of the men picked Sunaomi up and carried him. The sky was a clear, pale blue, the sun just rising over the eastern mountains. The path leveled out and led through a forest of beech and live oak. Summer wildflowers carpeted the floor, and bush warblers called their morning song, echoing and answering each other. Later it would be hot, but now the air was perfect, cooled by the rain, and still.

Takeo could hear the rustle in the leaves and the flap of wings that indicated the presence of the houou in the forest ahead. Here among the broad-leaved trees was a stand of paulownia, which the birds favored for nesting and roosting, though they were said to feed on bamboo leaves.

Now the path was easier and Sunaomi demanded to be put down, and to Takeo's surprise ordered the two men to wait there while he went ahead with Lord Otori.

When they were out of earshot, he said confidentially to Takeo, "I did not think Tanaka and Suzuki should see the houou. They might want to hunt them or steal their eggs. I've heard a houou's egg is very valuable."

"Your instinct is probably right," Takeo replied.

"They are not like Lord Gemba and Lord Makoto," Sunaomi said. "I don't know how to put it. They will see, but they will not understand."

"You put it very well," Takeo replied, smiling.

A curious fluting call came from above them in the canopy, followed by a harsh cry in answer.

"There they are," Takeo whispered, feeling as always the sense of astonishment and awe that the presence of the sacred birds aroused in him. Their call was like their appearance, beautiful and strange, graceful and clumsy. The birds were both inspiring and somehow comical. He would never get used to them.

Sunaomi was staring upward, his face rapt. Then one bird burst out from the foliage and fluttered to the next tree.

"It is the male," Takeo said. "And here comes the female."

Sunaomi laughed in delight as the second bird swooped across the clearing, its long tail silky, its eyes bright gold. Its plumage was made up of many colors, and as it landed on the branch one feather fluttered down.

The birds were there for no more than an instant. They turned their heads toward each other, called again, each in its distinct voice, looked briefly but intently toward Takeo, and then flew away into the forest.

"Ah!" Sunaomi gasped and ran after them, staring upward so that he missed his footing and fell facedown in the grass. When he stood, the feather was in his hand.

"Look, Uncle!"

Takeo approached the boy and took the feather. Once Matsuda had shown him a houou's feather, white pinioned, tipped with red. It had come from a bird that Shigeru had seen when he was a boy, and had been preserved at the temple ever since. This feather was deep gold in color, apart from the pure white quill.

"Keep it," he said to Sunaomi. "It will remind you of this day, and of the blessing you received. This is why we seek peace always, so the houou will never leave the Three Countries."

"I will give the feather to the temple," Sunaomi said, "as a pledge that I will return one day and study with Lord Gemba."

This boy has such fine instincts, Takeo thought. *I will bring him up as my son.*

fter Takeo had left with Sunaomi, Taku sat for a while on the veranda looking out over the rain-soaked garden, thinking about all his mother's cousin had told him. It disturbed him more than he had revealed, for it threatened to bring him into open conflict with his older brother, something he had hoped to avoid. *What a fool Zenko is,* he thought, *and always has been. Just like our father!*

At ten years old, in the moment just before the earthquake had shattered the city, he had watched his father betray Takeo. Zenko had blamed Takeo for Arai's death, but Taku had interpreted the whole scene differently. He already knew his father had ordered his mother's death in a fit of rage—he would never forget or forgive his readiness to throw away the lives of his sons. He had thought Takeo would kill Zenko—often afterward dreamed that he had—and could never understand Zenko's resentment that Takeo had spared his life.

He had hero-worshipped Takeo as a boy, and now, as a man, respected and admired him. Moreover, the Muto family had sworn allegiance to the Otori; he would never break that oath. Quite apart from the obligations of honor and loyalty, he would have to be as big a fool as Zenko—his position in the Three Countries was everything he could desire, giving him power and status and enabling him to take full advantage of all his talents.

Takeo had also taught him many things that he had learned from the

Kikuta. Taku smiled to himself, remembering the many times he had succumbed to the Kikuta sleep until he had learned to evade it—and even use it himself. There was a strong bond between the two of them; they were alike in many ways, and both knew the conflicts caused by mixed blood.

Still, an older brother was an older brother, and Taku had been brought up to respect the hierarchy of the Tribe. He might be prepared to kill Zenko, as he had told Takeo, but he would not insult him by ignoring his right to have a say in who would take over the leadership of the Muto family. He decided he would suggest his mother, Shizuka, Kenji's niece. It might be an acceptable compromise.

His mother's husband, Dr. Ishida, would take Zenko's younger son to Hagi. He could take letters or verbal messages to Shizuka. Ishida, Taku believed, was trustworthy enough. His main weakness was a certain innocence, as if he found it hard to comprehend the depth of wickedness possible in human nature. Perhaps he had taught himself to ignore it in Lord Fujiwara, whom he had served for many years, and was all the more shocked by it when it emerged. Apart from the courage it must take to go off on his explorations, he was not physically brave, and did not like fighting.

Taku himself would stay close to Zenko and Kono, possibly even travel with Kono to the West, where he would arrange a meeting with Sugita Hiroshi, his oldest friend. It was important that Kono take a true picture of the Three Countries back to the capital, making it clear to the Emperor and his general that Lord Otori was supported unconditionally in Maruyama and Inuyama, and that Zenko stood alone.

Reasonably satisfied with these decisions, he went to the stables to see how the old horse, Ryume, had recovered from the journey. He was pleased with what he found there—whatever his brother's faults, his knowledge and care of horses was unparalleled. Ryume had been groomed—mane and tail were free of mud and untangled; the horse looked dry, well fed, and content. Despite his age, he was still a fine horse, and the grooms admired him openly, even treated Taku with greater deference on his account.

He was still petting the horse and feeding him carrots when Zenko came into the stable area. They greeted each other with their usual show of warmth.

"You still have Raku's son," Zenko said, putting his hand out and rubbing the horse's brow. Taku remembered Zenko's jealousy when they had returned to Hagi in the spring with the two beautiful colts, one Hiroshi's and one his, a clear indication of Takeo's fondness for them both, only serving to emphasize his coldness toward Zenko.

"I will give him to you," he said on an impulse. "He is not too old to get foals." Apart from his children, he could not have offered his brother anything more precious. He hoped the generosity of the gesture would soften Zenko's feelings toward him.

"Thank you, but I will not accept him," Zenko said. "He was a gift to you from Lord Otori, and anyway, I think he is too old to breed."

"Like Lord Otori," he remarked as they returned to the residence, "who has to get his sons from younger men."

Taku perceived that this was meant to be a joke, but it had a bitter ring to it. *Truly my brother construes everything as an insult,* he thought.

"It is a great honour to you and your wife," he said mildly, but Zenko's face was dark.

"Is it an honor, or are they now hostages?" he demanded.

"That surely rather depends on you," Taku replied.

Zenko made some noncommittal reply and dropped the subject.

"I suppose you will go to the Muto family home for the funeral ceremonies?" he said when they were seated inside.

"I believe Lord Takeo wishes to conduct a ceremony in Hagi. Our mother is there, and since there is no corpse to bury . . ."

"No corpse? So where did Kenji die? And how do we know he is dead? It would not be the first time he disappeared to suit his own purposes."

"I am sure he is dead." Taku glanced at his brother and went on, "He was in ill health—he may have died of the lung illness, but the mission he was undertaking was extremely dangerous, and he had arranged to come immediately to Inuyama if he had been successful. I am telling you this in confidence. The official story will be that he passed away from the disease."

"I suppose it was at the hands of the Kikuta?" Zenko said after a long silence.

"What makes you think that?"

"I may bear our father's name, brother, but that doesn't alter the fact that I am as much one of the Tribe as you. I have contacts among the Muto—and among the Kikuta, come to that. Everyone knows that Akio's son is Kenji's grandson. I imagine Kenji longed to see him—he was an old man, his health was failing. Akio, they say, has never forgiven him or Takeo for Kotaro's death. I am just drawing conclusions from the facts. I have to, because Takeo does not confide in me as he does in you."

Taku noted again the resentment in his brother's voice, but it concerned him less than his comment that he had contacts with the Kikuta. Could it be true, or was Zenko merely boasting?

He waited in silence to see what else Zenko would reveal.

"Of course there was the gossip in the Muto village about the boy," Zenko went on. "That Takeo was the father, not Akio." He spoke idly, but Taku was aware of the deep interest beneath the words.

"Only Muto Yuki would know for sure," he replied. "And she died shortly after the child was born."

"Yes, I remember," Zenko said. "Well, whoever the father is, the boy is Kenji's grandson, and the Muto family have an interest in him. If I am to become the Master, I shall contact the Kikuta about him."

"I believe it would be better to leave the question of who is to succeed Kenji until we have discussed it with our mother," Taku said politely. "I would be surprised if I had to remind you that the Master of the family usually possesses high skills."

Zenko flushed in anger, his eyes three-cornered. "I have many Tribe skills, little brother. They may not be as showy as yours, but they are very effective!"

Taku made a slight—and insincere—movement with his head to show submission, and they moved on to safer subjects. After a little while Lord Kono joined them; they ate the midday meal together and then went with Hana and the two younger boys to see the kirin. Afterward Dr. Ishida was invited back to the residence to become better acquainted with Chikara before taking him to Hagi.

ISHIDA HAD SEEMED very nervous on meeting Kono, and had become even more tense as the nobleman questioned him about his time in Fujiwara's household. He accepted the invitation with reluctance, and arrived somewhat late for the evening meal—already, Taku realized with apprehension, quite drunk.

Taku himself was tense, disturbed by his conversation with Zenko and aware of all the undercurrents in the room as they ate. In his habitual way, he gave no sign of this, conversing lightly but courteously with Kono, complimenting Hana on the food and her sons, and trying to draw Ishida into innocuous subjects such as the customs of the Gen nomads or the life cycle of whales. He had a guarded, somewhat barbed relationship with his sister-in-law, whom he did not particularly like or trust but whose intelligence and spirit he could not help admiring—and no man could help responding to her beauty. Taku recalled how they had all been besotted by her when they were boys—he, Zenko, and Hiroshi. They had followed her around like dogs with their tongues hanging out, and had competed for her attention.

It was common knowledge that Kono's father had preferred men to women, but Taku saw nothing to indicate that the son took after him. Indeed, he thought he saw a natural enough attraction behind Kono's attention to Hana. *Impossible not to desire her,* he thought, and wondered fleetingly what it would be like to wake in the dark with her alongside him. He could almost envy Zenko.

"Dr. Ishida took care of your father," Hana remarked to Kono. "And now he looks after Lord Otori's health."

Taku heard both duplicity and malevolence in her voice, and desire gave way to dislike. He was thankful he had recovered from his infatuation— and had never suffered another. He thought gratefully of his own straightforward wife, whom he knew he could trust and whom he missed already. It was going to be a long, tedious summer.

"With great success," Zenko said, "Dr. Ishida has saved Lord Otori from death on many occasions."

"My father always had the highest regard for your skill," Kono said to Ishida.

"You flatter me unduly. My skill is negligible."

Taku thought Ishida would say no more on the matter, but after another deep draught of wine the doctor went on, "Of course, Lord Otori's case is quite fascinating, from the point of view of a man like myself who is interested in the workings of the human mind." He paused, drank deeply, then leaned forward and said confidentially, "Lord Otori believes no one can kill him—he has made himself immortal."

"Indeed?" Kono murmured. "That sounds a little grandiose. Is it some kind of a delusion?"

"In a way, yes. A very useful one. There was some prophecy made— Taku, you were there when your poor uncle—"

"I don't remember," Taku said swiftly. "Chikara, how do you feel about a sea voyage with a kirin?"

Chikara gulped at being addressed directly by his uncle, and before he could reply, Zenko inquired, "What prophecy?"

"That Lord Otori can only die at the hands of his own son." Ishida drank again. "Why was I talking about that? Oh yes, the effects of strong belief on the body. He believes he cannot be killed, and his body responds by healing itself."

"Fascinating," Kono said smoothly. "Lord Otori does seem to have survived many attacks on his life. Have you known other similar cases?"

"Well, yes," Ishida said, "in my travels in Tenjiku, where there are holy men who can walk on flame and not get burned, and lie on beds of nails with no harm to their skin."

"Did you know of this, brother?" Zenko demanded quietly, while Kono pressed Ishida for more traveler's tales.

"It is no more than a popular superstition," Taku said lightly, inwardly wishing all the torments of hell on the drunken doctor. "The Otori family are the target of endless gossip and speculation."

"My sister was the subject of such hearsay," Hana said. "She was supposed to bring death to any man who desired her, but Lord Takeo has survived the danger quite well. Heaven be thanked," she added, glancing at Taku.

The laughter that followed was slightly uncomfortable, as more than one person present recalled that Lord Fujiwara had married Kaede, against her will, and had not survived.

"Yet everyone knows of the Five Battles," Zenko went on. "And the earthquake—'Earth delivers what Heaven desires.'" He saw Kono's quizzical look and explained. "A prophecy was made by a holy woman, which was confirmed by Takeo's victories in the war. The earthquake was held to be a sign from Heaven, favoring him."

"Yes, so he told me," Kono said, mockery in his voice. "So convenient for the victor to have a useful prophecy at hand." He drank and then said more seriously, "In the capital an earthquake is usually seen as a punishment for evil conduct, not a reward."

Taku did not know whether to speak and reveal to Kono where his loyalties lay, or to say nothing and seem to be in support of his brother. He was rescued by Ishida, who spoke with great emotion. "The earthquake saved my life. And that of my wife. In my opinion the evil were punished."

Tears sprang into his eyes, and he wiped them away on his sleeve. "Forgive me, I did not mean to insult the memory of either of your fathers." He turned to Hana. "I should retire. I am very tired. I hope you will excuse an old man."

"Of course, Father," she said, addressing him with courtesy, for he was her husband's stepfather. "Chikara, take grandfather to his room and tell the maids to assist him."

"I'm afraid he had a little too much to drink," she apologized to Kono after the boy had helped the doctor to his feet and they had left.

"He is a most interesting man. I am sorry he is to go to Hagi. I hoped

to have many conversations with him. He knew my father better than anyone alive, I think."

And was fortunate not to die at his hands, Taku thought.

"The prophecy is interesting, is it not?" Kono said. "Lord Otori has
no sons, I believe."

"He has three daughters," Taku said.

Zenko laughed, a short, conspiratorial burst. "Officially," he said.
"There is more gossip about Takeo . . . but I must not be indiscreet!"

Kono raised his eyebrows. "Well, well!" he said.

As Kenji would say, that's torn it, Taku thought. *Uncle, what am I going to do
without you?*

· 14 ·

 iyoshi Kahei accompanied Takeo to Hagi with his old-est son, Katsunori. The city was his hometown, and he was glad to have the chance to see his relatives. Takeo, on the other hand, knew he would need Kahei's advice on how best to counter the growing threat from the capital, Miyako, from the Emperor and his general, and how he should spend the winter of preparation.

It was hard to think of winter now, at the end of the plum rains, with all the heat of summer still to come. Other concerns should take prece-dence over war: the harvest, the usual anxieties about plague and other hot-weather illnesses and what measures could be taken to prevent them, the conservation of water in case of late summer drought. But all of these matters lost their urgency when he allowed himself to think of seeing Kaede and his daughters.

They rode across the stone bridge at the end of a day of sun and show-ers, like the fox's wedding. Takeo was aware of the clammy cling of his clothes—he had been soaked to the skin so often on the journey he could hardly remember how it felt to be dry. Even the lodging places had been humid, smelling of damp and mildew.

Over the sea, the sky was a clear translucent blue, turning yellow in the west as the sun set. Behind them, the mountains were covered in heavy clouds, and thunder rumbled, making the horses startle despite their fatigue.

The animal he was riding was nothing special; he missed his old horse, Shun, and wondered if he would ever find another like him. He would talk to Mori Hiroki about horses, and also to Shigeko. If they were to go to war, they would need more horses . . . but he did not want to go to war.

The Miyoshi brothers left him at the gate. He dismounted in the main bailey; the horses were led away, and, taking only Sunaomi, he walked through the gardens. Word had gone ahead to the castle. Kaede waited for him on the long veranda that surrounded the residence. The sound of the sea filled the air, and doves were calling from the roofs. Her face was alight with joy.

"We did not expect you so soon! What weather to ride in! You must be exhausted. And you are soaking wet."

The pleasure her affectionate scolding roused in him was so intense that for a moment he wanted to stand there forever. Then it was replaced by the desire to hold her, to lose himself in her. But first the news must be broken, to Kaede to Shizuka.

Shigeko came running from the interior of the residence. "Father!" she cried, and knelt to remove his sandals. Then she noticed the boy, who was standing back in shyness.

"Can this be our cousin?" she said.

"Yes, Sunaomi is going to live with us for a while."

"Sunaomi!" Kaede exclaimed. "But why? Is his mother all right? Has something happened to Hana?"

He saw her concern for her sister and wondered how much he could tell her of his suspicions.

"She is well," he replied. "I will tell you the reasons for Sunaomi's visit later."

"Of course. Come inside. You must bathe at once, and put on dry clothes. Lord Takeo, do you think you are still eighteen years old? You take no concern for your health!"

"Is Shizuka here?" he inquired as Kaede led him along the veranda to the rear of the residence, where a pool had been constructed around a hot spring.

"Yes, what has happened?" Kaede glanced up at his face and said,

"Shigeko, tell Shizuka to come to us shortly. Ask the maids to bring clothes for your father."

Shigeko's face was serious as she bowed and left them. He could hear her light tread on the boards; he heard her speak to her sisters. "Yes, Father is home. But you are not to go to him yet. Come with me. We are to find Shizuka."

They were alone. The light was leaching from flowers and shrubs. Around the pools and streams a late iris or two gleamed. Sky and sea merged into each other in the mist of evening. Around the bay fires and lamps began one by one to sprinkle the darkness. Kaede said nothing as she helped him remove his clothes.

"Muto Kenji is dead," he said.

She took water from the pool in a bamboo bucket and began to wash him. He saw tears begin to form in her eyes and spill down her cheeks. Her touch was both soothing and almost unbearable. Every part of his body seemed to hurt. He longed for her to put her arms around him and hold him, but first he had to speak to Shizuka.

Kaede said, "It is a terrible loss. How did it happen? Did he succumb to the sickness?"

He heard himself say, "It seems mostly likely. He was traveling beyond the borders. There are no clear details. Taku came to tell me in Hofu."

He did not linger as long as he would have liked in the hot water, but emerged and dressed quickly. "I must speak to Shizuka alone," he told Kaede.

"Surely you have no secrets from me?"

"They are Tribe matters," he said. "Kenji was the Master of the Muto family. Shizuka is going to have to choose his successor. It is not to be discussed with outsiders."

He saw that she was not pleased, that she wanted to stay with him.

"There are many other things you and I need to talk about," he said to placate her. "We will be alone later. I must tell you about Sunaomi. And I had a visit from Lord Fujiwara's son . . ."

"Very well, Lord Takeo. I will order a meal to be prepared for you," she said, and left him.

When he returned to the main room of the residence, Shizuka was already there. He spoke without any preliminary greeting. "No doubt you can guess why I am here. I have come to bring you the news that your uncle is dead. Taku came to Hofu to tell me, and I thought you should know at once."

"Such news is never welcome," Shizuka replied formally, "but it is not unexpected. I thank you, cousin, for your thoughtfulness, and for your honoring my uncle in this way."

"I think you know what he has been to me. We have no corpse, but we will further honor him with a ceremony here or in Yamagata, whichever you think is the most fitting."

"I thought he might have died in Inuyama," she said slowly. "He was living there, was he not?"

No one had known of Kenji's mission save he himself and Taku. He regretted now that he had not told Shizuka earlier. "Come closer," he said. "I must tell you all I know, because it affects the Tribe."

Before she could move, a maid came with tea. Shizuka poured it for him. While Takeo drank, she rose, looked quickly around the room, opened the closet doors, then stepped onto the veranda and peered beneath it.

She came back to Takeo and sat before him, knee to knee. "Can you hear anyone breathing?"

He listened. "No, we seem to be alone."

"Your daughters have become adept eavesdroppers, and can hide themselves away in the narrowest of spaces."

"Thank you. I do not want my daughters or my wife to overhear us. I told Kaede Kenji died from the lung illness; that he had gone to seek treatment beyond the Eastern borders."

"And the truth?"

"He went to try to negotiate with the Kikuta. After the episode at Inuyama we thought we might use Gosaburo's children to put pressure on them to make a truce." He sighed, and went on. "Kenji wanted to see Yuki's child, his grandson. Taku knows only that he died in the Kikuta village where Akio and the boy have been hiding for some years."

"Takeo, you should tell Kaede all this . . ."

He did not allow her to continue. "I am telling you because it concerns the Muto family, of which you are now the senior member. There is no need for Kaede, or anyone outside the Tribe, to know."

"Better she should hear it from you than from anyone else," Shizuka said.

"I have kept it all secret for too long to be able to speak of it to her now. It is all past—the boy is Akio's son; my daughter is my heir. In the meantime, there is the question of the Muto family and the Tribe. Kenji and Taku worked closely together: Kenji's knowledge and skills were unparalleled. Taku has great skills, but I think you will agree there is a certain unsteadiness about him—I wonder if he is old enough to lead the Tribe. Zenko is your older son and Kenji's direct heir, and I do not want to insult and annoy him or give him any pretext for . . ." He broke off.

"For what?" Shizuka prompted him.

"Well, I think you know how much your son resembles his father. I am worried about his intentions. I do not intend to allow him to return us to civil war again." He spoke with intensity, then smiled at Shizuka and went on more lightly: "So I have arranged for his sons to spend some time with us. I thought you would like to see your grandsons."

"I have already seen Sunaomi," Shizuka said. "It is indeed a great pleasure. Is Chikara to come too?"

"Your husband will bring him by ship, along with a fabulous creature that is said to be a kirin," Takeo said.

"Ah, Ishida is back; I'm happy to hear it. To tell you the truth, Takeo, I would be quite content with my quiet life, companion to Kaede and your children, wife to my dear doctor . . . but I think you are going to make other demands on me."

"You are as perceptive as ever," he replied. "I want you to become head of the Muto family. Taku will work with you as he worked with Kenji, and Zenko must of course defer to you."

"The head of the family is known as the Master," Shizuka reminded him. "There has never been a woman 'Master.' 'Mistress' has quite a different meaning!" she added.

"You may be called, simply, the head, or whatever you like. It will set an excellent precedent. I intend to introduce this into the local districts too—we will start with the Middle Country and spread outward. There are already many areas where women of merit and ability stand in for their husbands. They will be recognized and given the same authority as men."

"So you will strengthen the country from the roots upward, and these women will be your daughter's support?"

"If she is the sole woman ruler, she will have to become like a man. If other women are in positions of power, we may see change flow throughout the Three Countries."

"You are still a visionary, cousin!" Shizuka said, smiling despite her grief.

"You will do as I ask, then?"

"Yes, partly because my uncle once hinted that this would also be his wish. And at least until Taku settles down and Zenko comes to his senses. I believe he will, Takeo, and I'm grateful to you for your careful handling of him. But whatever the outcome, the Muto family will stay faithful to you and your family." She bowed formally to him. "I will swear that to you now, Lord Otori, as their head."

"I know what you have already done for Lord Shigeru and the Otori. I owe you a huge debt," Takeo said with emotion.

"I'm glad we have this chance to speak alone," she went on, "as we must also talk about the twins. I had hoped to ask my uncle about something that happened recently, but maybe you will know how to deal with this."

She told him about the episode with the cat, how it had slept and never woken.

"I knew Maya had this skill," she said, "as she had shown signs of it during the spring. Once or twice I even felt myself growing dizzy when she looked at me. But none of the Muto know much about the Kikuta sleep, though there are many superstitions attached to it."

"It is like a powerful medicine," Takeo replied. "A small amount is beneficial, but too strong a draught can kill. People make themselves open to it through their own weakness, their lack of self-mastery. I was taught how to control it in Matsue—and I learned there that the Kikuta never look at their own infants directly, for a young child has no defense against the gaze. I suppose a young cat would be as defenseless. I never tried it on a cat, only on dogs—and grown ones at that."

"You never heard of a transference between the dead and the one who has made them sleep?"

The question made the back of his neck prickle with unease. It had started raining again, and now the drumming grew louder on the roof.

"Usually it is not the sleep that kills," he said carefully. "It is used only to disable—death must always be by some other means."

"Is that what they taught you?"

"Why are you asking this?"

"I am troubled by Maya. She shows signs of being possessed. It has happened among the Muto, you know. Kenji himself was called the Fox when he was young; he was said to have been possessed by a fox spirit— even to have married a fox as his first wife—but apart from my uncle I don't know of any recent transformations. It's almost as though she drew the cat's spirit into herself. All children are like animals, but they should become more human as they grow up; Maya is becoming less. I can't talk to Kaede about it; Shigeko already suspects there is something wrong. I am glad you have returned."

He nodded, deeply perturbed by this news. "Your grandsons show no sign of Tribe skills," he remarked.

"No, and I am quite relieved. Let them be Zenko's sons, warriors. Kenji always said the skills would disappear within two generations. Perhaps, in the twins, we are seeing the last spurt of flame before the lamp dies."

These last flames can cast grotesque shadows, Takeo thought.

NO ONE DISTURBED them during this conversation. Takeo was half-consciously listening all the time for the breath, the slight sound of a joint moving, the soft tread that would reveal an eavesdropper, whether it was one of his daughters or a spy, but all he could hear was the rain falling, the distant thunder, and the ebbing tide.

However, when they had finished and he was walking toward Kaede's room along the gleaming corridor, he heard an extraordinary sound ahead of him, a kind of growling and snarling, half-human and half-animal. Then a child's voice shrieking in fear, and the pad of feet. He turned the corner and Sunaomi ran into him.

"Uncle! I am sorry!" The boy was giggling with excitement. "The tiger's going to get me!"

Takeo saw the shadows first, thrown against the paper screen. For a moment he saw clearly the human shape, and behind it another with flattened ears, clawed paws and lashing tail. Then his twin daughters came tearing around the corner, and they were both just girls, even though they were snarling. They stopped dead when they saw him.

"Father!"

"She's the tiger!" Sunaomi squealed.

Miki saw her father's face, pulled at Maya's sleeve and said, "We were just playing."

"You are too old for these games," he said, masking his concern. "This is no way to greet your father. I expected to find you grown into young women."

As always, his displeasure deflated them completely.

"We're sorry," Miki said.

"Forgive us, Father," Maya pleaded, with not a trace of tiger in her voice.

"It was my fault too," Sunaomi added. "I should have known better. They are only girls, after all."

"I can see I need to have a serious talk with you both. Where is your mother?"

"She is waiting for you, Father. She said we might be allowed to eat with you," Miki whispered in a small voice.

"Well, I suppose we must welcome Sunaomi into our family. You may eat with us. But no more turning into tigers!"

"But people are supposed to feed themselves to tigers," Maya said as they walked alongside him. "Shigeko told us the story." She could not resist whispering to Sunaomi, "And what tigers like best is little boys."

But Sunaomi had taken his uncle's reprimand to heart, and did not respond.

Takeo had intended to talk to the twins that night, but by the time the meal was over he was aching with fatigue and longing to be alone with Kaede. The girls behaved impeccably throughout the meal, were kind to their young cousin and faultlessly polite to their parents and older sister. He saw they had all his talents of mimicry, and wondered if that would be sufficient to carry them through a conventional marriage—even to Sunaomi, for example. Or would they not need to marry, but be able to use their talents within the Tribe, perhaps eventually taking over from Shizuka . . . ? Certainly Shizuka had had the most freedom of any woman he had known to make her own decisions—and her actions had changed the course of history within the Three Countries. Moreover, she had had men as she pleased, and sons—and now, as head of the Tribe, would wield more power than any other woman apart from Kaede herself.

HE LOOKED UP at Kaede now in the dim lamplight, the familiar curve of her cheekbone just visible, the outline of her head. She had wrapped her sleeping robe around her and sat cross-legged on the mattress, her slender limbs faintly white against the silken bedcovers. He lay with his head on her lap, feeling the heat of her body, remembering how he had lain like this as a child with his mother, with the same sense of abandonment and trust. She stroked his hair gently, rubbing up under his neck, dissolving what remained of tension.

They had fallen on each other as soon as they were alone, hardly speaking, seeking the closeness and the self-annihilation, always so familiar, always so new and strange, that came with the act of love. They shared their grief at Kenji's death, but did not speak of it, nor of her sense of exclusion from his Tribe secrets or their anxiety about their daughters, but all these concerns fueled the wordless intensity of their passion, and as always, when the passion receded, miraculously some healing had taken place. Her coolness had evaporated; his grief seemed bearable; they spoke with no barriers between them.

There was much to discuss, and first came his suspicions of Zenko and his reasons for taking the two Arai boys into their household.

"Surely you will not adopt them legally?" Kaede exclaimed.

"How would you feel if we did?"

"I already feel toward Sunaomi like my own child—but Shigeko is to be your heir?"

"There are many possibilities—a marriage even, when he is old enough. I don't want to do anything in a hurry. The longer we can delay a decision, the more likely Zenko is to come to his senses and calm down. But I am afraid he is being encouraged by the Emperor and his supporters in the East. We have your kidnapper to thank for that!"

He told her about his meeting with Lord Kono. "They have labeled me as a criminal. Because Fujiwara was a nobleman he escapes all censure for his crimes!"

"Your insistence on a new system of justice probably terrifies them," Kaede observed. "For until now no one has dared judge a man like Fujiwara or call him to account. I knew he could have me killed on a sudden whim. No one would refuse to obey him; no one would think he had done wrong. That sense of being owned by a man, of having less value than a painting or a precious vase—for he would kill a woman with far greater ease than deliberately destroy one of his treasures—I can hardly put into words how it sapped my will and paralyzed my body. Now in the Three Countries a woman's murder is treated as seriously as a man's, and no one escapes our justice because of their birth or rank. Our warrior families have accepted this, but beyond our borders both warriors and noblemen will see it as an affront."

"You remind me how much there is at stake. I will never abdicate as the Emperor has requested, but nor do I want us to enter into war. Yet if we are to fight eventually in the East, the sooner we do so, the better." He told her about the problems with firearms, and Fumio's mission. "Kahei of course thinks we should prepare for war at once—we have time to mount a campaign before winter. But at Terayama the Masters all advised against it. They say I should go to the capital next spring with Shigeko, and that magically everything will be solved."

He was frowning now. She rubbed her fingers on his forehead, smoothing away the lines.

"Gemba has a new line in showy tricks," he said. "But I think it will take more than that to pacify the Emperor's general, Saga Hideki, the Dog Catcher."

he following day was spent in making preparations for Kenji's funeral service, and in dictating letters. Minoru was kept busy all day, writing to Zenko and Hana to inform them of Sunaomi's safe arrival; to Sugita Hiroshi, requesting him to come to Hagi as soon as possible; to Terada Fumifusa, informing him of Takeo's return and his son Fumio's whereabouts; and finally to Sonoda Mitsuru in Inuyama, telling him only that no decision had yet been made about the fate of the hostages; it would be discussed at the coming meeting.

Takeo and Minoru were then brought up to date by Kaede on all the current issues pertaining to the city of Hagi and its inhabitants, Minoru making careful records of the decisions they came to. At the end of a long, hot, and tiring day, Takeo went to bathe, and sent orders for his younger daughters to come to him there.

They slipped naked into the steaming water; they were just beginning to show signs of womanhood, their bodies no longer childlike, their hair long and thick. They were more subdued than usual, still apparently unsure if he had forgiven their boisterous behavior of the previous day.

"You look tired," he said. "You have been working hard today, I hope."

"Shizuka was very strict today." Miki sighed. "She says we need more discipline."

"And Shigeko made us do so much writing," Maya complained. "If I had no fingers like you, Father, would Lord Minoru do my writing for me?"

"I had to learn to write, as you have to," he said. "And it was harder for me, because I was much older. The younger you are, the easier it is to learn. Be thankful you have such good teachers!"

His voice was stern, and Miki, who had been touching the scar that ran from the side of his neck across his chest and was about to ask him to tell the story of the fight, thought better of it and said nothing.

Takeo spoke more gently. "A lot is demanded of you. You have to learn the way of the warrior, as well as all the secrets of the Tribe. I know it is not easy. You have many talents—you must be very careful how you use them."

Miki said, "Is it because of the cat?"

"Tell me about the cat," he replied.

They exchanged a glance but did not answer.

Takeo said, gesturing toward his private parts, floating limp, innocent, in the water, "I carried you there; you come from me. You are marked as I am as Kikuta. There is nothing you cannot tell me. Maya, what happened with the cat?"

"I didn't mean to hurt it," Maya began.

"You must not lie to me," he reminded her.

She went on, "I wanted to see what would happen. I thought it might hurt the cat, but I didn't mind." Her voice was serious; she looked directly at him. One day she would challenge him, but now her look was still that of a child. "I was angry with Mori Hiroki."

"He looked at us," Miki explained. "Everyone does. As if we were demons."

"He likes Shigeko and he doesn't like us," Maya said.

"And that's the same with everyone," Miki said, and as if his silence unleashed something within her, she began to cry. "Everyone hates us because there are two of us!"

The twins rarely cried. It was yet another trait that made them seem unnatural.

Maya was also crying. "And Mother hates us because she wanted one boy, and she got two girls!"

"Chiyo told us that." Miki gulped.

He felt his heart twist for them. It was easy to love his oldest daughter; he loved these two all the more, because they were not easy to love, and he pitied them.

"You are very precious to me," he said. "I have always been glad that there are two of you and that you are girls. I would rather have two girls than all the sons in the world."

"When you are here, it's all right. We feel safe, and we don't want to do bad things. But you are away so much of the time."

"I would keep you with me if I could—but it is not always possible. You have to learn to be good even when I am not here."

"People shouldn't look at us," Maya said.

"Maya, from now on it is you who must be careful how you look. You know the story—I have often told you—about my encounter with the ogre Jin-emon?" Takeo asked.

"Yes," they said together, with enthusiasm.

"I looked into his eyes and he fell asleep. This is the Kikuta sleep, which is used to disable your enemy. This is what you did to the cat, Maya. But Jin-emon was huge, as tall as the castle gate and heavier than an ox. The cat was small and young, and the sleep killed it."

"It's not really dead," Maya said, coming close to him, hanging off his left arm. "It came into me."

Takeo tried to make no sign of shock or alarm, not wanting to silence her now.

"It came to live with me," Maya said. "It doesn't mind. Because it couldn't talk before, and now it can. And I don't mind either. I like the cat."

"But Jin-emon didn't come into you, did he, Father?" Miki said. It was no more strange to them than invisibility, or the second self, and perhaps no more harmful.

"No, because in the end I cut his windpipe and throat with Jato. He died from that, not from the sleep."

"Are you angry about the cat?" Maya said.

He knew they trusted him, and knew he must not lose that trust, that they were like shy wild animals who would flee at a moment. He recalled the months of misery he had endured with the Kikuta, the brutality of the training.

"No, I am not angry," he said calmly.

"Shizuka was very angry," Miki muttered.

"But I need to know everything—in order to protect you, and to stop you hurting other people. I am your father and your senior in the Kikuta family. You owe me your obedience on both counts."

"This is what happened," Maya said. "I was angry with Mori Hiroki. I saw how he loved the cat. I wanted to pay him back for not looking at us. And the cat was sweet. I wanted to play with it. So I looked in its eyes, and I couldn't stop looking. It was sweet, but I wanted to hurt him, and I couldn't stop." She broke off, and looked helplessly at him.

"Go on," he said.

"I drew it in. From its eyes, through my eyes. It came leaping into me. It yowled and mewed. But I couldn't stop looking. And then the cat was dead. But it was still alive."

"And?"

"And Mori Hiroki was sad, and that made me happy." Maya gave a deep sigh, as if she had completed reciting a lesson. "That's all, Father, I promise you."

He touched her cheek. "You were honest with me. But you see how confused your emotions were. Your mind was not clear, as it must be when you use any of the Tribe skills. When you look into other people's eyes, you will see their weaknesses and their lack of clarity. That is what makes them vulnerable to your gaze."

"What will happen to me?" Maya said.

"I don't know. We have to watch you to find out. You acted wrongly; you made a mistake. You will have to live with the consequences. But you must promise me never to use the Kikuta sleep on anyone, until I say you may."

"Kenji would know," Miki said, and began to cry again. "He told us about animal spirits and how the Tribe use them."

"I wish he wasn't dead," Maya said through her own renewed sobs.

And Takeo felt his own eyes grow hot, for his teacher, now lost to him, and for his twin daughters, whom he had not been able to protect from a possession whose outcome he had no way of foreseeing.

Both girls were close to him, their limbs, in the steaming water, so like his in the texture and color of the skin, brushing against him.

"We don't have to marry Sunaomi, do we?" Maya asked him, calmer now.

"Why? Who says you should?"

"Sunaomi told us he is to be betrothed to one or the other of us!"

"Only if he is very naughty indeed," Takeo replied. "As a punishment!"

"I don't want to be betrothed to anyone," Miki said.

"One day you may change your mind," Takeo teased her.

"I want to marry Miki," Maya said, beginning to giggle.

"Yes, we'll marry each other," Miki agreed.

"Then you will have no children. You need a man to make children."

"I don't want children," Miki said.

"I hate children," Maya agreed. "Especially Sunaomi! You won't make Sunaomi your son, will you, Father?"

"I have no need of sons," Takeo replied.

Kenji's funeral was held the following day, and a stone was erected for him at the Hachiman shrine next to Tokoji, which soon became a place of pilgrimage for the Muto family and other members of the Tribe. Kenji had passed into the spirit world, like Shigeru, like Jo-An. All three had seemed more than human in their lifetime. Now they inspired and protected those who still lived in the midst of the world.

· 16 ·

he plum rains ended and the great heat of summer began. Shigeko rose early every day before sunrise and went to the shrine on the riverbank to spend an hour or so with the black colt while the air was still cool. The two old mares nipped and kicked him and taught him manners; he had become calmer in their company, and gradually he seemed to accept her, whickering when he saw her and showing signs of affection.

"He has never done that to anyone," Mori Hiroki remarked, watching the colt rub his head against Shigeko's shoulder.

"I would like to give him to my father," she replied. "He has had no horse he likes since Shun died."

"He is ready to be broken in," Hiroki said. "But you should not attempt it, certainly not alone. I am too old and slow now, and your father is too busy."

"But I must do it," Shigeko argued. "He has come to trust me." Then the thought leaped into her mind. *Hiroshi is coming to Hagi. We can break the horse in together. And Father can ride him next year when we travel to Miyako.*

She named the horse Tenba, for he had something heavenly about him, and when he galloped around the meadow, he seemed to fly.

So the hot days passed. The children swam in the sea and continued their studies and training, happy because their father was home, and though government affairs kept him busy most of the day, he always spent some time with them in the warm evenings when the sky was deep black and the stars huge, and the faint breath of the wind from the sea cooled the residence.

For Shigeko, the next great event of the summer was the arrival of Sugita Hiroshi from Maruyama. He had lived with the Otori household until he reached the age of twenty and had then moved to Maruyama, where he ran the domain that was her mother's and would one day be hers. It was like the return of a beloved older brother for all three girls. Every time she received a letter, Shigeko expected to read that Hiroshi was married, for he was twenty-six years old and had not yet taken a wife. It was inexplicable, but to her only half-admitted relief, when he rode into Hagi he came alone, and there was no mention of any wife or betrothed left behind in Maruyama. Waiting until she could question Shizuka alone, she tried to bring the subject up casually. "Shizuka, how old were your sons when they married?"

"Zenko was eighteen, and Taku seventeen," Shizuka replied. "Not particularly young."

"And Taku and Sugita Hiroshi are the same age, are they not?"

"Yes, they were born in the same year—your aunt Hana was also born that year." Shizuka laughed. "All three boys hoped to marry Hana, I think. Hiroshi in particular had always had a yearning to be Hana's husband— he idolized your mother and thought Hana very like her. Taku got over his disappointment swiftly, but it's common gossip that Hiroshi never did, and that is why he has never married."

"How very unusual," Shigeko said, half-wanting to continue the conversation, and half-astonished at the pain it caused her. Hiroshi in love with Hana? And to the extent that he could not bring himself to marry anyone else?

"If a suitable alliance had presented itself, no doubt your father would have arranged a marriage," Shizuka said. "But Hiroshi's position is unique.

He is both too high in rank and not high enough. His closeness to your family is almost that of a son of the house, yet he has no hereditary lands of his own. He will give Maruyama over to you this year."

"I hope he will continue to serve me there," Shigeko said. "But I can see I will have to find him a wife! Does he have a mistress or concubine?"

"I suppose so," Shizuka replied. "Most men do!"

"Not my father," Shigeko said.

"No, nor did Lord Shigeru." Shizuka's eyes took on a faraway, pensive look.

"Why are they so different from other men, I wonder."

"Maybe no other woman appeals to them. And I suppose they do not want to cause their beloved the pain of jealousy."

"Jealousy is a terrible feeling," Shigeko said.

"But luckily you are too young to have such emotions," Shizuka replied. "And your father will choose wisely when it comes to your husband. In fact, he will be so particular about it, I wonder if he will ever find anyone good enough."

"I would be happy never to marry," Shigeko declared, but she knew that this was not wholly true. Ever since she had reached womanhood she had found herself troubled by dreams, and by longings for a man's touch, the feel of the strong body aligned with her own, the intimacy of hair, skin, and smell.

"It's a shame girls are not permitted to take lovers as boys are," she said.

"They have to be a little more discreet about it," Shizuka replied, laughing. "Is there already someone you desire, Shigeko? Are you older than I think?"

"Of course not. I just want to know what it's like—the things men and women do together, marriage, love . . ."

She studied Hiroshi carefully that evening as he ate the evening meal. He did not look like someone driven mad by love. He was not particularly tall, about the same height as her father but more powerfully built and fuller in the face. His eyes were long in shape and lively in expression, his hair thick and completely black. He seemed in an excellent humor, over-flowing with optimism about the coming harvest and eager to share the results of his innovative techniques in drilling men and horses. He teased the twins and flattered Kaede, made jokes with Takeo and reminisced about the old days, the retreat in the typhoon and the battle for Hagi. Once or twice in the course of the evening she fancied she felt his eyes on her, but when she glanced at him, he was always looking away, and he spoke directly to her only once or twice, addressing her with formality. His face became less animated then, taking on a calm, almost remote expression. It reminded her of the way her teachers at the temple looked while meditating; and she recalled that, like herself, Hiroshi had been trained in the Way of the Houou. It consoled her a little—they would always be comrades, though they could be nothing more; he would always understand her and support her.

Just before they retired, he asked her about the young horse, for she had already written to him on the matter.

"Come to the shrine tomorrow and you can see him," she said.

He hesitated for a moment, and then said, "With great pleasure. Let me escort you." But the tone of his voice was cool, and the words formal.

THEY STROLLED SIDE by side across the stone bridge, as they had so often when she was a young child and he not quite a man. The air was still, the light clear and golden, as the sun rose above the Eastern mountains and turned the unruffled surface of the river into a gleaming mirror whose reflected world seemed more real than the one in which they walked.

Usually two of the castle guards accompanied her, keeping a respectful few paces ahead and behind, but today Hiroshi had dismissed them. He was dressed ready for riding, in trousers and leggings, and wore a sword in his belt. She was in similar clothes, her hair tied back with cords, and as usual in Hagi she was armed only with the hidden short stick. She talked about the horse, and Hiroshi's reserve gradually dissolved, until he was arguing with her as he might have done five years ago. Perversely, this disappointed her as much as his formality.

He sees me as a little sister, just like one of the twins.

The morning sun lit up the old shrine; Hiroki was already up and Hiroshi greeted him with pleasure, for he had spent many hours as a boy in the older man's company, learning the skills of horsebreaking and breeding.

Tenba heard Shigeko's voice and neighed from the meadow. When they went to look at him, he trotted up to her but put his ears back and rolled his eyes at Hiroki.

"He is both fierce and beautiful," Hiroshi exclaimed. "If he can be tamed, he will make a marvelous war horse."

"I want to give him to Father," Shigeko told him. "But I don't want Father to take him to war! Surely we are at peace now?"

"There are some storm clouds on the horizon," Hiroshi said. "That is why I have been summoned here."

"I hoped you had come to see my horse!" she said, daring to tease him.

"Not only your horse," he replied quietly. To her surprise when she glanced at him, a wave of color had swept into his neck.

She said after a moment of awkwardness, "I hope you have time to help me break him in. I don't want anyone else to do it—he trusts me now, and that trust must not be broken, so I must be present at all times."

"He will come to trust me too," Hiroshi said. "I will come here whenever your father can spare me. We will work on him together, in the way we have both been taught."

The Way of the Houou was the way of the male and female elements of the world—gentle strength, fierce compassion, the dark and the light, shadow and sun, the hidden and the exposed. Gentleness alone would not tame a horse like this. It would also need a man's strength and resoluteness.

They started that morning, before the heat intensified, accustoming the horse to Hiroshi's touch, on his head, around his ears, on the flanks, and under the belly. Then they laid soft ribbons across his back and neck, finally tying one loosely around his nose and head—his first bridle. He sweated and his coat shuddered, but he submitted to their handling.

Mori Hiroki watched them with approval, and afterward, when the colt had been rewarded with carrots and Shigeko and Hiroshi with cold barley tea, said, "In other parts of the Three Countries and beyond, horses are broken in swiftly and forcefully, often with cruelty. The animals are beaten into submission. But my father always believed in a gentle approach."

"And that's why the Oteri horses are renowned," Hiroshi said. "They are so much more obedient than other horses, more reliable in battle, and with greater stamina, as they are not wasting energy fighting the rider and trying to bolt! I have always used the methods I learned from you."

Shigeko's face was glowing. "We will succeed in taming him, won't we?"

"I have no doubt of it," Hiroshi replied, returning the smile unguardedly.

akeo knew of his daughter's partnership with Sugita Hiroshi in breaking in the black colt—though he did not know the horse was for him—as he knew almost everything, not only in Hagi but throughout the Three Countries. Messengers ran or rode in relays between the cities, and homing pigeons were used to send urgent news from ships at sea. He thought Hiroshi like an older brother to his daughter; he worried occasionally about his future and his unmarried status, casting around in his mind for a suitable and useful match for the young man who had served him so loyally since childhood. He had heard the common talk about Hiroshi's infatuation with Hana; he did not altogether believe it, knowing Hiroshi's strength of character and intelligence—yet Hiroshi evaded all marriage prospects and seemed to live more chastely than a monk. He resolved to make renewed efforts to find a wife for him among the warrior families in Hagi.

One hot afternoon in the seventh month, shortly before the Festival of the Weaver Star, Takeo, Kaede, Shigeko, and Hiroshi went across the bay to the residence of Terada Fumifusa. This was his old friend Fumio's father, the former pirate chief who now maintained and supervised the fleet, both merchant vessels and warships, that gave the Three Countries their eminence in trade and their security from attack by sea. Terada was now about fifty years old, yet showed little sign of the usual infirmities of age.

Takeo valued his shrewdness and pragmatism, as well as the combination of boldness and vast knowledge that had led to the establishment of trade and the encouragement of craftsmen and artists from faraway lands to settle, work, and teach in the cities of the Three Countries. Terada himself did not care much for the lavish treasures he had acquired during his years of piracy—his grudge against the Otori clan had been his driving force, and the downfall of Shigeru's uncles his greatest desire. But after the battle for Hagi and the earthquake he had rebuilt his old house under the influence of his son and his daughter-in-law, Eriko, a young niece of the Endo family. Eriko loved painting, gardens, and objects of beauty. She wrote poetry in exquisite brushwork, and had made a residence of splendor and charm across the bay from the castle, near the volcano crater, where the unusual climate enabled her to cultivate the exotic plants that Fumio brought back from his voyages as well as the medicinal herbs that Ishida liked to experiment with. Her artistic nature and sensibility had made her a favored friend of Takeo and Kaede, and her oldest daughter was especially close to Shigeko, as the two girls were born in the same year.

Small pavilions had been constructed over the streams in the garden, and the cool sound of flowing water filled the air. The pools were a mass of mauve and cream lotus flowers, shaded by strange trees shaped like fans from the Southern Islands. The air was redolent of aniseed and ginger. The guests all wore light summer robes in brilliant colors, rivaling the butterflies that flitted among the flowers. A late cuckoo was calling its fractured song from the forest, and cicadas shrilled ceaselessly.

Eriko had introduced an old game in which the guests composed poems, read them, and then sent them floating on little wooden trays for the group in the next pavilion to read. Kaede excelled at this sort of poetry, with her huge knowledge of classical allusions and her quick mind, but Eriko came close to her. They strove to surpass each other in friendly rivalry.

Cups of wine were also floated in the slow-moving water, and every now and then one or another of the guests would reach out and hand it to a companion. The rhythm of the words and the sound of laughter mingled with the water, the insects, and the birds, producing in Takeo a rare moment of pure enjoyment, dissolving his concerns and lightening his grief.

He was watching Hiroshi, who sat with Shigeko and Eriko's daughter, Kaori, in the next pavilion. Kaori was almost of marriageable age—perhaps this would be a good match; he would discuss it with Kaede later. Kaori took after her father, plump and full of good health and spirits. She was laughing now, with Shigeko, at Hiroshi's efforts.

But through the laughter and all the other sounds of this peaceful afternoon, he heard something else, perhaps the flutter of a bird's wing. He looked up into the sky and saw a small flock of specks far in the southeast. As they came closer, it was clear that they were white homing pigeons returning to the Terada residence where they had been hatched.

The birds returned all the time, for all Terada's ships carried them, yet the direction from which these came filled him with unease, for to the southeast lay the free city of Akashi . . .

The pigeons fluttered overhead toward the dovecotes. Everyone looked up to watch them. Then the party resumed with apparently the same lightheartedness, but Takeo was conscious now of the heat of the afternoon, of the sweat in his armpits, of the rasp of the cicadas.

A servant came from the house, knelt behind Lord Terada, and whispered to him. Terada looked toward Takeo and made a slight gesture with his head. They both rose at the same time, made a brief apology to the gathering, and went with the servant to the house. Once on the veranda, Terada said, "Messages from my son." He took from the servant pieces of folded paper, made from silk, lighter than feathers, and they pieced together the words.

"Failure. Weapons already in Saga's hands. Returning at once."

Takeo looked from the shade of the veranda toward the bright scene in the garden. He heard Kaede's voice as she read, heard the laughter that greeted her grace and wit.

"We must prepare for a council of war," he said. "We will meet tomorrow and decide what must be done."

THE COUNCIL CONSISTED of Terada Fumifusa, Miyoshi Kahei, Sugita Hiroshi, Muto Shizuka, Takeo, Kaede, and Shigeko. Takeo told them of his meeting with Kono, the Emperor's demands, the new general, and the smuggled weapons. Miyoshi Kahei naturally was in favor of immediate action—a swift summer campaign, the deaths, ideally, of Arai Zenko and Lord Kono, followed by a concentration of troops on the Eastern borders, which could advance on the capital in the spring, rout the Dog Catcher, and persuade the Emperor to think again about threatening and insulting the Otori.

"Your ships might also blockade Akashi," he said to Terada. "We should bring the port under our control to prevent any more disasters from Arai."

Then he recalled Shizuka's presence and remembered Zenko was her son, and somewhat belatedly begged her pardon for his bluntness. "Yet I cannot retract my advice," he said to Takeo. "While Zenko undermines you in the West, you cannot hope to deal with the threat from the East."

"We have Zenko's son with us now," Kaede said. "We feel that this will help control him and make him biddable."

"He is hardly a hostage, though," Kahei replied. "The essence of holding hostages is to be prepared to take their lives. I don't want to insult you, Takeo, but I don't believe you could bring yourself to order the child's death. His parents, of course, know that he is as safe with you as in his mother's arms!"

"Zenko has sworn yet again that he will be loyal to me," Takeo said. "I cannot attack him without provocation or warning. I prefer to give him my trust, in the hope that he deserves it. And we must make every effort to maintain peace through negotiation. I will not bring civil war on the Three Countries."

Kahei pressed his lips together and shook his head, his face dark.

"Your brother, Gemba, and the others at Terayama have advised me to placate the Emperor, to visit Miyako next year and plead my case to him in person."

"By which time Saga will have equipped his army with firearms. At least let us seize Akashi and prevent him trading in niter. Otherwise you will go straight to your death!"

"I am in favor of acting decisively," Terada said. "I agree with Miyoshi. Those merchants at Akashi have gotten altogether above themselves. A free city, indeed! They're an insult. It would be a pleasure to teach them a lesson." He seemed to miss the days when his ships virtually controlled all trade along the northern and western coasts.

"Such an action would antagonize and infuriate our own merchants," Shizuka said. "And we rely on their support for provisions as well as niter and iron ore. It would be very hard to fight a war without that support."

"Everywhere the merchant class is becoming dangerously powerful," Terada grumbled. It was an old complaint with him, as it was, Takeo knew, with Miyoshi Kahei and many other warriors, who resented the growing wealth and prosperity that trade brought to the townspeople. Yet that prosperity, in his opinion, was one of the greatest underpinnings of peace.

"If you do not strike now, it will be too late," Kahei said. "That is my advice."

"Hiroshi?" Takeo addressed the young man, who up till now had been silent.

"I understand Lord Miyoshi's point of view," Hiroshi said. "And in many ways he has the most reason on his side. According to the art of war, his strategy has much to recommend it. But I have to submit to the wisdom of the Masters of the Way of the Houou. Send messages to the Emperor announcing your intended visit, when you will make your decision known to him. This will put off any planned attack on his part. I would recommend, like Kahei, strengthening the army in the East, preparing for attack while not inciting it. We must build up our forces of foot soldiers carrying firearms, and drill them to face similarly armed soldiers, for undoubtedly by next year Saga will have considerable numbers of weapons. That we cannot prevent. As for your brother-in-law, I believe the ties of family will be stronger than any grudge he may bear you or any ambition to oust you. Again I would advise you to take your time, and do nothing hastily."

Hiroshi has always been a clever strategist, Takeo thought. *Even as a child!*

He turned to his daughter. "Shigeko?"

"I agree with everything Lord Hiroshi has said," she replied. "If I come with you to Miyako, I believe the Way of the Houou will prevail, even with the Emperor."

· *18* ·

hen in Hagi, Shizuka lived in the castle residence, and consequently Takeo saw her several times a day, in the company of Kaede or their children. There was no need to arrange formal meetings, nor did he see the need to announce to the world her appointment to the headship of the Tribe. The skills and talents of the Tribe might now come under the control of the state, in his person, but they were still kept secret. He found this division suited his warrior advisers, who as always were happy to take advantage of the services provided by the Tribe while preferring to stay aloof from sorcery. Taku, of mixed blood like himself, understood all this perfectly.

It was easy enough to have informal talks with Shizuka, in the garden, on the veranda, or on the sea wall. A few days after the council of war, on the morning of the Star Festival, they met as if by chance as he was going from the residence toward the castle itself. Minoru followed Takeo as usual with the writing implements, but stepped away to allow them to speak privately.

"I had a message from Taku," she said quietly. "Late last night. Ishida and Chikara left Hofu at the last full moon. The weather has been settled and fine; they should arrive any day now."

"That's good news," he replied. "You must be looking forward to your husband's return." Then he said, for there was no reason why this news should be secret, "What else?"

"Apparently Zenko gave permission for the foreigners to come with them. Two of them are on board, with their translator—the woman."

Takeo frowned. "What is the purpose of their visit?"

"Taku does not say. But he thought you should be forewarned."

"It's annoying," Takeo said. "We will have to receive them with all sorts of ceremony and splendor, and pretend to be impressed by their paltry gifts and uncouth speeches. I don't want them feeling they have the freedom to go where they will. I prefer to keep them confined to one place—Hofu did very well. Find them somewhere uncomfortable to live, and have them watched at all times. Do we have anyone who speaks their language?"

Shizuka shook her head.

"Well, someone must learn it as soon as possible. Their translator must teach us while she is here." He was thinking rapidly. He had not wanted to see Madaren again; he had a sense of discomfort that she was reappearing so soon in his life. He feared the complications that her presence would inevitably cause, but if he had to use a translator it might as well be she—whom he had some connection with, possibly some hold over.

He thought of Kaede, who learned so quickly, who had mastered the languages of Shin and Tenjiku so she could read the classic works of history, literature, and the scriptures. He would ask her to learn the foreigners' language from Madaren, and he would tell her the translator was his sister . . . the idea that he would have one less secret from her made him curiously happy.

"Find some bright girl who can be their servant," he told Shizuka. "Let her make every effort to come to understand what they say. And we will arrange lessons here as well."

"Do you intend to learn, cousin?"

"I doubt I have the aptitude," Takeo replied. "But I am sure Kaede has. And you too."

"I fear I am too old," Shizuka replied, laughing. "Ishida, however, has quite an interest, and has been compiling a list of scientific and medical words."

"Good. Let him continue this work with them. The more we can learn from them the better. And see if you can find out more details from your husband about their real purposes, and about how close they are to Zenko.

"Taku is well?" he added as an afterthought.

"He seems to be. Just a little frustrated at being stuck in the West, I think. He is about to leave with Lord Kono to inspect the estates, and intends to go on from there to Maruyama."

"Is that so? Then Hiroshi had better be there to meet them," Takeo said. "He can take the same ship back again, and take news of our decisions to Taku."

THE SHIP WAS spotted out at sea two days later. Shigeko heard the bell from the hill above the castle ring out as she and Hiroshi worked with the colt. Tenba accepted the bit and allowed her to lead him with the soft reins, but they had not yet tried him with a saddle or any weight on his back other than a light padded cloth that still made him flinch and kick.

"A ship is coming," she said, trying in vain to see against the bright dawn light. "I hope it is Dr. Ishida's."

"If it is, I must return to Maruyama," Hiroshi said.

"So soon!" Shigeko could not help exclaiming, and then, embarrassed, said quickly, "Father says he is bringing me some special present, but he will not tell me what it is." *I sound like a child,* she thought, exasperated with herself.

"I've heard him talk about it," Hiroshi replied, treating her like a child, she thought.

"Do you know what it is?"

"It is a secret!" he said teasingly. "I can't reveal Lord Otori's secrets."

"Why should he tell you and not me?"

"He did not tell me," he said, relenting. "Only that he hoped for fine weather and a calm voyage for it."

"It's some animal," Shigeko exclaimed in pleasure. "A new horse! Or maybe a tiger cub! The weather has been beautiful. I'm always happy when it is fine weather for the Star Festival."

She recalled the beauty of the recent still, moonless night, the brilliant splash of stars, the one night of the year when the Princess and her lover can meet across the magical bridge built by magpies.

"I used to love the Star Festival when I was young," Hiroshi said. "But now it makes me feel sad. For there are no magical bridges, not in real life."

He is speaking of himself and Hana, Shigeko thought. *He has suffered for so long. He should be married. He would get over it if he had a wife and children.* Yet she could not bring herself to suggest he marry.

"I used to imagine the Star Princess with your mother's face," he said. "But maybe the Princess is like you, taming the horses of Heaven."

Tenba, who had been walking docilely between them, suddenly took fright at a dove fluttering from the eaves of the shrine and jumped backward, pulling the ribbon through Shigeko's hands. She went quickly after him to soothe him, but he was still flighty, and plunged past her, striking her with his shoulder and frightening himself more. She nearly fell, but Hiroshi somehow put himself between her and the horse, and she was aware of his strength for a moment, and longed with an intensity that startled her to be held by him. The colt ran with high steps, the reins dangling. Hiroshi said, "Are you all right? He did not step on you?"

She shook her head, suddenly riven by emotion. They stood close, not touching. She found her voice.

"I think we have done enough for today. We will just make him walk quietly again. Then I must go home and prepare to receive my gift. Father will want to make a ceremony of it."

"Of course, Lady Shigeko," he replied, once more cool and formal. The colt allowed him to approach, and Hiroshi led him back to Shigeko. The air stirred slightly in the breeze and the doves fluttered overhead, but the young horse walked quietly between them, head lowered. Neither of them said anything.

DOWN AT THE dockside, the usual early morning bustle of activity had quieted. Fishermen paused from unloading their nighttime catch of silver sardines and shiny blue-scaled mackerel. Merchants halted the loading of bales of salt, rice, and silk onto the wide-beamed junks, and a crowd gathered on the cobbles to welcome the ship from Hofu with its unusual cargo.

Shigeko had just had time to return to the residence and change into garments more suitable for welcoming whatever her present was to be. Luckily it was only a short walk from the castle gate to the harbor steps, along the beach, past the little house under the pines where the famous courtesan Akane had once entertained Lord Shigeru, the sweet-smelling shrubs she had planted still scenting the air. Shizuka had waited for her, but her mother stayed behind, saying she felt a little unwell. Takeo had already gone ahead with Sunaomi. When they joined him, she could see her father was in a state of some excitement—he kept looking sideways at her and smiling. She hoped her reaction would not disappoint him, and resolved that no matter what the gift was, she would pretend it was her heart's desire.

However, as the ship approached the wharf, and the strange animal could be seen clearly—its long neck, its ears—Shigeko's amazement was as great and as unfeigned as the rest of the onlookers', and her delight when Dr. Ishida led the creature carefully down the gangplank and presented it to her was inexpressible. She was enchanted by the softness and strange pattern of its coat, by its dark and gentle eyes, fringed with long, thick lashes, by its delicate, graceful gait and its calm composure as it surveyed the unfamiliar scene before it.

Takeo was laughing with pleasure, both with the kirin itself and with Shigeko's reaction. Shizuka was welcoming her husband with undemonstrative affection, and the little boy, Chikara, awed by the reception and the crowd, recognized his brother's face and struggled to hold back tears.

"Be brave," Dr. Ishida admonished him. "Greet your uncle and cousin properly. Sunaomi, look after your little brother."

"Lord Otori," Chikara managed to say, bowing deeply. "Lady . . ."

"Shigeko," she prompted him. "Welcome to Hagi!"

Ishida said to Takeo, "We have brought some other passengers, less welcome perhaps."

"Yes, I was forewarned by Taku. Your wife will show them where they are to be lodged. I will tell you later what our plans are for them. I hope I may prevail on you to keep them entertained in the meantime."

The foreigners—two of them, the first ever in Hagi—appeared on the gangplank, causing no less astonishment than the kirin. They wore strange puffed trousers and long boots of leather; gold gleamed at neck and breast. One had a swarthy face half obscured by a dark beard; the other was paler-skinned and his hair and beard were the color of pale rust. This man's eyes were pale, too, green as green tea; at the sight of the hair and the light eyes a shiver ran through the crowd, and Shigeko heard several whispers of, "Can they be ogres?" "Ghosts." "Goblins."

They were followed by a small woman who seemed to be instructing them in the appropriate courtesies. At her whisper they both bowed in a strange, rather ostentatious manner, and then spoke in their harsh language.

Her father acknowledged them with a slight gesture of the head. He was no longer laughing; he looked stern, magnificent in his formal robes, embroidered with the heron, and black lacquer hat, his features composed and impassive. The foreigners might be taller and of larger frame, but to Shigeko's eyes Lord Otori was far more impressive.

The woman dropped to the ground before him, but he, with great graciousness Shigeko thought, indicated that she might stand and speak to him.

Shigeko was holding the silk cord that was attached to the kirin's collar, and her attention was taken up by the marvelous creature, but as she listened to her father speak a few words of welcome to the strangers and the woman translate, then reply, she thought she heard something unusual in the voice. She looked at the woman, at her gaze, which was fixed on Takeo's face. *She knows Father,* Shigeko thought. *She dares to look directly at him.* There was something in that look, some familiarity bordering on insolence, which troubled her and put her on her guard.

THE CROWD AT the quayside were then faced with the vexing question whether to follow the extraordinary kirin, which Ishida and Shigeko led toward the shrine, where it would be shown to Mori Hiroki and presented to the river god, and where an enclosure would be prepared for it; or the equally extraordinary foreigners, who with a line of servants carrying a large number of boxes and bales, were escorted by Shizuka to the tiny boat that would take them across the river to their lodging alongside the old temple building of Tokoji.

Fortunately the city of Hagi had a large number of inhabitants, and when the crowd divided more or less in half, each procession was composed of a sizeable throng. The foreigners found this more annoying than the kirin—they showed signs of ill-humor at the constant staring, and would be even more irritated by the distance of their lodging place from the castle and the guards and other restrictions placed on them for their protection. The kirin walked as it always did, with a deliberate, graceful step, aware of everything, alarmed by nothing, inexhaustibly gentle.

"I am in love with it already," Shigeko said to her father as they neared the shrine. "How can I ever thank you?"

"You must thank Dr. Ishida," Takeo replied. "It is his gift to us—a precious gift, too, for he is as attached to it as you are, and has been acquainted with it for a long time. He will show you how to look after it."

"It is a wonderful thing to have in Hagi," Mori Hiroki exclaimed when he saw it. "How blessed are the Three Countries!"

And Shigeko thought so too. Even Tenba seemed captivated by the kirin, running to the bamboo fence to inspect it and touching noses gently with it. The only sad thing was that Hiroshi was leaving. But when she remembered the moment earlier that morning, she thought perhaps it was for the best that he was going home.

hen Takeo returned to the residence after the welcome of
the kirin, he went straight to Kaede, concerned for her
state of health, but she seemed recovered and was seated
on the veranda on the northern side of the house, where
the sea breeze brought a certain coolness. She was talk-
ing with Taro, the eldest son of the carpenter Shiro, who had returned to
Hagi with his father to rebuild the city after the earthquake, and who now
spent his time carving statues from wood.

Takeo greeted him cheerfully, and Taro replied without undue ceremony, for their past history had bound them together in friendship, and
Takeo deeply admired the other man's skill, unequaled in the Three Countries.

"For some time I have had an idea of how I might create a figure of the
Goddess of Mercy," Taro said, looking at his hands as though he wished
they might speak for him. "Lady Otori has a suggestion."

"You know the house near the seashore," Kaede said. "It has been
empty for years, ever since Akane died. People say it is haunted by her
spirit, that she used spells to try to bind Lord Shigeru to her and in the
end was trapped by her own dark magic. Sailors say she lights lamps on the
rocks to give false messages to ships, for she hates all men. Let us tear the
house down and have the garden purified. Taro and his brother will build

a new shrine there for Kannon, and the statue he makes of her will bless the seashore and the bay."

"Chiyo told me Akane's story when I was a boy," Takeo replied. "But Shigeru never spoke of her, nor of his wife."

"Maybe the departed spirits of both women will find rest," Taro said. "I picture a small building—we will not need to cut down the pine trees but will build among them. A double roof, I think, with deep curves like this, and interlocking elbow joints to support it."

He showed Takeo the sketches he had made of the building. "The lower roof balances the upper, giving it an appearance of strength and gentleness. I hope to give the Blessed One the same attributes. I wish I could show you a sketch of her, but she remains hidden within the wood until my hands discover her."

"Will you carve from one tree?" Takeo asked.

"Yes, I am in the process of choosing the piece now."

They discussed the variety of tree, the age of the wood and such matters. Then Taro left them.

"It is a fine plan." Takeo said to Kaede when they were alone. "I am delighted with it."

"I believe I have a special reason to be thankful to the goddess," she said quietly. "This morning's sickness, which has passed quickly . . ."

He grasped her meaning and felt again the familiar mixture of delight and terror, that their deep love for each other should have created another life, launched another being into a new cycle of birth and death. It was the thought of death that caused the terror, awaking all the fears from the past when twice his children had threatened her life.

"My dearest wife," he murmured, and since they were alone, he embraced her.

"I am embarrassed," she said, laughing a little. "It seems so old to be bearing a child! Shigeko is already a woman. Yet I am so happy too. I thought I would never conceive again, that our chances of having a son were gone."

"I have told you many times, I am happy with our daughters," he said. "If we have another girl, I will be delighted."

"I don't want to speak the words," Kaede whispered. "But this one I am sure is a boy."

He held her against him, wondering at the miracle of the new creature already growing inside her, and they remained in silence for some time, breathing in each other's closeness. Then the sound of voices from the garden, the maids' tread on the boards of the veranda, drew them back to the everyday world.

"Did the kirin arrive safely?" Kaede inquired, for Takeo had already revealed the nature of the surprise to her.

"Yes, its appearance was everything I could have hoped for. Shigeko fell in love on the spot. The entire populace was silenced in astonishment."

"To silence the Otori is no mean feat!" Kaede replied. "I expect they have recovered their tongues and are already making up songs about it. I will go and see it for myself later."

"You must not go out in the heat," Takeo said swiftly. "You must not exert yourself at all. Ishida must come and see you at once, and you must do everything he tells you."

"Ishida also arrived safely. I am glad. And little Chikara?"

"He was very seasick—he is ashamed about it. But very happy to see his brother." Takeo was silent for a moment, and then said, "We will delay the question of adoption until the birth of our child. I do not want to raise expectations that cannot be met later, or to create complications for the future."

"This is wise," Kaede agreed. "Though I fear Zenko and Hana will be disappointed."

"It is only a delay, not an outright refusal," Takeo pointed out.

"You have grown wise and cautious, husband!" she said, laughing.

"Just as well," he replied. "I hope I have mastered the rashness and thoughtlessness of my younger self." He was weighing what he should say next, and, coming to a decision, said, "There were other passengers from Hofu. Two of the foreigners and a woman who interprets for them."

"For what purpose have they come here, do you think?"

"To increase their opportunities for trade, I suppose; to see a little more of a country that is a complete mystery to them. I haven't had a chance to speak to Ishida yet. He may know more. We need to be able to understand them. I hoped you might learn their language, with the help of the woman who has come with them, but I do not want to place any extra demands on you at this time."

"Studying, learning a language is one of the things I delight in," Kaede replied. "It seems an ideal occupation at a time when other activities must be curtailed. I will certainly do it. But who is the woman who has come with them? It interests me that she has mastered a foreign tongue."

Takeo said in a distant voice, "I do not want to shock you, but I must tell you. She is from the East, and had lived for some time in Inuyama. She was born in the same village I was, to the same mother. She is my sister."

"One of the two you believed to be dead?" Kaede said in astonishment.

"Yes, the younger girl, Madaren."

Kaede frowned. "It is a strange name."

"It is common enough among the Hidden. She took some other name, I believe, after the massacre. She was sold into a brothel by the soldiers who killed her—my—mother and sister. She ran away to Hofu, and worked in another brothel, where she met the foreigner called Don João; she speaks their language well."

"How do you know all this?"

"We happened to see each other in an inn in Hofu. I was in disguise, meeting Terada Fumio in the hope, vain as it turned out, of intercepting smuggled weapons. We recognized each other."

"But it must be years . . . ?" Kaede was staring at him, partly in sympathy, partly in disbelief.

"I am sure it is she. We met one more time, briefly, and I was convinced of it. I had inquiries made about her and learned something of her life. I told her I would provide for her, but I did not want to see her again. The gulf between us had become too vast. But now she has come here. . . . It is natural that she should be drawn to the foreigners, for their religion is in essence the same as the beliefs of the Hidden. I will not recognize her as my relative, but rumors may well spread, and I wanted you to hear the truth from me."

"Presumably she may be very useful to us, both as an interpreter and as a teacher. Can you prevail on her to become a spy?" Kaede seemed to be making an effort to master her surprise and speak rationally.

"I am sure she will be a source of information, wittingly or not. But information flows in both directions. She may prove a useful way to plant ideas in the minds of the foreigners. So I must ask you to treat her accordingly, with kindness, even respect, but do not reveal any secrets to her, and never speak to her of me."

"Does she look like you? I am longing to see her now."

He shook his head. "She looks like her mother."

Kaede said, "You sound so cold. Was it not a thrill to find her alive? Do you not want to bring her into your family?"

"I thought she was dead. I grieved for her with the others. Now I don't know how to treat her—I have become someone quite different from the boy who was her brother. The gap between our rank and status has become huge. Moreover, she is a fervent believer; I believe in nothing, and will never adhere to our childhood religion again. I suspect the foreigners want to spread their religion—to convert people. Who knows why? I cannot let any one of the many ways of believing hold sway over me, for I must protect them all from one another in case their arguments tear our society apart."

"No one watching you conduct the necessary ceremonies at temple and shrine would be convinced of your disbelief," Kaede said. "And what about my new shrine, and statue?"

"You know my skills as an actor," Takeo replied, with a sudden note of bitterness. "I am perfectly happy to pretend belief for the sake of stability. But if you are of the Hidden, there can ultimately be no pretense where belief is concerned. You are exposed to the all-seeing, pitiless gaze of

God." *If my father had not converted, he would still be alive,* he was thinking. *And I would have been someone else.*

"Surely the god of the Hidden is merciful?" Kaede exclaimed.

"To believers, maybe. Everyone else is damned to hell for eternity."

"I could never believe that!" Kaede said, after a moment's deep thought.

"Nor can I. But it is what the Hidden believe, and so do the foreigners. We must be very wary of them—if they think us damned already, they may feel justified in treating us with contempt or malice."

He saw Kaede tremble slightly, and feared she had been touched by some premonition.

n the eighth month came the Festival of the Dead. Seashore and riverbank were filled with throngs of people, their dancing shapes stark against the blaze of bonfires, and countless lamps floated on the dark water. The dead were welcomed, feasted, and farewelled with the customary mixture of sadness and joy, dread and elation. Maya and Miki lit candles for Kenji, whom they missed deeply, but their genuine grief did not keep them from their newest pastime, tormenting Sunaomi and Chikara. They had overheard the adult conversations and knew of the proposal to adopt one or both of the boys, and they saw Kaede's fondness for her nephews and imagined she preferred them because they were boys.

They were not told directly of Kaede's pregnancy, but in the way of alert, watchful children they discerned it, and the fact that it was not openly spoken of troubled them all the more. The summer days were long and hot; everyone grew irritable. Shigeko seemed to have advanced effortlessly ahead into adulthood and to have become distant. She spent more time with their father, discussing the visit to the capital the following year and other matters of state. Shizuka was occupied with the administration of the Tribe.

The twins were never allowed outside the castle grounds alone, and only on special occasions when accompanied, but they were already extremely skillful in the ways of the Tribe, and though they were not supposed to use these skills, because they felt bored and neglected they tried them out.

"What's the point of all that training if we never use our talents?" Maya grumbled quietly, and Miki agreed with her.

Miki could use the second self long enough to give the impression that Maya was in the room while Maya took on invisibility in order to creep up on Sunaomi and Chikara and terrify them with a ghostlike breath on the back of the neck, or sudden touch on the hair. They had obeyed the rule against roaming outside, but it irked them—both of them longed to explore the bustling, fascinating town, the forest beyond the river, the area around the volcano, the wooded hill above the castle.

"There are goblins there," Maya told Sunaomi, "with long noses and eyes on stalks!"

She pointed up the hill, where the dark trees formed an impenetrable mass. Two kites wheeled above them. The four children were in the garden at the end of the afternoon on the third day of the Festival. The day had been stifling; even in the garden, under the trees, it was still unbearably hot.

"I'm not afraid of goblins," he replied. "I'm not afraid of anything!"

"These goblins eat boys," Miki whispered. "They eat them raw, bit by bit!"

"Like tigers?" Sunaomi replied, mocking, irritating Maya even more. She had not forgotten Sunaomi's words to her father, his unconscious assumption of superiority: *They are only girls, after all.* She would pay him back for that. She felt the cat stir inside her, and flexed her hands.

"They can't get to us here," Chikara said nervously. "There are too many guards."

"Oh, it's easy to be brave when you're surrounded by guards," Maya said to Sunaomi. "If you were really brave, you would go outside alone!"

"I am not allowed to," he replied.

"You are scared to!"

"No, I'm not!"

"So go outside. I'm not afraid to. I've been to Akane's house, even though her ghost haunts it. I've seen her."

"Akane hates boys," Miki whispered. "She buries boys alive in her garden so the shrubs grow well and smell sweet."

"Sunaomi wouldn't dare go there," Maya said, showing her small white teeth in a half-smile.

"In Kumamoto I was sent to the graveyard at night to bring back a lantern," Sunaomi said. "I didn't see a single ghost!"

"So go to Akane's house and bring back a spray of flowers."

"That would be so easy," Sunaomi said scornfully. "Only I'm not allowed—your father said so."

"You're afraid," Maya said.

"It's not very easy to get out without being seen."

"It's easy if you're not scared. You're just making excuses." Maya stood and went to the edge of the sea wall. "You climb down here at low tide and walk over the rocks to the beach." Sunaomi had followed her, and she pointed to the clump of pine trees where Akane's house stood, empty and forlorn-looking. It was half-dismantled in preparation for the building of the new shrine—no longer a dwelling, not yet a temple, it suggested the in-between world of spirits. The tide was half full, the partly exposed rocks jagged and slippery. "You could go tonight." She turned and looked at Sunaomi, holding his gaze for an instant until his eyes began to roll.

"Maya!" Miki called warningly.

"Oh, forgive me, cousin! I forgot. I mustn't look at people. I promised Father." She gave Sunaomi a quick slap on the cheek to wake him up, and went back to Chikara.

"Do you know, if you gaze into my eyes you will go to sleep and never wake up!"

Sunaomi came running to his brother's defense. "Do you know that you would not be alive if you lived in Kumamoto? We kill twins there!"

"I don't believe anything you say," Maya replied. "Everyone knows the Arai are traitors and cowards."

Sunaomi drew himself up proudly. "If you were a boy I would kill you. But since you are only a girl, I will go to this house and bring back whatever you want."

At sunset the sky was clear, the air blue and luminous with no wind, but as the moon rose, one night past full, it drew with it from the east a strange dark mass of cloud that spread across the sky, obliterating the stars and finally swallowing the moon itself. Sea and land merged into one. The last fires still smoldered on the beach; there was no other light.

Sunaomi was the eldest son of a warrior family. He had been trained since infancy in self-discipline and the overcoming of fear. It was not difficult for him, though only eight years old, to stay awake until midnight. He was, despite his bold assurances, apprehensive—but more of disobeying his uncle than of physical danger or ghosts. The retainers who had accompanied him from Hofu were staying in one of the clan halls in the town, ordered there by Lord Otori—the castle guards were mainly on the gates and around the front walls. A patrol walked through the gardens at regular intervals. Sunaomi heard them go past the open doors of the room where he and Chikara slept, along with the two maids who took care of them. Both girls were fast asleep, one of them snoring slightly. He rose quickly, ready to say he was going to the privy if they woke, but neither stirred.

Outside, the night was still. Both castle and town slept. Below the wall, the sea murmured gently. Hardly able to discern anything, Sunaomi took a deep breath and began to feel his way down the great ramp of the wall. Made of huge stones fitted closely together, giving just enough space for a fingerhold, it curved outward slightly, toward the water. Several times he thought himself stuck, unable to go up or down; he thought of monsters that came up out of the sea, huge fish or giant octopuses that might at any moment pluck him into the darkness. The sea moaned, louder now. He could hear the swirl of water on the rocks.

When his feet, in the straw sandals, touched the surface of the rock, he slipped immediately and nearly fell straight into the water. Scrabbling to grab a handhold, he felt the sharp shells like knives beneath his palms and knees. A wave crept under him, setting the small cuts stinging. Clenching his teeth, he edged his way like a crab in the direction of the last smoldering fires, toward the shore.

The beach was a pale grayness; the waves hissed with a sudden gleam of white. When he reached the sand, it was a relief to feel its softness beneath his feet. It gave way to tussocks of stiff grass; he stumbled and continued on all fours into the small grove where the trunks of the pines loomed around him. An owl hooted overhead, making him jump, and its ghostly shape floated briefly ahead of him on soundless wings.

The glow of the fires was well behind him. He halted for a few moments, crouching beneath the trees. He could smell their resiny scent along with the smoke from the fires—and another heavy fragrance, sweet and enticing— the shrubs in Akane's garden, their perfume enhanced by boys' blood and bones.

Boys were frequently sent to graveyards or execution grounds at night to test their courage. Sunaomi had boasted to Maya that he had never seen a ghost. But that did not mean he did not believe in their existence— women with long necks like snakes and teeth sharp as cats', strange inhuman shapes with only one eye and no limbs, headless bandits who resented their cruel punishment, any one of the restless dead who sought to feed on human blood or human souls.

He swallowed hard, and tried to suppress the shivering that threatened to take over his limbs. *I am Arai Sunaomi,* he told himself, *son of Zenko, grandson of Daiichi. I am afraid of nothing.*

He forced himself to stand, and to walk forward, though his legs seemed as heavy as the tree trunks, and he badly needed to piss. He could just make out the walls of the garden, the curve of the roof behind them. The gate stood open; the walls were beginning to crumble.

As he stepped through the gate, he walked into a summer spider's web, the sticky threads clinging to face and hair. His breath was coming faster now, but he told himself, *I'm not crying, I'm not crying,* though he could feel the pressure of water building up behind his eyes, inside his bladder.

The house seemed completely dark. Something scuttled away across the veranda, a cat perhaps, or a large rat. He held his hands out in front of him as he followed the scent round the far side of the house and into the garden. The cat—it must have been a cat—yowled suddenly from the shadows.

He could see the blossom—the only thing visible in the darkness, a faint gleam. He set out toward it, hurrying now, desperate to pluck a spray and escape, but he tripped over a rock and fell full length, his mouth in the earth. Its smell and taste made him think of graves and corpses, and how he might soon lie buried in it, its taste his last living sensation.

Then he pushed himself up on all fours and spat out the earth. He stood, reached up, and snapped off a branch. The shrub instantly gave out another strong smell of sap, and Sunaomi heard footsteps on the veranda behind him.

As he spun round, his eyes were instantly dazzled by the light. All he could see was a half-formed shape, a woman, but only partly a woman, one who must have just struggled out of the grave. The shadows played over her; her arms were stretching out to him. The lamp rose a little; the light fell on her face. She had no eyes, no mouth, no nose.

His control broke. He screamed; the wetness burst out, running down his legs. He threw the branch from him.

"I'm sorry, Lady Akane. I'm sorry. Please don't hurt me. Don't bury me!"

"What on earth?" a voice exclaimed, a human voice, a man's voice. "What do you think you're doing here at this time of night?"

But Sunaomi was incapable of answering.

TARO, who had taken to sleeping at Akane's house while he worked on the statue, carried the boy at once back to the castle. Sunaomi was not harmed in any way, other than being severely frightened, and the following morning would not even admit to that, but a wound had been made in his heart, and though it healed, it left a scar of deep hatred toward Maya and Miki. From that time on, Sunaomi dwelt more and more on his grandfather's death, and the offenses against the Arai by the Otori clan. His childish mind sought ways to hurt Maya and Miki. He began to ingratiate himself with the women of the household, charming and delighting them; most of them adored boy children anyway, and he knew himself to be handsome and winning. He missed his mother, but knew instinctively that he could gain a high place in the affections of his aunt, Kaede, much higher than the twin girls.

TAKEO AND KAEDE were distressed and angered by this episode, for if Sunaomi had been killed or badly injured while in their care, quite apart from their own grief, for they had both become fond of him, their strategy to placate and contain their brother-in-law would have been completely destroyed. Takeo himself reprimanded Sunaomi for his disobedience and foolhardiness, and questioned him closely about his reasons, suspecting that he would never have thought of such a thing without some prompting. It did not take long for the truth to come out, and then it was Maya's turn to face her father's anger.

He was more alarmed for her this time, for she gave no sign of contrition, and her eyes were fierce and unrelenting, like an animal's. She did not cry, not even when Kaede expressed her own displeasure and slapped her hard several times.

"She is completely beyond reason," Kaede said, tears of exasperation in her own eyes. "She cannot stay here. If she is not to be trusted with the young boys…"

Takeo heard her concern for herself and the child she carried. He did not want to send Maya away—he thought she needed his protection and supervision, but he was too busy to devote much time to her, and he could not keep her constantly at his side.

"It is not right to want to send your own daughter away and favor other people's sons," Maya said quietly.

Kaede slapped her again. "How dare you speak to me, your mother, in that way? What do you understand of the affairs of state? Everything we do has a political reason. It will always be like this. You are the daughter of Lord Otori. You cannot behave like other children."

Shizuka said, "She does not know who she is—she has Tribe skills that she cannot use as a warrior's daughter. It's a shame to see them wasted."

Maya whispered, "Then let me be a child of the Tribe."

"She needs watching and training. But who knows about these things among the Muto? Even you, Shizuka, with your Kikuta blood, have no experience with this sort of possession," Takeo said.

"You yourself taught my son many Kikuta skills," Shizuka replied. "Maybe Taku is the best person."

"But Taku must stay in the West. We cannot bring him back here just for Maya's sake."

"Then send her to him."

Takeo sighed. "It seems the only solution. Can someone be spared to accompany her?"

"There is a girl she's recently come from the Muto village to Hagi with her sister. They are both in service in the foreigners' house at present."

"What's her name?"

"Sada—she is related to Kenji's wife, Seiko."

Takeo nodded. He remembered the girl now; she was tall and strongly built, and could pass as a man, a disguise she was often called on to use while engaged in Tribe work.

"You will go to Taku in Maruyama," he told Maya. "You will obey Sada in everything."

Sunaomi tried to avoid her, but before she left, Maya cornered him, whispering, "You failed the test. I told you the Arai were cowards."

"I went to the house," he replied. "Taro was there. He made me come back."

Maya smiled. "You did not bring back the branch!"

"There was no blossom!"

"No blossom! You picked a spray. Then you threw it away, and pissed yourself. I saw you."

"You weren't there!"

"Yes, I was."

Sunaomi shouted for the maids to come and punish her, but Maya was already running away.

s summer gave way to autumn, Takeo prepared to travel again. It was the custom for the country to be governed from Yamagata from the end of the ninth month until the winter solstice, but he was forced to leave earlier than he intended, for Matsuda Shingen died peacefully at the beginning of the month; Miyoshi Gemba brought the news to Hagi, and Takeo left at once, with Gemba and Shigeko, for Terayama. The records of the work that had occupied them through the summer—the policy decisions, agricultural and financial planning, codes of justice, and the carefully considered conclusions of tribunals—were dispatched in boxes and baskets on long trains of packhorses.

There was nothing to mourn in Matsuda's passing. His life had been long and full of achievement, his spirit one of purity and strength. He had taught Shigeru, Takeo, and Shigeko, and he left many disciples dedicated to continuing his vision. Yet Takeo missed him irrationally and deeply, and felt the loss as one more breach in the defenses of the Three Countries, through which wind would howl or wolf enter when winter came.

Makoto was installed as Abbot in his place, and took the name of Eikan, but Takeo continued to think of his old friend by his former name, and, after the ceremonies were completed and they traveled on to Yamagata, took some comfort from the knowledge that Makoto continued to support him as he had always done; and he thought again with longing of the time when he might retire to Terayama and spend his days in meditation and painting.

Gemba accompanied them on to Yamagata where the various matters of administration took up all of Takeo's attention. Shigeko attended most of the meetings with him, but rose early every morning to practice her horse riding and archery with Gemba.

Just before they departed for Maruyama in the first week of the tenth month, letters came from Hagi. Takeo read them eagerly, and shared the family news immediately with his oldest daughter.

"Your mother has moved with the little boys to Lord Shigeru's old house. And she has started learning the foreigners' language."

"From their interpreter?" Shigeko wanted to ask her father more, but Minoru was with them, as well as servants from the Miyoshi household, and Jun and Shin, as usual, outside but within earshot. However, later, when they walked in the gardens, she found herself alone with him.

"You must tell me more about the foreigners," she said. "Should they be allowed to trade in Maruyama?"

"I want them where we can watch them at all times," Takeo replied. "They will stay in Hagi for the winter. We need to learn as much as we can about their language, customs, and intentions."

"Their interpreter—there was something strange about the way she looked at you, almost as if she knew you well."

He hesitated for a moment. Leaves were falling in the tranquil garden, carpeting the ground with drifting gold. It was late afternoon, the mist rising from the moat mingling with wood smoke, blurring outlines and details.

"Your mother knows who she is, but no one else does," he said finally. "I will tell you, but keep it secret. Her name is Madaren; it is a name often used by the sect known as the Hidden. They share some of the beliefs of the foreigners, and used to be severely persecuted by the Tohan. Everyone in her family was killed, except her older brother, who was rescued by Lord Shigeru."

Shigeko's eyes widened and her pulse beat more rapidly. Her father smiled.

"Yes, it was me. I was called Tomasu then, but Shigeru renamed me Takeo. Madaren is my younger sister. We were born to the same mother, but from different fathers—my father, as you know, was from the Tribe. I thought she was dead for all these years."

"How extraordinary," Shigeko said, and with her characteristic swift sympathy, "How terrible her life must have been."

"She has survived, has learned a foreign language, has grasped every opportunity offered to her," Takeo replied. "She has done better than many. Now she is under my protection to a certain extent, and permitted to instruct my wife." After a moment, he added, "There have always been many Hidden in Maruyama. Lady Naomi gave them a safe haven, indeed was one of them. You will need to acquaint yourself with their leaders. Jo-An, of course, was also a believer, and many former outcastes still live in hamlets around the city."

She saw his face darken, and did not want to pursue a subject that brought back so many painful memories.

"I doubt I will live to even half Matsuda's age," Takeo continued with great seriousness. "The future safety of these people is in your hands. But do not trust the foreigners, nor Madaren, even though she is your relative. And remember to honor all beliefs, but follow none, for that is the only path for the true leader."

Shigeko reflected on this for a few moments, and then said, "May I ask you a question?"

"Of course. You know you may ask me anything at any time. I do not want to conceal anything from you."

"Prophecies justify your rule as ordained and blessed by Heaven. The houou nest again in the Three Countries. We even possess a kirin—one of the signs of a great and just ruler. Do you believe all this of yourself?"

"I believe all of it and none of it," Takeo replied. "I seem to balance my life between the two. I am deeply grateful for everything that Heaven has bestowed on me, but I will never take any of it for granted, nor, I hope, abuse the power entrusted to me.

"Old men grow foolish," he added lightly. "When that happens, you must encourage me to retire. Though, as I said, I do not expect to see old age."

"I want you never to die," she exclaimed, suddenly fearful.

"I will die happy knowing I am leaving everything in safe hands," he replied, smiling. But she knew he was masking many concerns.

A FEW DAYS later they crossed the bridge near Kibi, and Takeo was reminiscing with Gemba about the past—the flight from Terayama in the rain, the help given by Jo-An and the outcastes, and the death of the ogre Jinemon. The shrine on the bank had been dedicated to the fox god, but in some strange twist of belief Jo-An had become identified with this deity and was now also worshipped here.

"It was at that time that Amano Tenzo gave me Shun," Takeo said. He patted the neck of the black horse he was riding. "This fellow is nice enough, but Shun astonished me in our first fight together. He knew more about it than I did!"

"I suppose he is dead now?" Gemba questioned.

"Yes, he died two years ago. I've never seen another horse like him. Did you know he was Takeshi's horse? Mori Hiroki recognized him."

"I did not know that," Gemba replied.

Shigeko, however, had known it all her life, one of the legends that she had grown up with. The bay horse had been broken in by Lord Takeshi, Shigeru's younger brother, who had taken him to Yamagata. Takeshi had been murdered by Tohan soldiers, and the horse had disappeared until Amano Tenzo bought him and gave him to Takeo. She thought with pleasure of the secret gift she had for her father, already, she hoped, on its way to Maruyama, for she intended to present him with a surprise at the coming ceremony.

Thinking about legends and marvelous animals made an idea come into her mind. It seemed so brilliant she felt she must share it at once.

"Father, when we go to Miyako next year, let us take the kirin as a gift for the Emperor."

Gemba gave a shout of laughter. "What a perfect gift! Nothing like it will ever have been seen in the capital!"

Takeo turned in the saddle and stared at Shigeko. "It is a marvelous thought. But I gave the kirin to you. I do not want to demand it back again. And is it capable of making such a journey?"

"It travels well by ship. I could accompany it to Akashi. Maybe Lord Gemba or Lord Hiroshi will come with me."

"The Emperor and his court will be dazzled by such a present," Gemba said, his plump cheeks rosy with pleasure. "Just as Lord Saga will be disarmed by Lady Shigeko."

Shigeko, riding through the peaceful autumn countryside toward the domain that was to be hers, where she would see Hiroshi again, felt that they were indeed blessed by Heaven, and that the Way of the Houou, the way of peace, would prevail.

fter Muto Kenji's death, the old man's body was flung into a pit and covered with earth. Nothing marked the spot, but Hisao never had any difficulty finding it, for his mother guided his feet there. Often rain would fall in a sudden shower while he passed by, refracting the sun's light in fragments of rainbows on the high-floating clouds. He would gaze at them and pray silently for his grandfather's spirit, that it would have a safe passage through the world of the dead and an auspicious rebirth into the next life, and then lower his eyes to the mountain ranges that unfolded to the east and north, to see if another stranger was approaching.

He was half-relieved and half-sorry that the old man's spirit had passed on. It did not hang at the edge of his awareness like his mother's, making his head ache with incomprehensible demands. He had known his grandfather only for an hour, but he missed his presence. Kenji had taken his own life at the moment and in the manner of his own choosing; Hisao was glad his spirit had gone in peace, but he regretted the death, and though he never spoke of it resented Akio for causing it.

The summer passed and no one came.

Everyone in the village was anxious throughout the hot summer months, especially Kotaro Gosaburo, for nothing was heard about the fate of his children, who were still held in Inuyama castle. Rumors and speculation abounded—that they were half-dead from ill-treatment; that one or both had died; for a few days, thrillingly, that they had escaped. Gosaburo grew thin, his skin hanging in folds, his eyes dull. Akio was increasingly impatient with him; indeed, he was irritable and unpredictable with everyone. Hisao thought he would almost have welcomed news of the young people's execution, for it would have extinguished Gosaburo's hopes and hardened his resolve for revenge.

Autumn lilies blossomed in scarlet profusion over Kenji's body, though no one had planted the bulbs. Birds began their long flights south, and the nights were filled with the crying of geese and the beat of their wings. The moon of the ninth month was huge and golden. Maples and sumac turned crimson, beech copper, willow and ginkgo gold. Hisao's days were spent in repairing dikes before winter, distributing rotten leaves and dung on the fields, gathering firewood from the forest. His watering system had been a success: The mountain field yielded a fine crop of beans, carrots, and squash. He developed a new rake, which spread the manure more evenly, and experimented with the blades of axes, their weight, angle, and sharpness. There was a forge in the village, and Hisao went there whenever he had time to watch the smith and help blow up the heat with the bellows in the mysterious process of turning iron to steel.

Earlier in the seventh month, Imai Kazuo had been sent to Inuyama to discover the truth. He returned in mid-autumn with the welcome yet puzzling news that the hostages were still alive, still held in Inuyama castle. He had other news: that Lady Otori was with child and that Lord Otori was sending a splendid procession of messengers to the capital. The retinue had been in Inuyama at the same time as Kazuo, and was about to leave for Miyako.

Akio was less pleased with the first piece of news than he pretended, bitterly envious at the second, and deeply uneasy at the third.

"Why is Otori making approaches to the Emperor?" he questioned Kazuo. "What does it mean?"

"The Emperor has appointed a new general, Saga Hideki, who has been busy for the last ten years extending his control over the East. It seems finally a warrior has appeared who can challenge the Otori."

Akio's eyes gleamed with an unusual expression of emotion. "Something has changed; I sense it. Otori has become more vulnerable. He is responding to some threat. We must be part of his downfall—we cannot wait hidden away for someone else to bring the news of his death to us."

"There are signs of weakness," Kazuo agreed. "Messages to the Emperor, the young people still alive. . . . He has never hesitated to kill Kikuta before."

"Muto Kenji sniffed us out," Akio said thoughtfully. "Takeo must know where we are. I could not believe neither he nor Taku would let Kenji's death go unchallenged unless they were preoccupied with other more urgent matters."

"It is time for you to travel again," Kazuo said. "There are many Kikuta families in Akashi, and even here and there in the Three Countries, who need guidance, who will follow your lead if you are there in person."

"Then we will go first to Akashi," Akio said.

AS A CHILD Hisao's father had taught him some of the traveling theater skills of the Kikuta—playing the drum, juggling, singing the ancient ballads that country people love, of old wars, feuds, betrayals, and acts of revenge—that they had always used in their journeys across the Three Countries. In the week after Kazuo's return Akio started juggling training again; a large supply of straw sandals was prepared, dried persimmons and chestnuts were collected and packed, amulets taken out and dusted off, weapons sharpened.

Hisao was not a gifted performer—he was too shy and did not enjoy attracting attention, but Akio's combination of blows and caresses had made him skillful enough. He knew all the juggling routines and rarely made a mistake, just as he knew all the words to the songs, though people complained he mumbled and was hard to hear. The idea of traveling filled him with both excitement and trepidation. He looked forward to being on the road, leaving the village, seeing new things, but he was less enthusiastic about performing and uneasy about leaving his grandfather's grave.

Gosaburo had received Kazuo's news with joy, and questioned him closely. He did not speak directly to Akio at the time, but the night before their departure, when Hisao was preparing for sleep, he came to the door of the room and asked Akio if he might speak privately to him.

Akio was half-undressed, and Hisao could see his face scowl in the dim lamplight, but he made a slight gesture with his head, and Gosaburo stepped into the room, slid the door shut, and knelt nervously on the matting.

"Nephew," he said, as though trying to assert some authority of age. "The time has surely come for us to negotiate with the Otori. The Three Countries are growing rich and prosperous while we skulk here in the mountains with barely enough to feed ourselves and the prospect of another freezing winter ahead. We could be flourishing too—our influence could be extending with our trade. Call off the blood feud."

Akio said, "Never."

Gosaburo took a deep breath. "I am going to return to Matsue. I will leave in the morning."

"No one leaves the Kikuta family," Akio reminded him, his voice expressionless.

"I am rotting away here. We all are. Otori has spared the lives of my children. Let us accept his offer of truce. I will still be loyal to you. I'll work for you in Matsue as I always did, provide funds, keep records . . ."

"Once Takeo—and Taku, too—are dead, we will talk about truce," Akio replied. "Now get out. I am tired, and your presence is repulsive to me."

As soon as Gosaburo left, Akio doused the lamp. Hisao already lay on the mattress; the night was mild and he had not pulled the cover over him. Little fragments of light danced behind his eyelids. He thought briefly about his cousins and wondered how they would die in Inuyama, but mostly he was listening to Akio's movements, every cell, it seemed, aware, with a mixture of dread and arousal, physical longing for affection and an only half-acknowledged sense of shame.

Akio's anger made him rough and hasty. Hisao bit back any sound, conscious of the latent violence and afraid of provoking it against himself. Yet the act brought some fleeting release. Akio's voice was almost gentle when he told the boy to sleep, not to get up, no matter what he heard, and Hisao felt the brief moment of tenderness that he craved as his father caressed his hair, the back of his neck. After Akio left the room, Hisao buried himself under the quilt and tried to close his ears. There were a few muted sounds, someone gasping and struggling; a heavy thump, a dragging on boards, then on earth.

I am asleep, he told himself, over and again, until suddenly, before Akio returned, he had fallen into a sleep as deep and dreamless as death.

The next morning Gosaburo's body lay slumped in the laneway. He had been garroted in the way of the Tribe. No one even dared mourn him.

"No one leaves the Kikuta and goes unpunished," Akio said to Hisao as they prepared to depart. "Remember that. Both Takeo and his father dared to leave the Tribe. Isamu was executed for it, and Takeo will be too."

AKASHI HAD SPRUNG from the years of conflict and confusion, when merchants had profited from the needs of warriors for provisions and weapons; once they had become rich, they saw no reason to lose their wealth to the depredations of these same warriors, and had banded together to protect their goods and their trade. The city was surrounded by deep moats, and each of its ten bridges was guarded by soldiers from its own army. It had several great temples that protected and encouraged trade, both in the material and the spiritual realm.

As warlords rose to power, they sought beautiful objects and clothes, works of art, and other luxuries from Shin and beyond, and these the merchants of the free port gladly supplied. The Tribe families had once been more powerful merchants than any within the city, but the increasing prosperity of the Three Countries and the alliance with the Otori had led many of the Muto to move to Hofu, and even the remaining Kikuta had become more interested in trade and profit, during Akio's self-imposed isolation in the mountains, than in espionage and assassination.

"Those days are past," Jizaemon, the owner of a busy importing business, told Akio after welcoming him somewhat less than wholeheartedly. "We must move with the times. We can be more successful and exercise more control over events by supplying arms and other necessities of life, by lending money. Let's by all means encourage the preparation of war, while with luck avoiding its outbreak."

Hisao thought his father would react with the same violence as he had against Gosaburo, and he felt sorry. He did not want Jizaemon to die before he had shown Hisao some of the treasures he had acquired: mechanical gadgets that measured the hours, glass bottles and drinking vessels, mirrors, and delicious new foods, sweet and spicy, licorice and sugar—words he had never heard before.

The journey had been tedious. Neither Akio nor Kazuo were young anymore, and their performance as actors lacked fire. Their songs were old-fashioned and no longer popular. Their reception on the road had been grudging, and in one village hostile—no one wanted to give them lodging, and they had been forced to walk all night.

Hisao studied his father closely now, without appearing to, and saw that he was old. In the hidden village Akio had an innate power as the undisputed Master of the Kikuta family, feared and respected by everyone; here, in his old faded clothes, he looked like a nobody. Hisao felt a stab of pity, and then tried to extinguish it, since the pity, as always, opened him up to the voices of the dead. The familiar headache began—half the world slipped into mist; the woman was whispering, but he was not going to listen to her.

"Well, maybe you're right," he heard Akio say, as if from a distance. "But surely war cannot be avoided forever. We had heard of Otori's messengers to the Emperor."

"Yes, you only missed them by a few weeks; I've never seen such a lavish procession. Otori must be truly rich and, more than that, gifted with taste and refinement: They say that is his wife's influence . . ."

"And the Emperor has a new general?" Akio cut short the merchant's enthusiasm.

"Indeed, and what's more, cousin, the general has new weapons—or very soon will have. They say that's why Lord Otori is seeking the Emperor's favor."

"What do you mean?"

"For years the Otori have kept a strict embargo on firearms. But recently the embargo was broken, and firearms were smuggled out of Hofu—it is said with the direct help of Arai Zenko! You know Terada Fumio?"

Akio nodded.

"Well, Fumio arrived two days after the arms to try to get them back. He was furious; first he offered large sums of money, then he threatened to come back with a fleet and burn the city if they weren't returned. But it was too late—they were already on their way to Saga. And I can't tell you what it's done for the price of iron and niter. Sky high, cousin, sky high!"

Jizaemon poured another cup of wine and urged them to drink with him.

"No one cares about Terada's threats." He chuckled. "He's nothing but a pirate. He's smuggled far worse himself before now. And Lord Otori will never attack the free city, not while he needs his own merchants to feed and equip his army."

Hisao wondered at Akio's lack of response. His father simply drank deeply, and nodded in agreement at everything Jizaemon said, though his scowl deepened and his face grew darker.

Hisao woke in the night to hear his father whispering to Kazuo. He felt his whole body grow tense, and half-expected to hear again the dull sounds of murder, but the two men were talking about something else— about Arai Zenko, who had allowed firearms to escape the Otori net.

Hisao knew of Zenko's history—that he was the older son of Muto Shizuka, and Kenji's great-nephew, some sort of cousin to himself. Zenko was the only member of the Muto family not execrated by the Kikuta— he had not been involved in Kotaro's death, and was rumored to be not completely loyal to Takeo, despite being his brother-in-law. It was suspected that he blamed Takeo for his father's death, and even nursed a secret desire for revenge.

"Zenko is both powerful and ambitious," Kazuo whispered. "If he is seeking to ingratiate himself with Lord Saga, he must be preparing to move against the Dog."

"It's a perfect time to approach Zenko," Akio murmured. "Takeo is looking to threats from the East; if Zenko attacks from the West he will be caught between them."

"I feel Zenko will welcome an approach from you," Kazuo replied. "And, of course, since Muto Kenji's death, Zenko must be the next Master of the Muto family. What better time to go to the Muto to mend the rift in the Tribe, to bring the families back together?"

Jizaemon, glad perhaps to get rid of his visitors, provided them with letters of passage and fitted them out with the clothes and other appurtenances of merchants. He arranged for them to travel on one of his guild's ships, and within a few days they set sail for Kumamoto by way of Hofu, taking advantage of the fine, calm weather of late autumn.

· 23 ·

aya did not travel as the daughter of Lord Otori, but in her other fashion, disguised in the Tribe way. She was younger sister to Sada, and they were going to Maruyama to see their relatives there and find work after the death of their parents. Maya liked playing the part of this orphaned child, and it gratified her to imagine her parents dead, for she was still angry with them, especially with her mother, and deeply wounded by their preference for Sunaomi. Maya had seen Sunaomi reduced to a sniveling child by what he thought was a ghost—in reality an unfinished statue of the all-merciful Kannon. She despised his fear all the more, for it was trivial compared to what she had seen that same starless night, the third night of the Festival of the Dead.

It had been easy enough to follow Sunaomi using ordinary Tribe skills, but when she came to the beach something about the night and the smoldering fires, the intensity and grief of the Festival touched her deeply, and the cat's voice spoke inside her, saying, "Look what I can see!"

At first it was like a game—the sudden clarity of the dark scene, her huge pupils taking in every movement, the scuttling of small creatures and night insects, the quiver of leaves, the drops of spray borne by the breeze. Then her body softened and stretched into the cat's, and she became aware that the beach and the pine grove were full of phantoms.

She saw them with the cat's vision, their faces gray, their robes white,

their pale limbs floating above the ground. The dead turned their gaze
toward her and the cat responded to them, knowing all their bitter regrets,
their unending grudges, their unfulfilled desires.

Maya cried out in shock; the cat yowled. She struggled to return to her
own familiar flesh; the cat's claws scrabbled on the black shingle at the
sand's edge—it leaped into the trees around the house. The spirits followed
her, pressing round her, their touch icy on her pelt. She heard their voices
like the rustling of leaves in the autumn wind, full of sorrow and hunger.

"Where is our Master? Take us to him. We are waiting for him."

Their words filled her with terror, though she did not understand
them, as in a nightmare when a single obscure sentence chills the sleeper to
the bone. She heard the snap of the branch breaking, and saw a man come
out of the half-demolished house with a lamp in his hand. The dead retreated from the light, and it made her pupils narrow so that she could no
longer see them clearly. But she heard Sunaomi scream, and heard the
trickle of water as he pissed himself. Her contempt for his fear helped her
master her own, enough to retreat into the shrubs and return unseen to the
castle. She could not remember at what point the cat had left her and she
had become Maya again, just as it was not clear to her what had made the
cat shape manifest itself. But she could not rid herself of the memory of
the cat's ghost vision and the hollow voices of the dead.

Where is our Master?

She dreaded seeing and hearing that way again, and she tried to armor
herself against the cat's possession of her. She had inherited something of
the implacable nature of the Kikuta along with many of their talents. But
the cat came to her in dreams, demanding, terrifying, and enticing.

"YOU WILL MAKE an excellent spy!" Sada exclaimed after their first
night on the ship, when Maya recounted the gossip she had overheard the
day before—nothing sinister or dangerous, just individuals' secrets that
they might have preferred to remain unknown to the wide world.

"I would rather be a spy than have to get married to some lord," Maya replied. "I want to be like you, or like Shizuka used to be."

She gazed across the white-flecked water toward the East, where the city of Hagi already lay lost in the distance. Oshima also lay far behind them, only the clouds above the island volcano visible. They had passed it during the night, to Maya's regret, for she had heard many stories of the pirates' former stronghold and her father's visit to Lord Terada, and she wanted to see it for herself, but the ship could not afford any delay—the northeasterly wind would not hold for many more days, and they needed it to drive them to the coast of the West.

"Shizuka used to do whatever she pleased," Maya went on. "But then she got married to Dr. Ishida, and now she's just like any other wife."

Sada laughed. "Don't underestimate Muto Shizuka! She has always been so much more than she seems."

"She is Sunaomi's grandmother too," Maya grumbled.

"You are jealous, Maya; that's your trouble!"

"It's so unfair," the girl said. "If only I were a boy, it wouldn't matter if I were a twin. If I were a boy, Sunaomi would never have come to live with us, and Father would not be thinking of adopting him!" *And I would never have thought of daring the little coward to go to the shrine.* She looked at Sada. "Didn't you ever wish you were a man?"

"Yes, often, when I was a child. Even in the Tribe, where women have great freedom, boys seem to be valued more. I always set myself against them, always strove to beat them. Muto Kenji used to say that explained why I grew as tall and as strong as a man. He taught me to copy boys, use their speech, and ape their gestures. Now I can be either man or woman, and that's the way I like it."

"He taught us the same!" Maya exclaimed, for like all the Tribe children she had learned both men's and women's language and gestures, and could pass as either.

Sada studied her. "Yes, you could become a boy."

"Really, I am not sorry to be sent away," Maya confided in her. "Because I like you—and I love Taku!"

"Everyone loves Taku." Sada laughed.

But Maya had no opportunity to pick up more of the enticing, almost incomprehensible language of the sailors—some of them hardly older than she was—for the swell picked up, and to her annoyance she discovered she was not a good sailor. The dip and rise of the ship made her head ache and her body feel unbearable to her. Sada cared for her without fussing or words of sympathy, held her head while she vomited and sponged her face afterward, making her take tiny sips of tea to wet her lips, and, when the most violent phase had passed, laid her down and took her head on her lap, holding her long, cool hand against Maya's brow. Sada thought she could feel, just beneath the skin, the animal nature like a pelt, dark, solid, and heavy yet soft to the touch, calling out to be caressed. Maya experienced the touch as that of a nurse or a mother. She woke from the sickness when the ship rounded the cape just as the winds changed and the westerly came up to bring them to shore, and gazed at Sada's sharp face, with its high cheekbones like a boy's, and thought it would be happiness to lie forever in her arms, and felt her whole body stir in response. In that moment a passion came over her for the older girl, a combination of admiration and need—it was her first experience of love. She stretched against Sada, folded her arms around her, feeling the strong muscles like a man's, the surprising softness of the breasts. She nuzzled into the neck, half childlike, half animal-like.

"I take it this affection means you're feeling better?" Sada said, hugging her back.

"A little. It was awful. I will never go in a ship again!" She paused and then said, "Do you love me, Sada?"

"What sort of question is that?"

"I dreamed you did. But I'm never sure if it's me dreaming, or . . ."

"Or what?"

"Or the cat."

"What sort of dreams does the cat have?" Sada asked idly.

"Animal dreams." Maya was gazing at the distant shore the pine-topped cliffs that rose abruptly from the dark blue water, the black rocks fringed with gray-green and white waves. Within the bay, where the surface was calmer, and up into the estuary, wooden racks supported seaweed and shallow-hulled fishing boats were pulled up on the sand, where sea grass grew in tussocks. Men crouched on the shore, mending nets and keeping the fires lit that forced salt from seawater.

"I don't know about loving you," Sada teased. "But I do love the cat!" She reached out and rubbed Maya's neck as if she were petting a cat, and the girl's back arched in pleasure. Again Sada thought she could almost feel the fur under her fingers.

"If you keep doing that, I think I will turn into the cat," Maya said dreamily.

"I'm sure that will come in useful." Sada's tone was matter of fact and practical. Maya grinned. "That's why I love the Tribe," she said. "They don't mind if I'm a twin, or if the cat is possessing me. Whatever is useful to them is good. That's how I think. I'm never going to go back to life in a palace, or a castle. I'm going to stay with the Tribe."

"We'll see what Taku has to say about that!"

Maya knew Taku was the strictest of teachers and quite lacking in sentimentality, but she feared he would be swayed by his duty to her father and would therefore be inclined to treat her with favoritism. She did not know which would be worse—to be accepted by Taku only because she was an Otori daughter, or to be rejected by him as not being skillful enough. One moment she found herself thinking he would send her away, unable to help her; the next that he would be amazed by all she could do and all her potential. In the end his reception of her would be something between the two—not quite disappointing, but not overwhelming or flattering, either.

The sandy estuary was too shallow for their ship to enter, and they were lowered down on ropes to the flimsy fishing boats. The boats were narrow and unstable; the boatman laughed as Maya grabbed the gunwale, and tried to engage Sada in bawdy conversation as he poled them upstream toward the city of Maruyama.

The castle stood on a small hill above the river and the town that had spread around it. It was small and beautiful, white-walled and gray-roofed, looking in some way birdlike, as if it had just come to rest, its wings still spread, the setting sun tinging them pink. Maya knew it well and had often stayed there with her mother and sisters, but today it was not her destination. She kept her eyes lowered and spoke to no one, already half-consciously able to dissemble her features so no one would recognize her. Sada addressed her roughly from time to time, scolding her for dawdling, telling her not to scuffe her feet in the dirt. Maya answered her meekly, *yes older sister, of course older sister,* walking without complaining, though it was a long way and the bundle was heavy, and it was nearly dark by the time they came to a long, low house that extended all the way round the corner of the street. Its windows were barred with wooden slats, and its low tiled roof extended out in deep eaves. One side was a shop front, now closed and silent. Set into the other wall was a huge gate. Two men stood outside, armed with swords, each holding a long, curved spear.

Sada addressed one of them. "Are you expecting an invasion, cousin?"

"Here's trouble," he replied. "What are you doing? And who's the kid?"

"My little sister, you remember her?"

"That's never Mai!"

"No, not Mai, Maya. Let us in. I'll tell you all about it later. Is Taku in Maruyama?" she added as the gate was unbarred and they slipped in-side.

"Yes, he came a few days ago. Very grand, too, and in elevated com-pany. He is with Lord Kono, from Miyako, and Lord Sugita is entertain-ing them both. He hasn't dropped in like he usually does. We'll let him know you and your *sister* are here."

"Do they know who I am?" Maya whispered as Sada led her through the darkened garden to the entrance.

"They know. But they also know it is not their business to know, so they will say nothing to anyone."

She imagined how it would be, a man—perhaps a woman—in the guise of a soldier, a guard, or a servant. They would approach Taku casually, with some comment about a horse or a meal, and add a seemingly random sentence, and then Taku would know . . .

"What will they call me?" she said to Sada, stepping lightly onto the veranda.

"Call you? Who?"

"What is my secret name that only the Tribe know?"

Sada laughed almost soundlessly. "They will make something up. The Kitten, perhaps." *The Kitten came back tonight.* Maya could almost hear the maid's voice—she had decided it would be a woman—whisper in Taku's ear as she bent to wash his feet, or poured wine for him, and then . . . what would Taku do then?

She felt a slight touch of apprehension—whatever happened was not going to be easy.

She had to wait two days. She did not have time to be bored or anxious, for Sada kept her busy with the Tribe training that has no end, for the skills of the Tribe can always be improved, and no one, not even Muto Kenji or Kikuta Kotaro, has ever mastered them completely. And Maya was only a child—years lay ahead of her, standing motionless for long periods, stretching and folding her limbs to keep them completely supple, memory and observation training, the speed of movement that leads to invisibility and the command of the second self. Maya submitted to the discipline uncomplainingly, for she had decided that she loved Sada without reserve, and strove to please her.

At the end of the second day, after night had fallen and they had finished eating, Sada beckoned to Maya, who was gathering up the bowls and placing them on trays—for here she was no longer Lord Otori's daughter but the youngest girl in the household, and hence servant to everyone. She finished her task, carrying the trays to the kitchen, and then stepped outside onto the veranda. At the farther end, Sada stood holding a lamp. Maya could see Taku's face, half-lit, half in darkness.

She approached and dropped to her knees before him, but not before she had quickly studied what she could see of his face. He looked tired, his expression strained, even annoyed. Her heart sank.

"Lord Taku," she whispered.

He frowned more deeply, and made a gesture to Sada to bring the lamp closer. Maya felt the heat on her cheek, and closed her eyes briefly. The flame flickered behind her darkened lids.

"Look at me," Taku said.

His eyes, black, opaque, stared directly into hers. She held his gaze without blinking, making her mind go blank, not allowing anything to surface that might reveal her weaknesses to him, and at the same time not daring to search for his. But she could not foil him completely—she felt as if some beam of light, or of thought, had penetrated her, had seen a secret she had not known she held.

"Unnh," Taku grunted, but Maya could not tell if it was in approval or surprise. "Why has your father sent you to me?"

"He thinks I am possessed by a cat spirit," she said quietly. "He thought Kenji might have passed some of the Tribe's knowledge of these things on to you."

"Show me."

"I don't want to," she said.

"Let me see this cat spirit, if it is there." His voice was skeptical and dismissive. Maya responded with a flash of anger. It ran through her body, direct and non-human, making her limbs soften and stretch, rippling her coat; her ears flattened and she showed her teeth, prepared to spring.

"Enough," Taku said quietly, and touched her lightly on the cheek. The animal self subsided, and purred.

"You didn't believe me," Maya said blankly. She was shivering.

"If I didn't before, I do now," he replied. "Very interesting. And I daresay useful. The question is, just how shall we use you best? Have you ever taken on its form completely?"

"Once," she admitted. "I followed Sunaomi to Akane's shrine and watched him wet himself!"

Taku heard something beneath the bravado. "And?" he questioned.

Maya did not answer for a few moments; then she muttered, "I don't want to do it again! I don't like the feeling."

"Whether you like it or not has nothing to do with it," he said. "Don't waste my time. You must promise that you will do only what Sada or I tell you, no going off on your own, no risks, no secrets from us."

"I swear it."

"It's not a good time for all this," Taku said with some irritation to Sada. "I'm trying to keep Kono under control, and watch my brother's activities in case he makes any unexpected move. Still, if Takeo has requested it, I suppose I'd better keep her near me. You can come to the castle with me tomorrow. Dress her as a boy, but live here. You can be what you please, but she must live as a girl here. Most of the household already know who she is; she must be protected as far as possible as Lord Otori's daughter. I'll warn Hiroshi. Will anyone else recognize you?"

"No one ever looks at me directly," Maya told him. "Because I am a twin."

"Twins are rather special to the Tribe," he said. "But where's your sister?"

"She stayed in Hagi. She will go to Kagemura soon." Maya felt a sudden pang of longing for Miki, for Shigeko and her parents. *I am here like an orphan,* she thought, *or an exile. Maybe I'll be like father, discovered in a remote village, with more talent than anyone else in the Tribe.*

"Now go to bed," Taku told her abruptly. "There are things I have to discuss with Sada."

"Master." Maya bowed submissively to him and bade them both goodnight. No sooner had she re-entered the house than one of the maids seized her and sent her off to prepare the bedding. She unfolded the mats and spread the quilts, walking softly through the long, low rooms of the house. The wind had risen and whistled through all the cracks, autumn in its mouth, but Maya did not feel the cold. She was listening all the time to the muffled words from the garden. They had told her to go to bed and she had obeyed them, but they had not forbidden her to listen.

She had her father's acute hearing, and all year it had been growing more sensitive and more finely attuned. When she at last lay down, she set her ears, trying to filter out the whispering of the girls who lay on either side of her. Gradually they fell silent, their low voices replaced by the last of the summer insects, bewailing the coming cold and their own deaths.

She heard the hushed, feathery beat of the owl's wings as it floated through the garden, and breathed out almost inaudibly. Moonlight threw a latticed pattern on the paper screens; the moon tugged at her blood, making it race through her veins.

In the distance Taku said, "I brought Kono here that he might see the loyalty in Maruyama to the Otori. I'm afraid Zenko has let him believe that the Seishuu are on the verge of seceding once more, and that the West will not stand by Takeo."

"Surely Hiroshi is completely trustworthy?" Sada murmured.

"If he is not, I might as well cut my own throat," Taku said.

Sada laughed. "You would never take your own life, cousin."

"I hope I never have to. I might be forced to it out of sheer boredom if I have to put up with Lord Kono for much longer."

"Maya will be a welcome distraction, if it is boredom you fear."

"Or another responsibility that I could well do without!"

"What startled you when you looked in her eyes?"

"I was expecting a girl. What I saw was nothing like a girl—it is something unformed, waiting to find its shape."

"Is it a male spirit, or something to do with the cat possession?"

"I really have no idea. It seemed different. She is unique—probably very powerful."

"And dangerous?"

"Probably. To herself more than anything."

"You are tired." A note came into Sada's voice that made Maya shiver with a mixture of longing and jealousy.

Sada said, even more quietly, "Here, I will massage your brow."

There was a moment of silence. Maya held her breath. Taku let out a deep sigh. Some kind of intensity had fallen on the darkened garden, on the unseen couple. She could not bear to listen anymore, and pulled the quilt over her head.

A long time later, it seemed, she heard their footsteps on the veranda. Taku said in a low voice, "I did not expect that!"

"We grew up together," Sada replied. "It need not mean anything."

"Sada, nothing between us can be meaningless." He paused as if he would say more, but then said briefly, "I will see you and Maya tomorrow. Bring her to the castle at midday."

Sada came quietly into the room and lay down next to Maya. Pretending to be asleep, Maya rolled against her, breathing in her smell, mingled with Taku's, still on her. She could not decide which one she loved the most—she wanted to embrace them both. At that moment she felt herself theirs for life.

THE NEXT DAY, Sada woke her early and set about cutting her long hair to shoulder length and then pulling it back into a topknot, leaving the forehead unshaven, like a young boy not yet of age.

"You are not a pretty girl," she said, laughing. "But you make a very nice-looking boy. Scowl a bit more, and keep your lips together. You must not be too beautiful! Some warrior will spirit you away."

Maya tried to set her features in a more boyish way, but excitement and the unfamiliar feel of her hair and clothes, the male words in her mouth, made her eyes gleam and brought color into her cheeks.

"Calm down," Sada scolded her. "You must not draw attention to yourself. You are one of Lord Taku's servants; one of the lowest, too."

"What will I have to do?"

"Very little, I expect. Learn how to deal with boredom."

"Like Taku," Maya said without thinking.

Sada gripped her arm. "You heard him say that? What else did you hear?"

Maya stared back at her. For a moment she did not speak. Then she said, "I heard everything."

Sada could not prevent the smile curving her lips. "Never speak of it to anyone," she murmured, with complicity. She drew Maya close and embraced her. Maya hugged her back, felt the heat of her body, and wished she was Taku.

· 24 ·

ome men love love, but Muto Taku was not one of them, nor had he ever been smitten by the passion that wants to devote itself only to the beloved. He found such extreme emotions curious, even distasteful, and had always laughed at the infatuated, openly despising their weakness. When women professed to love him, as they often did, he detached himself from them. He liked women, and all the pleasures of the body one enjoyed with them, was fond of his wife and trusted her to run his household, bring up his children properly, and be loyal to him, but the idea of being faithful to her had never occurred to him. So the persistence of the memory of the sudden, unexpected intimacy with Sada disturbed him. It had been unlike anything in his experience, desire of such intensity, fulfillment so piercing and complete; her body, as tall and as strong as his, almost like a man's, yet a woman's; her responding desire for him, which yielded to him and at the same time seized him. He had hardly been able to sleep, longing only to feel her next to him, and now, talking to Sugita Hiroshi in the garden of the castle at Maruyama, he was finding it hard to concentrate on what his old friend was saying. *We grew up together. It need not mean anything,* she had said, and that had been part of the thrill, she moving from companion, almost sister, to lover. And he had said, with unknowing insight, *Nothing between us can be meaningless.*

He drew his attention back to his companion. They were the same age, turning twenty-seven in the new year, but whereas Taku had the wiry build and nondescript, mobile face of the Muto, Sugita Hiroshi was considered a handsome man, half a head taller than Taku and broader in the shoulder, with the pale skin and fine features of the warrior class. As boys they had squabbled and competed with each other for Lord Takeo's attention, had been lovers for one ecstatic summer, the year they had broken in the colts together, and since then had been tied by the bonds of deepest friendship.

It was early morning on what promised to be a brilliant autumn day. The sky was the clear pale blue of a bird's egg, the sun just beginning to lift the haze from the golden stubble of the rice fields. It was the first chance the two men had had to talk in private since Taku had arrived in the company of Lord Kono. They had been discussing the coming meeting between Lord Otori and Arai Zenko, which was to take place within the next few weeks in Maruyama.

"Takeo and Lady Shigeko must be here by next month's full moon," Hiroshi said, "but their arrival has been delayed somewhat, for they were to go to Terayama to visit Matsuda Shingen's grave."

"It is sad for Takeo to lose his two great teachers in the same year. He had barely gotten over Kenji's death," Taku remarked.

"Matsuda's passing was neither as sudden nor as shocking as Kenji's. Our Abbot was over eighty years, an extraordinary life span. And he has worthy successors. As your uncle has in you. You will become to Lord Takeo what Kenji always was."

"I already miss my uncle's skill and perception," Taku confessed. "The situation seems to become more complex every week. My brother's intrigues, which even I cannot completely fathom; Lord Kono and the demands from the Emperor; the refusal of the Kikuta to negotiate . . ."

"During my time in Hagi, Takeo seemed unusually preoccupied," Hiroshi said tentatively.

"Well, apart from his grief and these affairs of state, he has other concerns, I suppose," Taku replied. "Lady Otori's pregnancy, problems with his daughters."

"Is something wrong with Lady Shigeko?" Hiroshi interrupted. "She was in good health when I saw her recently . . ."

"Not as far as I know. It's the twin girls," Taku said. "Maya is here with me; I must warn you in case you recognize her."

"Here with you?" Hiroshi repeated in surprise.

"She's dressed as a boy. You probably won't even notice her. She's being looked after by a young woman, also in men's guise, a distant relative of mine. Sada is her name."

There was no need to speak her name, yet he could not help himself. *I am obsessed*, he thought.

"Zenko and Hana are coming," Hiroshi exclaimed. "Surely they will recognize her!"

"I suppose Hana might. Not much escapes her."

"No," Hiroshi agreed. They were silent for a moment, then both laughed at the same time.

"You know," Taku said, "people say you never got over her, and that is why you never married." They had never spoken of it before, but his curiosity had been kindled by his own new obsession.

"It's true at one time I fervently wanted to marry her. I thought I adored her, and I wanted so much to be part of that family—my own father, as you know, was killed in the war, and my uncle and his sons took their own lives rather than surrender to Arai Daiichi. I had no family of my own; when Maruyama settled down after the earthquake, I was living in Lord Takeo's household. My family's lands reverted to the domain. I was sent to Terayama to study the Way of the Houou. I was as foolish and conceited as any young man. I thought that Takeo would adopt me eventually, especially when no sons were born." He smiled in self-mockery but without bitterness. "Don't misunderstand me. I am not disappointed or distressed. I see my life's calling is to be of service; I am happy to be the steward of Maruyama and to hold it for Lady Shigeko. Next month she will receive her domain; I will soon return to Terayama, unless she needs me here."

"I am sure she will need you—at least for a year or two. No need to bury yourself at Terayama like a hermit. You should marry and have children of your own. As for land, Takeo—or Shigeko—would give you anything you asked for."

"Not quite anything," Hiroshi said quietly, almost to himself.

"So you *are* still pining after Hana."

"No, I rapidly recovered from that infatuation. Hana is a very beautiful woman, but I am glad it is your brother who is her husband, not myself."

"It would be better for Takeo if it were you," Taku said, wondering what else might keep Hiroshi from remarrying.

"They feed each other's ambitions," Hiroshi agreed, and deftly changed the subject. "But you still have not told me for what reason Maya is here."

"She needs to be kept apart—from her cousins, who are now in Hagi, and from her twin. And someone needs to be watching her constantly, which is why Sada came with her. I'll have to spend some time with her too. I can't explain all the reasons to you. I'm relying on you to cover my absence and entertain Lord Kono—and, incidentally, convince him of the Seishuu clans' complete loyalty to the Otori."

"Is the child in some danger?"

"She *is* the danger," Taku replied.

"But why does she not come openly, as Lord Otori's daughter, and stay here as she often has before?"

When Taku did not answer immediately, Hiroshi said, "You love intrigue for its own sake, admit it!"

"She is more useful if she is not recognized," Taku said finally. "Anyway, she's a child of the Tribe. If she is Lady Otori Maya, that is all she can be; in the Tribe she can take on many different roles."

"I suppose she can do all those tricks you used to tease me with," Hiroshi said, smiling.

"Those tricks, as you call them, have saved my life more than once!" Taku retorted. "Besides, I believe the Way of the Houou has a few tricks of its own!"

"The Masters, like Miyoshi Gemba, and Makoto himself, have many skills that seem supernatural, but are the result of years of training and self-mastery."

"Well, it's more or less the same with the Tribe. Our skills may be inherited, but they're nothing without training. But your Masters have prevailed on Takeo not to go to war, either in the East or the West?"

"Yes, when he comes, he will inform Lord Kono that our emissaries are on their way to Miyako to prepare for next year's visit."

"Do you think this visit is wise? Isn't Takeo simply placing himself in the power of this new general, the Dog Catcher?"

"Anything that avoids war is wise," Hiroshi replied.

"Forgive me, but these are strange words from the mouth of a warrior!"

"Taku, we both saw our fathers die in front of our eyes . . ."

"My father, at least, deserved to die! I will never forget that moment when I thought Takeo must kill Zenko . . ."

"Your father acted correctly, according to his beliefs and his code," Hiroshi said calmly.

"He betrayed Takeo after swearing alliance with him!" Taku exclaimed.

"But if he had not, sooner or later Takeo would have turned on him. It is the very nature of our society. We fight until we tire of war, and after a few years we tire of peace and so we fight again. We mask our bloodlust and our desire for revenge with a code of honor, which we break when it seems expedient."

"Have you truly never killed a man?" Taku said abruptly.

"I was taught many ways to kill, and learned battle tactics and war strategy before I was ten years old, but I have never fought in a real battle, and I have never killed anyone. I hope I never will."

"Find yourself in the midst of a fight and you'll change your mind," Taku said. "You'll defend yourself like all men do."

"Maybe. In the meantime I'll do everything in my power to avoid war."

"I'm afraid that between them my brother and the Emperor will bring you to it. Especially if they now have firearms. You can be sure they will not rest until they have tried out their new weapons for themselves."

There were signs of movement at the far end of the garden, and a guard ran forward and knelt before Hiroshi.

"Lord Kono is coming, Lord Sugita!"

In the nobleman's presence they both changed a little—Taku became more guarded, Hiroshi apparently more open and genial. Kono wanted to see as much of the town and the surrounding countryside as possible, and they made many excursions, the nobleman carried in his elaborate gilded lacquer palanquin, the two young men riding the horses, Raku's sons, who were as much old friends as they were. The autumn weather continued clear and brilliant, the leaves more deeply colored every day. Hiroshi and Taku took every opportunity to apprise Kono of the wealth of the domain, its secure defenses and number of soldiers, the contentment of its people, and its absolute loyalty to Lord Otori. The nobleman received all this information with his usual unperturbed courtesy, giving no indication of his real feelings.

SOMETIMES MAYA WENT on these trips, riding on the back of Sada's horse, occasionally finding herself close enough to Kono and his advisers to catch what they murmured to each other. The conversations seemed uninteresting and trivial, but she memorized them and repeated them word for word to Taku when he came to the house where she and Sada stayed, as he did every two or three days. They took to sleeping in a small room at the end of the house, for sometimes he came late at night, and no matter how late the hour he always wanted to see Maya, even if she was already asleep. She was expected to wake immediately, in the way of the Tribe, who control their need for sleep in the same way they control all their needs and desires, and she had to summon up all her energy and concentration for these nighttime sessions with her teacher.

Taku was often tired and tense, his patience short; the work was slow and demanding. Maya wanted to cooperate, but she was afraid of what might happen to her. Often she longed to be home in Hagi with her mother and sisters. She wanted to be a child; she wanted to be like Shigeko, with no Tribe skills and no twin. Being a boy all day exhausted her, but that was nothing compared to the new demands. She had found her earlier Tribe training easy—invisibility, the use of the second self came naturally to her, but this new path seemed far more difficult and more dangerous. She refused to let Taku lead her down it, sometimes with a cold sullenness, sometimes with fury. She came to regret bitterly the cat's death and its possession of her spirit; she begged Taku to remove it.

"I cannot," he replied. "All I can do is help you learn to control it, and master it."

"You did what you did," Sada said. "You have to live with it."

Then Maya was ashamed of her weakness. She had thought she would like being the cat, but it was darker and more frightening than she had expected. It wanted to take her into another world, where ghosts and spirits lived.

"It will give you power," Taku said. "The power is there—you must grasp it and exploit it!"

But though under his gaze and with his guidance she became familiar with the spirit that lived within her, she could not do what she knew he expected: take on its form and use it.

he full moon of the tenth month approached, and everywhere preparations began for the Autumn Festival. The excitement was heightened this year by the fact that Lord Otori himself and his oldest daughter, heir to Maruyama, Lady Shigeko, would be present for the Festival. Dancing began, the townspeople taking to the streets in throngs every evening in bright clothes and new sandals, singing, waving their hands above their heads. Maya had known that her father was popular, beloved even, but she had not fully realized to what extent until she heard it from the mouths of the people she now mingled with. The news also spread that the domain of Maruyama was to be formally presented to Shigeko now that she was of age. She would become Lady Maruyama.

It was like something from a legend, a name Maya had heard all her life, from Chiyo, from Shizuka, from the balladeers who sang and recited the tales of the Otori on street corners and riverbanks.

"It seems my mother is to lead the Tribe, Lady Shigeko will one day rule the Three Countries; you had better become a girl again before you are much older!" Taku teased her.

"I'm not interested in the Three Countries, but I would like to lead the Tribe!" Maya replied.

"You will have to wait until I am dead!" Taku laughed.

"Don't say such things!" Sada warned him, touching him on the arm.

He turned his head at once and looked at her in the way that both thrilled Maya and filled her with jealousy. The three of them were alone in the small room at the end of the Tribe house. Maya had not expected Taku so soon—he had been there the previous night.

"You see, I cannot stay away from you," he had said to Sada when she expressed her surprise, and then it was she who could not hide her pleasure, who could not keep herself from touching him.

The night was cold and clear, the moon, four days from full, already swollen and yellow. Despite the frosty air the shutters were still open; they sat close together near the small charcoal brazier, the bed quilts wrapped around them. Taku was drinking rice wine, but neither Sada nor Maya liked its taste. One small lamp barely dinted the room's darkness, but the garden was filled with moonlight and dense shadows.

"And then there is my brother," Taku whispered to Sada, no longer joking, "who believes it is his right to lead the Tribe, as Kenji's oldest male relative."

"I am afraid there are others, too, who feel it is wrong for Shizuka to be the Muto Master. A woman has never acted in this way before; people do not like to break with tradition. They mutter that it offends the gods. It is not that they want Zenko—they would prefer you, certainly, but your mother's appointment has caused divisions."

Maya listened carefully, saying nothing, aware of the heat of the fire on one side of her face, the chill air on the other. From the town came sounds of music and singing, drums beating with an insistent rhythm, sudden guttural shouts.

"I heard a rumor today," Sada went on. "Kikuta Akio has been seen in Akashi. He left for Hofu two weeks ago."

"We'd better send someone to Hofu at once," Taku said. "And find out where he is going and what his intentions are. Is he traveling alone?"

"Imai Kazuo is with him, and his son."

"Whose son?" Taku sat upright. "Not Akio's?"

"Apparently, a boy of about sixteen years. Why are you so shocked?"

"You don't know who this boy is?"

"He is Muto Kenji's grandson, everyone knows that," Sada replied.

"Nothing else?"

Sada shook her head.

"I suppose it is a Kikuta secret," Taku muttered. Then he seemed to recall Maya's presence.

"Send the girl to bed," he said to Sada.

"Maya, go and sleep in the maids' room," Sada ordered. A month ago she would have protested, but she had learned to obey Sada and Taku in everything.

"Good night," she murmured, and rose to her feet.

"Close the shutters before you go," Taku said. "It's getting chilly."

Sada stood to help her. Away from the fire Maya was cold, and once in the maids' room even colder. Everyone seemed to be asleep already; she found a space between two girls and crawled between them. Here in the Tribe house everyone knew she was female—it was only in the outside world that she had to keep up her disguise as a boy. She was shivering. She wanted to hear what Taku said; she wanted to be with him and Sada. She thought of fur, of the cat's thick, soft coat covering her, warming her through and through, and the shivering turned into something else, a ripple of power that ran over her, as the cat flexed its muscles and came to life.

She slipped from the covers and padded silently from the room, aware of her huge pupils and acute vision, remembering how the world looked, full of little movements that she never noticed before, listening all the time in part-dread for the empty voices of the dead. She was halfway down the passageway when she realized she was moving above the ground, and cried out a little in fear.

Men and women turned in their sleep, shuddering as they saw unbearable dreams.

I cannot open the doors, she thought, but the cat spirit knew better, and leaped at the shutters, flowing through them, floating across the veranda and entering the room where Sada and Taku lay entwined. She thought she would show herself to them, that Taku would be pleased with her and would praise her. She would lie down between them and be warmed by them.

Sada spoke half-lazily, resuming the earlier conversation, words that shocked Maya more deeply than anything in her life, but that resonated in the cat's undead spirit.

"The boy is truly Takeo's son?"

"Yes, and according to the prophecy will be the only person who can bring death to him."

So Maya learned of her brother's existence, and of the threat to her father. She tried to keep silent but could not prevent the yowl of horror and despair that forced itself from her throat. She heard Taku call, "What's there?" and heard Sada's cry of astonishment, and then she leaped through the screen and out into the garden as though she could run forever, away from everything. But she could not run from the spirits' voices that rustled through her pricked ears and into her fragile, liquid bones.

Where is our Master?

tori Takeo and Arai Zenko arrived in Maruyama within hours of each other, the day before the full moon. Takeo had come from Yamagata and brought most of the Otori court with him, including Miyoshi Kahei and his brother Gemba, a train of horses carrying the records of administration that needed to be dealt with while he was in the West, a large number of retainers, and his oldest daughter, Lady Shigeko. Zenko was accompanied by an equally large group of retainers, horses bearing baskets packed with lavish gifts and sumptuous clothes, Lady Arai's hawks and lap dog, and Lady Arai herself, in an exquisitely carved and decorated palanquin.

The arrival of these great lords, their retinues blocking the streets and filling the lodging houses, delighted the townspeople, who for the last month had been laying in extra supplies of rice, fish, beans, wine, and the delicacies of the region, and now hoped to make a great profit. The summer had been benign, the harvest particularly fruitful; Maruyama was to be given to a female heir and there was much to celebrate. Everywhere banners, floating in the gentle breeze, displayed the round hill of the Maruyama together with the Otori heron, and cooks vied with one another to create inventive meals of round shapes to honor the full moon.

Takeo looked on it all with great pleasure. Maruyama was dear to him, for it was here that he had spent the first few months of his marriage and had begun to put into practice all that he had learned of government and agriculture from Lord Shigeru. The domain had been nearly destroyed by the typhoon and earthquake during the first year of his reign. Now, sixteen years on, it was rich and peaceful: Its trade thrived, its artists flourished, its children were all well fed, the wounds of the civil war all apparently long since healed, and Shigeko would now take over this domain and rule it in her own right. He knew she was worthy of it.

He had to keep reminding himself he was here to meet the two men who might snatch it from her.

One of them, Lord Kono, was accommodated like himself within the castle residence. Zenko was in the most prestigious and luxurious residence just beyond the castle walls, once the home of Sugita Haruki, the domain's senior retainer, who with his sons had taken his own life rather than agree to surrender the town to Arai Daiichi. Takeo wondered if Zenko was aware of the house's history of loyalty, and hoped he might be influenced by the spirits of the steadfast dead.

Before the evening meal, when he was to meet these potential enemies, he sent for Hiroshi to speak with him privately. The younger man seemed calm and alert, yet filled with some deeper emotion that Takeo could not fathom. After discussing the following day's procedures and ceremonies, Takeo thanked him for his diligence. "You have spent many years in my family's service. We must reward you. Will you stay in the West? I will find an estate for you, and a wife. I had considered Lord Terada's granddaughter, Kaori. She is a fine young woman, a great friend of my daughter."

"To give me land in Maruyama would be to take it from someone else, or from Lady Shigeko," Hiroshi replied. "I have already mentioned to Taku that I will stay here while I am required—but my real desire is to be permitted to retire to Terayama and follow the Way of the Houou."

Takeo stared at him without replying immediately. Hiroshi met his eyes and glanced away. "As for marriage . . . I thank you for your concern, but I have truly no desire to marry, and I have nothing to offer a wife."

"Any family in the Three Countries would welcome you as a son-in-law. You do not value yourself enough. If Terada Kaori does not please you, let me find someone else. *Is* there someone else?"

"No one," Hiroshi replied.

"You know the great affection my whole family holds you in," Takeo went on. "You have been like a brother to my daughters; were we not so close in age I would regard you as a son."

"I must beg you, Lord Takeo, not to continue," Hiroshi pleaded. The color had mounted to his neck. He tried to hide his distress by smiling. "You are so content in your marriage, you want us all to share the same state! But I feel called to another path. My only request is to be allowed to follow it."

"I would never deny you that!" Takeo replied, and decided to drop the question of marriage for the time being. "But I have one request to make of you—that you will accompany us when we go to the capital next year. As you know, I am making this peaceful visit at the request of the Masters of the Way of the Houou. I want you to be part of it."

"It is a great honor," Hiroshi replied. "Thank you."

"Shigeko is to come with me, also on the Masters' advice. You must take care of her safety, as you always have done."

Hiroshi bowed without speaking.

"My daughter has suggested that we take the kirin—it will make an unparalleled gift for the Emperor."

"You would give away the kirin!" Hiroshi exclaimed.

"I would give away anything if it preserves the peaceful existence of our country," Takeo replied.

Even Shigeko? Neither of them spoke the words, yet they echoed in Takeo's mind. He did not know that he could answer yet.

Something from this conversation must have alerted him, for in the moments when he was not occupied with Lord Kono, Zenko, and Hana he found himself watching Hiroshi and his daughter during the evening meal with more attention than usual. They were both somewhat silent and grave, hardly addressing or looking at each other. He could not discern any particular feeling between them; he fancied Shigeko's heart to be untouched. But of course they were both adept at hiding their emotions.

The meal was formal and elegant, with the autumn specialties of the West—pine-tree mushrooms; tiny crabs and prawns, salted and crunchy; chestnuts and ginkgo nuts; all served on lacquer trays and pale fawn pottery from Hagi. Kaede had helped restore the residence to its former beauty—the mats were green-gold and sweet smelling; the floors and beams gleamed warmly; behind them stood screens decorated with the birds and flowers of autumn, plovers with bush clover, quail with chrysanthemums. Takeo asked himself what Kono thought of the surroundings, and how they compared to the Emperor's court.

He had apologized for his wife's absence, explaining her pregnancy, and had wondered if Zenko and Hana were disappointed at this news, for it would delay plans for adoption of either of their sons. He thought he discerned the slightest pause of discomfort before Hana began effusive congratulations, expressing her joy and hoping for a son for her sister. Takeo, in his turn, was careful to praise Sunaomi and Chikara—it was not difficult, for he was genuinely fond of both boys.

Kono said courteously, "I have received letters from Miyako. I understand you will visit the Emperor next year."

"If he will receive me, that is my intention," Takeo replied.

"I believe he will receive you. Everyone is curious about you. Even Lord Saga Hideki has expressed his desire to meet you."

Takeo was aware that Zenko was hanging on every word, though his eyes were cast downward. *And if they ambush and kill me there, Zenko will be waiting in the West, will advance with the Emperor's blessing . . .*

"Indeed Lord Saga is thinking about some sport, or contest. He writes to me that rather than shedding the blood of thousands of men, he would like to meet Lord Otori in some game—dog hunting, perhaps. It is his passion."

Takeo smiled. "Lord Saga has no knowledge of our remote affairs. He cannot be aware that my crippled hand prevents me from drawing a bow." *Luckily,* he could not help thinking, *for I have never had much skill with the bow.*

"Well, some other contest, perhaps. Your wife's confinement will prevent her from accompanying you?"

"Naturally. But my daughter is to come with me." Shigeko raised her head and looked at her father. Their eyes met and she smiled at him.

"Lady Shigeko is not yet betrothed?" Kono inquired.

"No, not yet," Takeo answered.

"Lord Saga is recently widowed." Kono's voice was cool and neutral.

"I am sorry to hear it." Takeo was wondering if he could bear to give his daughter to such a man—yet it could be a desirable alliance, and if it were to ensure the peace of the Three Countries . . .

Shigeko spoke, her voice clear and firm. "I look forward to meeting Lord Saga. Perhaps he will accept me as my father's substitute in any contest."

"Lady Shigeko is highly skilled with the bow," Hiroshi added.

Takeo recalled in amazement Gemba's words: *There will be some contest in Miyako . . . your daughter should also come. She must perfect her horse riding, using the bow. . . .* How had Gemba known this?

He looked across the room at Gemba, who was seated a little distance away next to his brother Kahei. Gemba did not meet his gaze, but a faint smile appeared on his plump face. Kahei looked more stern, masking his disapproval.

Yet this corroborates the Masters' advice, Takeo thought swiftly. *I will visit Miyako. I will accept Saga's challenge whatever it is. We will settle matters between us. There will be no war.*

Kono seemed as surprised as Takeo, though for a different reason. "I had not realized women in the Three Countries were so talented, or so bold," he said finally.

"Like Lord Saga, perhaps you do not know us well, yet," Shigeko replied. "All the more reason why we must visit the capital, so that you come to understand us." She spoke with courtesy, yet no one could miss the authority that lay behind her words. She showed no sign of unease at meeting the son of her mother's kidnapper, nor did she seem in the least intimidated by him. Takeo gazed on her in barely concealed admiration. Her long hair fell loose around her shoulders; her back was straight, her

skin almost luminescent against the pale yellow and gold of her robe, with
its brilliant maple leaves. He was reminded of the first time he had seen
Lady Maruyama Naomi—he had thought her like Jato, the sword, her
serene beauty masking her strength. Now he saw the same strength in his
daughter, and felt a kind of release deep within him. Whatever happened
to him, he had an heir. All the more reason to ensure the Three Countries
would be kept intact for her to inherit.

"I look forward to it greatly!" Kono exclaimed. "I hope I may be released from Lord Otori's hospitality to return to Miyako before your visit,
and to inform His Divine Majesty of all I have learned here." He leaned
forward and said with some fervor, "I can assure you all my reports will be
in your favor."

Takeo bowed slightly in assent, wondering how much of this speech
was sincerity, how much flattery—and what intrigues Kono and Zenko
might have been hatching together. He hoped Taku would know more, and
wondered where he was, why he was not present at the meal. Was Zenko,
aggrieved at Taku's presence and surveillance, deliberately excluding his
brother? And he was anxious to hear about Maya. He could not help wondering if Taku's absence were not connected to her—she was in some trouble; she had run away. . . . He realized his mind was wandering. He had not
heard Kono's last few sentences. He forced himself to concentrate on the
present.

There seemed no reason to detain the nobleman any longer in the
West; indeed, now might be the best time to send him home with his mind
full of the prosperity of the domains, the loyalty of the Seishuu—and the
beauty, character, and strength of his daughter. But he would have liked to
have heard for himself, from Taku, further details of Kono's sojourn in the
West, and of the nobleman's relationship with Zenko and Hana.

The festivities continued until late in the evening—musicians played
the three-stringed lute and the harp, while from the town the sounds of
drumming and singing echoed across the still waters of river and moat.
Takeo slept fitfully, his mind still full of anxieties for his daughters, for
Kaede and the unborn child, and he woke early, conscious of the pain in

his hand and a dull ache in most of his body. He called for Minoru to be wakened, and while he drank tea, went through what had been said the previous night, checking that everything had been recorded faithfully, for Minoru had been concealed behind a screen throughout the evening. Since Kono might be permitted to leave, arrangements should be made.

"Is Lord Kono to travel by ship or land?" Minoru asked.

"By ship, if he is to arrive before winter," Takeo replied. "There must already be snow on the High Cloud Range: He will not get there before the passes are closed. He may go by road to Hofu and embark from there."

"So he will travel with Lord Otori as far as Yamagata?"

"Yes, I suppose he should. We will have to put on another display for him there. You had better prepare Lady Miyoshi."

Minoru bowed.

"Minoru, you have been present at all my meetings with Lord Kono. His attitude toward me last night seemed changed in some way, did you not think so?"

"He seemed more conciliatory," Minoru replied. "He must have observed Lord Otori's popularity, the devotion and loyalty of the people. At Yamagata I am sure Lord Miyoshi will explain the size and strength of our armies. Lord Kono must take back to the Emperor the conviction that the Three Countries will not be relinquished easily, and . . ."

"Go on," Takeo prompted him.

"It is not my place to say it, but Lady Shigeko is unmarried, and Lord Kono will surely prefer to negotiate a marriage rather than start an unwinnable war. If he is to be the go-between, he must have the bride's father's trust and approval."

"Well, we will continue to flatter him and endeavor to impress him. Is there any word from Muto Taku? I had expected him last night."

"He sent apologies to his brother, saying he was unwell—nothing more," Minoru replied. "Shall I make contact with him?"

"No, there must be some reason for his non-appearance. As long as we know that he is still alive."

"Surely no one would attack Lord Muto, here in Maruyama?"

"Taku has offended many, in service to me," Takeo said. "Neither of us can ever be truly safe."

THE BANNERS OF the Maruyama, the Otori, and the Seishuu fluttered above the horse ground in front of the castle. The moat was packed with flat-bottomed boats filled with onlookers. Silk pavilions had been erected for those of higher class, and tasseled emblems hung from their roofs and from poles placed around them. Takeo sat on a raised platform within one of these pavilions, cushions and carpets strewn over its floor. On his right was Kono, on his left Zenko, and a little behind Zenko, Hana.

In front of them Hiroshi, mounted on the pale gray horse with the black mane and tail that Takeo had given him so many years ago, waited as still as a carving. Behind him, on foot, holding lacquer chests, stood the elders of the clan, all in heavy robes embroidered with gold, wearing black hats. Within the chests would be the treasures of the domain, and scrolls of genealogies chronicling Shigeko's descent through all the women of Maruyama.

Kaede should be here, Takeo thought with regret; he longed to see her, imagined himself recounting the scene to her, pictured the curve of her belly where their child was growing.

Takeo had had no part in planning the ceremony—it had all been done by Hiroshi, for it was an ancient ritual of Maruyama that had not been enacted since Lady Naomi inherited the domain. He scanned the gathering, wondering where Shigeko was, and when she would appear. Among the crowds in the boats he suddenly spotted Taku, dressed not in formal robes like his brother, Zenko, but in the ordinary faded clothes of a merchant. Beside him stood a tall young man and a boy who looked vaguely familiar. It took Takeo several moments to realize it was his daughter, Maya.

He felt astonishment—that Taku should have brought her here in disguise, that he had not recognized her—followed by swift, deep relief that she was alive and seemingly unharmed. She looked thinner, a little taller, her eyes more noticeable in her pointed face. The young man must be Sada, he thought, though her disguise was impenetrable. Taku must have been unwilling to leave Maya, or he would have come in his own guise. He must have known Takeo would spot them, if no one else did. What message was he conveying? He must see them—he would go to them tonight.

His attention was drawn back to the ceremony by the sound of horses' hooves. From the western end of the bailey came a small procession of women on horseback. They were the wives and daughters of the elders who waited behind Hiroshi. They were armed in the way of women of the West, with bows over their shoulders and quivers filled with arrows on their backs. Takeo marveled at the Maruyama horses, so tall and fine-looking, and his heart swelled even more as he saw his daughter on the finest-looking horse, in their midst—the black that she had broken in herself, and that she called Tenba.

The horse was overexcited and cavorted a little, tossing its head and rearing as she brought it to a halt. Shigeko sat as still as if she too were a carving; her hair, tied loosely back, was as black as the horse's mane and tail, and gleamed like his coat in the autumn sun. Tenba calmed and relaxed.

The women on horseback faced the men on foot, and at one and the same moment the elders all dropped to their knees, holding the boxes in outstretched hands and bowing deeply.

Hiroshi spoke in a loud voice. "Lady Maruyama Shigeko, daughter of Shirakawa Kaede and second cousin of Maruyama Naomi, we welcome you to the domain which has been held in trust for you."

He slipped his feet from the stirrups and dismounted, drew his sword from his belt and, kneeling before her, held it out in both hands.

Tenba startled for an instant at the man's sudden move, and Takeo saw Hiroshi break his composure in alarm. He realized it was far more than a vassal's concern for his lady. He recalled the weeks they had spent breaking in the horse together. His earlier suspicions were confirmed. He did not know his daughter's feelings, but there was no doubt about Hiroshi's. It seemed so obvious to him now he could not believe he had not realized it before. He was torn between irritation and pity—it was impossible to give Hiroshi what he wanted—yet he admired the young man's self-control and dedication. *It is because they were brought up together,* he thought. *She is fond of him, like a brother, but her heart is not touched.* But he watched his daughter closely as two of the women dismounted and came to hold Tenba's reins. Shigeko slid gracefully off the horse's back and faced Hiroshi. As he looked up at her, their eyes met. She smiled very slightly at him and took the sword from him. Then she turned and held it out toward each direction in turn, bowing over it to the crowd, to her vassals and her people.

A great shout rose, as if everyone present spoke in one voice, and then the sound broke, like a wave on a shingle, into bursts of cheering. The horses pranced in excitement. Shigeko thrust the sword in her belt and remounted, as did the other women. The horses galloped around the bailey, then fell into line along the straight edge, toward the target. Each rider dropped the reins on her horse's neck, took the bow, placed the arrow and drew, all in one swift, fluid movement. The arrows flew one after another, hitting the targets with a repetition of thunks. Finally Shigeko rode, the black horse flying like the wind, like a horse of Heaven, and her arrow hit true. She turned the horse and galloped back, pulling him to a halt in front of Takeo. She leaped from Tenba's back and spoke in a loud voice, "The Maruyama swear allegiance and loyalty to the Otori, and in recognition I present this horse to Lord Takeo, my father." She held out the reins in her hand, and bowed her head.

Another roar came from the crowd as Takeo rose and stepped down from the platform. He approached Shigeko and took the reins of the horse from her, more moved than he could say. The horse dropped its head and rubbed it against his shoulder. It was most obviously from the same line as Shigeru's horse Kyu, and Aoi, who had been fatally injured by the ogre Jin-emon. He was aware of the past all around him, the spirits of the dead, their approving gaze, and he felt pride and gratitude that he and Kaede had raised this beautiful child, that she had reached adulthood and come into her inheritance.

"I hope he will come to be as dear to you as Shun," she said.

"I have never seen a finer horse—and when he moves he seems to fly." He was already longing to feel the horse's strength beneath him, to begin the long mysterious bonding between creatures. *He will outlive me,* he thought with gladness.

"Will you try him?"

"I am not dressed for riding," Takeo said. "Let me lead him back, and we will ride out together later. In the meantime, I thank you from the bottom of my heart. You could not have given me a better gift."

NEAR THE END of the afternoon, when the sun was sinking toward the West, they rode in its path across the coastal plain toward the mouth of the river. The company consisted not only of Takeo, Shigeko, and Hiroshi—though the three of them would have preferred it—but also of Lord Kono, Zenko, and Hana. Zenko declared he was surfeited with feasting and ceremonies and needed a good gallop to clear his mind. Hana wanted to take out the hawks, and Kono confessed to sharing her passion for hawking. Their route took them past the outcastes' village, which Takeo had established long ago, when Jo-An was still alive. The outcastes still tanned hides here, and were shunned on that account but were left in peace, protected by the laws of the Three Countries. Now the sons of the men who built the bridge that enabled Takeo to escape from the Otori army worked alongside their fathers and uncles; the young people looked as well fed and healthy as the old.

Takeo stopped to greet the headman of the village with Hiroshi and Shigeko, while the others rode on. When they caught up with the hunting party, the hawks were already released, hovering high over the grasses, which swayed like the waves of the sea, the last rays of the sun glowing through the tasseled heads.

Takeo had been getting the feel of the new horse, letting him extend his gallop across the plain. He was more excitable than Shun had been, possibly not quite as clever, but eager to please and equally responsive, and much faster. He shied once when a partridge shot under his feet with a whirring of its barred wings, and Takeo had to exert some force to remind him who was in control. *But I will not have to rely on him in battle*, he told himself. *Those days are over.*

"You have handled him well," he told Shigeko. "He seems to have no faults."

"Whatever disabilities Lord Otori has, they have not impaired his horsemanship," Kono commented.

"Indeed, I forget them when I am riding," Takeo said, smiling. Horse riding made him feel like a young man again. He felt he could almost like Kono, that he had misjudged him, and then chided himself for being so susceptible to flattery.

Above his head the four hawks wheeled, two stooping at the same time and plummeting to earth. One rose again, a partridge in its curved talons, the down fluttering; the other screeched in fury. It reminded him that as the strong feed on the weak, so would his enemies feed on him. He imagined them like hawks hovering, waiting.

They rode back at dusk, the full moon rising behind the plumed grasses, the rabbit shape clearly visible on the gleaming disk. The streets were thronged with people, shrines and shops overflowing, the air filled with roasting rice cakes, grilled fish and eels, sesame oil and soy. Takeo was gratified with the response of the crowd. The townspeople gave way respectfully, many kneeling spontaneously or shouting his and Shigeko's names, but they were not cowed, nor did they stare after him with the desperate, hungry look that had followed Lord Shigeru all those years ago, of which he himself had once been the target. They no longer needed a hero to save them. They saw their prosperity and peace as their rightful way of living, achieved by their own hard work and intelligence.

astle and town had fallen silent. The moon had set; the night sky was spangled with brilliant stars. Takeo sat with Minoru, two lamps burning near them, going over the evening's conversation and the young man's impressions.

"I am going out for a while," Takeo said when they had finished. "I must see Taku before I leave, and that must be within the next two days if we are to get Kono to Hofu before winter. Stay here, and if anyone should come asking for me, pretend we are conducting some urgent and confidential business and cannot be disturbed. I will be back before dawn."

Minoru was used to such arrangements and made no response beyond bowing. He helped Takeo change into the dark clothes he often wore at night. Takeo wound a scarf around his head to hide his face, took two flasks of wine, a short sword, and the holster of throwing knives, and hid them inside his garments. He stepped out onto the veranda and disappeared into the night.

If Kono could see me now, he thought as he passed the nobleman's rooms and heard him breathing deeply in sleep. But he knew no one would see him, for he was cloaked in the invisibility of the Tribe.

If horse riding made him feel young again, so did this—he had left the Tribe; his family, the Kikuta, had pursued him nearly half his life; but the deep pleasure the ancient skills bring had never left him. At the end of the garden he listened intently for a few moments and, hearing no sound leaped to the top of the wall between the garden and the first bailey. He ran along the top of the wall to the opposite side and dropped down to the horse ground within the second bailey. The banners still hung there, limp under the starlight. He thought it too cold for swimming, so after crossing to the farther side scaled the wall there and followed it around to the main gate. The guards were awake—he could hear them talking as he crossed the wide, curved roof, but they did not hear him. He ran over the bridge, let visibility return on the far side, and walked swiftly into the maze of streets beyond.

He knew the house where Taku would be—the old Muto residence. At one time he had known every Tribe house in Maruyama, its position, size, and inhabitants. He still felt deep regret at the way he had used this knowledge when he had first come to Maruyama with Kaede; determined to demonstrate his ruthlessness to the Tribe, he had pursued them, had killed or executed most of them. He had thought the only way to deal with the evil was to eradicate it, but now if he had that time over, surely he would try to negotiate without shedding blood. . . . The dilemma still faced him: If he had shown weakness then, he would not now be strong enough to impose his will with compassion. The Tribe might hate him for it, but at least they did not despise him. He had bought enough time to make his country secure.

At the shrine at the end of the street he stopped, as he always did, and placed the flasks of wine in front of the Muto family's god, asking for forgiveness from the spirits of the dead.

Muto Kenji forgave me, he told them, *and I him. We became close friends and allies. May you be the same to me.*

Nothing broke the silence of the night, but he sensed he was not alone. He shrank back into the shadows, his hand on the sword's hilt. Leaves had already fallen from the trees, and he could hear a slight rustling, as if some creature were moving across them. He peered toward the sound, and saw the leaves scatter gently under the unseen tread. He cupped his hands over his eyes to open the pupils further, and then looked sideways out of the corner of his left eye to detect invisibility. The creature was staring at him, its eyes green in the starlight.

Just a cat, he thought, *a trick of the light*—and then realized with a jolt of surprise that its gaze had trapped his; he felt the shock of pure fear. It was something supernatural, some ghostly being that dwelt in this place, sent by the dead to punish him. He felt he was about to be plunged into the Kikuta sleep, that their assassins had caught up with him and were using this ghostly being to corner him. He himself moved into the almost supernatural state that attack of any sort induced in him. It was second nature to him now to defend himself instantly, to kill before he was killed. Summoning up all his own power, he broke its gaze, fumbling for the throwing knives. The first came into his hand and he hurled it, saw the starlight catch it as it spun, heard the slight impact and the creature's cry of pain. It lost invisibility at the same moment as it leaped toward him.

Now the sword was in his hand. He saw the tawny throat and bared teeth. It was a cat, but a cat with the size and strength of a wolf. One set of claws raked his face as he dived sideways and turned to come up close enough to stab it in the throat, losing invisibility himself in order to focus on the blow.

But the cat twisted away. It cried in an almost human voice, and through the shock and fear of the fight he heard something he recognized.

"Father," it cried again. "Don't hurt me! It's me, Maya."

The girl stood before him. It took all his strength and will to halt the knife thrust that nearly cut his daughter's throat. He heard his own desperate yell as he forced his hand to turn the blade away. The knife fell from his fingers. He reached out to her and touched her face, felt the wet of blood or tears or both.

"I nearly killed you," he said, and wondered with a sense of horror and pity whether she could be killed, aware of the tears in his own eyes, and when he raised his sleeve to wipe them away, he felt the sting of the scratch, the blood dripping from his face. "What are you doing here? Why are you out here on your own?" It was almost a relief to express his confusion in anger. He wanted to slap her, as he might have done when she misbehaved as a child, but what had happened to her had put her beyond childhood. And it was his blood that made her what she was.

"I'm sorry, I'm sorry." She was crying like a child, incoherent with distress. He pulled her into his arms and held her tightly, surprised by how much she had grown. Her head came up to the center of his breastbone; her body was lean and hard, more like a boy's than a girl's.

"Don't cry," he said with assumed calmness. "We will go and see Taku, and he will tell me what has been happening to you."

"I'm sorry because I'm crying," she said in a muffled voice.

"I thought you might be sorry because you tried to kill your own father," he replied, leading her by the hand through the shrine gate and into the street.

"I did not know it was you. I could not see you. I thought you were some Kikuta assassin. As soon as I recognized you, I changed. I can't always do that immediately, but I'm getting better. I did not need to cry, though. I *never* cry. Why did I cry then?"

"Perhaps you were happy to see me?"

"I am," she assured him. "But I have never cried for joy. It must have been the shock. Well, I'll never cry again!"

"There is nothing wrong with crying," Takeo said. "I was also crying."

"Why? Did I hurt you? It must be nothing compared to the wounds you have already suffered." She touched her own face. "You hurt me worse."

"And I am deeply sorry. I would rather die than hurt you."

She has changed, he was thinking; *even her speech is more abrupt, more unfeeling.* And there was some stronger accusation behind her words, something more than the physical wound. What other grievance did she hold against him? Was it resentment at being sent away, or something else?

"You should not be out here alone."

"It is not Taku's fault," Maya said quickly. "You must not blame him."

"Who else do I blame? I entrusted you to him. And where is Sada? I saw the three of you together earlier today. Why is she not with you?"

"Wasn't it wonderful?" Maya said, evading his questions. "Shigeko looked so beautiful. And the horse! Did you like your present, Father? Were you surprised?"

"Either they are negligent or you are disobedient," Takeo said, refusing to be distracted by her sudden childish speech.

"I was disobedient. But it's as if I have to be. Because I can do things no one else can do, so there is no one to teach me. I have to find out on my own." She shot a glance up at him. "I suppose Father has never done that?"

Again he sensed a deeper challenge. He could not deny it, but he decided not to answer, faced now—for they were approaching the gate of the Muto residence—with the problem of how to get inside. His face was smarting, and his body ached from the sudden, intense fight. He could not see Maya's wound clearly, but could picture its jagged edge—it must be treated immediately. It would scar, almost certainly, leaving her with an identifiable mark.

"Is the family here trustworthy?" he whispered.

"I have never asked myself!" Maya replied. "They are Muto, Taku's relatives and Sada's. Surely they are?"

"Well, we will soon find out," Takeo muttered, and rapped on the barred gate, calling to the guards within. Dogs began barking furiously.

It took a few moments to convince them to open the gate—they did not recognize Takeo immediately, but they knew Maya. They saw the blood in the light of their lamps, exclaimed in surprise and called for Taku—but, Takeo noticed, none of them touched her. Indeed, they avoided coming close to her, so she stood as if surrounded by an invisible fence.

"And you, sir, are you hurt too?" One of the men held the lamp up so its light fell on his cheek. He made no effort to dissemble his features; he wanted to check their reaction.

"It is Lord Otori!" the man whispered, and the others all immediately dropped to the ground. "Come in, lord." The man holding the lamp stood aside, lighting the threshold.

"Get up," Takeo said to the prostrate men. "Bring water, and some soft paper or silk wads to staunch the bleeding." He stepped over the threshold, and the gate was swiftly shut and barred behind him.

The household was awake by now; lamps were lit within, and maids came out, blinking sleepily. Taku came from the end of the veranda, dressed in a cotton sleeping robe, a padded jacket flung over his shoulders. He saw Maya first, and went straight to her. Takeo thought he was going to hit her—but Taku beckoned to the guard to bring the light, and, holding Maya's head in both hands, tilted it sideways so he could see the wound in her cheek.

"What happened?" he said.

"It was an accident," Maya replied. "I got in the way."

Taku led her to the veranda, made her sit down, and knelt next to her, taking a wad of paper from the maid and soaking it in water. He bathed the wound carefully, calling for the light to be held closer.

"This looks like a throwing knife. Who was out there with a throwing knife?"

"Sir, Lord Otori is here," the guard said. "He is also hurt."

"Lord Takeo?" Taku peered toward him. "Forgive me, I did not see you. You are not badly hurt?"

"It's nothing," Takeo said, moving toward the veranda. At the step, one of the maids came forward to take off his sandals. He knelt next to Maya. "It may be hard to explain how I came by it, though. The marks will be visible for a while."

"I am sorry," Taku began, but Takeo held up a hand to silence him.

"We'll talk later. See what you can do for my daughter's wound. I am afraid it will leave a noticeable scar."

"Get Sada," Taku ordered one of the maids, and a few moments later the young woman came, also from the far end of the veranda, dressed like Taku in a sleeping robe, her shoulder-length hair loose round her face. She looked quickly at Maya and went into the house, returning with a small box.

"It's a salve Ishida prepares for us," Taku said, taking it and opening it. "The knife was not poisoned, I hope?"

"No," Takeo replied.

"Luckily it missed the eye. It was you who threw it?"

"I'm afraid so."

"At least we don't have to go searching for some Kikuta assassin." Sada held Maya's head still while Taku spread the paste over the wound; it seemed slightly sticky, like glue, and held the edges of the cut together. Maya sat without flinching, her lips curved as if she was about to smile, her eyes wide open. There was some strange bond between the three of them, Takeo thought, for the scene held a deep charge of emotion.

"Go with Sada," Taku told Maya. "Give her something to make her sleep," he said to Sada. "And stay with her all night. I will speak with her in the morning."

"I am very sorry," Maya said. "I did not mean to hurt my father."

But her tone managed to suggest the opposite.

"We will devise a punishment that will make you sorrier still," Taku said. "I am very angry, and I am sure Lord Otori is too."

"Come closer," he then said to Takeo. "Let me see what she did to you."

"Let's go inside," Takeo replied. "It is better that we speak in private."

Telling the maids to bring fresh water and tea, Taku led the way to the small room at the end of the veranda. He folded the sleeping mats and pushed them to the corner. One lamp still burned, and next to it stood a flask of wine and a drinking bowl. Takeo surveyed the scene without saying anything.

"I had expected to see you before now," he said, his voice cold. "I did not expect to meet my daughter in this way."

"There is really no excuse," Taku replied. "But let me treat your wound first; sit down, here, drink this." He poured the last of the wine into the bowl and handed it to Takeo.

"You don't sleep alone, but you drink alone?" Takeo emptied the bowl at one gulp.

"Sada doesn't like it." Two maids came to the door, one with water, one with tea. Taku took the bowl of water and began to bathe Takeo's cheek. The scratches stung.

"Bring some more wine for Lord Otori," Taku told the maid. "Quite a lot of blood," he murmured. "The claws went deep."

He fell silent as the maid returned with another flask. She filled the drinking bowl and Takeo drained it again.

"Do you have a mirror?" he asked her.

She nodded. "I will bring it for Lord Otori."

She returned with an object wrapped in a dull-brown cloth, knelt and handed it to Takeo. He unwrapped it. It was unlike any mirror he had ever seen, long-handled, round, the reflective surface brilliant. He had rarely seen his own reflection—and never so clearly—and was now amazed by it. He had not known how he looked—very like Shigeru when he had last seen him, but thinner and older. The claw marks on his cheek were deep, scarlet-edged, the blood drying darker.

"Where did this mirror come from?"

The maid glanced at Taku and murmured, "From Kumamoto. A trader brings things from time to time, a Kuroda man, Yasu. We buy knives and tools from him—he brought this mirror."

"Have you seen this?" Takeo asked Taku.

"Not this particular one. I have seen something similar in Hofu and Akashi. They are becoming quite popular." He tapped the surface. "It is glass."

The backing was some metal that Takeo did not immediately recognize, carved or molded into a pattern of interwoven flowers.

"It was made overseas," he said.

"It looks like it," Taku agreed.

Takeo looked again at his reflection. Something about the foreign mirror was bothering him. He made an effort to put it from him now.

"These marks will not fade for a long time," he said.

"Unn," Taku agreed, dabbing at the wound with a wad of clean paper to dry it; he then began to apply the sticky salve.

Takeo gave the mirror back to the maid. When she had left, Taku said, "What was it like?"

"The cat? The size of a wolf, and possessing the Kikuta gaze. You have not seen it yourself?"

"I have sensed it within her, and a few nights ago Sada and I caught a glimpse of it. It can pass through walls. It is extremely powerful. Maya has been resisting it in my presence, though I have tried to persuade her to let it appear. She has to learn to control it—at the moment it seems to take her over when her guard is down."

"And when she is alone?"

"We cannot watch her all the time. She must be obedient; she must be held responsible for her own actions."

Takeo felt anger blaze suddenly. "I did not expect that the two people to whom I entrusted her would end up sleeping together!"

"I did not expect it, either," Taku said quietly. "But it happened and will continue."

"Perhaps you should return to Inuyama, and your wife!"

"My wife is a very practical woman. She knows I have always had other women, in Inuyama and on my travels. But Sada is different. I don't seem to be able to live without her."

"What idiocy is this? Don't tell me you are bewitched!"

"Maybe I am. I may as well tell you that wherever I go, she will come with me, even to Inuyama."

Takeo was astonished, both that Taku should be so infatuated and that he made no effort to conceal it.

"I suppose this explains why you have stayed away from the castle."

"Only partly. Until the previous episode with the cat, I was there every day with Hiroshi and Lord Kono. But Maya was very distressed and I did not want to leave her. If I brought her with me, Hana would be sure to recognize her, ask questions about her. The fewer people to know about this possession, the better. It's not the sort of report that Kono should take back to the capital. I am thinking of your plans for your older daughter's marriage. I don't want to give Hana and Zenko any more weapons to use against you. I don't trust either of them. I've had some disturbing conversations with my brother about the headship of the Muto family. He is determined to insist on his right to succeed Kenji, it seems, and there are some—I don't know how many—who are not happy with the idea of a woman in authority over them."

So he had been right in his instinct not to trust the Muto unquestioningly.

"Would these same malcontents accept you?" Takeo asked.

Taku poured more wine for them both, and drank. "I don't want to offend you, Lord Takeo, but these things have always been decided within the family, not by outsiders."

Takeo took his own cup and drank without replying. Finally he said, "You are full of bad news tonight. What else do you have to tell me?"

"Akio is in Hofu, and, as far as we can find out, plans to winter in the West—I fear he is going to Kumamoto."

"With—the boy?"

"It seems so." Neither of them spoke for a few moments. Then Taku said, "It would be easy enough to get rid of them in Hofu, or on the road. Let me arrange it. Once Akio is in Kumamoto, if he contacts my brother, he will find a welcome there, even a refuge."

"No one is to lay a hand on the boy."

"Well, only you can decide that. One other thing I've learned is that Gosaburo is dead. He wanted to negotiate with you for his children's lives, so Akio killed him."

For some reason this news, and the bluntness of Taku's delivery, shook him profoundly. Gosaburo had ordered the deaths of many—one, at least, Takeo had carried out himself—but that Akio should turn on his uncle, as well as Taku's suggestion that he himself should have his own son killed, reminded him forcefully of the relentless cruelty of the Tribe. Through Kenji, he had kept them in check, but now his control of them was being challenged. They had always claimed that warlords might rise and fall, but the Tribe went on forever. But how would he deal with this intractable enemy who would never negotiate with him?

"Therefore you must come to a decision about the hostages in Inuyama," Taku said. "You should order their execution as soon as possible. Otherwise the Tribe will scent weakness, and that will cause more dissent."

"I will discuss it with my wife when I am back in Hagi."

"Don't leave it too long," Taku urged him.

Takeo wondered if Maya should return with him—but he feared for Kaede's peace of mind, and her health during her pregnancy. "What will we do with Maya?"

"She can stay with me. I know you feel that we have let you down, but despite tonight we are making progress with her. She is learning to control the possession—and who knows what use we may be able to make of her. She tries to please Sada and me—she trusts us."

"But surely you do not plan to stay away from Inuyama all winter?"

"I should not move too far from the West. I need to keep an eye on my brother. Maybe I will winter in Hofu—the climate is milder, and I can hear all the gossip that comes through the port."

"And Sada will go with you?"

"I need Sada, especially if I am to take Maya."

"Very well." *His private life is none of my business,* Takeo thought. "Lord Kono will also go to Hofu. He is returning to the capital."

"And you?"

"I hope to get home before winter. I will stay in Hagi until our child is born. Then in the spring I must go to Miyako."

TAKEO RETURNED TO Maruyama castle just before dawn, drained by the events of the night, wondering what he was doing as he summoned up all his flagging energy to take on invisibility, scale the walls, and get back to his room undetected. His earlier pleasure in the skills of the Tribe had faded. Now he felt only distaste for that dark world.

I am too old for this, he told himself as he slid open the door and stepped inside. *What other ruler sneaks around his own country at night in this way, like a thief? I escaped the Tribe once, and thought I had left it forever, but it still enmeshes me, and the legacy I have passed on to my daughters means I will never be free.*

He was deeply disturbed by all he had uncovered and, above all, by Maya's state. His face smarted; his head ached. Then the mirror came back to him. It indicated foreign goods were being traded in Kumamoto. But

the foreigners were supposed to be confined to Hofu, and now Hagi—
were there other foreigners in the country? If they were in Kumamoto,
Zenko must be aware of it, yet he had said nothing about it—neither had
Taku. The idea that Taku was hiding something from him filled Takeo with
anger. Either Taku was hiding it or he did not know. The affair with Sada
also troubled him. Men become careless when they are ensnared by passion. *If I cannot trust Taku, I am doomed. They are brothers, after all . . .*

The room was light already by the time he slept.

When he woke, he ordered arrangements to be made for his departure,
and instructed Minoru to write to Arai Zenko, requesting that he wait on
Lord Otori.

It was afternoon when Zenko came, carried in a palanquin and accompanied by a train of retainers, all in splendid dress, the bear's paw of Kumamoto clearly displayed on robes and banners. Even in the few months
since they had met at Hofu, Zenko's appearance and retinue had changed.
He had become more like his father than ever, physically imposing and
with increased self-confidence. His demeanor, his men and all their garments and weapons, spoke of lavishness and self-regard.

Takeo himself had bathed and dressed with care for this meeting, putting on the formal robes that seemed to increase his stature with their stiff
wide shoulders and long sleeves. But he could not mask the wound on his
cheek, the raking slashes and Zenko exclaimed when he saw it, "But what
happened? You are hurt? Surely there has not been some attack on you? I
had heard no news of it!"

"It's nothing," Takeo replied. "I walked into a branch in the garden last
night." *He will think I was drunk, or with a woman,* he thought, *and will despise me
even more.* For he caught in Zenko's expression scorn as well as dislike and
resentment.

The day was cool and damp, rain having fallen in the morning. The red
leaves of the maples had turned darker and were beginning to drift downward. Now and then, gusts of wind blew suddenly through the garden,
making the leaves flutter and dance.

"When we met in Hofu earlier this year, I promised we would discuss the question of adoption at this time," Takeo said. "You will understand that my wife's pregnancy makes it advisable to delay any formal proceedings."

"Of course we all heartily hope that Lady Otori gives you a son," Zenko replied. "Naturally, my sons would never take precedence over yours."

"I am aware of the trust you have placed in my family," Takeo said. "And I am deeply grateful to you. I regard Sunaomi and Chikara as my own children . . ." He thought he saw Zenko's disappointment, and felt, *I must offer him something.* He paused for a moment.

He had promised the opposite to his daughters, and he did not approve of betrothing children while they were still young, yet he found himself saying, "I would like to propose that Sunaomi and my youngest daughter, Miki, be betrothed when they come of age."

"It is a very great honor." Zenko did not sound overwhelmed by this suggestion, though his words were entirely appropriate. "I will discuss your unsurpassed kindness with my wife when we receive the formal documents of all the offer entails—what estates they will receive, where they are to live, and so on."

"Of course," Takeo said, thinking, *And I must discuss it with my wife.* "They are both still very young. There is plenty of time." *At least the offer is made. He cannot claim that I have insulted him.*

Shigeko, Hiroshi, and the Miyoshi brothers joined them shortly after this, and the discussion moved on to the military defenses of the West, the threat or lack of it posed by the foreigners, the produce and materials in which they wanted to trade. Takeo mentioned the mirror, asking idly if many such objects were to be purchased in Kumamoto.

"Perhaps," Zenko replied evasively. "They are imported through Hofu, I suppose. Women love such novelties! I believe my wife has received several as gifts."

"So there are no foreigners in Kumamoto?"

"Of course not!"

Zenko had brought records and accounts of all his activities: the weapons he had forged, the niter he had purchased; everything seemed to be in order, and he repeated his protestations of fealty and allegiance.

Takeo could do no more than accept the records as genuine, the protestations as sincere. He spoke briefly about the proposed visit to the Emperor,
knowing that Kono would have already discussed it with Zenko; he emphasized its peaceful nature, and told Zenko that both Hiroshi and
Shigeko would accompany him.

"What about Lord Miyoshi?" Zenko asked, glancing at Kahei. "Where
will he be next year?"

"Kahei will stay in the Three Countries." Takeo replied. "But he will
move to Inuyama until my safe return. Gemba comes with us to Miyako."

No one mentioned that most of the forces of the Middle Country
would be waiting on the Eastern borders under Miyoshi Kahei's command,
but it would not be possible to keep this news from Zenko. Takeo thought
fleetingly of the dangers of leaving the Middle Country unprotected—yet
both Yamagata and Hagi were almost impossible to take by siege, and they
would not be undefended. Kaede would hold Hagi against any attack, and
Kahei's wife and sons would do the same in Yamagata.

They continued talking until late in the evening, while wine and food
were served. As Zenko took his leave, he said to Takeo, "There is one more
thing we should discuss. Will you step outside on the veranda? I should
like it to be in private."

"Certainly," Takeo agreed with affability. It was raining again; the wind
was cold. He was tired, craving sleep. They stood under the cover of the
dripping eaves.

Zenko said, "It is about the Muto family. My impression is that many
in my family, throughout the Three Countries, while they have the greatest
respect for my mother and yourself, feel it is—how can I put it?—unlucky,
even wrong, to have a woman as their head. They consider me to be Kenji's
oldest male relative, and therefore his heir." He glanced at Takeo. "I don't
want to offend you, but people know of the existence of Kenji's grandson,
Yuki's boy. There are whisperings that he should inherit. It could be a sensible move to institute me quickly as head of the family—it would silence
these whisperings and reassure those in favor of upholding tradition." A
slight smile of satisfaction played briefly on his face.

"The boy is of course heir to the Kikuta," he went on. "Better to keep him away from the Muto."

"No one knows if he is alive or not, let alone where he is," Takeo said, all pretense at affability stripped from him.

"Oh, I think they do," Zenko whispered, and, noticing Takeo's immediate reaction of anger, added, "I am only trying to assist Lord Otori in this difficult situation."

If he were not my brother-in-law, if his mother were not my cousin and one of my oldest friends, I would order him to take his own life! I must do it. I cannot trust him. I must do it now, while he is in Maruyama and in my power.

Takeo was silent while the conflicting thoughts raged. Finally he said, striving for mildness, "Zenko, I must advise you not to push me any further. You have vast estates, sons, a beautiful wife. I have offered you a deeper alliance with my family through marriage. I value our friendship and hold you in the highest esteem. But I will not allow you to challenge me . . ."

"Lord Otori!" Zenko protested.

"Or to bring civil war on our country. You have sworn allegiance to me; you owe me your life. Why do I have to keep repeating this? I am weary of it. For the last time, I am advising you to return to Kumamoto and enjoy this life you owe me. Otherwise I will demand that you end it."

"You will not consider my thoughts on the Muto inheritance?"

"I insist that you support your mother as head of the family and obey her. Anyway, you have always chosen the way of the warrior—I do not understand why you are interfering with the workings of the Tribe now!"

Zenko was as furious now, and masked it less successfully. "I was raised by the Tribe. I am as much a Muto as Taku."

"Only when you see some political advantage in it! Do not think you can continue unchecked to undermine my authority. Never forget I hold your sons as hostages to your loyalty."

It was the first time Takeo had directly threatened the boys. *Heaven forfend I have to make good this threat,* he thought. *Yet surely Zenko would not risk his sons' lives.*

"All my suggestions are only to make the whole country stronger, and to support Lord Otori," Zenko said. "I am sorry I spoke. Please forget it."

They had been outside alone as two individuals. When they returned, they seemed to Takeo to assume their roles as if in some drama, driven by the hand of fate to play out their parts to the end; the audience room, decorated with gold embossments on the pillars and beams, filled with retainers in their resplendent robes, had become the setting. Masking their mutual anger, they made their farewells with icy politeness. Zenko's departure from Maruyama was planned for the following day, Takeo's for the day after.

"**AND THEN YOU** will be alone in your domain," he said to Shigeko before they retired.

"Hiroshi will be here to advise me, at least until next year," she replied. "But what happened to you last night, Father? Who gave you that wound?"

"I must have no secrets from you," he said. "But I do not want to disturb your mother at this time, so make sure she does not hear of it." He told her briefly about Maya, about the possession and its results. She listened in silence, expressing neither shock nor horror, and he felt curiously grateful to her.

"Maya will be in Hofu with Taku for the winter," he said.

"Then we will keep in touch with them. And we will watch Zenko carefully too. You must not worry too much, Shigeko. In the Way of the Houou we often encounter things like this animal possession. Gemba knows much about them, and he has taught me."

"Should Maya go to Terayama?"

"She will go there when the time is right." Shigeko was smiling gently as he continued. "All spirits seek the higher power that can control them and give them peace."

A shiver ran down his spine. She seemed like a stranger, enigmatic and wise. He was suddenly reminded of the blind woman who had spoken the prophecy, who had called him by his water name and known him for who he was. *I must go back there,* he thought. *I will make a pilgrimage to the mountain, next year after my child is born, after my journey to the capital.*

He felt Shigeko had the same spiritual power. His own spirit lightened as he embraced his daughter and bade her good night.

"I think you should tell Mother," Shigeko said. "You should have no secrets from her. Tell her about Maya. Tell her everything."

·28·

umamoto, the castle town of the Arai, lay to the far south-west of the Three Countries, surrounded by mountains rich in iron ore and coal. These resources had led to the establishment of a flourishing industry of all forms of ironware, pots and tea kettles, and above all sword-making, with many renowned swordsmiths and forges, as well as, in recent years, the even more profitable business of making firearms.

"At least," grumbled the old man, Koji. "It would be profitable if the Otori permitted us to produce enough to meet the demand. Blow up the heat, boy."

Hisao pumped at the handle of the huge bellows and the furnace glowed even more fiercely, with a white heat that scorched his face and hands. He did not mind, for winter had come since they had arrived at Kumamoto two weeks before; a biting wind blew off the iron-gray sea, and every night was frosty.

"What right do they have to dictate to the Arai what we can and can't make, what we're allowed to sell and what's forbidden!" Koji went on.

Hisao heard the same discontent everywhere. His father told him, with some glee, that Arai's retainers fomented rumors constantly, stirring up old grievances against the Otori, questioning why Kumamoto now obeyed Hagi when Arai Daiichi had won the whole of the Three Countries in battle, unlike Otori Takeo, who had simply been lucky, taking advantage of a convenient earthquake, and bringing about the shameful death of Lord Arai by the same firearm that he now denied to the clan.

Akio and Hisao learned on their arrival in Kumamoto that Zenko was not there—he had been summoned to Maruyama by Lord Otori.

"Treats him like a servant," the innkeeper said on their first night, at the evening meal. "Expects him to drop everything and come running. Isn't it enough that Otori holds his sons as hostages?"

"He likes to humiliate both his allies and his enemies," Akio said. "It gratifies his own vanity. But he has no real strength. He will fall, and the Otori with him."

"There will be celebrations in Kumamoto on that day," the other man replied, taking up the dishes and returning to the kitchen.

"We will wait until Arai Zenko returns," Akio said to Kazuo.

"Then we will need some funds," Kazuo said. "Especially with winter at hand. Jizaemon's money is almost gone."

Hisao already knew that there were few Kikuta families this far West, and those had lost much of their power and influence during the years of the Otori rule. However, a few days later a sharp-featured young man came to call on Akio, greeting him with both deference and delight, addressing him as Master and using the secret language and signs of the Kuroda family. His name was Yasu; he was from Hofu and had fled to Kumamoto after some unpleasantness there involving the smuggling of firearms.

"I became a dead man!" he joked. "Lord Arai was to have me executed on Otori's orders; but luckily he valued me too much, and made a substitution."

"Are there many like you who serve Arai?"

"Yes, many. The Kuroda have always gone with the Muto, as you know, but we've many links with the Kikuta too. Look at the great Shintaro! Half Kuroda, half Kikuta."

"Murdered by the Otori, like Kotaro," Akio observed quietly.

"There are many deaths still unavenged," Yasu agreed. "It was different while Kenji was alive, but since his death, when Shizuka became the head of the family—everything's changed. No one's happy. First, because it's not right to be led by a woman, and second, because Otori arranged it. Zenko should be the head—he's the oldest male heir—and if he doesn't want to take it on, being a great lord, then it should be Taku."

"Taku is hand in glove with Otori, and was involved in Kotaro's death," Kazuo said.

"Well, he was only a child, and can be forgiven—but it's wrong for the Muto and Kikuta to be so estranged. That's Otori's doing too."

"We are here to mend bridges and heal wounds," Akio told him.

"That's exactly what I hoped. Lord Zenko will be delighted, I can tell you."

Yasu paid off the innkeeper and took them to his own lodgings, at the back of the shop where he sold knives and other kitchen utensils, cooking pots, kettles, hooks, and chains for hearths. He loved knives, from the great cleavers cooks used in the castle to tiny blades of exquisite sharpness for taking the living flesh from fish. When he discovered Hisao's interest in all kinds of tools he took him to the forges he bought from. One of the smiths, Koji, needed an assistant, and Hisao found himself apprenticed to him. He liked it, not only for the work itself—he was skillful at it, and it fascinated him—but also because it gave him more freedom, and took him away from Akio's oppressive company. Since leaving home, he saw his father with new eyes. He was growing up. He was no longer a child to be dominated and bullied. In the new year he would turn seventeen.

In some complex scheme of debts and obligations, his work for Koji paid for their food and lodging, though Yasu often professed he would take nothing from the Kikuta Master, that the honor of being allowed to be of assistance was sufficient. Yet Hisao thought he was a calculating man who gave away nothing—if Yasu helped them now, it was because he saw some profit in it in the future. And Hisao also saw how old Akio had become, and how antiquated his thinking was, as if it had been frozen in time in the years of isolation in Kitamura.

He realized how Akio was flattered by Yasu's attention, that his father craved respect and status in a way that seemed almost old-fashioned in the bustling, modern city, which had flourished in the long years of peace. The

Arai clan were full of confidence and pride. Their lands now stretched right across the West. They controlled the coast and the shipping lanes. Kumamoto was full of traders—and even a handful of foreigners, not only from Shin and Silla but also, it was said, from the Isles of the West, the barbarians with their acorn eyes and thick beards, and their utterly desirable goods.

Their presence in Kumamoto was hinted at, whispered of, for the whole city knew of Otori's unreasonable prohibition on anyone dealing with the barbarians directly—all trade had to go through the Otori clan's central government, administered from Hofu, the only port where foreign ships officially were allowed to land. This was widely believed to be because the Middle Country wished to keep the profits to itself, as well as the inventions, so practical and useful, and in the question of armaments so effective, so deadly. The Arai smoldered beneath the unfairness.

Hisao had never seen a barbarian, though the artifacts he had been shown by Jizaemon had sparked his interest in them. Yasu often called by the forge at the end of the day to give new orders, collect a fresh supply of knives, deliver wood for the furnaces. One day he was accompanied by a tall man in a long cloak with a deep hood that hid his face. They came at the end of the day; dusk was falling and the leaden sky threatened snow. It was around the middle of the eleventh month. The blaze of the fire was the only color in a world turned black and gray by winter. Once off the street, the stranger let his hood fall back and Hisao realized with surprise and curiosity that he was a barbarian.

The barbarian could hardly talk to them—he knew only a few words, but both he and Koji were the sort of men who spoke with their hands, who understood machinery better than language, and as Hisao followed them round the forge he realized he was like that too. He grasped the barbarian's meaning as quickly as Koji did. The stranger was absorbed by all their methods, studied everything with his quick light eyes, sketched their fireplaces, bellows, cauldrons, molds, and pipes; later, when they drank hot wine, he brought out a book, folded in a strange way, printed, not written, and showed pictures, which were clearly of forging. Koji pored over them, his brow furrowed, his fingers scratching behind his ears. Hisao, kneeling to one side, peering in the dim light, could feel his own excitement increasing as the pages turned. His head was spinning with all the possibilities revealed before his eyes. The details of forging techniques gave way to careful illustration of the products. On the final pages were several firearms— most were the long cumbersome muskets he was already familiar with, but one, at the bottom of the page, slipped in among them like a foal between its mother's legs, was small, barely a quarter of their length. He could not prevent his forefinger from reaching out and touching it.

The barbarian chuckled. "Pistola!" He mimed, hiding it inside his clothes, then brought it out and aimed it at Hisao.

"Pa! Pa!" He laughed. "Morto!"

Hisao had never seen a more beautiful thing, and instantly desired it.

The man rubbed his fingers together, and they all understood him. Such weapons were expensive. But they could be made, Hisao thought, and he determined to learn how to make one.

Yasu sent Hisao away while he discussed financial matters. The boy tidied up the forge, damped down the fire, and prepared all the materials for the following day. He made tea for the men and filled their wine bowls, and then went home, his mind full of ideas. But either the ideas themselves, the unaccustomed wine, or the bitter wind after the heat of the forge had set his head aching, and by the time he got to Yasu's house he could see only half the building, only half the display of knives and axes.

He stumbled over the step, and as he recovered his balance, he saw the woman, his mother, in the misty void where half the world should have been.

Her face was pleading, full of tenderness and horror. He felt sick as the strength of her appeal hit him. The pain became unbearable. He could not help groaning, and then he realized he was going to vomit, fell to his hands and knees, crawled to the threshold, and heaved into the gutter.

The wine was sour in his mouth; his eyes watered painfully, the sleety wind freezing the tears on his cheeks.

The woman had followed him outside and hung above the ground, her outline blurred by the haze and the sleet.

Akio, his father, called from inside. "Who's there? Hisao? Close the door, it's freezing."

His mother spoke, her voice inside his mind as piercing as ice. "You must not kill your father."

He had not known that he wanted to. He was frightened, then, that she knew all his thoughts, his hatred as well as his love.

The woman said, "I will not let you."

Her voice was intolerable, jangling all the nerves in his body, setting them on fire. He tried to scream at her. "Go away! Leave me alone!"

Through his own moaning, he was aware of footsteps approaching, and heard Yasu's voice.

"What on earth!" the man exclaimed, and then called to Akio, "Master! Come quickly! Your son . . ."

They carried him inside and washed the vomit from his face and hair.

"The fool drank too much wine," Akio said. "He should not drink. He has no head for it. Let him sleep it off."

"He hardly had any wine," Yasu said. "He can't be drunk. Maybe he is sick?"

"He gets headaches now and then. He's had them since he was a child. It's nothing. They go away in a day or two."

"Poor lad, growing up without a mother!" Yasu said, half to himself, as he helped Hisao lie down and covered him with the quilt. "He's shivering; he's freezing. I'll brew something for him to help him sleep."

Hisao drank the tea and felt warmth gradually return; the shivering abated, but the pain did not, nor did the woman's voice. Now she hovered in the dark room—he did not need lamplight to see her. He understood dimly that if he listened to her the pain would lessen, but he did not want to hear what she had to say. He drew the pain around him as his defense against her, and thought about the marvelous little firearm and how he longed to make it.

The pain made him savage, like a tortured animal. He wanted to inflict it on someone else.

The tea dulled the edge of his feelings, and he must have dozed for a short time. When he woke, he heard Akio and Yasu talking, heard the chink of the wine bowls and the small noises their throats made as they drank.

"Zenko has returned," Yasu was saying. "I can't help feeling a meeting between you would bring benefits to everyone."

"That is the main reason we came here," Akio replied. "Can you arrange it?"

"I am sure I can. Zenko himself must long to heal the divisions between Muto and Kikuta. And, after all, you are related by marriage, are you not? Your son and Zenko must be cousins."

"Has Zenko any Tribe skills?"

"None that anyone knows of. He takes after his father—he's a warrior. Not like his brother."

"My son has few skills," Akio admitted. "He has learned some things, but he has no innate talents. It's been a great disappointment to the Kikuta. His mother was highly talented, but she passed nothing on to her son."

"He is good with his hands. Koji speaks quite highly of him—and Koji never praises anyone."

"But that is not going to make him a match for Otori."

"Is that what you hoped? That Hisao would be the assassin to finally get the better of Takeo?"

"I will have no peace until Otori is dead."

"I understand your feelings, but Takeo is both skillful and lucky. That's why you must talk to Zenko. An army of warriors might succeed where the Tribe's assassins have failed."

Yasu drank again and chuckled. "On the other hand, Hisao likes guns. A gun is stronger than any Tribe magic, I'm telling you. He may yet surprise you!"

ou say he threatened the boys directly?" Lady Arai drew her fur outer garment around her. The sleet that had blown off the sea all week since their return from Maruyama had finally turned to snow. The wind had dropped and the flakes were falling gently and steadily.

"Don't worry," her husband, Zenko, replied. "He is just trying to bully us. Takeo will never harm them. He is too weak to bring himself to do it."

"It must be snowing in Hagi," Hana said, staring out at the distant sea and thinking of her sons. She had not seen them since they left in the spring.

Zenko said, ill-will coloring his voice, "And in the mountains. With any luck Takeo will be stuck in Yamagata and will not be able to return to Hagi before spring. The snow is early this year."

"At least we know Lord Kono is safely on his way to Miyako," Hana remarked, for they had received messages from the nobleman before he left Hofu.

"Let's hope he is preparing a warm reception for Lord Otori next year," Zenko said, and gave his short, explosive laugh.

"It was amusing to see Takeo lulled by his flattery," Hana murmured. "Kono is certainly a very accomplished and plausible liar!"

"As he said before he left," Zenko remarked, "Heaven's net is wide, but its mesh is fine. Now the net is to be drawn tighter. Takeo will be caught in it eventually."

"I was surprised by my sister's news," Hana said. "I thought she would be past childbearing." She stroked the surface of the fur, and wanted to feel it against her skin. "What if she does have a son?"

"It is not going to make a great deal of difference, if all goes according to plan," Zenko replied. "Neither will this betrothal between Sunaomi and their daughter."

"Sunaomi must never marry a twin!" Hana agreed. "But we will maintain the pretense for the time being."

They smiled at each other with complicity.

"The only good thing Takeo ever did was giving me you in marriage," Zenko said.

It was a grave mistake on his part, Hana was thinking. *If he had yielded to me and taken me as a second wife, how different everything would be. I would have given him sons; without me Zenko would be just another of his barons, no threat to him. He will pay for it. And Kaede too.*

For Hana had never forgiven Takeo for rejecting her, nor her sister for deserting her when she was a child. She had adored Kaede, had clung to her when grief for her parents' deaths had almost deranged her—and Kaede had left her, had ridden off one spring morning and never come back. After that, Hana and her older sister, Ai, had been held in Inuyama as hostages, and would have been put to death there had Sonoda Mitsuru not saved them.

"You are not past childbearing!" Zenko exclaimed. "Let us make many more sons—a whole army of them."

They were alone in the room, and she thought he would be moved to begin there and then, but at that moment a voice called outside. The door slid open and a manservant said quietly, "Lord Arai, Kuroda Yasu is here with another man."

"They have come despite the weather," Zenko said. "Give them something to drink, but make them wait a little before you bring them in, and make sure we are undisturbed."

"Kuroda comes openly these days?" Hana asked.

"Taku is safely in Hofu—no one will be spying on us now."

"I have never liked Taku," Hana said abruptly.

A faint look of discomfort crossed Zenko's large face. "He is my brother," he reminded her.

"Then his first loyalty should be to you, not to Takeo," she retorted. "He deceives you every day, and you take no notice of it. He has been spying on you most of this year, and you may be sure he intercepts our letters too."

"That will all change soon," Zenko said with composure. "We will settle the matter of the Muto inheritance. Taku will have to obey me then, or . . ."

"Or what?"

"The punishment in the Tribe for disobedience has always been death. I could not change that rule even for my own kin."

"Taku is popular, though; you've often said so yourself. And your mother is too. Surely many will not go against them?"

"I believe we will have some support. And if Kuroda's companion is who I think he is, much of it will be quite powerful."

"I can't wait to meet him." Hana smiled slightly.

"I'd better tell you a little about him. He is Kikuta Akio; he's been Master of the Kikuta family ever since Kotaro's death. He married Muto Kenji's daughter, Yuki; after she died he more or less went into hiding with her son." He paused and stared at Hana, his heavy-lidded eyes bright.

"Not *his* son?" she said, and then, "Not Takeo's?"

He nodded, and laughed again.

"How long have you known this?" Hana said. She was both astonished and excited by this revelation, her mind already seeking ways to use it.

"I heard all the rumors in the Muto family when I was a boy. Why else would Yuki have been forced to take poison? The reason the Kikuta killed her must have been because they did not trust her. And why else would Kenji have gone over to the Otori, with four of the five families? Kenji believed Takeo would reclaim him, one day, or at least protect him. The boy—they call him Hisao, apparently—is Takeo's son."

"My sister does not know this, I am sure of it." Hana felt a small inner glow of pleasure at the thought.

"Maybe you can tell her at the right time," her husband suggested.

"Oh, I will," Hana agreed. "But why has Takeo never sought him out?"

"I believe there are two reasons: He does not want his wife to know, and he fears his son will be the one to kill him. As Dr. Ishida so kindly revealed to us, there was a prophecy to that effect, and Takeo believes it."

Hana could feel her pulse quickening. "When my sister learns this news, it will drive them apart. She has longed for a son for years—she will never forgive Takeo for this hidden boy."

"Many men have mistresses and illegitimate children, and their wives forgive them."

"But most wives are like me," Hana replied. "Realistic and practical. If you have other women, it does not bother me. I understand men's needs and desires, and I know I will always come first with you. My sister is an idealist—she believes in love. Takeo must too—he has never taken another woman—and that is why he has no sons. More than that, both of them have been influenced by Terayama and what they call the Way of the Houou. Their realm is held in balance by their union—by the merging of the male and the female. Break that union and the Three Countries will fall apart."

She added, "And you will inherit all your father fought for, with the blessing of the Emperor, and the support of his general."

"And the Tribe will no longer be divided," Zenko said. "We will recognize this boy as heir to both the Kikuta and the Muto families, and through him control the Tribe ourselves."

Hana heard footsteps outside. "They are coming now," she said.

Her husband called for more wine, and when it came, Hana dismissed the maids and served the visitors herself. She knew Kuroda Yasu by sight, and had taken advantage of the luxuries he imported from the Isles of the South—aromatic woods, textiles from Tenjiku, ivory, and gold. She herself owned several mirrors, made with the hard, brilliant glass that showed a person's true reflection. It pleased her that these treasures were kept concealed in Kumamoto. She never displayed them in Hofu. Now she had this hard, bright secret too, one that would reveal Takeo as he truly was.

She studied the other man, Akio. He took one glance at her, then sat with lowered eyes, outwardly humble, but she recognized at once that he was not a humble man. He was tall and lean; despite his age, he looked very strong. He emanated a sense of power, which aroused a flicker of interest in her. She would not like him as an enemy, but he would make a ruthless and relentless ally.

Zenko greeted the men with great courtesy, managing to defer to Akio as head of the Kikuta without relinquishing anything of his own status as overlord of the Arai.

"The Tribe has been divided for too long," he said. "I deeply regret the split, and Kotaro's death. Now Muto Kenji is dead, it is time for those wounds to be healed."

"I believe we have a common cause," Akio replied. His speech was abrupt, with the accent of the East. Hana felt he would remain silent rather than use flattery, and was not susceptible to flattery himself, nor to any of the usual bribes or persuasions.

"We can speak openly here," Zenko said.

"I have never hidden what I most desire," Akio said. "Otori's death. He has been indicted by the Kikuta for absconding from the Tribe, and for Kotaro's murder. It outrages our family, our ancestors and traditions, and the gods, that he still lives."

"People say he cannot be killed," Yasu remarked. "But surely he is only a man."

"I once had my knife against his throat." Akio leaned forward, his eyes intense. "I still don't understand how he got away. He has many skills—I should know; I trained him in Matsue—he has evaded all our attempts against him."

"Well," Zenko said slowly, exchanging a look with Hana. "I learned something earlier this year that you may not have heard. Very few people know of it."

"Dr. Ishida told us," Hana said. "He is Takeo's physician, and has treated many of his wounds. He learned it from Muto Kenji."

Akio raised his head and looked directly at her.

"It seems Takeo believes only his own son can kill him," Zenko continued. "There was some prophecy to that effect."

"Like the Five Battles?" Yasu asked.

"Yes, that was used to justify his murder of my father and his seizure of power," Zenko said. "The other words were kept hidden."

"Lord Otori has no sons, though," Yasu said into the silence, looking from one to the other. "Though certain things are whispered . . ." Akio sat completely still, his face expressionless. Hana again felt the quick lick of excitement in her belly.

Akio addressed Zenko, his voice lower and rougher than ever. "You know about my son?"

Zenko moved his head very slightly in acquiescence.

"Who else knows of this prophecy?"

"Apart from those in this room and Ishida, my brother, and possibly my mother, though she has never mentioned it to me."

"What about at Terayama? Kubo Makoto may know—Takeo tells him everything," Hana murmured.

"It's possible. Anyway, very few. And what matters is that Takeo believes it," Zenko said.

Yasu took a quick gulp of wine and said to Akio, "So all those rumors *were* true?"

"Yes. Hisao is Takeo's son." Akio drank as well, and for the first time seemed almost to smile. It was more painful and more alarming, Hana thought, than if he had wept and cursed. "He does not know. He has no Tribe skills. But now I see that it will be easy for him to kill his father."

Yasu slapped the matting with his open palm. "Didn't I tell you the boy would surprise you? That's the best joke I've heard in years."

Suddenly all four of them were seized with uproarious laughter.

· 30 ·

 aede had decided to stay in Hagi for the winter, until her child was born, and Shizuka and Dr. Ishida stayed with her. They all moved from the castle into Lord Shigeru's old house by the river—the house faced south, catching all the winter sunshine, and was easier to keep warm during the long cold days. Chiyo still lived there, bent double, old beyond reckoning but still able to brew her healing teas and to tell stories about the past, and what she had forgotten Haruka filled in, as merry and bold as ever. Kaede retired from public life to a certain extent. Takeo and Shigeko had left for Yamagata; Maya had been sent with the Muto girl, Sada, to Maruyama, to Taku; Miki to the Tribe village of Kagemura. It gave Kaede pleasure to think of all three girls occupied in such serious training, and she prayed often for them, that they would learn to develop and control their different talents, and that the gods would protect them from accident, illness, or attack. It was easier, she thought with sorrow, to love her twin daughters from a distance, when their unnatural birth and strange talents could be overlooked.

She was not lonely, for she had Shizuka and the little boys to keep her company, as well as the girls' pets, the monkey and the lion dogs. In the absence of her daughters she lavished all her care and affection on her nephews. Sunaomi and Chikara enjoyed the move, too, away from the formalities of castle life. They played on the riverbank and on the fish weir.

"It's as if Shigeru and Takeshi lived again," Chiyo said with tears in her eyes as she listened to the shouts of the children from the garden or their footsteps on the nightingale floor, and Kaede enfolded her swelling belly in her arms and thought of the child growing there, for Sunaomi and Chikara had no Otori blood in their veins, but her son would have. Her son would be Shigeru's heir.

Several times a week Kaede took the boys to the shrine, for she had promised Shigeko she would keep an eye on Tenba and the kirin and make sure the horse did not forget everything he had learned. Ishida usually accompanied her, for his affection for the kirin was as strong as ever, and he could hardly bear to let a day go past without checking on its welfare. Mori Hiroshi saddled and bridled Tenba and lifted Sunaomi onto his back, and Kaede led him around the meadow. The horse seemed to scent something in her pregnant body and loved to walk gently beside her, nostrils flared, nuzzling her from time to time.

"Am I your mother?" she chided him, but his trust delighted her, and she prayed her son would be as bold and as handsome. She thought of her horse, Raku, and of Amano Tenzo—both long dead, yet surely their spirits would live as long as there were Otori horses.

Then Shigeko wrote to send for the horse, for she had decided to present him to her father, asking her mother to keep it a secret. Tenba was prepared for the journey and sent with the young groom by ship to Maruyama. Kaede was afraid the kirin would fret when its companion had gone, and Ishida shared her concern. The kirin did seem somewhat dispirited, but this only seemed to increase its affection for its human companions.

Kaede wrote often, for she still loved the art of writing—letters to her husband in reply to his; to Shigeko and Miki, urging them to work hard and obey their teachers; to her sisters, telling Hana of the good health and progress of her sons and inviting them both to visit her in the spring.

But she did not write to Maya, telling herself there was no purpose since Maya was living in secret somewhere in Maruyama, and letters from her mother would only endanger her.

She went to the other shrine, where Akane's old house had stood, and admired the slender, graceful figure that slowly emerged from the wood while the new home was erected around it.

"She looks like Lady Kaede," Sunaomi said, for she insisted he always came with her to face the place of his shame and fear. Mostly he had regained his confidence and high spirits, but at the shrine she saw traces of the humiliation and the scars it had left, and she prayed that the spirit of the goddess would emerge from the wood and bring healing.

Shortly after Takeo had left for Yamagata, Fumio returned. During Takeo's absence and Kaede's semi-withdrawal, he and his father acted as their representatives. One of their most annoying and persistent problems was what to do with the foreigners who had so inconveniently arrived from Hofu.

"It's not that I dislike them," Fumio told Kaede one afternoon in the middle of the tenth month. "As you know, I am used to foreigners; I enjoy their company and find them interesting. But it's hard to know what to do with them, day after day. They are very restless; and they were not too pleased when they learned Lord Otori was no longer in Hagi. They want to meet him, negotiate with him; they are getting quite impatient. I have told them nothing can be arranged until Lord Otori returns to Hagi. They demand to know why they cannot go to Yamagata themselves."

"My husband does not want them to travel throughout the country," Kaede replied. "The less they know about us, the better."

"I agree—and I don't know what understanding they came to with Zenko. He allowed them to leave Hofu, but for what purpose I don't know. I've been hoping they might send letters that would reveal something, but their interpreter cannot write much—certainly nothing that Zenko could read."

"Dr. Ishida could offer to be their scribe," Kaede suggested. "That would save you the trouble of intercepting their letters."

They smiled at each other.

"Perhaps Zenko just wanted to get rid of them," Kaede went on. "Everyone seems to find them something of a burden."

"Yet there is much to gain from them too—great knowledge and wealth, as long as we control them and not the reverse."

"For that purpose I must begin my language lessons," Kaede said. "You must bring the foreigners and their interpreter here to discuss it."

"That will certainly give them something to do through the winter," Fumio agreed. "I will impress on them what a great honor it is to be invited into the presence of Lady Otori."

The meeting was arranged, and Kaede found herself awaiting it with some trepidation—not on the foreigners' account but because she had no idea how she should behave toward their interpreter, the child of a peasant family, a woman from a house of pleasure, a follower of the strange beliefs of the Hidden, her husband's sister. She did not want to be brought into contact with this part of Takeo's life. She did not know what to say to such a person, or even how to address her. All her instincts, heightened by her pregnancy, warned her against it, but she had promised Takeo she would learn the foreigners' language, and she could think of no other way.

Of course, she had to admit, she was curious, too—mostly, she told herself, about the foreigners and their customs, but in fact she wanted to see what Takeo's sister looked like.

HER FIRST THOUGHT, when Fumio ushered the two large men, followed by the small woman, into the room, was, *She is nothing like him,* and she was conscious of a deep relief that no one would suspect a connection. She spoke formally to the men, welcoming them, and they bowed, while standing, before Fumio indicated that they should be seated.

Kaede herself sat with her back to the long wall of the room, facing toward the veranda. The trees, touched by the first frosts, were just past their finest moment of color, and the ground was carpeted with their crimson leaves, contrasting with the cloud-gray stone of rocks and lanterns. On her right, a scroll hung in the alcove, the calligraphy her own, from one of her favorite poems about the autumn bush clover for which the city of Hagi was named. The allusion was of course completely lost on the foreigners and their interpreter.

The men sat somewhat awkwardly with their backs to the scroll. They had removed their footwear outside, and she noted the long skin-tight clothing that covered their legs, disappearing beneath the hem of their strange outer garments, which were puffed out, making their hips and shoulders unnaturally large. The material was mostly black, with colored patches stitched into it—it did not appear to be silk, cotton, or hemp. The woman crawled to the space they left at Kaede's side, touched her head to the matting, and stayed low.

Kaede continued her covert study of the men, aware of their unfamiliar smell that filled her with a vague disgust, but she was also intensely conscious of the woman at her side, of the texture of hair, the color of skin, so like Takeo's. The reality of it hit her like a slap that made her heart thud. This really was his sister. For a moment she thought she must react—she did not know whether she would cry, or faint—but fortunately Shizuka came into the room with bowls of tea and sweet bean cakes. Kaede regained her self-control.

The woman, Madaren, was even more overwhelmed, and her first attempts at translating were so subdued and muffled that both sides were completely at a loss as to what was actually said. They assumed courtesies and pleasantries, presents were received, the foreigners smiled a lot— rather terrifyingly—and Kaede spoke as gently and bowed as gracefully as possible. Fumio himself knew several words of the foreigners' language, and used them all, while everyone said *Thank you, A great pleasure,* and *Forgive me* in their own tongue many times over.

One of the men, it transpired, the one called Don João, was confusingly both warrior and merchant, the other a priest. It took a long time to converse because Madaren was so anxious not to insult Lady Otori that she spoke in an extremely convoluted and courteous fashion. After several lengthy exchanges about the foreigners' accommodations and needs, Kaede realized the winter was likely to pass without her learning anything.

"Take them outside and show them the garden," she said to Fumio. "The woman will stay here with me."

She told everyone else to leave them. Shizuka glanced questioningly at her as she withdrew.

The men seemed grateful enough to step outside, and while they talked in loud, somewhat strained but mostly good-natured tones, presumably about the garden, Kaede addressed Madaren quietly.

"You must not be afraid of me. My husband has told me who you are. It is better that no one else should know of it, but for his sake I will honor and protect you."

"Lady Otori is too condescendingly gracious," Madaren began, but Kaede stopped her.

"I have a request to make of you—and of the gentlemen you serve. You have learned their language; I want you to teach me. We will study every day. When I have learned to speak fluently, I will consider all their requests. The quicker I learn, the more likely these are to be met. I hope you understand me clearly. One of them must come with you, as I must also learn their writing, of course. Tell them that—frame it as a request in whatever way is pleasing to them."

"I am the lowest of the low, but I will do everything I can to fulfill Lady Otori's desires." Madaren prostrated herself again.

"Madaren," Kaede said, speaking the strange name for the first time. "You are to be my teacher. There is no need to use excessive formality."

"You are very kind," Madaren said. She was smiling slightly as she sat up.

"We will begin our lessons tomorrow," Kaede said.

MADAREN CAME EVERY day, crossing the river by boat and walking through the narrow streets to the house by the river. The daily lessons became part of the household routine, and she became absorbed into its rhythm. The priest, Don Carlo, came with her about twice a week, and taught both women to write in what he called the alphabet, using the finest brushes.

Having reddish hair and beard, and pale green-blue eyes like the sea, he was an object of constant curiosity and wonder, and usually arrived with a trail of children and other people who had nothing better to do. He himself was equally curious, would occasionally seize a child and examine its clothes and footwear, studied every plant in the garden, and often took Madaren out into the fields to interrogate the astonished farmers about crops and seasons. He kept many notebooks, in which he made lists of words and sketches of flowers, trees, buildings, and farming implements.

Kaede saw most of these, for he brought them with him to use as teaching tools, and would often sketch something quickly to explain a word. He was obviously intelligent, and she felt shamefacedly amazed by this, for when she had first set eyes on him, his strange appearance had made her think of him as not quite human.

The language was difficult: Everything about it seemed to be back to front, and it was hard to remember the masculine and feminine forms and the way the verbs changed. One day when she was feeling particularly discouraged, she said to Madaren, "I will never master it. I don't know how you managed it." It was particularly galling that Madaren, a woman of low birth and no education, should have become so fluent.

"Well, I learned under circumstances that are not an option for Lady Otori," Madaren said. Once she had gotten over her shyness, her natural, life-hardened, practical self began to emerge. Their conversation became more relaxed, especially if Shizuka was present, as she usually was. "I made Don João teach me in bed."

Kaede laughed. "I don't think my husband had that sort of thing in mind."

"Don Carlo is free," Shizuka said teasingly. "Maybe I should try language lessons. Would you recommend the foreigners' techniques, Madaren? You hear such gossip about their parts; I would like to find out the truth for myself."

"Don Carlo does not care for that sort of thing," Madaren said. "He does not seem to desire women—or men, for that matter. In fact, he disapproves strongly. In his eyes, the act of love is what he calls a sin—and love between men particularly shocking."

It was a concept that neither Shizuka nor Kaede could quite understand.

"Maybe when I know more of his language, Don Carlo will explain it," Kaede said, joking.

"Don't ever speak of such things to him," Madaren begged. "It will embarrass him beyond belief."

"Is it something to do with his religion?" Kaede said, somewhat hesitantly.

"It must be. He spends a great deal of time in prayer, and often reads aloud from his holy books on attaining purity and controlling the desires of the body."

"Does not Don João believe the same things?" Shizuka asked.

"Part of him does, but his desires are stronger. He satisfies himself, and then hates himself for it."

Kaede wondered if this strange behavior extended to Madaren herself, but did not like to ask her directly, just as she did not want to question her about her beliefs, though she was curious to know how similar they were to the foreigners'. She observed the young woman closely when the two men were present, and thought that they did indeed despise her, though both needed her skills and depended on her, and one lusted after her body. She thought the relationship strange and distorted, with manipulation, even exploitation, on both sides. She found herself curious about Madaren's past, what strange journey had brought her to this place. Often when they were alone together, she was on the verge of asking her what her memories were, and what Takeo was like as a child. But the intimacy such questions would presuppose was too threatening.

Winter drew in. The eleventh month brought heavy frosts; despite the padded clothes and braziers it was hard to stay warm. Kaede no longer dared take exercise with Shizuka—the memory of her miscarriage was always with her, and she dreaded losing this child. Wrapped in fur rugs, she had little to do but study and talk to Madaren.

Just before the moon of the eleventh month letters came from Yamagata. She and Madaren were alone; Shizuka had taken the boys to see the kirin. She murmured her apologies for interrupting the lesson and went at once to her own study—the room where Ichiro used to read and write—and read the letters there. Takeo wrote at length—or rather he had dictated, for she knew Minoru's hand—informing her of all the decisions that had been made. There were still many preparations to discuss with Kahei and Gemba about the visit to the capital—he was waiting for news from Sonoda about the reception of the messengers. He felt obliged to spend the New Year there.

Kaede was severely disappointed—she had hoped Takeo would have returned before the snows closed the mountain passes. Now she was afraid he would be delayed until the thaw. When she went back to Madaren, she was distracted and felt even her memory was failing her.

"I hope Lady Otori has not had bad news from Yamagata?" Madaren inquired when Kaede made her third elementary mistake.

"Not really. I had hoped my husband would return sooner, that is all."

"Lord Otori is well?"

"He seems in good health, thank Heaven." Kaede paused and then said abruptly, "What did you call him, when you were children?"

"Tomasu, lady."

"Tomasu? It sounds so strange. What does it mean?"

"It is the name of one of the great teachers of the Hidden."

"And Madaren?"

"Madaren was a woman who, they say, loved the son of God when he walked on earth."

"Did the son of God love her?" Kaede said, remembering their former conversation.

"He loves us all," Madaren replied with great seriousness.

Kaede's interest at that moment was not in the strange beliefs of the Hidden, but in her husband, who had grown up among them.

"I don't suppose you remember much about him. You must have been still a child."

"He was always different," Madaren said slowly. "That's what I remember most. He didn't look the same as the rest of us, and he didn't seem to think in the same way. My father was often angry with him; our mother would pretend to be angry, but she adored him. I was always running after him, pestering him. I wanted him to notice me. I think that's why I noticed him when I saw him in Hofu. I dreamed about him constantly. I pray for him all the time."

She fell silent, as if she feared she had said too much. Kaede herself was slightly shocked, though she could not quite explain to herself why.

"We had better resume our studies," she said in a cooler voice.

"Of course, lady," Madaren agreed submissively.

That night there was a heavy snow, the first of the year. Kaede woke in the morning to the unfamiliar white light, and almost wept. For it meant the passes would indeed be closed, and Takeo would stay in Yamagata until spring.

KAEDE WAS INTERESTED in the foreigners, and the more she learned of their language the more she realized she needed to know what they believed in in order to understand them. Don Carlo seemed equally eager to understand her, and when the snow fell, preventing him from going into the fields to conduct his research, he came more frequently with Madaren and their conversations became more involved.

"He watches me in a way that in normal men would be desire," she remarked to Shizuka.

"Maybe he should be warned about your reputation!" Shizuka replied. "At one time that desire meant death to any man!"

"I have been married for sixteen years, Shizuka! I hope that reputation has been laid to rest by now. Anyway, it is not desire, for we know Don Carlo does not feel such natural urges."

"We know nothing of the sort! We only know he does not *act* on them," Shizuka pointed out. "But if you want to hear my opinion, I think he is hoping to win you over to his religion. He does not desire your body; he desires your soul. He has started talking about Deus, has he not? And explaining the religion of his country?"

"How strange," Kaede said. "What difference can it make to him what I believe?"

"Mai, the girl we sent to work for them, says Lady Otori's name is often introduced into conversation between them. Mai's grasp of their language is not perfect yet, but she feels they hope to win trade and believers, in equal measure, and eventually to gain new land for themselves. This is what they do all over the world."

"From what they say, their own country lies a huge distance away—a year or more of sailing," Kaede said. "How can they bear to live so far from home for so long?"

"Fumio says it is a characteristic of all such merchants and adventurers. It makes them very powerful, and dangerous."

"Well, I cannot imagine adopting their strange beliefs." Kaede dismissed the idea with scorn. "It seems like nonsense to me!"

"All beliefs can seem like madness," Shizuka said. "But they can seize people suddenly, almost like the plague. I have seen it happen. Be on your guard."

Shizuka's words made Kaede remember the time when she was Lord Fujiwara's wife, and how she had passed the long days in a mixture of prayer and poetry, holding all the while to the promise the goddess had made to her while she lay in the deep Kikuta sleep as though encased in ice. *Be patient: He will come for you.*

She felt the child kick within her. Now all her patience was strained to its limit by the pregnancy, the snow, Takeo's absence.

"Ah, my back aches," she sighed.

"Let me massage it. Lean forward." As Shizuka's hands worked on Kaede's muscles and spine, she said nothing, and the silence grew more intense, as though she had fallen into a kind of reverie.

"What are you thinking about?" Kaede questioned.

"Ghosts from the past I often used to sit with Lord Shigeru in this very room. Several times I brought messages from Lady Maruyama—she was a believer, you know."

"In the teachings of the Hidden," Kaede said. "I feel the foreigners' religion, while it seems to be the same, is more dogmatic and intransigent."

"All the more reason to treat it with suspicion!"

Throughout the winter, Don Carlo introduced her to more words: *hell*, *punishment*, *damnation*, and she remembered what Takeo had said about the all-seeing God of the Hidden and the mercilessness of his gaze. She realized how Takeo had chosen to ignore that gaze, and it made her admire and love him all the more.

For surely the gods were good, and wanted life to continue for all beings in harmony, the seasons passing, night following day and summer winter, and, as the Enlightened One himself taught, death itself no more than a pause before the next birth . . .

This she tried to explain with her limited vocabulary to Don Carlo and, when words failed, took him to look at the finished carving of the all-merciful Kannon in the shrine that had been built for her.

It was a sudden mild day in early spring. The plum blossoms still hung like tiny flakes of snow to the bare branches in Akane's garden; the snow underfoot was moist and melting. Despite her dislike of the conveyance, Kaede was carried in the palanquin; she was in the seventh month of pregnancy and was slowed by the weight of the child. Don Carlo rode in a separate one behind her, and Madaren followed him.

The carpenters, under Taro's leadership, were putting the finishing touches to the shrine, taking advantage of the warmer weather. Kaede was pleased to see that the new building had stood up to the winter well, sheltered by its double roof, the two curves perfectly balanced as Taro had promised they would be, their upward thrust reflected by the protective umbrella of the pines. Snow still lay on the roof, dazzling against the blue sky; melting icicles dripped from the eaves, refracting the light.

The transoms over the side doors were shaped like leaves, and delicate tracery let light into the building. The main door stood open, and the winter sun fell in splashes on the new floor. The wood was the color of honey and smelled as sweet.

Kaede greeted Taro, and stepped out of her sandals onto the veranda.

"The foreigner is interested in your work," she told Taro, and looked behind her to where Don Carlo and Madaren were approaching the shrine building.

"Welcome," she said to the priest in his language. "This is a special place for me. It is new. This man made it."

Taro bowed, and Don Carlo made an awkward gesture with his head. He looked more than usually uncomfortable, and when Kaede said, "Come inside. You must see this man's most beautiful work," he shook his head and replied, "I will look from here."

"You cannot see," she persisted, but Madaren whispered, "He will not go in; it is against his beliefs."

Kaede felt a flash of anger at his rudeness, not comprehending at all the reasons behind it, but she was not going to give in so easily. She had listened to him all winter, and had learned much from him. Now he was going to listen to her.

"Please," she said. "Do as I tell you."

"It will be interesting," Madaren encouraged him. "You will see how the building is constructed and how the wood is carved."

He pulled off his footwear with a show of reluctance, Taro helping him with encouraging smiles. Kaede stepped inside the shrine; the finished statue stood before them. One hand, against her breast, held a lotus flower; the other lifted up the hem of her robe with two slender fingers. The folds of the robe were carved with such exquisite skill they almost seemed to sway in the breeze. The goddess's eyes looked downward, her expression both stern and compassionate, her mouth archaic in its smile.

Kaede put her hands together and bowed her head in prayer—for her unborn child, for her husband and daughters, and for Akane's spirit, that it might finally find rest.

"She is very beautiful," Don Carlo said, with a kind of wonder, but he did not pray.

Kaede told Taro how much the foreigner admired the statue, exaggerating his praise to make up for his earlier rudeness.

"It is nothing to do with me," Taro replied. "My skills are mediocre. My hands listen to what is inside the wood, and help it find its way out."

Kaede tried to translate this as best she could. Taro, with gestures and sketches, showed Don Carlo the inner construction of the roof, how the struts gave each other mutual support. Don Carlo then brought out his own notebook and drew what he saw, asking the names of the different woods, and what each joint was called.

His eyes strayed often back to the goddess, and then to Kaede's face.

As they left, he murmured, "I did not think I would find a Madonna in the Orient."

It was the first time Kaede had heard either word, and she did not know their meaning but she saw something had increased Don Carlo's interest in her; it disturbed her. She felt the child kick suddenly and violently, and longed for Takeo to return.

· 31 ·

he scars left by the claw marks on his face had almost faded when Takeo returned to Hagi at the end of the third month. The snows had barely melted—the winter had been long and harsh. With all the passes closed between the cities of the Three Countries he had not even been able to receive letters, and his anxiety for Kaede had been extreme. He was glad Ishida had stayed with her during her pregnancy, yet regretted the physician's absence as the bitter weather set all his old wounds aching, and the soothing draught was soon finished. He had spent the long hours of his enforced stay mainly with Miyoshi Kahei, discussing the strategy for the coming spring and the visit to the capital, and going through the records of the administration of the Three Countries. Both lifted his spirits— he felt he was well prepared for whatever might happen on the visit. He would go peacefully, but he would not leave his country undefended. And the administration records confirmed once again how strong the country was, right down to village level, where the system of elders and headmen chosen by the peasants themselves to represent them could be mobilized to defend themselves and their land.

The spring weather, the prospect of returning home, the joy of riding through the awakening countryside all added to his sense of well-being. Tenba had wintered well, hardly losing any weight or condition. His winter coat had been brushed away by the horse boys, who treasured him as much as Takeo did, and his black body gleamed like lacquer. His joy to be out on the road, heading in the direction of his birthplace, made him prance and cavort, nostrils flared, mane and tail streaming.

"BUT WHAT HAPPENED to your face?" Kaede asked when they were alone, tracing the faint marks with her fingers.

Takeo had arrived that morning. The air was still cool, the wind fresh; the roads had been muddy, often flooded. He had gone straight to the old house, where Chiyo and Haruka had greeted him with delight, had bathed, and eaten with Kaede, Ishida, and the little boys. Now he and Kaede sat in the upstairs room, the shutters open, the sound of the river in their ears, and everywhere the smells of spring.

How can I tell her? He looked at her with concern. She was so close to her time, no more than three or four weeks away. He recalled what Shigeko had said: *You should tell Mother. You should have no secrets from her. Tell her everything.*

He said, "I rode into a branch. It's nothing."

"It looks like a scratch from an animal. I know, you grew lonely in Yamagata and found a passionate woman!" She was teasing him in her pleasure at having him home.

"No," he replied, more seriously. "You know I have told you many times, I will never lie with anyone but you."

"For the rest of your life?"

"For the rest of my life."

"Even if I die before you?"

He laid his hand gently over her mouth. "Don't say such things."

He pulled her into his arms and held her close for a while without speaking.

"Tell me everything," she said finally. "How was Shigeko? I rejoice to think of her as Lady Maruyama now."

"Shigeko is fine. I wish you could have seen her at the ceremony. She reminded me so much of Naomi. But I realized, watching them together, that Hiroshi is in love with her."

"Hiroshi? It's not possible. He has always treated her like a little sister. Did he tell you so?"

"Not in so many words. But I have no doubt that is why he has avoided marriage."

"He hopes to marry Shigeko?"

"Would it be such a bad thing? I believe Shigeko is very fond of him."

"She's still only a girl!" Kaede said, sounding as if she was angered at the idea.

"She is the age you were when we met," Takeo reminded her.

They stared at each other for a moment. Then Kaede said, "They should not be together in Maruyama. It is expecting far too much of them!"

"Hiroshi is much older than I was! I am sure he has much more self-control. And they are not expecting their lives to end hourly." *Our love was a blind passion,* he was thinking. *We hardly knew each other. We were possessed by the intense madness that the constant expectation of death induces. Shigeko and Hiroshi know each other like brother and sister. It is not a bad foundation for marriage.*

"Kono hinted at a political alliance through marriage with the Emperor's general, Saga Hideki," he told Kaede.

"It is an idea we cannot dismiss lightly," she said, giving a deep sigh. "I am sure Hiroshi would make a fine husband, but such a marriage would be throwing Shigeko away, and bringing us no advantages that we do not already have."

"Well, she will come with me to Miyako; we will meet Saga and decide then."

He went on to tell her how matters stood with Zenko, and they decided Hana should be invited to spend the summer in Hagi. She would be able to spend time with her sons and keep Kaede company after the birth of the child.

"And I expect you are now fluent in the new language," Takeo said.

"I have made progress," Kaede said. "Both Don Carlo and your sister are good teachers."

"Is my sister well?"

"Yes, mainly. We have all had colds, but nothing serious. I like her—she seems a good person, and clever, despite having no education."

"She is like our mother," Takeo said. "Do the foreigners correspond with Hofu or Kumamoto?"

"Yes, they write often. Dr. Ishida sometimes helps them, and naturally we read everything."

"You understand it all?"

"It is very hard. Even if I know every word, I still cannot grasp the meaning. I have to be very careful not to alert Don Carlo—he takes an intense interest in everything I say, and weighs every word. He writes a lot about me, my influence over you, my unusual power as a woman." She fell silent briefly. "I think he hopes to convert me to his religion, and reach you through me. Madaren must have told him about your birth into the Hidden. Don Carlo almost thinks you are a fellow believer and will allow him to preach and Don João to trade freely in the Three Countries."

"Trade is one thing, desirable as long as we control it and it is on our terms. But I will not allow them to preach, or to travel."

"Did you know there are already foreigners in Kumamoto?" Kaede inquired. "Don João received a letter from one of them. They were business acquaintances, it seems, back in their homeland."

"I suspected it." He told her about the mirror he had been shown in Maruyama.

"I have one the same!" Kaede called for Haruka, and the maid brought the mirror, wrapped in a heavy silk cloth.

"Don Carlo gave it to me," Kaede said, unwrapping it.

Takeo took it and looked in it with the same sense of unfamiliarity and shock.

"It worries me," he said. "What else is being traded through Kumamoto that we do not know of?"

"Another good reason to have Hana here," Kaede said. "She cannot resist showing off her new acquisitions, and will boast of Kumamoto's superiority. I am sure I can induce her to tell me more."

"Is Shizuka not here? I would like to talk to her about this matter, and about Zenko."

"She left as soon as the snow melted, to go to Kagemura. I have been worried about Miki in this bitter weather, and Shizuka had things to discuss with the Muto family."

"Will Miki return with her?" Takeo was seized by longing to see his youngest daughter.

"It is not yet decided." Kaede patted the small lion dog that lay curled beside her. "Kin will be glad when she comes back—he misses the girls. Did you see Maya?"

"I did." Takeo was not sure how to go on.

"You are concerned for her too? Is she all right?"

"She is all right. Taku is teaching her. She seems to be learning self-control and discipline. But Taku has become enmeshed in some kind of infatuation with the girl."

"With Sada? Have all these young men gone mad? Sada! That is the last person I would have expected Taku to lose his head over. I did not think she cared for men—she looks like a man herself."

"I should not have told you," Takeo said. "Do not let it distress you. You must think of your health."

Kaede laughed. "I am more astonished than distressed. As long as they are not distracted from their work, let them love each other. What harm does it do? That sort of passion cannot be halted—it will burn itself out eventually."

"Ours did not," Takeo said.

Kaede took his hand and placed it on her belly.

"Our son is kicking," she said, and he felt the child move strongly within her.

"I don't really want to speak of it," he said. "But we must come to a decision about the hostages that we still hold in Inuyama, the Kikuta who attacked you last year. Their father was himself killed by the family last year, and I do not believe the Kikuta will ever negotiate with me. Justice demands that they be put to death for their crime. I think it is time to write to Sonoda. It must be seen to be according to the law, not as an act of revenge. Maybe I should be there to witness it—I am considering asking it to be done when I go through Inuyama on my way to the capital."

Kaede shivered. "It is a bad omen for a journey. Tell Sonoda to do it himself—he and Ai are our representatives in Inuyama. They can witness it on our behalf. And do it immediately. There must be no more delay."

"Minoru will write this afternoon." He was grateful to her for her decisiveness.

"Sonoda has written recently, by the way. Your retinue of messengers has returned to Inuyama. They were received by the Emperor himself, and shown considerable honor. They were accommodated by Lord Kono all winter, and he speaks nothing but praise of you and the Three Countries."

"His attitude did seem changed toward me," Takeo said. "He knows how to be charming, how to flatter. I do not trust him, but I must still go to Miyako as if I did."

"The alternative is too terrible to consider," Kaede murmured.

"You understand very well what that alternative is."

"Indeed: to attack and defeat Zenko quickly in the West and prepare for war against the Emperor in the East. Think of the cost. Even if we can win two such difficult campaigns, we bring war on two-thirds of our country—and on a personal level destroy our own relatives and deprive Sunaomi and Chikara of their parents. Their mother is my sister, and I love her and her sons dearly."

He drew her close to him again, and touched his lips to the nape of her neck, still scarred after all those years, still beautiful to him.

"I will never let that happen, I promise you."

"But there are forces at work that even you, my dear husband, cannot control." She nestled against him. Their breath rose and fell in unison.

"I wish we could stay here like this forever," she said in a low voice. "I feel completely happy now, at this moment; but I am afraid of what the future holds."

NOW EVERYONE WAS waiting for the child to be born, but before Kaede went into seclusion Takeo wanted to have at least one meeting with the foreigners to clarify matters between them, reach some mutually satisfactory agreement on trade, and remind them who was the ruler of the Three Countries. He was concerned that during his absence, when Kaede was preoccupied with the infant, the foreigners would look to Kumamoto to grant them access to other districts and other resources.

The days grew warmer; ginkgo and maple leaves unfurled, brilliant and fresh. Suddenly cherry blossoms were everywhere, splashes of pure white on the mountainside, deep pink in the gardens. Birds returned to the flooded rice fields, and the noise of frogs filled the air. Aconite and violets flowered in the woods and gardens, followed by dandelions, windflowers, daisies, and vetch. The first cicadas were heard, and the fluting call of the bush warbler.

Both Don Carlo and Don João came, with Madaren, to the meeting, which was held in the main room of the house, looking out over the garden, where the stream and the waterfalls splashed and the red and gold carp swam lazily in the pools, leaping occasionally for spring insects. Takeo would have preferred to receive them in the castle with elaborate ceremony and a greater display of wealth, but he felt Kaede should not be put to the stress of going there, and they were both of the opinion that she should be present to help explain exactly what both parties meant.

It was a difficult task. The foreigners were more importunate than they had been previously. They were tired of being confined to Hagi, impatient to start real trade and, though they did not state it so baldly, to start making money. Madaren was made more nervous by Takeo's presence, seemed to dread offending him, yet at the same time to want to impress him. He himself was less than comfortable, suspecting that the foreigners, for all their protestations of respect and friendship, looked down on him, knowing that Madaren was his sister—did they know? Had she told them?

Kaede had said they knew he was born into the Hidden. . . . The interpretation slowed the discussions down; the afternoon dragged on.

He asked them to state clearly what they hoped to be granted within the Three Countries, and Don João explained that they hoped to establish regular trade. He praised the beautiful products, the silk, lacquerware, mother of pearl, and the celadon and porcelain imported from Shin. All of these, he said, were much sought after and highly prized in his own distant country. In return, he could offer silver, glassware, cloth from Tenjiku, aromatic woods and spices, and, naturally, firearms.

Takeo replied that all of this was perfectly acceptable—the only condition being that trade was to be conducted solely through the port of Hofu and under the supervision of his own officials, and that firearms were to be imported only with his or his wife's permission.

The foreigners exchanged glances when this was translated to them, and Don João replied, "It is customary among our people to be allowed to travel and trade freely wherever we choose."

Takeo said, "Maybe someday that will be possible. We know that you can pay well with silver, but if too much silver comes into our country, the value of everything must go down. We must protect our own people, and take things slowly. If trade with you turns out to be profitable to us, we will expand it."

"On these terms it may not be to our profit," Don João argued. "In which case we will leave altogether."

"That may be your decision," Takeo agreed politely, knowing inwardly that it was most unlikely.

Don Carlo then raised the issue of religion, and asked if they would be allowed to build a temple of their own in either Hofu or Hagi, and if the local people might join them in their worship of Deus.

"Our people are allowed to worship as they please," Takeo replied. "There is no need for special building. We have provided you with accommodation. You may use a room there. But I advise you to be discreet. Prejudices still exist, and the practice of your religion must remain a private affair. It must not be allowed to disrupt the harmony of society."

"We had hoped Lord Otori would recognize ours as the one true religion," Don Carlo said, and Takeo thought he heard a deeper fervency come into Madaren's voice as she translated.

He smiled, as if dismissing the idea as too absurd even to discuss. "There is no such thing," he replied, and saw that his words disturbed them.

"You should return to Hofu," he said, thinking he would write to Taku. "I will arrange a ship with Terada Fumio—he will accompany you. I will be away most of the summer, and my wife will be fully occupied with our child. There is no reason for you to stay in Hagi."

"I will miss Lady Otori's company," Don Carlo said. "She has been both pupil and teacher, and excellent as both."

Kaede spoke to him in his own language; Takeo marveled at her fluency in the strange sounds.

"I thanked him and said he, too, had been diligent as a teacher, and hoped he would continue to learn from us," she said aside to Takeo.

"He prefers to teach rather than be a pupil, I think," he whispered, not wanting Madaren to hear him.

"There are many things in which he is convinced he knows the truth," Kaede replied as quietly.

"But where is Lord Otori going for so long, so soon after the birth of your child?" Don João inquired.

The whole city knew—there was no reason to keep it from them. "I have to visit the Emperor."

When this was translated, it seemed to cause the foreigners some consternation. They questioned Madaren carefully, glancing toward Takeo with surprise.

"What are they saying?" He leaned toward Kaede and spoke in her ear.

"They did not know the Emperor existed," she murmured. "They had assumed you were what they call the king."

"Of the Eight Islands?"

"They don't know about the Eight Islands—they thought the Three Countries were all there was."

Madaren said, hesitantly, "Forgive me, but they would like to know if they would be permitted to accompany Lord Otori to the capital."

"Are they mad?" He added quickly, "Don't translate that! Tell them these things have to be arranged months in advance. It is not possible at this time."

Don João insisted. "We are the representatives of the king of our country. It is only right that we should be allowed to present our credentials to the ruler of this land, if it is not, as we had assumed, Lord Otori."

Don Carlo was more diplomatic. "Perhaps we should, in the first instance, send letters and gifts. Perhaps Lord Otori would be our ambassador."

"It's a possibility," Takeo conceded, inwardly determining to do no such thing. However, Don João and Don Carlo had to content themselves with this vague agreement, and after accepting some refreshments from Haruka, they made their farewells, promising to send the letters and presents before Takeo left.

"Remind them how opulent these gifts must be," Takeo told Madaren, for usually what the foreigners considered adequate fell far short of what was customary. He reflected with pleasure, tinged with some regret, on the impression the kirin was bound to make. Kaede had ordered the preparation of bolts of beautiful silk, and they were already packed in soft paper wrappings along with the finest examples of pottery, including tea bowls, caddies made of gold and black lacquer. She had also chosen a landscape painting by Sesshu. Shigeko would bring horses from Maruyama and scrolls of calligraphy in gold leaf, iron tea kettles and lamp stands, all designed to honor the Emperor and display the wealth and standing of the Otori, the extent of their trade, the riches of their realm. He doubted anything the foreigners could provide would be worth carrying as far as the capital, even to give to some under-minister.

He had stepped out into the garden as the foreigners retreated, bowing in their stiff, awkward way, rather than accompanying them to the gate, and did not notice for a moment that Madaren had come after him. It angered him, for he thought he had made it clear that he did not wish to be approached by her, yet he realized that she had been associating closely with his wife all winter and had gained a certain familiarity with the household. He in his turn felt he had certain obligations toward her; he regretted his own coolness, that he did not feel more affection for her, at the same time thinking fleetingly, gratefully, that if anyone saw them they would assume only that she spoke to him as an interpreter, not as his relative.

She called his name; he turned to her and, when she seemed unable to continue, said, trying to sound kind, "Tell me what I can do for you? Do you have any needs that are not met? Do you need money?"

She shook her head.

"Shall I arrange a marriage for you? I will find a suitable shopkeeper or merchant. You will have your own establishment, your own family eventually."

"I do not want any of those things," she replied. "Don João needs me. I cannot leave him."

He thought she might thank him, and was surprised when she did not. Instead she spoke abruptly, awkwardly. "There is one thing I desire above everything. Something only you can give me."

He raised his eyebrows slightly and waited for her to continue.

"Tomasu," she said, tears starting in her eyes, "I know you have not completely turned from God. Tell me that you are still a believer."

"I am not a believer," he said calmly. "I meant what I told you just now—there is no one true religion."

"When you spoke those terrible words, God sent me a vision." The tears were pouring down her face. There was no doubt of her distress or her earnestness. "I saw you burning in hell. The flames were devouring you. That is what awaits you after death, unless you come back to God."

He remembered the revelation that had come to him after the terrible poison-fever that had taken him to the very threshold of the next world. He would believe nothing, so that his people might believe whatever they chose. He would never abandon that stance.

"Madaren," he said gently, "you must not speak to me of these things. I forbid you ever to approach me in this way again."

"But your eternal life is at stake; your soul. It is my duty to try to save you. Do you think I do this lightly? Look how I am shaking! I am terrified to say these words to you. But I must!"

"My life is here, in this world," he said. He made a gesture at the garden, in all its spring beauty. "Is this not enough? This world into which we are born, and in which we die, to return, body and soul, into the great cycle, the seasons of life and death? This is wonder and miracle enough."

"But God made the world," she said.

"No, it makes itself; it is far greater than you think."

"It cannot be greater than God."

"God, the gods, all our beliefs, are created by humans," he said, "far smaller than this world that we live in the midst of." He was no longer angry with her, but he could see no reason why he was detained here by her, continuing this pointless discussion.

"Your masters are waiting for you. You had better return to them. And I forbid you to disclose anything about my past to them. I think you realize by now that that past is closed. I have cut myself off from it. My circumstances make it impossible for me to return. You have enjoyed my protection and I will continue to extend it to you, but it is not unconditional."

He felt chilled, despite the warm day, by his own words. What did he mean; what did he intend to do with her? Execute her? He remembered, as he did almost every day, the death, at his hands, of Jo-An, the outcaste who had also seen himself as a messenger of the Secret God. No matter how deeply he regretted the act, he knew that he would do it again with no more hesitation. He had killed his past, his childhood beliefs with Jo-An, and none of them could be resurrected.

Madaren also was subdued by his speech. "Lord Otori." She bowed to the ground as if recalling her true place in his world, not his sister but lower than the maids of his household—like Haruka, who had been waiting half-hidden on the veranda, and now, as he turned to go inside, stepped into the garden.

"Is everything all right, Lord Takeo?"

"The interpreter had some questions," he said. "Then she seemed to become unwell. Make sure she is recovered, and see that she leaves as soon as possible."

erada Fumio had spent the winter in Hagi with his wife and children. Shortly after the meeting with the foreigners, Takeo went to their house on the other side of the bay. The sheltered gardens, warmed by the hot springs surrounding the volcano, were already bright with azaleas and peonies, and other more exotic plants that Fumio brought back for Eriko from distant islands and remote kingdoms—orchids, lilies, and roses.

"You should come with me one day," Fumio said as they strolled through the garden and he related the provenance and history of each plant. "You have never left the Three Countries."

"I don't need to, when you bring the world to me," Takeo replied. "But one day I would like to—if I ever retire or abdicate."

"Are you considering such a thing?" Fumio studied him, his lively eyes scanning his face.

"We will see what happens in Miyako. I hope above all to resolve matters without fighting. Saga Hideki has proposed a contest—my daughter is determined to be my stand-in—and she and everyone else are already convinced that the outcome will be in my favor."

"You will wager the Three Countries on one single contest? Better by far to prepare for war!"

"As we decided last year, we *will* prepare for war. It will take a month at least for me to get to the capital. In that time Kahei will assemble our armies on the Eastern border. I will abide by the contest, win or lose, but on certain conditions that I will discuss with Saga. Our forces are there only if my conditions are not met, or if they break faith with us."

"We should move the rest of the fleet from Hagi to Hofu," Fumio said. "Thus we control the Western part of the sea, and can strike at Kumamoto if necessary."

"Yes, our greatest danger is that Zenko will take advantage of my absence and move into open revolt. But his wife is to come to Hagi; his sons are already there. It's my opinion that he will not be so foolhardy as to risk their lives. Kaede agrees with me, and she will exert all her influence on Hana. You and your father must go with the fleet to Hofu; be prepared for attack from the sea. Taku is there, and will keep you informed of whatever happens. And you can take the foreigners with you."

"They are to return to Hofu?"

"They are to set up a trading house there. You can help them with that, and keep an eye on them. The Muto girl, Mai, will also go with them."

Takeo went on to tell his old friend his concerns about such foreigners as there might already be in Kumamoto, the mirror and what else might be entering the country through that city.

"I'll find out what I can," Fumio promised. "I've got to know Don João quite well this winter, and am coming to understand their speech. Luckily he is not a discreet man, particularly after a few flasks of wine.

"Speaking of wine," he added. "Let's drink a few cups ourselves. My father wants to see you, of course."

FOR A FEW hours Takeo put aside all his anxieties and enjoyed the wine, the food Eriko prepared, fresh fish and spring vegetables, the company of his friend and of the old pirate Fumifusa, and the beautiful garden.

He returned to the house by the river, still in this calm and cheerful frame of mind, and his spirits were further lifted when he heard Shizuka's voice as soon as he walked into the garden.

"You did not bring Miki with you?" he asked when he had joined her in the upper room. Haruka served them tea and then left them alone.

"I was in two minds about it," Shizuka replied. "She wanted very much to see you again. She misses you, and her sister. But she is at the age where she is learning rapidly. It seemed unwise not to take advantage of that. And since you will be away all summer, and Kaede will be busy with the new baby . . . Anyway, it's good for her to learn obedience."

"I had hoped to see her before I left," Takeo replied. "Is she well?"

Shizuka smiled. "Flourishing. She reminds me of Yuki at that age. Full of confidence. She has blossomed in Maya's absence, as a matter of fact— it's been good for her to emerge from her sister's shadow."

The mention of Yuki's name sent Takeo into something of a reverie. Noticing it, Shizuka said, "I heard from Taku at the end of the winter. He told me Akio has been in Kumamoto with your son."

"It's true. I don't want to speak of it openly here, but his presence in Zenko's castle town has many implications that you and I must discuss. Do the Muto elders support you?"

"I have been told of some dissent," Shizuka replied. "Not in the Middle Country, but from both East and West. I am surprised Taku has not returned to Inuyama, where he could exert some control over the Tribe in the East. I should go there myself, but I am reluctant to leave Kaede at this time, especially if you are to depart so soon."

"Taku has become obsessed with the girl we sent to look after Maya," Takeo said, feeling the same flash of anger.

"I had heard rumors of that. I'm afraid my sons must both be a great disappointment to you, after everything you have done for them."

Her voice was measured, but he saw that she was genuinely distressed.

"I trust Taku completely," he said. "But such a distraction can only make him careless. Zenko is another question, but for the moment he is in check. However, it seems he is determined to claim the leadership of the Muto family, and that is going to bring him into direct conflict with you and Taku, and of course myself."

He paused, and then said, "I have tried to placate him; I have threatened him and commanded him, but he is determined to provoke me."

Shizuka said, "He grows more like his father every year. I cannot forget that Arai ordered my death, and would have watched you kill his sons, in his quest for power. My advice, both as head of the Muto and as an old friend of the Otori, is to get rid of Zenko quickly, before he gathers any more support. I will arrange it myself. You only have to order it."

Her eyes were bright, but she shed no tears.

"The first day we met, Kenji said I should learn ruthlessness from you," Takeo replied, amazed that she should advise him so coolly to kill her elder son.

"But neither Kenji nor I were truly able to instill it in you, Takeo. Zenko knows this, which is why he is not cowed by you, nor does he respect you."

Her words stung surprisingly, but he answered mildly, "I have committed myself and this country to a path of justice and peaceful negotiation. I will not let Zenko's challenge divert that."

"Then arrest him and try him for plotting against you. Make it legal, but act swiftly." She watched him for a few moments, and when he did not reply went on, "But you will not follow my advice, Takeo; you do not need to say anything. Of course, I am grateful to you for sparing my son's life, but I fear the cost to us all will be beyond bearing."

Her words made the cold touch of premonition brush against his spine. The sun had set and the garden was transformed by the blue light of evening. Fireflies flickered above the stream, and he saw Sunaomi and Chikara come splashing through the water under the wall—they must have been playing on the riverbank. Hunger had driven them home. How could he take the life of their father? He would only set the boys against him and his family, and prolong the feud.

"I have offered to betroth Miki to Sunaomi," he remarked.

"It is a very good move." Shizuka made a visible effort to speak more lightly. "Though I don't think either of the children will be grateful to you! Don't mention it to anyone; Sunaomi will hate the idea. He was deeply upset by the episode last summer. When he is older, he will realize what an honor it is."

"It is too early to announce it formally—maybe when I return at the end of the summer."

He thought from her expression that Shizuka was going to remind him again that he might have no country to return to, but they were interrupted by a cry from the far end of the house, where the women's rooms were. Takeo heard Haruka's footsteps running the length of the veranda, making the nightingale floor sing.

In the garden the boys stood and stared after her.

"Shizuka, Dr. Ishida," Haruka was shouting. "Come quickly! Lady Otori's pains have begun."

THE CHILD, as Kaede had known all along, was a boy. The news was celebrated instantly in the city of Hagi, though with a certain restraint, for infancy was a dangerous time, and a child's hold on life tenuous and fragile. Yet the birth had been swift, and the baby was strong and healthy. There seemed every reason to be confident that Lord Otori would have a son to inherit. The curse that people whispered had been caused by the birth of twins had been lifted.

The news was received with equal rejoicing over the next few weeks throughout the Three Countries, at least in Maruyama, Inuyama, and Hofu. Possibly the joy was less than heartfelt in Kumamoto, but Zenko and Hana professed all the appropriate sentiments and sent splendid gifts, silk robes for the baby, a small sword belonging to the Arai family, and a pony. Hana made preparations for her journey to Hagi later in the summer, eager to see her own sons and to keep her sister company while Takeo was away.

When the period of Kaede's confinement was over, and the house had been purified according to custom, she brought the child to his father and placed him in his arms.

"This is what I have wanted all my life," she said. "To give you a son."

"You have already given me more than I could have ever hoped for," he replied with emotion. He was unprepared for the wave of tenderness that filled him for the tiny, red-faced, black-haired creature—and for the sense of pride. He loved his daughters, and had not thought he wanted for anything, but to hold his son filled some hitherto unrecognized need. The corners of his eyes grew hot, yet he could not stop smiling.

"You are happy!" Kaede exclaimed. "I was afraid . . . you have so often told me you did not want sons, that you were content with our daughters, I had almost come to believe you."

"I am happy," he replied. "I could die at this moment."

"I feel the same," she murmured. "But let us not talk of dying. We are going to live and watch our son grow."

"I wish I did not have to leave you." He was gripped suddenly by the idea that he might abandon the journey to Miyako. Let the Dog Catcher attack if he wanted to; the armies of the Three Countries would repel him easily, and deal with Zenko too. He was astonished at the strength of the feeling; he would fight to the death to protect the Middle Country so that this Otori child would inherit it. He examined the thought carefully, and then put it from him. He would try the ways of peace first, as he had resolved; if the trip were postponed now, he would seem both arrogant and cowardly.

"I wish it too," Kaede said. "But you must go." She took the child from him and gazed into his face, her own face suffused with love. "I will not be lonely with this little man by my side!"

akeo had to leave almost immediately in order to complete most of the journey before the onset of the plum rains. Shigeko and Hiroshi arrived from Maruyama, and Miyoshi Gemba from Terayama. Miyoshi Kahei had already left for the East as soon as the snow melted, with the main Otori army, fifteen thousand men from Hagi and Yamagata; a further ten thousand would be mustered by Sonoda Mitsuru in Inuyama. Since the previous summer, stores of rice and barley, dried fish, and soy paste had been put aside and dispatched to the Eastern borders to provide for these huge numbers of men. Luckily the harvest had been bountiful—neither the army nor those they left behind would starve.

In all the arrangements for the journey, the most taxing was how to transport the kirin. She had grown even taller, and her coat had darkened to the color of honey, but her calmness and tranquility were unchanged. Dr. Ishida was of the opinion that she should not walk the whole way, that the mountains of the High Cloud Range would be too arduous for her. In the end it was decided that Shigeko and Hiroshi would take her by ship as far as Akashi.

"We could all go by ship, Father," Shigeko suggested.

"I have never been beyond the borders of the Three Countries," Takeo replied. "I want to see the terrain and the paths through the range for myself; if typhoons come in the eighth and ninth months, that is the way we will have to return. Fumio is going to Hofu—he will take you, and the kirin, as well as the foreigners."

The cherry blossoms had all fallen and the petals had been replaced by the new green leaves when Takeo and his retinue rode out from Hagi, through the mountain passes and along the coast road to Matsue. He had made this journey many times since the day he, a mute boy on the back of a retainer's horse, had traveled in the other direction with Lord Shigeru, but it never failed to bring back memories of the man who had saved his life and adopted him.

I say I believe in nothing, he thought, *but I pray often to Shigeru's spirit; never more so than now, when I need all his wisdom and courage.* The new rice was just beginning to appear above the surface of the flooded fields, which glittered dazzlingly in the sunshine. On the bank, where two paths crossed, stood a small shrine; he saw that it was to Jo-An, who in some districts had become merged with the local deities and was now worshipped by travelers. How strange were people's beliefs, he thought with wonder, remembering his conversation with Madaren of a few weeks ago—the conviction that had compelled her to speak to him. The same conviction that had sustained Jo-An in all his efforts for Takeo's sake—and now Jo-An had become a saint to those who would have despised him in real life, and whom he considered unbelievers.

He glanced at Miyoshi Gemba, who rode alongside him, as calm and cheerful a companion as might ever be wished for. Gemba's life had been dedicated to the Way of the Houou; it had been one of hardship and self-mastery, yet it had left no physical signs of suffering. Gemba was smooth-skinned, his body well covered; as he rode he often seemed to fall into a meditative trance, and occasionally emitted a low humming noise, like distant thunder or the growl of a bear. Takeo found himself talking about Sunaomi, whom Gemba had met at Terayama, telling him of his plan to betroth the boy to his daughter.

"He will become my son-in-law. Surely that will gratify his father!"

"Unless Sunaomi himself has the feelings of a devoted son toward you, a betrothal will do nothing," Gemba replied.

Takeo was silent, recalling what had happened at the shrine, the hostility between the cousins, fearing Sunaomi had been scarred by it.

"He saw the houou," he said finally. "I believe he has good instincts."

"Yes, I thought so too. Well, send him to us. We will look after him, and if there is any good in him, it will be nurtured and developed."

"I suppose he is old enough now—he turned nine this year."

"Let him come when we return."

"He lives with me as my nephew, as my future son, yet he is a hostage to his father's loyalty. I dread the thought that I may one day have to order his death," Takeo confessed.

"It will not come to that," Gemba said.

"I will write to my wife tonight with this suggestion."

Minoru had accompanied Takeo as usual, and that night at their first stop Takeo dictated letters to Kaede, and to Taku in Hofu. He felt the need to talk to Taku, to hear firsthand news from the West, and requested him to come to Inuyama—they would meet there. For Taku it would be an easy journey by ship from Hofu and then along the river in one of the flat-bottomed barges that plied between the castle town and the coast.

"You may come alone," he dictated. *"Leave your charge and her companion in Hofu. If it is impossible for you to get away, write to me."*

"Is that wise?" Minoru inquired. "Letters can be intercepted, especially . . ."

"Especially what?"

"If the Muto family are no longer sure where their loyalties lie?"

For Takeo relied on the networks of the Tribe to carry correspondence at speed between the cities of the Three Countries, young men of great stamina relaying letters from town to town. It was something else that he had always depended on Taku to control.

He stared now at Minoru, doubt beginning to creep through him. His scribe knew more of the secrets of the Three Countries than anyone.

"If the Muto family choose Zenko, which way will Taku go?" he said quietly.

Minoru raised his shoulders very slightly, but his lips were pressed firmly together and he did not reply directly. "Shall I write your last sentence?" he asked.

"Insist that Taku come in person."

This conversation remained in the back of Takeo's mind as they continued their journey toward the East. *I have outwitted the Kikuta for so long,* he thought. *Can I really escape the Muto too, if they turn against me?*

He began even to suspect the loyalty of the Kuroda brothers, Jun and Shin, who accompanied him as usual. He had trusted them completely till now—though they could not use invisibility, they could perceive it, and they had been trained in the fighting techniques of the Tribe by Kenji himself. Their vigilance had protected him many times in the past, but if they had to choose between himself and the Tribe, he asked himself again, which way would they go?

He remained constantly alert, always listening for the slightest sound that heralded an attack. The horse, Tenba, caught his mood—over the months Takeo had ridden him they had formed a strong bond, almost as strong as that with Shun. Tenba was as responsive and intelligent, but more highly strung. Both man and horse arrived in Inuyama tense and tired, with the hardest part of the journey still to come.

Inuyama was filled with excitement and activity; the arrival of Lord Otori and the mustering of the army meant merchants and armorers were kept busy day and night; money and wine flowed equally. Takeo was welcomed by his sister-in-law, Ai, and her husband, Sonoda Mitsuru.

Takeo was fond of Ai, admiring her gentleness and the kindness of her nature. She did not have the almost supernatural beauty of her sisters, but her appearance was attractive. It had always pleased him that she and Mitsuru had been able to marry, for they genuinely loved each other. Ai had often told the story of how the guards at Inuyama had come to put her and Hana to death when they heard of Arai's death and the destruction of his army, but Mitsuru had taken command of the castle, hidden the girls away in safety, and negotiated the surrender of the East to the Otori. In his gratitude, Takeo had arranged the marriage with Ai, which it was obvious both sides desired.

Takeo had trusted him for years—they were bound by close ties of marriage, and Mitsuru had grown into a pragmatic, sensible man who, while not lacking in personal bravery, disliked the senseless destruction of warfare. Many times he had brought his skills at negotiating into Takeo's service—together with his wife, he shared Takeo's vision of a prosperous country as well as his refusal to tolerate either torture or bribery.

But Takeo's tiredness made him suspicious of everyone around him. *Sonoda is from the Arai clan,* he reminded himself. *His uncle, Akita, was Arai's second-in-command. What vestiges of loyalty does he still harbor toward Arai's son?*

He was made more uneasy by the fact that there was no sign of Taku, nor any word from him. He sent for Taku's wife, Tomiko; she had had letters from him in the spring, but nothing recently. She did not seem worried, however; she was used to her husband's long, unexplained absences.

"If there was anything wrong, Lord Otori, we would hear of it soon enough. Affairs must be keeping him in Hofu—probably something he does not want to commit to paper."

She glanced at Takeo and said, "I've heard about the woman, of course, but I expect that sort of thing. All men have their needs, and he is away for a long time. It isn't anything serious. It never is with my husband."

His unease increased, if anything, and was compounded when he asked after the execution of the hostages, only to be told that they were still alive.

"But I wrote weeks ago, ordering it to be done immediately."

"I am very sorry, Lord Otori; we did not receive—" Sonoda began, but Takeo cut him off.

"Did not receive, or chose to ignore?" He realized he spoke more bluntly than he should. Sonoda struggled to hide his own offended reaction.

"I can assure you," he said, "if we had received the order, we would have acted on it. I had been wondering why it had been delayed for so long. I would have had it done myself, but my wife has been in favor of mercy."

"They seem so young," Ai said. "And the girl . . ."

"I had hoped to spare their lives," Takeo replied. "If their family was prepared to negotiate with us, they would not have to die. But they have made no gesture, sent no word. To delay any longer must seem like weakness."

"I will arrange for it tomorrow," Sonoda assured him.

"Yes, it must be so," Ai agreed. "Will you attend?"

"Since I am here, I must," Takeo replied, for he himself had made the ruling that executions for treason had to be witnessed by someone of the highest rank, himself or one of his family or senior retainers. He felt it emphasized the legal distinction between execution and assassination, and since he found such scenes sickening, he hoped witnessing them would keep him from ordering them indiscriminately.

It was done the next day, with the sword. When they were brought into his presence, before their eyes were blindfolded he told them their father, Gosaburo, was dead, executed by the Kikuta, presumably because he had wanted to negotiate for their lives. Neither of them made any response; probably they did not believe him. There was a sudden glint of tears in the girl's eyes; otherwise both young people faced death bravely, even defiantly. He admired their courage and regretted their wasted lives, reflecting with sorrow that they were related to him by blood—both, he could not help noticing, bore the straight line of the Kikuta on their palms—and that he had known them when they were children.

The decision had been made jointly with Kaede, and on the advice of his senior retainers. It was in accordance with the law. Yet he wished it could have been otherwise, and the deaths seemed indeed like a bad omen.

· 34 ·

hroughout the winter, Hana and Zenko met often with Kuroda Yasu to discuss the further opening up of trade with the foreigners, and they were pleased when Yasu reported the return of Don João and Don Carlo to Hofu at the end of the fourth month. They were less pleased with the news that Terada Fumio had brought the Otori fleet into the inland sea and now controlled the waterways.

"The foreigners' ships, they boast, are far better than ours," Yasu said. "If we could only call on them!"

"If they had some inducement to side with us against Takeo . . ." Hana said, thinking out loud.

"They want trade, and they seek conversions to their religion. Offer them either—or both. They will give you anything you want in return."

This comment stayed in Hana's mind as she made preparations for her own journey to Hagi. When she thought of confronting her sister with her secret, she felt both excitement and trepidation, a kind of destructive glee. But she did not underestimate Takeo, as her husband was inclined to. She recognized the strength and attraction of his character that had always won him the love of the people and loyal supporters in all walks of life. It was quite possible he would win the Emperor's favor also, and return with the protection of his blessing. So she had pondered through the winter on further strategies to underpin her husband's struggle for revenge and

power, and when she heard that the foreigners had returned with their interpreter she determined to go to Hagi by way of Hofu.

"You should come with us," she said to Akio, for he also had been a
frequent visitor to the castle during the winter, reporting on news from the
rest of the country, and on the progress Hisao and Koji were making in
forging. Hana's blood always quickened in his presence. She found his
pragmatic ruthlessness attractive.

He looked at her now in his usual calculating way. "Yes, I don't mind.
I'll bring Hisao, of course."

For once, they were alone together. It was still cold—it had been a late
and fickle spring—but the air held the scent of blossom and new growth
and the evenings were lighter. Akio had come to see Zenko, who had taken
out men and horses on some training exercise. He had seemed reluctant
to stay, but Hana had pressed him, offering him wine and food, serving
him herself, cajoling and flattering him, making it impossible for him to
refuse.

She had thought him impervious to flattery, but she could see that her
attentions pleased and in some way softened him. She wondered what it
would be like to sleep with him; though she did not think she ever would,
the idea excited her. She was wearing an ivory-colored silk robe, decorated
with pink and red cherry blossoms and cranes: it was the sort of flamboyant pattern that she loved. Really it was too cold for such a garment, and
her skin felt icy, but it was already the fourth month, and the idea that she
was heralding spring pleased her—she was still young, her blood rising
with the same impulse that pushed the shoots from the earth, the bud
from the twig. Full of confidence in her own beauty, she dared to question
him, as she had longed to all winter, about the boy who passed as his son.

"He does not resemble his father in the least," she remarked. "Is he like
his mother?"

When Akio did not reply immediately, she pressed him. "You should
tell me everything. The more I can disclose to my sister, the stronger the
effect will be on her."

"It's all a long time ago," he said.

"Yet do not pretend you have forgotten it! I know how jealousy carves its story with a knife in our hearts."

"His mother was an unusual woman," he began slowly. "When it was suggested that she sleep with Takeo—it was when the Tribe first got their hands on him and no one trusted him; none of us thought he would stay—I was almost afraid of telling her. To ask Yuki to do such a thing— it was common enough in the Tribe, and most women did what they were told, but it seemed like an insult to Yuki. When she agreed, I realized at once that she wanted him. I had to watch her seduce him—not once but many times. I had not realized I would feel such pain, or such hatred for him. I had never really hated anyone before; I killed because it was expedient, not out of personal emotion. He had what I most wanted, and he threw it away. He left the Tribe. If he ever feels the smallest part of what I felt, it will be only justice."

He glanced up at Hana. "I never slept with her," he said. "I regret that more than anything. If I had been able to, just once. . . . But I would not touch her while she was carrying his child. And then I made her kill herself. I had to—she never stopped loving him; she would never have brought the boy up to hate him in the way I have. I knew he must be part of my revenge, but as he grew, showing no sign of any talents, I could not see how. For a long time I thought it was hopeless—time and again, far more skillful assassins than Hisao failed. Now I know Hisao will be the one. And I will be there to witness it." He stopped abruptly.

The words had poured from him. *He has kept this bottled inside him for all these years,* Hana thought, chilled by all he said, yet flattered and excited that he confided in her.

"When Takeo returns from the East, Kaede will have been informed of all this," she said. "It will drive them apart. She will never forgive him. I know him—he will flee from her and from the world; he will seek refuge in Terayama. The temple is barely guarded. No one will be expecting you. You can surprise him there."

Akio's eyes were half closed. His breath came in a deep sigh. "It is the only thing that will assuage my pain."

Hana was seized by the desire to draw him to her, to ease some of the pain. She was sure she could console him for the death—she hesitated to name it murder—of his wife. Yet she prudently decided to save this pleasure for the future. She had something else that she wanted to discuss with Akio.

"Hisao has succeeded in forging a weapon small enough to be carried concealed?" she said. "No one will get close enough to Takeo to kill him with the sword, but the firearm can be used from some distance, isn't that right?"

Akio nodded and spoke more calmly, as if relieved to change subjects. "He has tried it out on the seashore. It has a longer range than a bow, and the bullet is much faster than an arrow." He paused for a moment. "Your husband is particularly interested in the use of this weapon, because of the way his father died. He wants Takeo to die as shamefully."

"It has a certain justice about it," Hana agreed. "Quite pleasing. But to be completely certain of success, surely you will give Hisao some rehearsal? I would suggest a trial run to assure everything works, that he does not lose his nerve, that his aim is true under stress."

"Does Lady Arai have anyone in mind?" Akio looked directly at her, and as their eyes met her heart jumped with excitement.

"As a matter of fact, I do," she said quietly. "Come a little closer and I will whisper his name."

"There's no need," he replied. "I can guess."

But he moved closer anyway, so close she could smell his breath and hear his heartbeat. Neither of them spoke or moved. The wind rattled the screens, and from the port came the cries of gulls.

After a few moments she heard Zenko's voice from the courtyard.

"My husband is back," she said, rising to her feet, not sure if she was relieved or disappointed.

LORD AND LADY Arai moved frequently between Kumamoto and Hofu; their arrival in the port city shortly after the foreigners' return was therefore no cause for surprise. The ship the foreigners came in had left almost at once for Akashi with Lady Maruyama Shigeko, Sugita Hiroshi, and the fabled kirin, which was farewelled with pride and sorrow by the people of Hofu, who had taken a proprietorial interest in it ever since its first astonishing arrival in their port. Terada Fumio set sail shortly after, to join his father, Fumifusa, off the cape, along with the Otori fleet.

The foreigners had often been guests at Lord Arai's residence; the fact that they were invited again immediately seemed unremarkable. Conversation flowed more easily, for the interpreter had grown bolder and more confident, and Don Carlo had become quite fluent.

"You must think us very foolish," he said, "for we did not know of the Emperor. Now we realize we should have approached him, for we are the representatives of our king, and monarchs should deal with monarchs."

Hana smiled. "Lord Kono, who has recently returned to the capital himself, and whom you have met here, I believe, is related to the imperial family, and assures us Lord Arai enjoys the Emperor's favor. Unfortunately, Lord Otori's assumption of the leadership of the Three Countries could be considered unlawful, which is why he has gone to plead his case."

Don João in particular looked interested when this was translated. "Then perhaps Lord Arai can help us approach His Imperial Majesty?"

"It will be my great pleasure," Zenko replied, flushed with anticipation as much as with wine.

The woman, their interpreter, translated this, and then said several more sentences. Don Carlo smiled somewhat sorrowfully, Hana thought, and nodded his head two or three times.

"What did you say?" she questioned Madaren directly.

"Forgive me, Lady Arai. I spoke of a religious matter to Don Carlo."

"Tell us more. My husband and I are interested in the ways of the foreigners, and open to their beliefs."

"Unlike Lord Otori, alas," Don Carlo said. "I had thought he would be sympathetic, and I held great hopes for the salvation of his beautiful wife, but he has forbidden us to preach openly or to build a church."

"We would be interested in hearing about these things," Hana said po-

litely. "And in return would like to know how many ships your king now has
in the Southern Isles, and how long it would take to sail here from there."

"You have some new scheme." Zenko said that night when they were alone.

"I know a little about the foreigners' beliefs. The reason why the Hidden have always been hated is because they obey the Secret God rather
than any worldly authority. The foreigners' Deus is the same, demanding
total allegiance."

"I have sworn that allegiance many times to Takeo," Zenko said. "I do
not like the idea of being known as an oath-breaker, like Noguchi; to tell
you the truth, it is the only thing that still restrains me."

"Takeo has rejected Deus—it is clear from what we heard tonight.
What if Deus was to choose you to punish him?"

Zenko laughed. "If Deus brings me ships and arms as well, I'm prepared to make a deal with him!"

"If both the Emperor and Deus order us to destroy Takeo, who are we
to question or to disobey?" Hana said. "We have the legitimacy; we have
the instrument." Their eyes met, and they were both seized again by the
same uncontrollable mirth.

"I HAVE ONE more scheme," Hana said later, when the town was quiet,
and she lay in her husband's arms, drowsy and sated.

He was almost asleep. "You are a treasure house of good ideas," he
replied, caressing her lazily.

"Thank you, my lord! But don't you want to hear it?"

"Can't it wait till morning?"

"Some things are better spoken of in the dark."

He yawned and turned his head toward her. "Whisper your scheme in
my ear and I will consider it while I dream."

When she had told him, he lay for a long time so silent he might have
been sleeping, yet she knew he was wide awake. Finally he said, "I will give
him one more chance. He is, after all, my brother."

espite Sada's best efforts, and Ishida's sticky salve, the wound on Maya's face left a scar as it healed, a faint mauvish outline on the cheekbone, like the shadow of a perilla leaf. She was punished in various ways for her disobedience, made to perform the lowliest tasks in the household, forbidden to speak, deprived of sleep and food, and she bore all this without rancor, fully aware that she deserved it for attacking and wounding her father. She did not see Taku for a week, and though Sada cared for the wound, she did not speak to her or give her the hugs and caresses that Maya longed for. Alone for much of the time, shunned by everyone, she had many opportunities to reflect on what had happened. She kept returning to the fact that when she had realized her assailant was her father, the tears had burst from her eyes. Yet usually she never cried— the only other time she could remember had been in the hot spring, with Takeo and Miki, when she had told him about putting the cat to sleep with the Kikuta gaze.

It is only in Father's presence that I shed tears, she thought.

Perhaps the tears had been partly of rage. She remembered her anger at him, for the son he had never mentioned, for all the other secrets he might have kept from her, for all the deceptions between parents and children.

But she also remembered that her gaze had dominated his, that she had heard his light tread and perceived him when he was invisible. She saw how the cat's power added to and enhanced her own. The power still frightened her, but every day, as the lack of sleep, food, and speech honed her, its attraction grew, and she began to glimpse how she would control it.

At the end of the week, Taku sent for her and told her that they would be leaving the next day for Hofu.

"Your sister, Lady Shigeko, is bringing horses," he said. "She wants to say good-bye to you."

When Maya simply bowed without answering, he said, "You may speak now—the punishment is over."

"Thank you, Lord Taku," she replied submissively, and then, "I'm really sorry."

"It's the sort of thing we've all done; somehow children survive these episodes. I'm sure I've told you of the time your father caught me in Shuho."

Maya smiled. It was a story she and her sisters had loved to hear when they were younger. "Shizuka often told us, to remind us to be obedient!"

"It seems to have had the opposite effect! We were both lucky it was your father we were dealing with. Don't forget, most adults from the Tribe will kill without thinking twice, child or not."

Shigeko brought two elderly Maruyama mares, sisters, for Maya and Sada, one bay, one, to Maya's delight, pale gray with black mane and tail, very similar to Taku's old horse, Ryume, Raku's son.

"Yes, the gray can be yours," Shigeko said, noticing the light in Maya's eyes. "You must take good care of her during the winter." She looked at Maya's face: "I will be able to tell you and Miki apart now." Drawing Maya aside, she said quietly, "Father told me what happened. I know it is hard for you. Do exactly what Taku and Sada tell you. Keep your eyes and ears open when you get to Hofu. I am sure you will be useful to us there." The sisters embraced; after they parted, Maya felt strengthened by Shigeko's trust in her. It was one of the things that sustained her during the long winter in Hofu, when the cold wind blew constantly from the sea, bringing no proper snow but sleet and icy rain. The cat's fur was warm, and she was often tempted to use it, at first still warily, then with increasing confidence as she learned to make the cat spirit submit to her will. There were still many elements of the spaces between the worlds that terrified her— the hungry ghosts with their insatiable cravings and her awareness of a kind of intelligence that sought her, only half-knowing it. It was like a light shining in the darkness. Sometimes she glanced toward it and felt its appeal, but mostly she shunned its gleam, remaining in the shadows. Occasionally she would catch fragments of words, whispers that she could not quite make out.

Something else that occupied her thoughts throughout the winter was the matter that had made her so angry with her father—the mysterious boy who was her half-brother, of whom no one ever spoke, who Taku had said would kill him—her father! When she thought about this boy, her emotions became confused and uncontrollable; the cat spirit threatened to take over her will and do what it desired—run toward the light, listen to the voice, recognize it and obey it.

She often woke screaming from nightmares, alone in the room, for Sada spent every night now with Taku. Maya would lie awake till daybreak, afraid to close her eyes, shivering with cold, longing to feel the cat's warmth and dreading it.

Sada had arranged for them to live in one of the Muto houses between the river and Zenko's mansion. It had formerly been a brewery, but the increase in customers as Hofu became more prosperous had made it necessary for the family to move to larger premises, and this building was used now only for storage.

As in Maruyama, the Muto family provided guards and servants, and Maya continued to dress like a boy outside the house but was treated like a girl within. She recalled Shigeko's instructions and kept her ears open, listened to the whispered conversations around her, wandered through the port when the weather was good enough, and told Taku and Sada most of what she heard. But she did not tell them everything—some of the rumors shocked and angered her and she did not want to repeat them. Nor did she dare question Taku about the boy who was her brother.

Maya saw Shigeko again briefly in the spring, when her sister sailed with the kirin and Hiroshi on their journey to Miyako. She had become closely acquainted with all the details of Taku's passion for Sada, and she studied her sister and Hiroshi to see if they also showed the same symptoms. It seemed a lifetime ago when she and Miki had teased Shigeko about Hiroshi—had it only been a young girl's crush, or did her sister still love the young man who was now her senior retainer? And did he love her? Like Takeo, Maya had noticed Hiroshi's swift reaction when Tenba had shied during the ceremony at Maruyama, and had drawn the same conclusions. Now she was not so sure—on the one hand, Shigeko and Hiroshi seemed both distant and formal with each other; on the other, they seemed to know each other's thoughts, and a kind of harmony existed between them. Shigeko had assumed a new authority, and Maya no longer dared tease her or even question her.

In the fourth month, after Shigeko and Hiroshi had left with the kirin for Akashi, Taku became preoccupied with the demands of the foreigners, who had returned from Hagi and were eager to establish a permanent trading post as soon as possible. It was around this time that Maya became fully conscious of changes that had been happening slowly since the first days of spring. They seemed to confirm the disturbing rumors she had started hearing in the winter.

Since childhood she had lived in the belief that the Muto family were unswervably loyal to the Otori, and that the Muto controlled the loyalty of the Tribe—apart from the Kikuta, who hated her father and sought his death. Shizuka, Kenji, and Taku were all Muto and had been her closest advisers and teachers all her life. So she was slow to understand and accept the signs in front of her eyes.

Fewer messengers came to the house; information was delivered so late as to be useless. The guards sniggered behind Taku's back about his obsession with Sada, a man-woman who had weakened and deranged him. Maya found herself burdened with more of the household work as the maids became lazy, even insolent. As she grew more suspicious, she followed them to the inn and heard the tales they told there—that Taku and Sada were sorcerers, and that they used a cat ghost in their spells.

It was in the inn that she heard other conversations among the Muto, Kuroda, and Imai—after fifteen years of peace, during which time ordinary merchants and peasants had enjoyed an unprecedented increase in prosperity, influence and power, the Tribe were regretting the old days, when they had controlled trade, money-lending, and commodities, and when warlords had competed for their skills.

The uncertain allegiances that Kenji had held together by the force of his character, his experience, and his guile were beginning to fall apart, and to re-form now that Kikuta Akio had emerged from the long years of isolation.

Maya heard his name several times in the early days of the fourth month, and each time her interest and curiosity grew. One night, a little before the full moon, she stole away to the inn on the riverbank; the town was even livelier than usual, for Zenko and Hana had returned with all their retinue, and the inn was crowded and the atmosphere rowdy.

Maya liked to conceal herself under the veranda, using invisibility to slip beneath it; tonight it was too noisy to hear much even with her sharp ears, but she caught the words Kikuta Master, and realized Akio himself was within.

She was astonished that he would dare appear openly in Hofu, and even more amazed that so many people whom she knew to be from the Tribe not only tolerated his presence but were seeking him out, making themselves known to him. She realized that he was here under Zenko's protection, and even heard Zenko referred to as the Muto Master. She recognized it as treachery, though she did not yet know its full extent. She had used her Tribe skills undetected all winter, and had become arrogant about them. She felt inside her upper garment for her knife, and without any clear idea of what she intended to do with it, took on invisibility and went to the door of the inn.

All the doors were wide open, catching the breeze from the southwest. Lamps burned smokily, and the air was full of rich smells: grilled fish and rice wine, sesame oil and ginger.

Maya scanned the different groups; she knew immediately who Akio was, because he saw her, penetrating her invisibility in an instant. She realized in that moment how truly dangerous he was, how weak she was in comparison, how he would kill her without hesitation. He leaped up from the floor and seemed to fly toward her, releasing the weapons as he moved. She saw the glint of the knives, heard them whistle through the air, and without thinking dropped to the ground. Everything changed around her—she saw with the cat's vision; she felt the texture of the floor beneath her pads; her claws scrabbled on the boards of the veranda as she fled back into the night.

Behind her she was aware of the boy, of Hisao. She felt his gaze seeking her, and heard the fragments of his voice forming into the words she had dreaded understanding. *Come to me. I have been waiting for you.*

And the cat wanted only to return to him.

MAYA FLED TO the only protection she knew, to Sada and Taku, rousing them from deep sleep. They tried to calm her as she struggled to regain her true form, Sada calling her name while Taku stared into her eyes, seeking to bring her back, fighting her powerful gaze. Finally her limbs went limp; she seemed to sleep for a few moments. When her eyes opened, she was rational again, and wanted to tell them everything.

Taku listened in silence as she related what she had heard, noting that despite her distress her eyes were dry, admiring her self-control.

"So something is linking Hisao and the cat?" he asked finally.

"It is he who is calling the cat," she said in a low voice. "He is its master."

"Its master? Where did you get that word from?"

"It's what the ghosts say, if I let them."

He shook his head in something like wonder. "Do you know who Hisao is?"

"He is Muto Kenji's grandson." She paused and then said without emotion, "My father's son."

"How long have you known this?" Taku asked.

"I heard you tell Sada, in Maruyama last autumn," Maya replied.

"The first time we saw the cat," Sada whispered.

"Hisao must be a ghost master," Taku said, hearing Sada's slight intake of breath, sensing the hairs bristle at the back of his neck. "I thought such things existed only in legends."

"What does that mean?" Maya said.

"It means he has the ability to walk between the worlds, to hear the voices of the dead. The dead will obey him. He has the power to placate them or incite them. It is far worse than we imagined."

Indeed, he felt for the first time real fear for Takeo, a primitive dread of the supernatural, as well as deep unease at the treachery Maya's account had revealed, and anger at his own complacence and lack of vigilance.

"What should we do?" Sada asked quietly. Her arms were around Maya; she held her close. Maya's bright tearless eyes were fixed on Taku's face.

"We must take Maya away," he replied. "But first I will go to my brother, make one last demand of him, and find out how deep his involvement with Akio is, and how much they know about Hisao. My guess is they have not discovered his gift. No one knows about these things in the Tribe anymore—all our reports have indicated that Hisao is believed to have no Tribe skills."

Did Kenji know? he found himself thinking, realizing yet again how much he missed the old Master, and in a rare moment of self-judgment how deeply he had failed to replace him.

"We will go to Inuyama," he said. "I will try to see Zenko tomorrow, but we must go anyway. We must get Maya away."

"We have heard nothing from Lord Takeo since Terada came from Hagi," Sada said uneasily.

"It had not worried me before, but now it concerns me," Taku replied, gripped by the sensation that everything was beginning to unravel.

LATER THAT NIGHT, though he would hardly admit it to himself, let alone speak of it to Sada or to anyone else, the conviction grew in him that

Takeo was doomed, that the net was tightening around him and there
would be no escape. As he lay awake, conscious of Sada's long body beside
him, hearing her steady breathing, watching the night pale, he pondered
what he should do. It made sense to obey his older brother, who would
take over the leadership of the Tribe—or even hand it on to Taku himself.
The Muto and Kikuta would be reconciled; he would not have to give up
Sada or his own life. All the pragmatic instincts of the Muto urged him to
follow this path. He tried to weigh in his head the probable costs. Takeo's
life, certainly. Kaede's, possibly the children's—maybe not Shigeko, unless
she took up arms, but Zenko would consider the twins too dangerous. If
Takeo fought it out, a few thousand Otori warriors, which did not concern
him unduly. Hiroshi . . .

It was the thought of Hiroshi that brought him up short. As a boy he
had always had a secret envy of Hiroshi, for his straightforward warrior
nature, his physical courage, his unshakeable sense of honor and loyalty.
Taku had teased him and competed with him, always trying to impress
him; had loved him more than any other human being until he had met
Sada. He knew Hiroshi would take his own life rather than abandon Takeo
and serve Zenko, and he could not bear the thought of Hiroshi's look
when he realized Taku had defected to Zenko's side.

What a fool my brother is, he thought, not for the first time, resenting
Zenko all the more for placing him in this intolerable position. He drew
Sada closer to him. *I never imagined I would fall in love,* he thought as he woke
her gently and, though he did not know it, for the last time. *I never imagined
I would play the noble warrior.*

TAKU SENT MESSAGES the next morning, and received an answer before midday. He was addressed with all the usual courtesies, and invited to
the Hofu residence to eat the evening meal with Zenko and Hana. He
spent the next few hours preparing for the journey, yet not openly, for he
did not want to draw attention to his departure. He rode to the residence

with four of the men who had accompanied him from Inuyama, feeling he could trust them more than those supplied by the Muto in Hofu.

As soon as he met his brother, Taku noticed a change in him. Zenko had grown his mustache and beard, but above that he showed a new confidence, a greater swagger. He noticed, too, though he did not remark on it immediately, that Zenko wore elaborate prayer beads round his neck, carved from ivory, similar to those worn by Don João and Don Carlo, who were also present at dinner. Before the meal, Don Carlo was asked to say a blessing, during which Zenko and Hana sat with folded hands, bowed heads, and expressions of great piety.

Taku noticed the new warmth between the foreigners and Zenko, the mutual flattery and attention, heard how often the name of Deus was introduced into the conversation, and realized with a mixture of astonishment and distaste that his brother had been converted to the foreigners' religion.

Been converted or pretended to? Taku could not believe that Zenko was sincere. He had always known him as a man with no religious beliefs and no spiritual interest—in this respect like himself. *He has seen some advantage to himself: It must be military,* he thought, and anger began to rise in him as he thought of all that the foreigners might bestow in the way of firearms and ships.

Zenko noticed his growing discomfort, and, when the meal was over, said, "There are matters I must discuss with my brother. Please excuse us for a little while. Taku, come into the garden. It is a beautiful night—the moon is nearly full."

Taku followed him, every sense alert, tuning his hearing for the unfamiliar tread, the unexpected breath. Were the assassins already concealed in the garden, and his brother leading him within easy reach of their knives? Or their guns? And his flesh recoiled at the thought of the weapon that brought death from afar, that not even all his Tribe skills could detect.

Zenko said, as if reading his thoughts, "There is no reason for us to be enemies. Let us not try to kill each other."

"I believe you are carrying out some intrigue against Lord Otori," Taku replied, masking his anger. "I cannot imagine for what reason, since you have sworn allegiance to him and owe him your life, and since these actions imperil your own family—my mother, myself—even your sons. Why is Kikuta Akio in Hofu under your protection, and what evil pact have you made with these people?" He gestured toward the residence where the conversation could be heard—like shrikes squawking, he thought sourly.

"There is no evil in it," Zenko replied, ignoring the question about Akio. "I have seen the truth of their beliefs and have chosen to follow them. That freedom is allowed throughout the Three Countries, I believe."

Taku saw his white teeth in his beard as he smiled. He wanted to strike out, but controlled himself.

"And in return?"

"I'm surprised that you don't know already, but I'm sure you can guess." Zenko looked at him, then stepped closer, taking him by the arm. "Taku, we are brothers, and I care for you, despite what you think. Let us speak very frankly. Takeo has no future—why go down with him? Join me; the Tribe will be united again. I told you I was in contact with the Kikuta. It's no secret I've found Akio very reasonable, a pleasure to deal with. He will overlook your role in Kotaro's death—everyone knows you were only a child. I will give you whatever you want. Takeo caused our father's death. Our first duty under Heaven is to avenge that."

"Our father deserved his death," Taku replied, biting back the words, *And so do you.*

"No, Takeo is an imposter, a usurper, and a murderer. Our father was none of those things—he was a true warrior."

"You look at Takeo as if at a mirror," Taku said. "You see your own reflection. It is you who are the usurper."

His fingers twitched, longing to reach for his sword, and his body tingled as he prepared to go invisible. He was sure Zenko would try to have him killed now. He was tempted, so strongly he was not sure he could resist, to strike the first blow, but something restrained him: a reluctance, deeper than he had realized, to take his brother's life, and a memory of Takeo's words: *That brother should kill brother is unthinkable. Your brother, like everyone else, including yourself, my dear Taku, must be contained by law.*

He breathed out deeply. "Tell me what you want from Lord Otori. Let us negotiate together."

"There is nothing that can be negotiated except by his overthrow and death," Zenko replied, displaying his rage. "In this you are either with me or against me."

Taku retreated a little into caution. "Let me consider it. I will talk to you again tomorrow. And you, too—reflect on your actions. Does your desire for vengeance warrant unleashing civil war?"

"Very well," Zenko said. "Oh, before you go—I forgot to give you these." He drew a bamboo container from inside his robe and held it out. Taku took it with foreboding—he recognized it as a letter carrier, used across the Three Countries. The ends were sealed with wax and stamped with the Otori crest, but this one had been opened.

"It is from Lord Otori, I believe," Zenko said, and laughed. "I hope it will influence your decision."

Taku walked swiftly from the garden, expecting at any moment to hear the rush through the air of arrow or knife, and left the residence without any further farewells. His own guards waited at the gate with the horses. He took Ryume's bridle and mounted swiftly.

"Lord Muto," the man beside him said quietly.

"What is it?"

"Your horse was coughing earlier, as though he could not breathe."

"It's probably the spring air. It is heavy with pollen tonight." He dismissed the man's anxieties, having far greater ones of his own.

At his own lodging place he told the men not to unsaddle the horses, but to keep them ready, and to prepare the two mares for the journey. Then he went inside to where Sada was waiting for him. She was still dressed.

"We are leaving," he told her.

"What did you discover?"

"Zenko has not only made some deal with Akio, he is also in alliance

with the foreigners. He professes to have accepted their religion, and in return they are arming him." He held out the letter holder to her. "He has
intercepted Takeo's correspondence. That is why we have heard nothing
from him."

Sada took the tube and drew out the letter. Her eyes raced over it. "He
asks you to go at once to Inuyama—but this will already be weeks late.
Surely he will have left by now?"

"We must still go there—we will leave tonight. The moon is bright
enough to ride by. If he has left Inuyama, I must follow him across the
borders. He must return and bring the armies back from the East. Wake
Maya; she will have to come with us. I can't leave her to be discovered by
Akio. In Inuyama you will both be safe."

MAYA WAS DREAMING one of the strangely colored animal dreams
in which her brother, whose face she had now glimpsed, appeared in different guises, sometimes accompanied by spirits. He was always murderous, armed with fearful weapons, and he always looked at her in a manner
she found inexplicably chilling, as though there were some complicity between them, as though he knew all her secrets. He had some kind of cat
soul like hers. This night he was whispering her name, which frightened
her, for she had not known that he knew it. She woke to find it was Sada,
speaking quietly in her ear.

"Get up, get dressed. We are leaving."

Unquestioning, she did as she was told, for the winter months had
taught her obedience.

"We are going to Inuyama to see your father," Taku said as he swung
her up onto the mare's back.

"Why are we going in the middle of the night?"

"I didn't feel like waiting till morning."

As the horses trotted down the street toward the high road, Sada said,
"Will your brother allow you to leave?"

"That is why we are going now. He may have us ambushed or pursued. Be armed, and prepared to fight. I suspect some trap."

Hofu was not a walled city, and its trade and port activities meant people came and went at all hours, following the moon and the tides; on a night like this, at the beginning of spring with the moon nearly full, there were other travelers on the road, and the small group—Taku, Sada, Maya, and the four guards—was not stopped or questioned. Shortly after dawn they halted at an inn to eat the first meal and drink hot tea.

As soon as they were alone in the small eating room, Maya said to Taku, "What has happened?"

"I'll tell you a little for your own safety. Your uncle Arai and his wife are concocting a plot against your father. We thought we could contain him, but the situation has suddenly grown more threatening. Your father should return at once."

Taku's face was lined with fatigue, and his voice more serious than she had ever heard it.

"How can my uncle and aunt behave in this fashion, when their sons live in our household?" Maya demanded, outraged. "My mother should be told at once. The boys should die!"

"You are hardly your father's child," Sada said. "Where does this fierceness come from?" But her voice was affectionate and admiring.

"Your father hopes no one will have to die," Taku told her. "That is why we must bring him back. Only he has the prestige and strength to prevent the outbreak of war."

"Anyway, Hana is to leave for Hagi this very day." Sada drew Maya close and sat with her arms round her. "She is to spend the summer with your mother and your little brother."

"That is worse! Mother should be warned. I'll go to Hagi and tell her what Hana is really like!"

"No, you will stay with us," Taku replied, placing his arm around Sada's shoulders. They sat in silence for a few moments. *Like a family*, Maya thought. *I'll never forget this: the food that tasted so good when I was so hungry, the fragrant scent of tea, the feel of the spring breeze, the light changing as huge white clouds race*

across the sky. Sada and Taku with me, so alive, so brave, the sense of the days on the road,
stretching ahead. The danger . . .

The day continued fair and fine. Around noon the breeze died down,
the clouds disappeared into the northeast, the sky was a clear, brilliant
blue. Sweat began to darken the horses' necks and flanks as they left the flat
coastal plain and began to climb toward the first pass. The forest deepened
around them; occasionally an early cicada made a tentative strumming.
Maya began to feel tired. The rhythm of the horse's gait, the warmth of
the afternoon, made her drowsy. She thought she was dreaming, and suddenly saw Hisao; she snapped awake.

"Someone is following us!"

Taku held up his hand, and they halted. All three of them heard it—
the drumming of hoofbeats, coming up the slope.

"Ride on with Maya," Taku said to Sada. "We will delay them. There
are not too many, a dozen at most. We will catch up with you."

He spoke a quick order to the men; unslinging their bows, they turned
their horses off the road and vanished among the trunks of bamboo.

"Go," he ordered Sada; reluctantly she set her horse into a canter and
Maya followed. They rode fast for a while, but as the horses began to tire,
Sada halted and looked back.

"Maya, what do you hear?"

She thought she heard the clash of steel, the whinnying of horses,
shouts, and battle cries, and another sound, cold and brutal, that echoed
through the pass, sending birds fluttering into the air, screeching in alarm.
Sada heard it too.

"They have firearms," she exclaimed. "Stay here—no, ride on, hide. I
must go back. I can't leave Taku."

"Nor can I," Maya muttered, turning the weary mare back in the direction they had come, but at that moment in the distance they saw a cloud
of dust and heard the galloping hooves, saw the horse's gray coat and black
mane.

"He's coming," Sada cried in relief.

Taku's sword was in his hand, his arm covered in blood—his own or someone else's, it was impossible to know. He shouted something when he saw them, but Maya could not make out the words, for even as he uttered them, the horse, Ryume, was falling; it was on its knees, then on its side. It happened so quickly—Ryume had dropped dead, throwing Taku onto the road.

Immediately Sada galloped toward him, the mare snorting and wild-eyed in the presence of death. Taku struggled to his feet. She pulled the mare to a halt beside him, seized his outstretched arm, and swung him up behind her.

He's all right, Maya thought with the clarity of relief. *He could not do that if he were injured.*

Taku was not badly injured, though there were many dead on the road behind him, his own men and most of the assailants. He could feel one cut smarting on his face, another on his sword arm. He was aware of the strength of Sada's back as he held her, and then the shot rang out again. He felt it hit him in the neck and tear through him; and then he was falling, and Sada fell with him, and the horse on top of them. From a great distance he heard Maya screaming. *Ride, child, ride,* he wanted to say, but there was no time. His eyes were filled with the dazzle of the blue sky above him—the light spun and dwindled. Time had come to an end. He hardly had time to think, *I am dying, I must concentrate on dying,* before the darkness silenced his thoughts forever.

Sada's mare scrabbled to her feet and trotted back to Maya's, whinnying loudly. Both mares were skittish, ready to bolt, despite their tiredness. With her Otori nature, Maya was thinking of the horses; she must not let them escape. She leaned over and caught Sada's mare's dangling reins. But then she did not know what to do next. She was trembling all over; the horses were, too, and she could not tear her eyes away from where the three bodies lay in the road. The horse, Ryume, farther from her, then Sada and Taku entwined together in death.

She rode back toward them, dismounted and knelt beside them, touching them, calling their names.

Sada's eyes fluttered—she was still alive.

The anguish in Maya's chest threatened to choke her. She had to open her mouth and scream, "Sada!" As if in response to the scream, two figures appeared suddenly in the road, just beyond Ryume. She knew she should run from them, should take on invisibility or cat form and escape into the forest. She was from the Tribe—she could outwit anyone. But she was paralyzed from shock and grief; furthermore, she did not want to live in this new heartless world that had let Taku die beneath a blue sky and bright sunshine.

She stood between the two mares, holding their reins in each hand. The men came toward her. She had barely glimpsed them the night before, in the dimly lit interior of the inn, but she knew them at once. They were both armed, Akio with sword and knife, Hisao with the firearm. They were from the Tribe—they would not spare her because she was a child. *I should at least fight,* she thought, but stupidly she did not want to let go of the mares.

The boy stared at her, holding the firearm toward her, while his companion turned the bodies over. Sada moaned slightly. Akio knelt, took his knife in his right hand, and swiftly cut her throat. He spat on Taku's peaceful face.

"Kotaro's death is nearly fully avenged," he said. "The two Muto have paid. Only the Dog left."

The boy said, "But who's this, Father?" His voice was puzzled, as though he thought he knew her.

"A horse boy?" the man said. "Bad luck for him!"

He came toward her and she tried to stare into his eyes, but he would not look at her. A terrible fear took hold of her. She must not allow him to capture her. She only wanted to die. She dropped the mares' reins and, startled, they both pranced backward. Maya drew her knife from her belt and raised her hand to plunge it into her throat.

Akio moved faster than she had ever seen a human move, even faster than the previous night, flying toward her and grasping her wrist. Her knife fell from her hand as he bent her wrist back.

"But what horse boy tries to cut his own throat?" he said mockingly. "Like a warrior's woman?"

Holding her with one iron-strong hand, he pulled at her garments and thrust his other hand between her legs. She screamed and struggled as he opened her fist. He smiled when he saw the straight line across her palm.

"So!" he exclaimed. "Now we know who was spying on us last night."

Maya thought her life was over. However, he went on, "This is Otori's daughter, one of the twins—she is marked as Kikuta. She may prove very useful to us. Therefore we will spare her for now." He addressed Maya. "You know who I am?"

She knew but would not answer.

"I am Kikuta Akio, the Master of your family. This is my son, Hisao."

She already knew him, for he looked exactly as he did in her dreams.

"It's true—I am Otori Maya," she said, addressing Hisao. "What's more, I am your sister . . ."

She wanted to tell him more, but Akio transferred his grip to her neck, felt for the spot on the artery, and held her until she lost consciousness.

· 36 ·

higeko had sailed many times between Hagi and Hofu, but she had never been farther east, along the protected coast of the Encircled Sea as far as Akashi. The weather was fine, the air brilliantly clear, the breeze from the south gentle yet strong enough to fill the ship's new sails and send them scudding through the green-blue water. In every direction small islands rose abruptly from the sea, their slopes dark green with cedars, their shores white-fringed. She saw vermilion-red shrine gates glowing in the spring sunshine, the dark cypress-roofed temples, the sudden white walls of a warrior's castle.

Unlike Maya she had never been seasick, even on the roughest voyages between Hagi and Maruyama, when the northeasterlies raced across the iron-gray sea, carving its flecked surface into cliffs and chasms. Ships and sailing delighted her, the smell of the sea, of the ship's rigging and timbers, the sounds of sail flapping, wake splashing, and wood creaking, the song of the hull as it drove through the water.

The ship's holds were filled with all manner of presents, as well as decorated saddles and stirrups for Shigeko and Hiroshi, and formal and ceremonial robes, all newly embroidered, dyed and painted by the most skilled craftsmen of Hagi and Maruyama. But the most important gifts stood on the deck itself, under a straw shelter: the horses bred at Maruyama, each fastened by two ropes to the head and a strap under the belly; and the kirin, held with cords of red silk. Shigeko spent much of the day next to the animals, proud of the horses' health and beauty, for she had raised them herself—the two dapples, one light, one dark, the bright chestnut, and the black. They all knew her and seemed to take pleasure in her company, following her with their eyes when she left to walk around the deck, and whickering to her. She had no qualms about parting with them. Such fine horses would be valued and well treated, and while they might not forget her, they would not pine for her. But she was more troubled about the kirin. The exotic creature, for all its gentleness, did not have the easygoing nature of a horse. "I am afraid it will fret when it is separated from us, and all its other companions," she said to Hiroshi on the after- noon of the third day of their voyage from Hofu. "See how it constantly turns its head back in the direction of home. It seems to be looking yearn- ingly for someone—Tenba, maybe."

"I've noticed it tries to approach you closely, whenever you are near," Hiroshi replied. "It will indeed miss you. I am surprised you can bring yourself to part with it."

"I have only myself to blame! It was my suggestion. It is a consummate gift—even the Emperor must be astonished and flattered by it. But I wish it were a carving, in ivory or some precious metal, for then it would have no feelings, and I would not worry about it being lonely."

Hiroshi looked intently at her. "It is, after all, only an animal. It may not suffer as much as you think. It will be well looked after, and well fed."

"Animals are capable of deep feelings," Shigeko retorted.

"But it will not have the same emotions that humans have when they are separated from those they love."

Shigeko's eyes met his; she gazed firmly at him for a few moments. He was the first to look away.

"And maybe the kirin will not be lonely in Miyako," he said in a low voice, "because you will be there too."

She knew what he meant, for she had been present when Lord Kono had told her father of Saga Hideki's recent loss, a loss that had left him, the most powerful warlord in the Eight Islands, free to marry.

"If the kirin is to be the consummate gift for the Emperor," he continued, "what better gift for the Emperor's general?"

She heard the bitterness in his voice, and her heart twisted. She had known for some time that Hiroshi loved her as deeply as she loved him. A rare harmony existed between them, as if they knew each other's thoughts. They were both trained in the Way of the Houou, and had attained deep levels of awareness and sensitivity. She trusted him completely. Yet there seemed no point in speaking of her feelings, or even fully recognizing them—she would marry whomever her father chose for her. Sometimes she dreamed that he had chosen Hiroshi, and woke suffused with joy and desire. She lay in the dark, caressing her own body, longing to feel his strength against it, fearing that she never would, wondering if she might not make her own choices now that she was ruler of her own domain and simply take him as her husband; knowing that she would never go against her father's wishes. She had been brought up in the strict codes of a warrior's family—she could not break them so easily.

"I hope I never have to live away from the Three Countries," she murmured. The kirin stood so close she could feel its warm breath on her cheek as it bent its long neck down to her. "I confess, I am anxious about all the challenges that await me in the capital. I wish our journey were over—yet I want it never to end."

"You showed no sign of anxiety when you spoke so confidently to Lord Kono last year," he reminded her.

"It's easy to feel confident in Maruyama, when I am surrounded by so many people who support me—you, above all."

"You will have that support in Miyako too. And Miyoshi Gemba will also be there."

"The best of my teachers—you and he."

"Shigeko," he said, using her name as he had when she was a child. "Nothing must diminish your concentration during this contest. We must all put aside our own desires in order to allow the way of peace to prevail."

"Not put them aside," she replied, "but transcend them." She paused, not daring to say more. Then suddenly she was seized by a memory: the first time she had seen the houou, both male and female birds together, when they had returned to the forests around Terayama to nest in the paulownia trees and raise their young.

"There is a bond of great strength between us," she said. "I have known you all my life—maybe even in a former life. Even if I am married to someone else, that bond must never be broken."

"It never will be, I swear it. The bow will be in your hand, but it is the spirit of the houou that will guide the arrows."

She smiled then, confident that their minds and thoughts were one.

Later, when the sun was descending toward the west, they went to the stern deck and began the ancient ritual exercises that flowed through the air like water, yet turned muscle and sinew to steel. The sun's glow tinged the sails, rendering the great heron crest of the Otori golden; the banners of Maruyama fluttered from the rigging. The ship seemed bathed in light, as though the sacred birds themselves had descended on it. The western sky was still streaked with crimson when in the east rose the full moon of the fourth month.

 few days after this full moon Takeo left Inuyama for the
East, farewelled with great enthusiasm by the towns-
people. It was the season of the spring festivals, when the
earth came alive again, sap rose in the trees and in men
and women's blood. The city was possessed by feelings of
confidence and hope. Not only was Lord Otori on his way to visit the Emperor—a semi-mythical figure for most people—but he left behind a
son—the unhappy effect of twin daughters was removed at last. The
Three Countries had never been so prosperous. The houou nested at Terayama, Lord Otori was to present the Emperor with a kirin. These signs
from Heaven confirmed what most people already saw in their plump children and fertile fields—that the evidence of a just ruler is in the health and
contentment of the people.

Yet all the cheering, the dancing, the flowers, and the banners could
not dispel Takeo's feelings of unease, though he attempted to hide them,
maintaining constantly the calm, impassive expression that was now habitual. He was most troubled by Taku's silence, and all that it might imply:
Taku's defection or his death. Either one was a disaster, and in either case,
what had become of Maya? He longed to return and find out for himself,
yet each day's journey took him farther away from any likelihood of receiving news. After much deliberation, some of which he shared with Minoru,
he had decided to leave the Kuroda brothers in Inuyama, telling them that

they would be more use to him there, and that they were to send messengers immediately if any news came from Taku.

"Jun and Shin are not happy," Minoru reported. "They asked me what they had done to lose Lord Otori's trust."

"There are no Tribe families in Miyako," Takeo replied. "Really, I have no need of them there. But you know, Minoru, that my trust in them has been eroded—not through any failing of theirs, simply that I know their first loyalty will be to the Tribe."

"I think you could have more confidence in them," Minoru said.

"Well, maybe I am saving them from a painful choice, and they will thank me one day," Takeo said lightly, but in fact he missed his two Tribe guards, feeling naked and unprotected without them.

Four days out of Inuyama they rode past Hinode, the village where he had rested with Shigeru on the morning after their flight from Iida Sadamu's soldiers and the burning village of Mino.

"My birthplace lies a day's journey from here," he remarked to Gemba. "I have not been this way in nearly eighteen years. I wonder if the village still exists. It was there that Shigeru saved my life."

Where my sister Madaren was born, he reminded himself, *where I was raised as one of the Hidden.*

"I wonder how I dare appear before the Emperor. They will all despise me for my birth."

He and Gemba rode side by side on the narrow track, and he spoke in a low voice so that no one else would hear. Gemba glanced at him and replied, "You know I have brought from Terayama all the documents that testify to your descent: that Lord Shigemori was your grandfather, and that your adoption by Shigeru was legal—and endorsed by the clan. No one can question your legitimacy."

"Yet the Emperor already has."

"You bear the Otori sword, and have been blessed with all the signs of Heaven's approval." Gemba smiled. "You probably weren't aware of the astonishment in Hagi when Shigeru brought you home—you were so like Takeshi. It seemed like a miracle—Takeshi had lived with our family for some time before he died. He was my elder brother Kahei's best friend. It was like losing a beloved brother. But our grief was nothing to Lord Shigeru's, and it was the final blow of many."

"Yes, Chiyo told me the story of his many losses. His life seemed full of grief and undeserved ill-fortune, yet he gave no sign of it. I remember something he said the night I first met Kenji: *I am not made for despair.* I often think of those words, and of his courage when we rode to Inuyama under the eye of Abe and his men."

"You must tell yourself the same thing. You are not made for despair."

Takeo said, "That is how I must appear, yet, as with so much of my life, it is a pretense."

Gemba laughed. "It's lucky your many skills include mimicry. Don't underestimate yourself. Your nature is possibly darker than Shigeru's, but it is no less powerful. Look at what you have achieved—nearly sixteen years of peace. You and your wife have brought together all the warring factions of the Three Countries; between you you hold the realm's well-being in perfect balance. Your daughter is your right hand; your wife supports you completely at home. Have confidence in them. You will impress the Emperor's court as only you can. Believe me." Gemba fell silent and after a few moments resumed his patient humming.

The words were more than comforting; they acted as some kind of release, not allaying the anxiety but enabling Takeo to dominate it, and eventually to transcend it. As the man's mind and body relaxed, so did the horse's: Tenba lowered his neck and lengthened his stride as the miles were swallowed up, day after day.

Takeo felt all his senses awaken: His hearing became as acute as when he was seventeen; the eye and hand of the artist began to reassert themselves. When he dictated letters at night to Minoru, he yearned to take the brush from him. Sometimes he did, and in the same way as he wrote, supporting the maimed right hand with the left and holding the brush between his two remaining fingers, he would sketch quickly some scene imprinted on his mind during the day's ride: a flock of crows flying among cedars, a chain of geese like foreign writing above a curiously shaped crag, a flycatcher and a bellflower against a dark rock. Minoru gathered the sketches and sent them with the letters to Kaede, and Takeo recalled the drawing of the flycatcher he had given her so many years ago at Terayama. The disability had prevented him from painting for a long time, but learning to overcome it had honed his natural talent into a unique and striking style.

The road from Inuyama to the border was well maintained and broad enough for three to ride abreast. Its surface was trodden smooth, for Miyoshi Kahei had come this way just a few weeks previously with the advance guard of the army, about one thousand men, most of them horsemen, as well as supplies on packhorses and oxcarts. The rest would move up from Inuyama over the next few weeks. The border country was mountainous. Apart from the pass through which they would travel, the peaks were inaccessible. To keep so large an army in readiness throughout the summer would demand huge resources, and many of the foot soldiers came from villages where the harvest would not be brought in without their labor in the fields.

Takeo and his retinue met up with Kahei on an upland plain just below the pass. It was still cold, the grass splashed with white in places with the last of the snow, the water in streams and pools icy. A small border post was established here, though not many travelers made the journey from the East by land, preferring to sail from Akashi. The High Cloud Range provided a natural barrier behind which the Three Countries had sheltered for years, ignored by the rest of the country, neither ruled nor protected by their nominal Emperor.

The encampment was orderly and well prepared: the horses on their lines, men well armed and trained. The plain had been transformed, with palisades erected in arrowhead formation along each flank and storehouses swiftly constructed to protect the provisions from weather and animals.

"There is enough room at the head of the plain for bowmen," Kahei said. "But we also have sufficient firearms when the foot soldiers come up from Inuyama to defend the road for miles behind us, as well as the surrounding countryside. We will set up a series of blockades. But if they fall out into the surrounding terrain, we will use horses and swords."

He added, "Do we have any idea what weapons they have?"

"They have had barely a year to acquire or forge firearms and train men to use them," Takeo replied. "We must be superior in that. We must have bowmen too—firearms are too unreliable in the rain or wind. But I hope to be able to send messages to you. I will find out all I can—except that I must at all times appear to be seeking peace; I must not give them any excuse to attack. All our preparations are in defense of the Three Countries; we do not threaten anyone beyond our borders. For this same reason we will not fortify the pass itself. You must remain on the plain in a purely defensive position. We cannot be seen to provoke Saga or challenge the Emperor."

"It will be strange actually to set eyes on the Emperor," Kahei remarked. "I envy you—we hear about him from childhood; he is descended from the gods, yet for years I for one did not believe he actually existed."

"The Otori clan is said to descend from the imperial family," Gemba said. "For when Takeyoshi was given Jato, one of the Emperor's concubines, pregnant at the time with his child, was also bestowed on him, to be his wife." He smiled at Takeo. "So you share the same blood."

"Somewhat diluted after so many years," Takeo said lightheartedly. "But maybe since he is my relative he will look on me kindly. Many years ago Shigeru told me it was the weakness of the Emperor that allowed warlords like Iida to flourish unchecked. It is my duty therefore to do all I can to strengthen his position. He is the legitimate ruler of the Eight Islands." He looked out toward the pass and the ranges beyond, which were turning deep purple in the evening light. The sky was a pale blueish white, and the first stars were appearing. "I know so little of the rest of them—how they are governed, if they prosper, if their people are content. These are all matters to find out about—and discuss."

"It is Saga Hideki with whom you will have to discuss them," Gemba said. "For he controls two-thirds of the country now, including the Emperor himself."

"But we will never allow him to control the Three Countries," Kahei declared.

Takeo did not disagree openly with Kahei, but privately, as always, he had been thinking deeply about the future of his country and how he might best secure it. He had overseen its recovery from the destruction and loss of life of the civil war and the earthquake. While he had no intention of handing it over to Zenko, he also had no desire to see it torn apart and fought over again. He did not believe the Emperor was a deity to be worshipped, but he recognized the essential place of the imperial throne as a symbol of unity, and was prepared to submit to the Emperor's will, to preserve peace and increase the unity of the whole country.

But I will not give up the Three Countries to Zenko. He returned over and again to this conviction. *I will never see him rule in my place.*

They crossed the pass as the moon waned, and, before it was full again, approached Sanda, a small town on the road between Miyako and Akashi. As they descended into the valleys, as well as surveying their return route—and where a small force of men might turn and fight a pursuer if necessary—Takeo studied the state of the villages, the systems of agriculture, the health of the children, often riding off the road into the surrounding districts. He was amazed to find that he was not unknown to the villagers—they reacted as if a hero from a legend had suddenly appeared among them. At night he heard blind singers recount tales of the Otori—Shigeru's betrayal and death, the fall of Inuyama, the battle of Asagawa, the retreat to Katte Jinja, and the capture of the city of Hagi. And new songs were made up about the kirin, for it was waiting for them at Sanda, with Lord Otori's beautiful daughter.

The land had been badly neglected—he was shocked by the half-ruined houses, the uncultivated fields. He learned on the way, by questioning the farmers, that all the local domains had been fought over savagely in the last stand against Saga before they capitulated to him two years earlier. Since then, compulsory armed service and labor had sapped the villages of manpower.

"But at least we have peace now, and we can thank Lord Saga for that," one older man told him. He wondered at what cost, and would have liked to have asked them more, but, as they approached the town, felt it was a mistake to appear too familiar, and rejoined his retinue in a more formal manner. Many of the people followed him, hoping to see the kirin with their own eyes, and by the time they reached Sanda they were accompanied by a huge crowd, made even larger by the townspeople who flocked out to meet him, waving banners and tassels, dancing and beating drums. Sanda was a town that had grown up as a marketplace and had no castle or fortifications. It showed signs of damage from the war, but most of the burned shops and dwellings had been rebuilt. There were several large lodging houses near the temple; in the main street in front of them Takeo was met by a small group of warriors, carrying banners marked with the twin mountain peaks of the Saga clan.

"Lord Otori," said their leader, a large thick-set man who reminded Takeo unpleasantly of Abe, Iida's chief henchman. "I am Okuda Tadamasa. This is my eldest son, Tadayoshi. Our great lord and Emperor's general bids you welcome. We have been sent to escort you to him." He spoke formally and courteously, but before Takeo could reply, Tenba whinnied loudly and above the tile-roofed wall of the garden of the largest inn the kirin's fan-eared, huge-eyed head on its long patterned neck appeared, causing the crowd to shout in one excited voice. The kirin's eyes and nose seemed to search for its old companion. It saw Tenba and its face softened as though it smiled; and it seemed to the crowd as if it smiled at Lord Otori.

Even Okuda could not help glancing toward it. An expression of amazement flitted briefly across his face. He clenched his muscles in an effort to control himself, his eyes popping. His son, a young man about eighteen years old, was grinning openly.

"I thank you and Lord Saga," Takeo said calmly, ignoring the excitement as if a kirin were as ordinary a creature as a cat. "I hope you will honor me by eating with my daughter and myself this evening."

"I believe Lady Maruyama is waiting inside for you," Okuda said. "It will give me the greatest pleasure."

They all dismounted. The grooms ran forward to take the horses' reins. Maids hurried to the veranda's edge with bowls of water to wash the travelers' feet. The innkeeper himself appeared, an important figure in the town's government. He was sweating with nervousness; he bowed to the ground, then leaped to his feet, organized the maids and menservants with many hissed instructions and much hand-flapping, and ushered Takeo and Gemba into the main guest room.

It was a pleasant enough room, though far from lavish. The matting was new and sweet-smelling, and the inner doors opened onto a small garden that contained some ordinary shrubs and one unusual black rock, like a miniature double-peaked mountain.

Takeo gazed on it, listening to the bustle of the inn all around him: the anxious voice of the owner, the activity in the kitchen as the evening meal was prepared, Tenba's whinny from the stables, and finally his daughter's voice, her step outside. He turned as the door slid open.

"Father! I could not wait to see you!"

"Shigeko," he said, and then with great affection, "Lady Maruyama!"

Gemba had been sitting in the shade on the inner veranda. He now rose to his feet and echoed Takeo. "Lady Maruyama!"

"Lord Miyoshi! I am so pleased to see you."

"Hmm, hmm," he said, smiling broadly and humming with pleasure. "You look well."

Indeed, Takeo thought, his daughter was not only at the peak of youthful beauty but radiated the power and confidence of a mature woman, of a ruler.

"And your charge arrived in good health, I see," Takeo said.

"I have just come back from the kirin's enclosure. She was so happy to see Tenba. It was quite touching. But are you well? You have had a more difficult journey. You are not in too much pain?"

"I am well," he replied. "In this mild weather the pain is bearable. Gemba has been the best of companions, and your horse is a marvel."

"You will have had no news from home?" Shigeko said.

"That's right, but since I have not been expecting any, the silence has not concerned me. But where is Hiroshi?" he asked.

"He is overseeing the horses and the kirin," Shigeko replied, calmly. "With Sakai Masaki, who came with us from Maruyama."

Takeo studied her face, but it revealed no emotion. After a moment he asked, "Was there any message from Taku at Akashi?"

Shigeko shook her head. "Hiroshi was expecting something, but none of the Muto people there had heard from him. Can there be something wrong?"

"I don't know; he has been silent for so long."

"I saw him and Maya briefly in Hofu before we left. Maya came to see the kirin. She seemed well, more settled, more accepting of her gifts and more able to control them."

"You see this possession as a gift?" he said, surprised.

"It will be," Gemba said, and he and Shigeko smiled at each other.

"So tell me, my Masters," Takeo said, masking with irony his slight annoyance that they should exclude him. "Should I be worrying about Taku and Maya?"

"Since you can do nothing for either of them from here," Gemba explained, "there is no point in wasting your energy on worrying about them. Bad news travels fast—you will hear it soon enough."

Takeo recognized the wisdom of this, and tried to put the matter from his mind. But in the nights that followed, as they traveled on toward the capital, he often saw his twin daughters in dreams, and in that other shadow world he was aware that they were undergoing some strange ordeal. Maya shone like gold, drawing all light from Miki, who in his dreams seemed as fine and sharpened as a dark sword. Once he saw them as the cat and its shadow—he called to them, but though their heads turned they took no notice of him but raced away along a pale road on silent feet until they were out of earshot and beyond his protection. He woke from these dreams with an aching sense of loss that his daughters were no longer children, that even his baby son would eventually grow to manhood and challenge him, that parents bring children into this world only to be supplanted by them, that the price of life is death.

Each day the night was shorter, and as the light strengthened each morning, Takeo, returning from the dream world, regathered his determination and his strength to deal with the task that faced him, to dazzle his opponents and win their favor, to retain his country and preserve the Otori clan, above all to prevent war.

he journey continued without incident. It was the best time of year to travel, the days lengthening toward the solstice, the air clear and mild. Okuda seemed deeply impressed by everything—by the kirin, by the Maruyama horses, by Shigeko, who chose to ride alongside her father. He questioned Takeo closely about the Three Countries, their trade, their administration, their ships, and Takeo's truthful answers made his eyes pop even more.

News of the kirin had gone ahead of them, and as they approached the capital, the crowds became thicker as the townspeople poured out to welcome it. They made a day's outing of it, bringing their wives and children in brightly colored clothes, spreading mats, and erecting scarlet sunshades and white tents, eating and drinking merrily. Takeo felt all this festivity as a blessing on his journey, dispelling the bad omen of the executions at Inuyama, and this impression was reinforced by Lord Kono, who sent invitations to Takeo to visit him on their first night in the capital.

The city lay in a bowl on the hills; a great lake to the north supplied it with fresh water and much fish, and two rivers flowed through it, crossed by several beautiful bridges. It was built like the ancient cities of Shin, on a rectangle with avenues running north to south, crossed by streets. The Imperial Palace was situated at the head of the main avenue, next to the great shrine.

Takeo and his retinue were lodged in a mansion not far from Kono's own residence, with stabling for the horses and a hastily constructed enclosure for the kirin. Takeo dressed with considerable care for the meeting, and rode in one of the sumptuous lacquered palanquins that had been transported by ship from Hagi to Akashi. Gifts for Kono were carried by a train of servants. The local products of the Three Countries were a testimony to prosperity and good rulership, whatever Kono had enjoyed or admired during his stay in the West—one of Taku's minor forms of espionage.

"Lord Otori has come up to the capital as the sun approaches its zenith," Kono exclaimed. "It could not be a more auspicious time. I have the highest hopes for your success."

This is the man who brought the news that my rule was illegal and the Emperor demanded my abdication and exile, Takeo reminded himself. *I must not be distracted by his flattery.* He smiled and thanked Kono, saying, "All these things are in the hands of Heaven. I will submit to the will of His Divine Majesty."

"Lord Saga is most anxious to meet you. Perhaps tomorrow is not too early? He would like to see matters settled before the rains begin."

"Certainly." Takeo could see no point in delay. Indeed he was eager to learn Saga's exact terms. The rains would no doubt keep him in the capital until the seventh month—he suddenly saw himself the loser in the contest. What would he do then? Skulk in the damp and dreary city until he could creep home and arrange his own exile? Or take his own life, leaving Shigeko alone in Saga's hands, at his mercy? Was he really about to gamble an entire country, and his life and hers, on the outcome of a contest?

He gave no sign of these misgivings, but spent the rest of the evening admiring Kono's collection of treasures and discussing painting with the nobleman.

"Some of these were my father's," Kono said, as one of his companions unwrapped the silk coverings of the precious objects. "Of course, most of his collection was lost . . . But we will not recall those unhappy times. Forgive me. I have heard that Lord Otori himself is an artist of great talent."

"No talent at all," Takeo replied. "But painting gives me great pleasure, though I have very little time for it."

Kono smiled and pursed his lips knowingly.

No doubt he is thinking I will soon have all the time in the world, Takeo reflected, and he could not help smiling, too, at the irony of his situation.

"I will be bold enough to beg you to give me one of your works. And Lord Saga would be delighted to receive one too."

"You flatter me too much," Takeo replied. "I have brought nothing with me. A few sketches done on the journey I have already sent home to my wife."

"I am sorry I cannot persuade you," Kono exclaimed with warmth. "In my experience, the less the artist displays his work, the greater the talent. It is the hidden treasure, the concealed skill, that is the most impressive and the most valued.

"Which brings me," he went on smoothly, "to your daughter—surely Lord Otori's greatest treasure. She will accompany you tomorrow?"

It seemed to be only partly a question. Takeo inclined his head slightly.

"Lord Saga is looking forward to meeting his opponent," Kono murmured.

LORD KONO CAME the next day with the Okuda, father and son, and the other warriors of Saga's household, to escort Takeo, Shigeko, and Gemba to the great lord's residence. When they dismounted from the palanquins in the garden of a large and imposing mansion, Kono murmured, "Lord Saga asks me to apologize. He is having a new castle built— he will show it to you later. In the meantime he fears you will find his dwelling place somewhat humble—not at all what you are accustomed to in Hagi."

Takeo raised his eyebrows and glanced at Kono's face, but could see no hint of irony there.

"We have had the advantage of years of peace," he replied. "Even so, I am sure nothing we have in the Three Countries can compare with the splendors of the capital. You must have the most skilled craftsmen, the most talented artists."

"It's my experience that such people seek a calm environment in which to practice their art. Many fled the capital and are only now beginning to return. Lord Saga gives many commissions. He is a passionate admirer of all the arts."

Minoru also accompanied them with scrolls of the genealogy of those present and lists of the gifts for Lord Saga. Hiroshi begged to be excused, pleading he did not want to leave the kirin unguarded, though Takeo thought there were other reasons—the young man's awareness of his lack of status and land, his reluctance to meet the man to whom Shigeko might be married.

Okuda, dressed in formal clothes rather than the armor he had worn previously, led them down a wide veranda and through many rooms, each one decorated with flamboyant paintings, brilliant colors on gold backgrounds. Takeo could not help admiring the boldness of the design and the mastery of its execution. Yet he felt all the paintings were done to demonstrate the power of the warlord: They spoke of glorification; their purpose was to dominate.

Peacocks strutted beneath massive pine trees. Two mythical lions strode across one entire wall; dragons and tigers snarled at each other; hawks gazed imperiously from their vantage point on twin-peaked crags. There was even a painting of a pair of houou feeding on bamboo leaves.

In this final room Okuda asked them to wait for a little while, while he left with Kono. Takeo had expected this—indeed he often used the same ploy himself. No one should expect too easy an access to the ruler. He composed himself and gazed at the houou. He was sure the artist had never seen a live one, but was painting from legend. He turned his thoughts to the temple at Terayama, to the sacred forest of paulownia trees where even now the houou were raising their chicks. He saw in his mind's eye Makoto, his closest friend, who had devoted his life to the Way of the Houou, to the way of peace, felt the spiritual strength of Makoto's support, embodied in his present companions, Gemba and Shigeko. All three of them sat without speaking, and he felt the energy of the room intensify, filling him with a steady confidence. He set his ears as he had once long ago in Hagi castle when made to wait in a similar way; then he had overheard the treachery of Lord Shigeru's uncles. Now he heard Kono talking quietly to a man he presumed was Saga, but they spoke only in commonplaces of insignificant matters.

Kono has been alerted to my hearing, he thought. *What else has Zenko revealed to him?*

He recalled his past, known only to the Tribe; how much did Zenko know?

After a while Okuda returned with a man whom he introduced as Lord Saga's chief steward and administrator, who would escort them to the audience room, receive the lists of presents prepared by Minoru, and oversee the scribes as they recorded the proceedings. This man bowed to the ground before Takeo and addressed him in terms of greatest courtesy.

A polished and covered boardwalk took them through a small exquisite garden to another building, even grander and more beautiful. The day was growing warmer, and the trickle of water from pools and cisterns gave an enticing sense of coolness. Takeo could hear caged birds whistling and calling somewhere in the depths of the house, and thought that they must be Lady Saga's pets, then recalled that the warlord's wife had died the previous year. He wondered if it had been a tragic loss for Saga, and felt a moment of fear for his own wife, so far away—how could he bear her death? Would he be able to live without her? Take another wife for reasons of state?

Recalling Gemba's advice, he put the thought from him, concentrating all his attention on the man he was at last to meet.

The steward fell to his knees, sliding the screens apart and touching his head to the ground. Takeo stepped into the room and prostrated himself. Gemba followed him, but Shigeko waited on the threshold. Only when the two men had received the command to sit up did she move gracefully into the room and sink to the floor beside her father.

Saga Hideki sat at the head of the room. The alcove on his right held a painting in the mainland style of Shin. It might even be the famous *Evening Bell from a Distant Temple,* which Takeo had heard of but never seen. Compared to the other rooms, this room was almost austere in its decoration, as though nothing should compete with the powerful presence of the man himself. The effect was extraordinary, Takeo thought. The ostentatious paintings were like the decorated scabbard—here the sword was exposed, needing no decoration, only its own sharp and deadly steel.

He had thought Saga might be a brutal and unreflecting warlord; now he changed his mind. Brutal he might be, but not unreflecting—a man who controlled his mind as stringently as his body. There was no doubt he was facing a formidable opponent. He bitterly regretted his own disability, his lack of skill with the bow, and then heard a very faint hum from his left, where Gemba sat in relaxed composure. And he saw suddenly that Saga would never be defeated by brute force, but by some subtlety, some shift in the balance of the life forces that the Masters of the Way of the Houou knew how to bring about.

Shigeko remained in a deep bow while the two men looked at each other. Saga must have been a few years older than Takeo, closer to forty than thirty, with the thick-set body of middle age. Yet he had a looseness about him that belied his years: He sat easily; his movements were fluid. He had the broad shoulders and huge muscles of a bowman, made broader by the flared wings of his formal robes. His voice was curt, the consonants clipped, the vowels shortened. It was the first time Takeo had heard the accent of the northeast region, Saga's birthplace. His face was broad and well-shaped, the eyes long and somewhat hooded, the ears surprisingly delicate, with almost no lobes, set very close to the head. He wore a small beard and a rather long mustache, both slightly grizzled, though his hair showed no traces of gray.

Saga's eyes searched Takeo's face no less keenly, flickered over his body, rested briefly on the black-gloved right hand. Then the warlord leaned forward and said, brusquely but amiably, "What do you think?"

"Lord Saga?"

Saga gestured toward the alcove. "The painting, of course."

"It's marvelous. It is Yu-Chien, is it not?"

"Ha! Kono advised me to hang it. He said you would know it, and that it would appeal to you more than my modern stuff. How about that one?"

He got to his feet and walked to the eastern wall. "Come and look."

Takeo rose and stood a little behind him. They were of almost equal height, though Saga was considerably heavier. The painting was a garden landscape showing bamboo, plum, and pine. It was also in black ink, understated and evocative.

"It is also very fine," Takeo said with unfeigned admiration. "A masterpiece."

"The three friends," Saga said, "flexible, fragrant, and strong. Lady Maruyama, please join us."

Shigeko stood and moved slowly to her father's side.

"All three can withstand the adversity of winter," she said in a low voice.

"Indeed," Saga said, returning to his seat. "I see such a combination here." He indicated that they should move closer to him. "Lady Maruyama is the plum, Lord Miyoshi the pine."

Gemba bowed at this compliment.

"And Lord Otori the bamboo."

"I believe I am flexible," Takeo replied, smiling.

"From what I know of your history, I believe so too. Yet bamboo can be extremely hard to eradicate if it happens to be growing in the wrong place."

"It will always grow back," Takeo agreed. "It is better to leave it where it is, and take advantage of its many and varied uses."

"Ha!" Saga gave his triumphant laugh again. His eyes strayed back to Shigeko, a curious expression in them, of both calculation and desire. He seemed to be about to address her directly, but then thought better of it and spoke to Takeo.

"Does this philosophy explain why you have not dealt with Arai?"

Takeo replied, "Even a poisonous plant can be put to some use, in medicine, for example."

"You are interested in farming, I hear."

"My father, Lord Shigeru, taught me to be, before his death. When the farmers are happy, the country is rich and stable."

"Well, I haven't had a lot of time for farming over the last few years. I've been too busy fighting. But food's been short this winter as a result. Okuda tells me the Three Countries produce more rice than they can consume."

"Many parts of our country practice double-cropping now," Takeo said. "It's true, we have considerable stores of rice, as well as soybeans, barley, millet, and sesame. We have been blessed by good harvests for many years, and have been spared drought and famine."

"You have produced a jewel. No wonder so many people are eyeing it covetously."

Takeo inclined his head slightly. "I am the legal head of the Otori clan, and hold the Three Countries lawfully. My rule is just and blessed by Heaven. I do not speak of these things to boast, but to tell you that while I seek your support, and the favor of the Emperor—indeed, am prepared to submit to you as the Emperor's general—it must be on conditions that protect my country and my heirs."

"We'll discuss all that later. First, let's eat and drink."

In keeping with the austere room, the food was delicate—the elegant seasonal dishes of the capital, each one offering an extraordinary experience to eye and tongue. Rice wine was also served, but Takeo tried to drink sparingly, knowing the negotiations might stretch on until nightfall. Both Okuda and Kono joined them for the meal, and the conversation was good-humored and wide-ranging, covering painting, architecture, the specialties of the Three Countries compared to those of the capital, poetry. Toward the end of the meal Okuda, who had drunk more than anyone else, expressed again his fervent admiration of the kirin.

"I long to see it with my own eyes," Saga said, and seemingly impulsively leaped to his feet. "Let us go there now. It is a pleasant afternoon. We will look at the ground where our contest is to take place." He took

Takeo's arm as they walked back to the main entrance and said confidentially, "And I must meet your champions. Lord Miyoshi will be one, I presume, and some other of your warriors."

"The second will be Sugita Hiroshi. The third you have already met. It is my daughter, Lady Maruyama."

Saga's grip tightened as he halted; he pulled Takeo around so he could look him directly in the face. "So Lord Kono reported, but I assumed it was a jest." He stared at Takeo, the hooded eyes piercing. Then he laughed abruptly, and lowered his voice further. "You intended to submit all along. The contest is only a formality for you? I see your reasoning—it saves you face."

"I don't want to mislead you," Takeo replied. "It is far from a formality. I take it extremely seriously, as does my daughter. The stakes could not be higher." But even as he spoke, he felt doubt stir in him. What had his trust in the Masters of the Way of the Houou led him into? He was afraid Saga would take Shigeko's substitution as an insult and refuse to negotiate at all.

However, after a moment of surprised silence, the warlord laughed again. "It will make a very pretty spectacle. The beautiful Lady Maruyama competes against the most powerful lord of the Eight Islands." He chuckled to himself as he released Takeo's arm and strode along the veranda, calling out in a loud voice, "Bring my bow and arrows, Okuda. I want to show them to my rival."

They waited under the deep eaves while Okuda went to the armory. He returned carrying the bow himself: It was over an arm-span long and lacquered in red and black. A retainer followed, holding the decorated quiver in which a bundle of tern arrows nestled. They were no less impressive, bound with gold-lacquered cord. Saga took one arrow from the quiver and held it out to show them, a hollow arrow of paulownia wood with a blunted end, fletched with white feathers.

"Heron's feathers," Saga said, running his finger very gently over them and glancing at Takeo, who was all too conscious of the heron crest of the Otori on the back of his robe.

"I hope Lord Otori does not take offense. Heron's feathers give the best flight, I've found."

He handed the arrow back to his retainer and took the bow from Okuda, stringing and flexing it with one effortless movement. "I believe it is almost as tall as Lady Maruyama," he said. "Have you ever taken part in a dog hunt before?"

"No, we do not hunt dogs in the West," she replied.

"It is a great sport. The dogs are so eager to join in! Really, one can't help but pity them. Of course, we do not aim to kill them. You must declare where you intend to hit. I would like to hunt a lion or a tiger. That would be a more worthy quarry!"

"Speaking of tigers," he went on with his characteristic rapid shift, giving the bow back and slipping into his sandals at the step. "We must remember to talk about trade. You send ships to Shin and Tenjiku, I believe?"

Takeo nodded in assent.

"And you have received the southern barbarians? They are of particular interest to us."

"We bring gifts from Tenjiku, Silla, Shin, and the Southern Isles for Lord Saga and for His Divine Majesty," Takeo replied.

"Excellent, excellent!"

The palanquin bearers had been lounging in the shade outside the gate. Now they leaped to their feet and bowed humbly while their masters climbed inside their elegant boxes and were conveyed, with no great degree of comfort, to the mansion that had become the Otori residence. The heron banners fluttered above the gate and along the street. The main building was situated on the western side of a large compound; the eastern side was taken up with stables, where the Maruyama horses stamped and tossed their heads, and in front of these stables, in an enclosure of bamboo posts roofed on one side with thatch, stood the kirin. Around the gate, quite a large crowd had gathered to try to get a glimpse of the kirin—children had climbed into the trees, and one enterprising young man was hurrying up with a ladder.

Lord Saga was the only person in the group who had not seen the fabulous creature before. Everyone stared at him in gleeful anticipation. They were not disappointed. Even Saga, with all his enormous self-control, could not prevent a look of utter astonishment crossing his face.

"It is much taller than I thought," he exclaimed. "It must be immensely strong, and swift."

"It is very gentle," Shigeko said, approaching the kirin. At that moment Hiroshi came from the stables leading Tenba, who was prancing and cavorting at the end of the rein.

"Lady Maruyama," he exclaimed. "I did not expect you back so soon." There was a moment of silence. Takeo noticed Hiroshi glance at Saga and go pale. Then the young man bowed as best he could while controlling the horse, and said awkwardly, "I have been riding Tenba."

The kirin had begun to pace with excitement when it saw the three creatures it loved the most.

"I will put Tenba back with her," Hiroshi said. "She misses him. After their separation she seems more attached to him than ever!"

Saga spoke to him as if he were a groom. "Bring the kirin out. I want to see it closer."

"Certainly, Lord," he replied with another deep bow, the color returning to his neck and cheeks.

"The horse is very good-looking," Saga remarked as Hiroshi tied Tenba to cords strung from each side of the corner of the stall. "Spirited. And quite tall."

"We have brought many horses from Maruyama as gifts," Takeo told him. "They are bred and raised by Lady Maruyama and her senior retainer Lord Sugita Hiroshi." As Hiroshi led the kirin out, the red silk cord in his hand, Takeo added, "This is Sugita."

Saga gave a perfunctory nod to Hiroshi; his attention was totally taken up by the kirin. He reached out and stroked the fawn-patterned skin. "Softer than a woman!" he exclaimed. "Imagine having this spread on your floor or bed." As if suddenly aware of the pained silence, he apologized, "Only after it died of old age, naturally."

The kirin bent its long neck down to Shigeko and gently nuzzled her cheek.

"You are its favorite, I see," Saga said, turning his admiring gaze onto her. "I congratulate you Lord Otori. The Emperor will be dazzled by your present. Nothing like it has ever been seen before in the capital."

The words were generous, but Takeo thought he heard envy and rancor in the other man's voice. After inspecting the horses further, and presenting two mares and three stallions to Lord Saga, they returned to Saga's residence, not to the austere room where they had been before but to one of the flamboyantly decorated audience halls, where a dragon flew across one wall and a tiger prowled across another. Saga did not sit on the floor here, but on a carved wooden seat from Shin, almost like an Emperor himself. More of his retainers attended the meeting; Takeo was aware of their curiosity toward himself and in particular toward Shigeko. It was unusual for a woman to sit among men in this fashion and take part in their discussions of policy. He felt they were inclined to take offense at such a breach of custom; yet the lineage of Maruyama was even more ancient than that of Saga and his Eastern clan, or of any of his vassals—as ancient as the imperial family, who were descended through legendary empresses from the Sun Goddess herself.

First they discussed the ceremonies surrounding the dog hunt, the days of feasting and rituals, the Emperor's procession, the rules of the contest itself. Two circles of rope were set up on the ground, one inside the other. In each round six dogs would be released, one at a time. The archer would gallop around the central ring; points were awarded as to where the dog was hit. It was a game of skill, not of butchery—severely wounded or dead dogs were considered undesirable. The dogs were white, so any blood showed immediately. Shigeko asked one or two technical questions—the width of the arena, whether there were any restrictions on the size of the bow or the arrows. Saga answered them precisely, humoring her and raising smiles among his retainers.

"And now we must proceed to the outcome," he said affably. "If Lady Maruyama wins, what are your conditions, Lord Otori?"

"That the Emperor recognize myself and my wife as the lawful rulers of the Three Countries; that you support us and our heirs; that you command Arai Zenko to submit to us. In return we will swear allegiance to you and the Emperor, for the sake of the unity and peace of the Eight Islands. We will provide food, men, and horses for your future campaigns, and open our ports to you for trade. The peace and prosperity of the Three Countries depend on our system of government, and this must remain unchanged."

"Apart from this last matter, which I would like to discuss with you further, that's all perfectly acceptable to me," Saga said, smiling confidently.

He is not troubled by any of my conditions, for he does not expect to have to consider them, Takeo reflected. "And Lord Saga's conditions?" he inquired.

"That you retire immediately from public life, and hand over the Three Countries to Arai Zenko, who has already sworn allegiance to me and is the legal heir of his father, Arai Daiichi; that you either take your own life or go into exile on Sado Island; that your son is sent to me as a hostage; and that you give me your daughter in marriage."

Both words and tone were insulting, and Takeo felt rage begin to simmer within him. He saw the expression on the men's faces, their shared awareness of the power and lust of their overlord, the gratification it caused them, their pleasure at his humiliation.

Why did I come here? Better to die in battle than to submit to this. He sat without moving a muscle, aware that he had no way out and no other options: either he agreed to Saga's proposals or he rejected them, fled the capital like a criminal, and prepared, if he and his companions lived long enough to make it back to the borders, for war.

"In either case," Saga went on, "I believe Lady Maruyama would be a fine wife for me, and I ask you to consider my offer very carefully."

"I heard of your recent loss, and I offer you my condolences," Takeo said.

"My late wife was a good woman. She gave me four healthy children and looked after all my other children—I believe the number is ten or twelve now. I think a marriage between our families has a great deal to recommend it."

All the pain that Takeo had felt when Kaede had been abducted from him swept up from his belly. It seemed outrageous that he should hand over his beloved daughter to this brutal man, older than himself, a man who already had several concubines, who would never treat her as a ruler in her own right, who simply wanted to own her. Yet this was the most powerful man in the Eight Islands; the honor and political advantage of such a marriage was huge. The offer had been made in public—the insult if he were to reject it outright would be no less public.

Shigeko sat with her eyes cast down, giving no indication of her reaction to the discussion.

Takeo said, "The honor is too great for us. My daughter is still very young, but I thank you from my heart. I would like to discuss the matter with my wife—Lord Saga may not be aware that she shares the government of the Three Countries equally with me—I am sure, like me, she will be overjoyed by such a union between us."

"I would have liked to spare your wife's life, since she has an infant child, but if she is your equal in government, she must also be your equal in death or exile," Saga said with some irritation. "Let us say that if Lady Maruyama should win, she may return to discuss her marriage with her mother."

Shigeko spoke for the first time. "I also have some conditions, if I may speak."

Saga glanced at his men and smiled indulgently. "Let us hear them, Lady."

"I ask Lord Saga to swear to preserve the female inheritance of the Maruyama. And as head of my clan, I will make my own choice in marriage, after consulting my senior retainers, as well as my father and my mother, as my liege lords. I am extremely grateful to Lord Saga for his generosity and the honor he bestows on me, but I cannot accept without the approval of my clan."

She spoke with resolve, yet with great charm, making it hard for anyone to take offense. Saga bowed to her.

"I see I have a worthy opponent," he declared, and a ripple of laughter ran through his men.

· 39 ·

he new moon of the sixth month hung in the eastern sky behind a six-layered pagoda as they returned to their residence. After he had bathed, Takeo sent for Hiroshi and told him of the day's discussions, leaving nothing out, and finishing with the marriage proposal.

Hiroshi listened in silence, saying only, "Of course it is not unexpected, and a great honor."

"Yet he is such a man . . ." Takeo said very quietly. "She will follow your advice, and that of my wife and myself. We have to consider her future life as well as what is best for the Three Countries. I suppose there is a small chance that we will not have to make a decision immediately." He sighed. "So much is resting on this contest—and everyone in Saga's camp has already decided the outcome!"

"Matsuda Shingen himself advised you to come to Miyako, did he not? You must have faith in his judgment."

"Yes, I must, and I do. Yet will Saga even abide by his own agreement? He is a man who hates to lose, and he is so confident of victory."

"The whole city is gripped with excitement about you, and Lady Shigeko, and the kirin. Already pictures of the kirin are being sold, and her image is being woven into cloth and embroidered on robes. When Lady Shigeko wins this contest, as she will, you will be supported—and protected—by the delight of the people. They are already making up songs about it."

"The people love, above all, tales of loss and tragedy," Takeo replied. "When I am in exile on Sado Island, they will listen to my melancholy story and weep, and enjoy it!"

The door slid open and Shigeko came into the room, followed by Gemba, who was carrying a black lacquered box with designs of the houou inlaid in gold. Takeo watched his daughter look at Hiroshi, saw their eyes meet with an expression of such mutual affection and trust that his heart twisted with regret and pity. *They are like a married couple already,* he thought, *tied by such deep bonds.* He wished he could give his daughter to this young man for whom he had such a high regard, who had been unfailingly loyal to him since childhood, whom he knew to be intelligent and brave, and who loved her deeply. Yet all these things could not equal the status and authority of Saga Hideki.

Gemba interrupted his thoughts. "Takeo, we thought you would like to see Lady Shigeko's weapons." He placed the box on the floor and Shigeko knelt beside it to open it.

Takeo said uneasily, "It is very small—surely it cannot contain bow and arrows."

"Well, it is small," Gemba admitted. "But Shigeko is not very tall: She must have something she can handle."

Shigeko took out a beautifully made miniature bow, a quiver, and then arrows, blunt-pointed and fetched with white and gold feathers.

"This is a joke?" Takeo said, his heart contracting in dread.

"Not at all, Father. Look, the arrows are fletched with houou feathers."

"There are so many birds this spring that we were able to collect enough feathers," Gemba explained. "They let them fall to the ground as if they offered them."

"This toy would hardly hit a sparrow, much less a dog," Takeo said.

"You don't want us to hurt the dogs, Father," Shigeko said, smiling. "We know how fond you are of them."

"It is a dog hunt!" he exclaimed. "Its purpose is to hit as many dogs as you can, more than Saga!"

"They will be hit," Gemba said. "But with these arrows there is no danger of hurting them."

Takeo remembered the flame that had burned up his irritation, and tried to suppress his irritation now. "Magic tricks?"

"Rather more than that," Gemba replied. "We will use the power of the Way of the Houou: the balance of male and female. As long as the balance is maintained, the power is invincible. It is this that holds the Three Countries together. You and your wife are the living symbols of it; your daughter is its outcome, its manifestation."

He smiled reassuringly, as if he understood Takeo's unspoken reservations. "The prosperity and contentment of which you are so rightly proud would not be possible without it. Lord Saga recognizes nothing of the power of the female element, and so he will be defeated.

Later, as they bade each other good night, Gemba added, "By the way, don't forget to offer Jato to the Emperor tomorrow." Seeing Takeo's look of astonishment, he went on, "It was requested, was it not, in Kono's first message?"

"Well, yes, but so was my exile. What if he keeps it?"

"Jato always finds its rightful owner, doesn't it? Anyway, you can't use it anymore. It's time to hand it on."

It was true that Takeo had not used the sword in battle since the death of Kikuta Kotaro and the loss of his fingers, but hardly a day had passed when he had not worn it, and he had become skilled enough in using his left hand to support his right, at least in practice combat. Jato had the deepest significance for him; it had been left to him by Shigeru and was the visible symbol of his legitimate rule. The idea of relinquishing it disturbed him so much he felt it was necessary, after changing into his night attire, to spend some time in meditation.

He dismissed Minoru and his attendants and sat alone in the darkened room, listening to the noises of the night and slowing his breath and his thoughts. Music and drums echoed from the riverbank, where the townspeople were dancing. Frogs were croaking in a pool in the garden, and crickets rasped among the bushes. Slowly he realized the wisdom of Gemba's advice—he would give Jato back to the imperial family from which it had come.

THE SOUND OF music and drums continued late into the night, and the next morning the streets filled again with men, women, and children dancing. Listening to them as he prepared for the audience with the Emperor, Takeo heard songs not only about the kirin but also about the houou:

> The houou nests in the Three Countries;
> Lord Otori has appeared in the capital.
> His kirin is a gift to the Emperor;
> His horses stir up our land.
> Welcome, Lord Otori!

"I went out last night to gauge the mood of the city," Hiroshi said. "I told one or two people about the houou feathers."

"It seems to have been very effective!" Takeo replied, holding out his arms for the heavy silk robe.

"People see your visit as a harbinger of peace."

Takeo did not reply directly, but he felt the sense of calm that he had achieved the previous night deepen. He recalled all his training, from Shigeru and Matsuda as well as from the Tribe. He became grounded and impassive; all unease left him.

His companions also seemed possessed by the same confidence and gravity. Takeo was transported in the ornately decorated palanquin. Shigeko and Hiroshi rode on the pale gray black-maned horses, Ashige and Keri, on either side of the kirin, each holding a scarlet silk cord attached to the kirin's collar of gold leaf–covered leather. The kirin walked as gracefully and unperturbed as ever, turning its long neck to look down on the adoring crowd. The shouts and excitement did not affect its composure, nor that of its attendants.

The Emperor had already made the short journey from the Imperial Palace to the Great Shrine in an elaborately lacquered carriage drawn by black oxen, and more carriages of noblemen and women milled around the entrance. The shrine buildings were all bright vermilion, newly restored and painted, and in front of them, within the gates, was a broad arena, the concentric circles already marked out in contrasting colors, where the contest would take place. The palanquin bearers trotted across this, followed by Takeo's retinue, guards good-naturedly keeping back the excited throng but leaving the outer gates open. Pine trees lined the sides, and beneath their branches wooden stands and silken tents and pavilions had been erected for the spectators, and hundreds of flags and banners fluttered in the breeze. Many people, warriors and noblemen, were already seated here, though the dog hunt would not take place until the following day, taking advantage of this excellent viewing point to get their first glimpse of the kirin. Women with long black hair, men wearing small formal caps, had brought silken cushions and sunshades, food in lacquered boxes. At the next gate the palanquin was lowered to the ground and Takeo stepped out. Shigeko and Hiroshi dismounted; Hiroshi took the reins of the horses and Takeo walked with his daughter and the kirin toward the main shrine building.

The white walls and red beams gleamed in the brilliant afternoon sun. At the steps Saga Hideki and Lord Kono waited with their attendants, all dressed in formal robes of great splendor, Saga's decorated with turtles and cranes, Kono's with peonies and peacocks. Bows and courtesies were exchanged, and then Saga led Takeo within, to a dim hall lit by hundreds of lamps, where on the top level of a stepped dais, behind a delicate bamboo curtain that shielded him from the profane eyes of the world, sat the Emperor, the embodiment of the gods.

Takeo prostrated himself, aware of the smoky smell of the oil, Saga's sweat masked by the sweet incense, and the fragrance of the Emperor's attendants, the Ministers of the Right and the Left, who sat on the steps below their sovereign.

This was as much as he expected, merely to be received into the presence of the Emperor, the first member of the Otori to be so honored since the legendary Takeyoshi.

Saga announced in a clear but deferential voice, "Lord Otori Takeo has come from the Three Countries to present a wonderful gift to your Majesty, and to assure your Majesty of his humble allegiance to your Majesty."

These words were repeated by one of the Ministers on the dais in a high-toned voice with many additions of elegant language and archaic courtesies. When he had finished, everyone bowed again, and a short silence ensued, during which Takeo felt certain the Emperor was scrutinizing him through the chinks in the bamboo.

Then from behind the curtain the Emperor himself spoke, in hardly more than a whisper.

"Welcome, Lord Otori. It is our great pleasure to receive you. We are aware of the ancient bond that exists between our families."

Takeo heard all this before it was relayed by the Minister, and he was able to shift his position slightly to study Saga's reaction. He thought he heard the slightest intake of breath from the man next to him. The Emperor's words were brief, but far more than he could have hoped for: recognition of both the lineage of the Otori and his own entitlement. It was a huge and unexpected honor.

He dared to say, "May I address your Majesty?"

The request was repeated, and the Emperor's assent relayed back.

Takeo said, "Many centuries ago your Majesty's ancestor gave this sword, Jato, to Otori Takeyoshi. It was handed on to me by my father, Shigeru, before his death. I was requested to return it to you, and I now humbly do so, offering it to you as a sign of my allegiance and my service."

The Minister of the Right conferred with the Emperor, and spoke again to Takeo.

"We accept your sword and your service."

Takeo went forward on his knees and took the sword from his belt. He felt a terrible pang of regret as he held it out in both hands.

Farewell, he said quietly in his mind.

The lowest of the ministers took Jato, and it was passed from official to official up the steps until the Minister of the Left took it and laid it down before the curtain.

It will speak; it will fly back to me, Takeo thought, but Jato lay on the ground, silent and immobile.

The Emperor spoke again, and Takeo heard in the voice not a god or even a great ruler but a flesh-and-blood human, full of curiosity, not easily swayed or manipulated.

"I would like to see the kirin now, with my own eyes."

There was a slight flurry of consternation, as no one seemed sure of the correct procedure to be followed. Then the Emperor actually stepped out from behind the screen and held out his arms for his attendants to support him down the steps.

He was clothed in robes of gold with scarlet dragons embroidered across the back and sleeves; they added to his stature, but Takeo had been right in his judgment. Beneath the splendor of the costume stood a rather small man of about twenty-eight years; his cheeks were plump, his mouth small and firm, showing self-will and shrewdness; his eyes sparkled with anticipation.

"Let Lord Otori come with me," he said as he walked past Takeo, and Takeo followed him, on his knees.

Shigeko was waiting outside with the kirin. She fell to one knee when the Emperor approached, and, with head bowed, held out the cord, saying, "Your Majesty, this creature is nothing compared to your greatness, but we offer it to you in the hope that you will look with favor on your subjects in the Three Countries."

The Emperor's expression was one of pure astonishment, possibly as much at being addressed by a woman as at the kirin. He took the cord carefully, glanced back at the courtiers, looked up at the kirin's long neck and head, and laughed in delight.

Shigeko said, "Your Majesty may touch her—she is very gentle," and the man-god put out his hand and stroked the soft fur of the fabulous creature.

He murmured, "The kirin only appears when the ruler is blessed by Heaven."

Shigeko replied as quietly, "So is Your Majesty blessed indeed."

"Is this a man or a woman?" the Emperor said to Saga, who had approached, in the same manner as Takeo, on his knees, for Shigeko had used the speech of a male ruler.

"Your Majesty, it is Lord Otori's daughter, Lady Maruyama."

"From the land where women rule? Lord Otori has brought many exotic things! Everything we hear of the Three Countries is true. How I should like to visit there, but it is not possible for me to leave the capital." He stroked the kirin again. "What can I give you in return?" he said. "I doubt I have anything that can compare." He stood as if deep in thought for a few moments, and then spun around and looked back as if struck by a sudden inspiration. "Bring me the Otori sword," he called. "I will bestow it on Lady Maruyama!"

Takeo remembered a voice from the past: *So it goes from hand to hand.* Kenji. The sword that Kenji had given to Shigeru after the defeat at Yaegahara, and that Yuki, Kenji's daughter, had brought to Takeo, had now been put into the hands of Maruyama Shigeko by the Emperor himself.

Takeo bowed to the ground again, and as he sat up, he saw the Emperor was observing him shrewdly. At that moment the temptation of absolute power glittered before him. Whoever was favored by the Emperor—or, to put it more bluntly, controlled the Emperor—controlled the Eight Islands.

That could be myself and Kaede, he thought. *We could vie with Saga—if we defeat him tomorrow in the contest, we could displace him. Our army is prepared. I can send messengers to Kahei to advance. We will drive him back to the north and into the sea. He will be the one in exile, not me!*

He entertained the fantasy for a few short moments, and then put it from him. He did not want the Eight Islands; he wanted only the Three Countries, and he wanted them to remain at peace.

THE REST OF the day was spent in feasting, recitals of music and drama, poetry competitions, and even a demonstration of the younger noblemen's favorite game of kick ball, in which Lord Kono proved himself to be unexpectedly adept.

"His languid demeanor hides his physical skill," Takeo remarked quietly to Gemba.

"They will all be worthy opponents," Gemba agreed serenely.

There was also a horse race just before sunset, which Lord Saga's team, mounted on the new Maruyama steeds, won easily, adding to the crowd's general admiration of the visitors, and the pleasure and astonishment at their unparalleled gifts.

Takeo returned to the mansion pleased and encouraged by the events of the day, though still anxious about the morrow. He had seen with his own eyes the skill and horsemanship of their opponents. He could not believe his daughter could defeat them. But Gemba had been right about the sword. He would have to trust him in the matter of the contest.

He had raised the oiled-silk curtains of the palanquin to enjoy the evening air, and as it was carried through the gate he saw, out of the corner of his eye, the shadowy outline of someone using invisibility. It astonished him, for he had not expected the Tribe to operate in the capital— none of his records, nor the Muto family's knowledge, had ever indicated that they had penetrated this far to the East.

He felt instinctively for his sword, realized that he was unarmed, had the immediate customary flash of curiosity as he faced again his own mortality—was this to be the assassination attempt that succeeded?—all in the instant it took before the palanquin was set down and he descended. Ignoring the attendants, he ran to the gate and searched the milling crowd with his eyes, wondering if he had been mistaken. His name was being chanted by many voices, but he thought he could distinguish one he recognized, and then he saw the girl.

He knew her at once as Muto, but it took him a moment or two to remember who she was: Mai, Sada's sister, who had been placed in the foreigners' household to learn their language and spy on them.

"Come inside at once," he commanded her.

Once they were within, he told the guards to close and bar the gates, then turned to the girl. She looked exhausted and travel-stained.

"What are you doing here? Do you bring news from Taku? Did Jun send you?"

"I must speak to Lord Otori in private," she whispered.

He saw the grief in the lines around her mouth and in the expression of her eyes, and his heart began to gallop in fear of what she had to tell him.

"Wait here. I will send for you directly."

He called for maids to help him change out of the formal robes, and then dismissed them, telling them to send the girl to him, to serve tea and then make sure he was left alone; not even his daughter, not even Lord Miyoshi, was to be admitted.

Mai came into the room and knelt before him. A maid came in with bowls of tea, and Takeo took one and put it into the girl's hands. Night was falling: despite the warmth of the evening she was pale and trembling.

"What has happened?" he said.

"Lord Taku and my sister are dead, lord."

Even though it was what he had expected, the news hit him like a physical blow. He stared at her, hardly able to speak, feeling the terrible tide of grief begin to well up through his veins. He made a gesture that she should continue.

"They were allegedly attacked by bandits a day's ride from Hofu."

"Bandits?" he said in disbelief. "What bandits are there in the Middle Country?"

"That is the official version put out by Zenko," Mai replied. "But Zenko is protecting Kikuta Akio. Rumor on the wind is that Akio and his son killed Taku in revenge for Kotaro's death. Sada died with him."

"And my daughter?" Takeo whispered, the tears beginning to force their way from his eyes.

"Lord Otori, no one knows where she is. She was not killed at the same time, but whether she escaped, or whether Akio has her . . ."

"Akio has my daughter?" he repeated stupidly.

"Maybe she escaped," Mai said. "But she has not found her way to Kagemura, or Terayama, or any of the other places where she might have fled."

"Does my wife know?"

"I don't know, lord."

He saw there was something else going on, some other reason why the girl had made this long journey, presumably without permission from anyone in the Tribe, and unknown to them, even to Shizuka.

"Taku's mother must surely have been told?"

"Again, I don't know. Something has happened to the Muto network, lord. Messages are misdirected, or read by the wrong people. People are saying they want to return to the old days, when the Tribe had real power. Kikuta Akio is very close to Zenko, and many among the Muto approve of their new friendship—they say it's like things used to be between Kenji and Kotaro, before . . ."

"Before I came along," Takeo stated bleakly.

"That's not for me to say, Lord Otori. The Muto swore allegiance to you, and Taku and Sada were loyal to you. That's enough for me. I left Hofu without telling anyone, hoping to catch up with Lady Shigeko and Lord Hiroshi, but they were always a few days ahead. I just kept following them, until I found myself in the capital. I have been six weeks on the road."

"I am very grateful to you." He recalled that she was also grieving. "And deeply sorry for your sister's death in the service of my family."

Her eyes went bright in the lamplight, but she did not cry.

"They were attacked with firearms," she said bitterly. "No one could have killed them with ordinary weapons. Taku was hit in the neck; he must have bled to death in seconds, and the same bullet knocked Sada from the horse, but she did not die from the fall—her throat was cut."

"Akio has firearms? Where did he get them from?"

"He has been in Kumamoto all winter. He must have been supplied by the Arai; they have been trading with the foreigners."

He sat in silence, remembering suddenly the feel of Taku's neck between his hands when he had woken and found him in his room, in Shuho. Taku had been a child of nine or ten; he had thickened his neck muscles to give the impression he was older and stronger than he really was. The memory, followed swiftly by so many others, nearly overwhelmed him. Covering his face with his hand, he fought to control sobbing. His grief was fueled by rage against Zenko, whom he had spared only to see him connive in his brother's death. *Taku wanted Zenko dead,* he remembered; *so even did Shizuka. And now we have lost the brother we could least spare.*

"Lord Otori," Mai said hesitantly. "Shall I call for someone to come to you?"

"No!" he said, regaining his self-mastery, the moment of weakness over. "You do not know our circumstances here. You must say nothing of this to anyone. Nothing must interfere with the arrangements for the next few days. There is to be a contest, involving my daughter and Lord Hiroshi. They must not be distracted in any way. They must not know of this until the contest is over. No one must know."

"But you should return to the Three Countries without delay! Zenko . . ."

"I will return as soon as possible, earlier than I had planned. But I cannot offend my hosts—Lord Saga, the Emperor himself—nor can I let Saga get a whiff of Zenko's treachery. At the moment I am in some favor—but that may change at any time. Once the contest is over and we know its outcome, I will make arrangements to return. It means we risk being caught in the rains, but it can't be helped. You will travel with us, of course, but for the time being I must ask you to stay away from this house. Shigeko might recognize you. It is only until after tomorrow. Then I will have to tell her, and Hiroshi, the news."

He made arrangements for Mai to be given money and found accommodation, and she departed, promising to return within two days.

Mai had barely left the residence when Shigeko returned with Gemba. They had been checking on the horses, preparing saddles and bridles for the next day, and discussing strategy. Shigeko, usually so self-controlled and calm, was brilliant with excitement from the events of the day and anticipation of the contest. He was relieved, for normally she would have observed his silence and his lack of high spirits, relieved too that it was too dark in the room for her to see his face.

She said, "I must give you back Jato, Father."

"Certainly not," he replied. "The Emperor himself gave it to you. It is yours now."

"Really, it is too long for me," she protested.

Takeo forced himself to smile. "Nevertheless, it is yours."

"I will give it to the temple until . . ."

"Until what," he prompted her.

"Either your son, or mine, is old enough to bear it."

"It will not be the first time it has rested there," he replied. "But it is yours, and confirms you as the heir not only to the Maruyama but also to the Otori."

Takeo realized as he spoke that the Emperor's recognition made the question of her marriage even more crucial. She would bring the Three Countries to whomever she married, with the Emperor's blessing. Whatever demands Saga made, he would not give in to them immediately, not before consulting Kaede.

He longed for Kaede now, not only for her body, with deep desire fueled by grief, but for her wisdom, her clarity, her gentle strength. *I am nothing without her,* he thought. He longed to be home.

It was not hard to persuade Shigeko to retire early, and Gemba also took himself off to bed, leaving Takeo alone to face the long night and the next day, filled with grief and anxiety, unable to give rein to either.

inoru came as always at first light, followed by the maids bringing tea.

"It promises to be a fine day," he said. "I have prepared records of everything that took place yesterday, and will likewise record everything that happens today."

When Takeo took the records without replying, the scribe said hesitantly, "Lord Otori does not look well."

"I slept badly, that's all. I must be well. I must continue to dazzle and impress. I cannot be otherwise."

Minoru raised his eyebrows very slightly, surprised by Takeo's bitter tone.

"Surely your visit has been a huge success?"

"We will know by the end of the day."

Takeo came to a sudden decision and said, "I am going to dictate something to you. Make no comment and tell no one. You need to be forewarned in order to arrange our return home somewhat earlier than anticipated."

Minoru prepared the inkstone and took up the brush without speaking. Dispassionately Takeo related all that Mai had told him the previous night, and Minoru wrote it down.

"I am sorry," he said when he had finished. Takeo looked reprovingly at him. "I am apologizing for my lack of skill. My hand trembled and the writing is very poor."

"It does not matter, as long as it is legible. Keep it safe—I will ask you to read from it later, tonight or tomorrow."

Minoru bowed. Takeo was aware of his scribe's silent sympathy; the fact that he had shared the news of Taku's death with another human being gave him a little relief from his anguish.

"Lord Saga has sent you a letter," Minoru said, producing the scroll. "He must have written last night. He shows you great honor."

"Let me see it." The writing reflected the man, bold and forceful, the new ink strokes black and emphatic, the style square.

"He congratulates me on the Emperor's graciousness toward me, and on the success of my gift, and wishes me good fortune today."

"He is alarmed at your popularity," Minoru said. "And afraid that if you lose the contest, the Emperor will still favor you."

"I will abide by our agreement, and I expect him to," Takeo replied.

"But he expects you to find some way of wriggling out from it, and so he sees no reason why he should keep it."

"Minoru, you have become too cynical! Lord Saga is a great warlord from an ancient clan. He has made this agreement publicly. He cannot go back on it without bringing dishonor on himself, and nor can I!"

"That is precisely how warlords become great," Minoru muttered.

THE STREETS WERE even more crowded than the day before, and people were already dancing frenetically. There was a feverish atmosphere; the day was hotter, with the humidity that heralded the plum rains. The arena in front of the Great Shrine was packed around all four sides with spectators: women in hooded robes, men in brightly colored clothes, children, all holding sunshades and fans. Within the red sand outer circles the horsemen waited—Saga's team had red cruppers and breast straps, Shigeko's white. The horses' saddles were inlaid with mother of pearl; their manes were plaited—their forelocks and tails flowed as shiny and silky as a princess's hair. A thick yellow straw rope divided the outer circle from the inner, where the sand was white.

Takeo could hear the yelping of excited dogs from the eastern side of the arena, where about fifty white dogs were penned in a small enclosure festooned with white tassels. At the back of the ground, a silken booth had been erected for the Emperor, who was hidden as before behind a bamboo blind.

Takeo was guided to a place a little to the right of this booth, and made welcome by the noblemen and women, warriors and their wives, some of whom he had met during the festivities of the previous day. The kirin's influence was already apparent—one man showed him an ivory toggle carved in its likeness, and several women wore hoods decorated with its image.

The atmosphere was that of a country picnic, lively and chattering, and he tried to take part in it wholeheartedly. But every now and then the scene would seem to fade and the sky darken, and his eyes and mind filled with the image of Taku, shot in the neck and bleeding to death.

He turned his attention to the living, to his representatives: Shigeko, Hiroshi, and Gemba. The two pale gray horses with black manes and tails contrasted strikingly with Gemba's black. The horses paced calmly around the ring. Saga himself was mounted on a large bay horse, his two supporters Okuda and Kono on a piebald and a chestnut. Their bows were huge compared to Shigeko's—and all three had arrows fletched with white and gray heron's feathers.

Takeo had never witnessed dog hunting before, and the rules were explained to him by his companions.

"You can only hit certain parts of the dog: back, leg, neck. You mustn't hit the head, the soft part of the belly, or the genitals, and you lose points if you draw blood, or if the dog dies. The more blood, the worse the shot. It's all about perfect control, which is very difficult to achieve when the horse is galloping, the dog is running, and the archer is powerful."

They rode in order of rank, from lowest to highest, the first pair Okuda and Hiroshi.

"Okuda will go first to show you how it is done," Saga said to Hiroshi, generously, for to ride second held a slight advantage.

The first dog was brought into the circle, Okuda also entered the ring and put his horse into a gallop, letting the reins fall on its neck as he brought his bow upward and set the arrow.

The dog's leash was slipped off, and it immediately began to prance about, barking at the galloping horse. Okuda's first arrow whistled past its ears, causing it to yelp in surprise and back away, its tail between its legs. The second arrow struck it on the chest.

"A good shot!" the man next to Takeo exclaimed.

The third shot caught the running dog in the back. The arrow was released with too much force—blood began to stain the white fur.

"Rather poor" was the verdict.

Takeo felt tension begin to build in him as Hiroshi entered the ring and Keri began to gallop. He had known the horse almost as long as he had known the man—nearly eighteen years. Could the gray withstand this sort of contest? Would he let his rider down? He knew Hiroshi was highly skilled with the bow, but could he compete with the top bowmen of the capital?

The dog was released. Perhaps it had been watching its fellow's fate and knew what was in store; it shot immediately out of the circle, pelting back to the other dogs. Hiroshi's first arrow missed it by a footspan.

The dog was captured, brought back, and released once more. Takeo could see it was terrified and snarling. *They must smell the blood and the fear,* he thought. *Or maybe they communicate with each other and warn each other.* Hiroshi was more prepared this time, but the arrow still failed to hit its mark.

"It's harder than it looks," Takeo's neighbor said sympathetically. "Takes years of practice."

Takeo stared at the dog as it was brought back for the third time, trying to will it to sit still. He did not want Hiroshi to hurt it, but he did want him at least to score one hit. The crowd went silent; beneath the sound of the galloping horse he could hear a very faint humming, the noise Gemba made when he was content.

No other human could hear it, but the dog could. It stopped struggling and yelping, and when it was released, it did not race away, but sat and scratched itself for a moment before getting up and walking slowly round the circle. Hiroshi's third arrow hit it in the flank, knocking it to the ground and making it yelp, but not drawing blood.

"That was an easy one! Okuda will win this round."

And so the judges decreed. Okuda's second hit, even though it drew blood, was scored higher than Hiroshi's two misses.

Takeo was preparing himself for another defeat—and then no matter how Shigeko fared, the contest would be decided. His eyes rested on Gemba, no longer humming in relaxed contentment, but looking as alert as he ever did. The black horse beneath looked alert too, gazing at the unfamiliar scene with pricked ears and large eyes. Lord Kono was waiting in the outer circle on his fine-boned high-spirited chestnut. He rode well, as Takeo already knew, and the horse was fast.

Since Hiroshi had lost the previous round, Gemba rode first this time. The next dog was more docile, and did not seem frightened of the galloping horse. Gemba's first arrow seemed to hover through the air and land gently on the dog's rump. A good hit, and no blood. His second shot was similar, again not drawing blood, but the dog was alarmed by now, running and zigzagging across the ground. Gemba's third shot missed.

Kono then came out on the chestnut, putting it into a showy gallop around the outer circle, sending the red sand flying. The crowd roared in appreciation.

"Lord Kono is very skillful and very popular," Takeo's neighbor informed him.

"He is indeed a joy to watch!" Takeo agreed politely, thinking, *I am losing everything, yet I will show neither anger nor grief.*

The dogs in the enclosure were getting more excited; the yelping turned to howling, and each dog released was made wilder by alarm. Nevertheless, Kono scored two perfect bloodless hits. On the third attempt the chestnut horse, overexcited by the cheers of the crowd, bucked slightly as Kono drew the bow, and the arrow sailed over the head of the dog and hit the side of the wooden platform beyond. Several youths jumped down to claim it, the lucky victor brandishing it over his head.

After a long discussion by the judges, the second bout was declared a draw.

"Now we might have an Emperor's decision," the man next to Takeo declared. "That's always very popular—it's how an overall draw is decided."

"That does not seem very likely, since I believe Lord Saga is considered to have the highest skills in this sport."

"You're right, of course. I just did not want to . . ." The man appeared overcome with embarrassment, and after a few moments' awkward silence he excused himself and walked away to join another group. He whispered to them, and Takeo heard his words clearly.

"Really, I cannot bear to sit next to Lord Otori while he faces his own death sentence. I can hardly enjoy the sport for pitying him!"

"It's being said that this contest is an excuse for him to retire without being defeated in battle. He does not mind—there's no need to feel sorry for him."

Then silence fell over the whole arena as Shigeko entered the circle and Ashige began to gallop. He could hardly bear to look at her, yet he could not tear his eyes away. After the male contestants she seemed tiny and fragile.

Despite the excitement of the crowd, the frantic barking of the dogs, and the rising tension, both woman and horse seemed completely relaxed, the horse's gait swift and smooth, the woman straight-backed and serene. Shigeko's miniature bow and arrows elicited gasps of surprise, which turned to admiration as the first one gently nudged the dog in the side. It snapped at it, as if at a fly, but was not hurt or frightened, and then it seemed to sense that this was a game, one that it was happy to play. It ran around the circle in perfect time with the horse. Shigeko leaned down and let the second arrow go as if it were her hand and she were stroking the creature's neck. The dog shook its head and wagged its tail.

Shigeko urged the horse to a faster gallop and the dog ran at its heels, mouth open, ears flying, tail plumed. They circled the arena three times like this; then she pulled the horse to a halt in front of the Emperor. The

dog sat behind her, panting. Shigeko bowed deeply, put the horse into a
gallop again, circling ever closer to the dog, which sat and watched her,
swiveling its head, its pink tongue lolling. The third arrow flew faster but
no less gently, hitting the dog with a barely audible sound just below its
head.

Takeo was overcome with admiration for her, for her strength and skill,
perfectly controlled, tempered by gentleness. He felt the corners of his
eyes grow hot, and feared pride would unloose what grief had not. He
frowned and held his face impassive, his muscles immobile.

Saga Hideki, the final contestant, now rode into the white sanded circle. The bay horse was pulling at the bit, fighting its rider, but the man
controlled it easily with his huge strength. He wore a black robe, with arrow quills emblazoned across the back, and a deerskin over each thigh to
protect his legs, the black scut hanging almost to the ground. When he
lifted his bow, the crowd gasped; when he set the arrow, they held their
breath. The horse galloped, foam flying from its mouth. The dog was released; barking and howling, it dashed across the ground. Saga's first arrow
flew faster than the eye could follow, perfectly judged. It hit the dog in the
side, knocking it over. The dog struggled to its feet, winded and dazed. It was
easy for Saga to hit it again with his second arrow, again drawing no blood.

The sun was in the western sky, the heat increasing as the shadows
lengthened. Despite the shouting all around him, the howling of the dogs,
the shrieking of children, an icy calm descended upon Takeo. He welcomed it, for it deadened all emotions, laying its frozen hand over grief, regret, and rage alike. He watched dispassionately as Saga galloped around
the circle again, a man in perfect control of mind and body, steed and
weapon. The scene became dreamlike. The final arrow flew, hitting the dog
in the side again with a dull, muted sound. *It must have drawn blood*, he
thought, but nothing stained the white fur or the pale sand.

Now everyone fell silent. He felt all eyes were on him, though he
looked at no one. He tasted defeat in his throat and belly, bitter, galling.
Saga and Shigeko must at least be equal. Two draws and one win—the victory would go to Saga.

But suddenly, before his eyes, as if continuing the dream, the white sand of the arena began to blossom red. The dog was bleeding terribly, from both mouth and anus. People exclaimed in shock. The dog arched its back, shook its head, scattering blood in an arc across the sand, yelped once, and died.

Saga's strength was too great, Takeo thought. He could not temper his male force—he could slow the arrow, but could not lessen its power. The two earlier blows had destroyed the dog's internal organs and killed it.

He heard the shouts and cheering as if from a great distance. He rose slowly to his feet, gazing toward the end of the arena, where the Emperor sat behind the bamboo screen. The contest had ended in a draw; the decision was now the Emperor's. Slowly the crowd fell silent. The contestants waited, motionless, the red team on the eastern side, the white team on the western, the long shadows of the horses' legs stretching right across the arena. Dogs still barked from the enclosure, but there was no other sound.

Takeo realized that during the course of the contest people had drawn away from him, not wanting to witness his humiliation too closely, or to share in his inauspicious fate. Now he waited alone to hear the outcome.

Whispering came from behind the screen, but he deliberately closed his ears to it. Only when the Minister appeared and he saw the official glance first toward Shigeko, and then, more nervously, at Saga, did he feel the first glimmer of hope.

"Since Lady Maruyama's team shed no blood, the Emperor awards the victory to the white team!"

Takeo dropped to his knees and prostrated himself. The crowd shouted in approval. When he sat up, he saw that suddenly the space around him had filled as people rushed to congratulate him, to be close to him. As the news spread throughout the arena and beyond, the singing started again.

> Lord Otori has appeared in the capital;
> His horses stir up our land.
> His daughter won a great victory;

Lady Maruyama shed no blood.
The sand is white. The dogs are white.
The white riders prevail.
The Three Countries live in peace;
So will all the Eight Islands!

Takeo looked toward Saga, and saw the warlord was gazing back at
him. Their eyes met, and Saga inclined his head in recognition of the victory.

It is not what he expected, Takeo thought, and remembered Minoru's
words. *He expected to remove me without fighting, but he has failed. He will grasp at any
excuse not to keep his word.*

LORD SAGA HAD arranged a great feast to celebrate his anticipated
victory; the feast took place as planned, but unlike the unfeigned delight
in the streets of the city, the rejoicing was not altogether sincere. Courtesy
prevailed, however, and Saga was generous in his compliments to Lady
Maruyama, making it clear that he now desired the marriage more than
ever.

"We will be allies, and you will be my father-in-law," he said, laughing
with forced jollity. "Though I believe I am your senior by a few years."

"It will be my great pleasure to call you son," Takeo said, with a slight
jolt of surprise as the word formed in his mouth. "But we must delay announcing the betrothal until my daughter has sought the opinion of her
clan. Including her mother." He glanced at Lord Kono and wondered what
the nobleman's true reaction was, beneath the polite exterior; what message
would he send to Zenko about the contest's outcome, and what was Zenko
doing right now?

The feast continued until late into the night. The moon had set and
the stars were huge, their light made diffuse and hazy by the moisture in
the air.

"I must ask you all to delay sleep a little longer," Takeo said when they returned to their residence, and led Shigeko, Gemba, and Hiroshi into the most secluded room of the house. All the doors stood open; water trickled in the garden and occasionally a mosquito whined. Minoru was summoned.

"Father, what is wrong?" Shigeko questioned urgently. "You have had bad news from home—is it Mother? The baby?"

"Minoru has something to read to you," he replied, and indicated that the scribe should begin.

He read without emotion, in his usual dry manner, but they were no less riven by the news. Shigeko wept openly. Hiroshi sat, face drained of color, as if he had been hit in the chest and winded. Gemba sniffed loudly and said, "You have kept this to yourself all day?"

"I did not want anything to distract you. I did not expect you to win. How can I thank you all? You were magnificent!" Takeo spoke with tears of emotion in his eyes.

"Luckily the Emperor was sufficiently impressed by you not to want to risk offending the gods by deciding against you. Everything has combined to convince him that you have the blessing of Heaven."

"I thought him sufficiently worldly to see in me a check on Saga's power," Takeo replied.

"That too," Gemba agreed. "Of course, he is a divine being—but he is no different from any of us, motivated by a mixture of idealism, pragmatism, self-preservation, and good intentions!"

"Your victory has bought us his favor," Takeo said. "But Taku's death means we should return as soon as possible. Zenko must be dealt with now."

"Yes, I feel it is time to return," Gemba said. "Not only because of Taku, but to forestall any further unraveling. There is something else amiss."

"Something to do with Maya?" Shigeko asked, fear in her voice.

"Possibly," Gemba replied, but would say no more.

"Hiroshi," Takeo said, "you have lost your closest friend . . . I am deeply sorry."

"I am trying to suppress my desire for revenge." Hiroshi's voice was harsh. "All I want is Zenko's death, as well as that of Kikuta Akio and his son. My instinct is to leave at once and hunt them down—but all my training in the Way of the Houou has been to refrain from violence. Yet how else do we deal with these murderers?"

"We will hunt them down," Takeo replied. "But it will be done with justice, and they will be executed according to law. I have been recognized by the Emperor, my rule confirmed by His Divine Majesty. Zenko no longer has any legal grounds for challenging me. If he does not genuinely submit, we will defeat him in battle and he will take his own life. Akio will be hanged like the common criminal he is. But we must leave swiftly."

"Father," Shigeko said, "I know you are right. But will a hasty departure not offend Lord Saga and the Emperor? And, to tell you the truth, I am concerned about the kirin. Her good health is essential to your continued good standing. She will fret if we all leave so suddenly. I had hoped to see her settled before we left. . . . Maybe I should stay here with her?"

"No, I will not leave you in Saga's hands," he said with a vehemence that surprised them all. "Am I to surrender all my daughters to my enemies? We have given the kirin to the Emperor. He and his court are responsible for her. We must leave before the end of the week—we will have the waxing moon to travel with."

"We will be riding into the rain, and may not see the moon at all," Hiroshi murmured.

Takeo turned to Gemba. "Gemba, you have proved yourself all-knowing so far. Will Heaven continue to favor us by delaying the plum rains?"

"We'll see what we can do," Gemba promised, smiling through his tears.

· 41 ·

I n the year since Takeo had asked her to take over the leadership of the Tribe, Muto Shizuka had traveled widely through the Three Countries, visiting the hidden villages in the mountains and the merchant houses in the cities where her relatives ran their varied and multilayered businesses of brewing rice wine, fermenting soybean products, money lending, and to a lesser extent spying, protectionism, and different forms of persuasion. The ancient hierarchies of the Tribe still persisted, with their vertical structure and their traditional family loyalties, which meant that even among themselves the Tribe kept their secrets and often went their own way.

Shizuka was usually greeted with courtesy and deference, yet she was aware that there was a certain surprise, even resentment, at her new position. If Zenko had supported her, it might have been different, but she knew that while he lived any dissatisfaction among the Muto family would be fomented into defiance. For that reason she felt obliged to maintain her contacts with all her relatives, to try to keep them loyal to her, to side with her against her eldest son.

She herself knew all too well how secrets might be kept and disobedience flourish within the Tribe; for, many years ago, she had revealed the workings of the Tribe to Lord Shigeru, and his meticulous records had enabled Takeo to outwit and control them. Kenji had known of her acts, and had chosen to overlook what could only be described as treachery, but she wondered, from time to time, who else might have suspected her. People in the Tribe had long memories, and were both patient and unrelenting when it came to revenge.

A month after Kaede's child was born, and shortly after Takeo had left for Miyako, Shizuka made preparations to set out again, first to Yamagata and then to Kagemura in the mountains behind Yamagata, and on to Hofu.

"Both Kaede and the little boy seem so healthy, I feel I can go before the plum rains," she said to Ishida. "You are here to take care of them; you will not travel this year while Fumio is away."

"The child is very strong," Ishida agreed. "Of course, you can never tell with infants—they often have only a tenuous grasp on life, and slip away unexpectedly. But this little boy seems like a fighter."

"He is a true warrior," Shizuka said. "Kaede adores him!"

"I've never seen a mother so besotted with her own child," Ishida admitted.

Kaede could hardly bear to be parted from the infant. She nursed him herself, which she had not done with her other children. Shizuka watched them with a mixture of envy and pity—the child's fierce concentration on sucking, the mother's equally intense protectiveness.

"What will his name be?" she said.

"We have not yet decided," Kaede replied. "Takeo fancies Shigeru, but the name has unhappy associations, and we already have Shigeko. Perhaps another of the Otori names, Takeshi, Takeyoshi. But he will not be named until he is two years old. So I call him my little lion."

Shizuka remembered how she had adored her own sons when they were children, reflecting on the disappointment and anxiety they caused her now.

When she had married Ishida, she had hoped for another child, a girl, but the years had passed and she had not conceived again. Now she hardly bled; her chances were nearly over, and indeed she no longer wanted her hopes to be fulfilled. Ishida had no children from his former marriage. His wife had died many years ago, and though he had wanted to marry again, being excessively fond of women, no one had ever been acceptable to Lord Fujiwara. He was as amorous and kind as ever, and, as Shizuka had told Takeo, she would have been quite content to live quietly with him in Hagi and continue to be Kaede's companion. But she had agreed to become the head of the Muto family, and therefore the nominal leader of the Tribe, and now the task was consuming her energy and time. It also meant that there were numerous matters she could not discuss with Ishida—she loved her husband, and he had many qualities that she admired, but discretion was not one of them. He talked too freely about everything that interested him, and had little concept of public and private subjects. He had enormous curiosity about the world and its creatures, humans and animals, plants and rocks and minerals, and would discuss his latest discoveries and theories with everyone he met. Rice wine loosened his tongue even further, and he invariably forgot what he had been babbling about the night before. He liked all the pleasures of peace—the plentiful food, his freedom to travel, interaction with the foreigners, the wonderful curiosities they brought from the far side of the world—to such an extent that he did not want to face the fact that peace was always under threat, that not everyone was to be trusted, that enemies might exist even within his own family circle.

So Shizuka did not confide in him her concerns about Taku and Zenko, and Ishida himself had almost forgotten the night in Hofu when he had drunkenly revealed to Zenko, Hana, and Lord Kono his theories on the power of the human mind, and the self-fulfilling effects of belief in prophecies, and how these applied to Takeo.

Sunaomi and Chikara were sad at her departure, but their mother, Hana, was expected in Hagi before the end of the month, and they were kept too busy with their education and training to miss their grandmother. Since they had been in Hagi, Shizuka had watched them closely for any sign of developing Tribe skills, but the boys seemed like normal warriors' sons, no different from the boys of their own age with whom they trained, competed, and squabbled.

Kaede hugged her, gave her a new cloak with a hood in the latest fashion and a horse from the stables, a mare that Shizuka had often ridden before. It was easier to obtain a horse than a traveling companion; she found herself missing Kondo Kiichi, who would have been perfect for such a journey, with his fighting skills and his loyalty. She regretted his death and, since he had no children, took it on herself to remember his spirit and pray for him.

There was no need for secrecy or disguise, yet her upbringing had made her cautious, and she refused Kaede's offer of an escort of Otori warriors. In the end she selected the man Bunta, who many years before had been her informant in Maruyama. He had worked as a groom for Lady Maruyama Naomi, had been in Inuyama at the time of her death, and had stayed there during the war. He had therefore escaped Takeo's purge of the Maruyama Tribe families, though he had lost relatives there. After the war and the earthquake he had found his way to Hagi and had been in the service of the Otori ever since. He was a few years younger than she was, from the Imai family. On the surface he was taciturn and obedient yet possessed some unusual skills: an adept pickpocket, a laconic storyteller who had the knack of extracting information, and an expert in street wrestling and bare-hand fighting who drank with the most hardened carousers yet never lost his head. Their shared past had created a bond between them, and she felt she could trust him.

Throughout the winter he had brought her snippets of information and, as soon as the snows melted, had gone at her request to Yamagata to find out, as he put it, which way the wind blew. The news he brought back was disturbing: Taku had not returned to Inuyama but was still in Hofu; Zenko was deeply involved with the Kikuta and considered himself the Master of the Muto family; the family itself was divided. These were the matters she had discussed with Takeo before his departure, but they had come to no decisions. The birth of his son, his preparations for the journey to Miyako, had taken up all Takeo's attention. Now she felt obliged to act herself, to do all she could to keep the Muto family loyal and to ensure the safety of the twins, Maya and Miki.

She loved them as if they were the daughters she had never had. She had cared for them when Kaede had taken so long to recover after their birth; she had overseen all their training in the ways of the Tribe; she had protected and defended them against all those who wished them ill.

She had one other aim that she was not sure she had the strength to fulfill, the one that she had put to Takeo and he had rejected. She could not help recalling another warlord, Iida Sadamu, from so long ago, and the plot to assassinate him. If only the world were as straightforward now. She had told Takeo that as the Muto Master and old friend to the Otori she had to advise him to get rid of Zenko. This was still her opinion when she thought clearly. But when she thought as a mother . . .

Takeo has told me he will not take Zenko's life, she thought. *There is no need for me to act against his wishes. No one can expect it of me.*

But in some secret part of her she expected it of herself.

She would discuss it with no one, but from time to time she took it out and looked at it steadily, accustoming herself to its darkness, its threat and its appeal.

Bunta's son, a boy of fifteen or sixteen, came with them, looked after the horses, bought the food, and rode on ahead to make arrangements at the next stopping place. The weather was fine, the spring planting finished, the rice fields pale green from the seedlings and blue from the reflected sky. The roads were safe and well maintained, the towns cheerful and prosperous, food plentiful and delicious—for on the high roads the horse stations vied with one another to produce local delicacies and specialties.

Shizuka marveled anew at Takeo and Kaede's achievements, at the richness and contentment of their country, and grieved at the lust for power and craving for revenge that threatened it.

For not everyone rejoiced at the land's stability and peacefulness. In Tsuwano the Muto family with whom she stayed grumbled at their lack of status among the merchants now that so many people were involved in trade. And in Yamagata, in Kenji's old house, now owned by one of her cousins, Yoshio, in the evening the conversation turned to the good old days, when Kikuta and Muto were friends and everyone feared and respected them.

Shizuka had known Yoshio almost all his life. He was one of the boys she had out-fought and outwitted during their childhood training in the hidden village. He treated her with familiarity and spoke openly to her. She did not know if she could count on his support, but at least he was honest with her.

"It was different while Kenji was alive," Yoshio said. "Everyone respected him, and could see his reasons for making peace with the Otori. Takeo had information that could have destroyed the Tribe, as he nearly did in Maruyama. Then, it was the expedient thing to do—it bought us time, and preserved our strength. But increasingly people are saying the Kikuta's demands for justice need to be heard: Takeo's guilty of the worst of offenses, absconding from the Tribe and killing the Master of his family. He's gotten away with it for all these years, but now between them Akio and Arai Zenko are in a position to execute judgment on him."

"Kenji swore allegiance to Takeo on behalf of the entire Muto family," Shizuka reminded him. "As has my son—many times. And I'm not only head of the Muto family because Takeo appointed me—it was Kenji's wish too."

"Kenji can't speak from the grave, can he? As far as most of us are concerned—I'm being honest with you, Shizuka. I've always admired you and liked you, too, even though you were an insufferable kid, but you grew out of that—you were even quite pretty for a while!" He grinned at her and poured her more wine.

"You can spare me the compliments," she returned, drinking the wine in one gulp. "I'm too old for all that now!"

"You drink like a man as well as fight like one!" he said with some admiration.

"I can lead like a man, too," she assured him.

"I don't doubt it. But, as I was saying, people in the Tribe resent the fact that Takeo appointed you. The Muto family affairs have never been decided by warlords—"

"Takeo is rather more than a warlord!" Shizuka protested.

"How did he get power? Like any other warlord, by grasping opportunities, dealing ruthlessly with his enemies, and betraying those he had sworn allegiance to."

"That is only one way of describing him!"

"It is the Tribe's way," Yoshio said, smiling broadly.

Shizuka said, "The evidence of his government is all around: fertile land, healthy children, rich merchants."

"Frustrated warriors and unemployed spies," Yoshio argued, gulping down his wine and filling their bowls again. "Bunta, you're very quiet. You tell Shizuka I'm right."

Bunta raised his bowl to his lips and gazed at Shizuka over its rim as he drank. "It's not only that Takeo appointed you, and that you're a woman. There are other suspicions about you, far graver ones."

Yoshio was no longer smiling, but sat with compressed lips, staring downward.

"People wondered how Takeo knew where to find the Tribe in Maruyama when he had never been there in his life. There were rumors that Lord Shigeru had recorded information on the Tribe for years; everyone knew that he and Kenji were friends, but Shigeru knew far more about the Tribe than he would have learned from Kenji. Someone was feeding him information."

Both men glanced at her when Bunta paused, but she made no response.

"People are saying it was you, and that's why Takeo made you head of the Muto family, to reward you for your years of treachery."

The word hung in the air like a blow.

"Forgive me," Bunta added hurriedly. "I'm not saying I am one of them; I just want to warn you. Of course Akio will take advantage of these rumors, which could be very dangerous for you."

"It's all a long time ago," Shizuka said with assumed lightness. "During Iida's rule, and in the civil war, many acted in a way that might be called treachery. Zenko's father turned on Takeo after vowing alliance with him, yet who could blame him? Everyone knew sooner or later the Arai would fight the Otori for control of the Three Countries. The Otori won—the Tribe went with the victor, as we always do, as we will continue to do."

"Unh," Yoshio grunted. "Now it looks as though the Arai will be challenging the Otori again. No one thinks Takeo is going to retire meekly into exile, whatever happens in the contest in Miyako. He'll come back and fight. He might defeat Zenko in the West, and possibly, though it's less likely, Saga in the East, but he can't win against both of them. We should go with the victor . . ."

"And then the Kikuta will have their revenge," Bunta said. "They've waited long enough for it. It goes to show, no one escapes the Tribe forever."

Shizuka heard the words like a ghostly echo, for she had said the same thing about Takeo's future to Kaede years ago, at Terayama.

"You can save yourself, Shizuka, and very likely the Muto family too. All you have to do is recognize Zenko as head of the family. We detach ourselves from Takeo before he's defeated; we don't get dragged down with him, and whatever secrets might lie in your past will remain buried."

"Taku will never agree to it," she said, voicing her thoughts.

"He will if you tell him to, as head of the family and his mother. He's got no choice. Anyway, Taku's a reasonable sort of fellow. He'll see it's for the best. Zenko will become Saga's vassal, the Tribe will be united again, we regain our power, and since Saga intends to bring all the Eight Islands under his rule, we will have interesting and lucrative employment for years to come."

And I will not have to seek my son's death, Shizuka thought.

SHE LEFT FOR the Muto village, Kagemura, the next day. It was the day after the full moon and she rode in a somber mood, disturbed by the previous night's conversation, fearing that the Muto family in the secret village would have the same views and urge her to follow the same course. Bunta said little, and she found herself angry and uncomfortable with him. How long had he suspected her? Ever since he had first started reporting to her on Shigeru's relationship with Maruyama Naomi? She had lived with the fear that her betrayal of the Tribe would be discovered for many years, but since she had admitted it to Kenji, and received his approval and forgiveness, the fear had receded. Now it surfaced again, making her alert and defensive in a way she had not been for years, prepared at any moment to have to fight for her life. She found herself assessing Bunta and the boy, working out how she would take them if they turned on her. She had not allowed her skills to diminish, still trained every day as she had done all her life, but she was no longer young; she could outfight most men with the sword but knew she could not match them in physical strength.

They came to the inn at nightfall and rose early the next morning, leaving the boy and the horses there, to walk on foot, as she had with Kondo, through the mountains. She had slept lightly, aware of every sound, and her heaviness of spirit had increased. The morning was misty, the sky overcast. She had an almost uncontrollable desire to weep. She could not stop thinking of Kondo—she had lain with him in this very place. She had not loved him, but he had touched her in some way. She had pitied him, and then he had appeared at the very moment when she thought her life was about to be brought to a slow and agonizing end, only to be burned to death in front of her eyes. His stolid, pragmatic character seemed to take on an almost unbearable tragic nobility. How pathetic he had been, and how admirable! Why was she so moved by his memory now? It was almost as if his spirit was reaching out to hers, to tell her something, to warn her.

Even the sudden sight of the Muto village in the hidden valley failed to delight her as it usually did. It was late afternoon when they arrived, but though the sun had come out briefly at midday, now that it was setting behind the steep mountain range, the mist was rising in the valley again. It was cold, making her glad of the hooded cloak she wore. The gates of the village were barred, and, it seemed to her, were opened reluctantly. Even the houses had a closed and hostile look about them, the wooden walls dark with moisture, roofs weighted down with stones.

Her grandparents had died years before, and the old house was now inhabited by families the age of her sons, with young children. She did not know any of them well, though she was familiar with their names, their talents, and most of the details of their lives.

Kana and Miyabi, grandmothers now, still ran the household, and they at least greeted her with unfeigned pleasure. She was less sure of the sincerity of the welcome from the other adults, though the children were excited by her arrival, especially Miki.

It was barely two months since Shizuka had last seen her—she was surprised by the change in the girl. She had grown taller and had lost weight, so that she appeared stretched and attenuated. The sharp bones in her face were more pronounced and her eyes glittered in their hollow sockets.

When they gathered in the kitchen to prepare the evening meal, she asked Kana, "Has Miki been unwell?" for spring was often the time of sudden fevers and stomach troubles.

"You should not be in here with us!" Kana scolded her. "You are the honored guest—you should be sitting with the men."

"I'll join them soon enough. Tell me about Miki."

Kana turned to look at the girl, who was sitting by the hearth, stirring the soup in an iron pot that hung over the fire on a fish-shaped iron hook.

"She's grown very thin," Kana agreed. "But she hasn't complained of anything, have you, child?"

"She never does," Miyabi added, laughing. "She's as tough as a man. Come here, Miki, let Shizuka feel your arms."

Miki came and knelt close to Shizuka without speaking. Shizuka closed her hands round the girl's upper arm. She felt like steel, no flesh at all, just muscle and bone.

"Is everything all right?"

Miki gave the slightest shake of her head.

"Come take a walk with me—you can tell me what's troubling you."

"She will talk to you when she will not talk to anyone else," Kana said in a low voice.

"Shizuka," Miyabi whispered even more quietly, "be on your guard. The young men . . ." She glanced toward the main room of the house where the male voices could be heard, muffled and indistinct, though Shizuka could pick out Bunta's. "There is some discontent," she said vaguely, obviously afraid of being overheard.

"So I have been told. It is the same in Yamagata, and Tsuwano. I am going on to Hofu, where I will discuss the whole situation with my sons. I will leave within a day or two."

Miki was still kneeling close to her, and Shizuka heard the slight intake of breath and felt the increased tension as the girl stiffened. She put her arm round Miki's shoulders, shocked by the sharpness and fragility of the bones beneath the skin, like a bird's wing.

"Come, get your sandals. We'll walk down to the shrine and greet the gods."

Kana gave Miki some rice cakes as an offering for the gods. Shizuka threw the hooded cloak over her shoulders; it had grown even colder. The moon shone dimly through the misty air, a huge halo around it, casting shadows across the street and beneath the trees that surrounded the shrine. Even though it was two days past the full moon of the fourth month, it was still too cold, high in the mountains, for frogs or cicadas to be heard. Only the owls called in their fractured mating song.

The shrine was lit with two lamps on either side of the altar. Miki placed the rice cakes in front of the statue of Hachiman, and they both clapped their hands and bowed three times. Shizuka had prayed here long ago for Takeo and Kaede, and now she made the same request, and she prayed for Kondo's spirit and told him of her gratitude.

"Will the gods protect Maya?" Miki said, staring up at the carved features of the statues.

"Did you ask them to?"

"Yes, I always do. And Father. But I don't see how they can answer everyone's prayers, when everyone wants different things. I pray for Father's safety, but many others pray for his death."

"Is it this that has made you so thin, worrying about your father?"

"I wish I was with him. And that Maya was too."

"Last time I saw you, you were so content, and doing so well. What's happened since then?"

"I don't sleep well. I am afraid of the dreams."

"What dreams?" Shizuka prompted her when she fell silent.

"Dreams where I am with Maya. She is the cat and I am its shadow. It takes everything from me and I have to follow it. Then I try to stay awake and I hear the men talking. They always talk about the same thing, about the Muto family, and whether the Master should be a woman, and Zenko, and the Kikuta. I used to love being here. I felt safe and everyone liked me. Now the men fall silent when I walk past; the other children avoid me. What's going on, Shizuka?"

"Men always grumble about something or other. They'll get over it," Shizuka replied.

"It's more than that," Miki said with great intensity. "Something bad is happening. Maya is in some terrible trouble. You know how we are together: We know what's happening to each other. We always have done. Now I can feel her calling for help, but I don't know where she is."

"She is in Hofu with Taku and Sada," Shizuka said with a confidence that masked her own unease, for it was true that the twins had always had an almost supernatural link with each other, had seemed to know each other's thoughts from afar.

"Will you take me with you when you go there?"

"Maybe I should."

Indeed, she thought. *I must. I cannot leave her here now, to be used against Takeo in any way. The sooner I speak to Taku and Zenko, the better. We must settle the question of leadership before this discontent gets out of hand.*

"We will leave the day after tomorrow."

SHIZUKA SPENT THE next day in consultation with the young men who now formed the core of the Muto family. They treated her with deference and listened to her politely, for her lineage, history, and talents all commanded their respect, and, in some cases, their fear. She was relieved that despite her age and her slight physical stature she could still exercise power and control over them. She repeated her intention of discussing the leadership question with Zenko and Taku, and emphasized that she would not relinquish her position as Master before Lord Takeo returned from the East, that it had been Kenji's wish and that she expected full obedience from them all according to the traditions of the Muto.

No one dissented, and no one argued when she told them Miki would be going with her, but on the road two days later, after they had retrieved the horses and were on their way back to Yamagata, Bunta said, "Of course, they know in the village now that you don't trust them. If you trusted them, you'd have left Miki there."

"I trust no one at the moment." They rode side by side, Miki ahead on the back of the boy's horse. Shizuka planned to borrow another horse for her from Lord Miyoshi's stables in Yamagata. It would make them both more flexible, safer.

She turned and looked at Bunta directly, challenging him. "Am I wrong? Should I trust you?"

"I'll be honest with you. It's all a question of what the Tribe decides. I'm not going to cut your throat while you sleep, if that's what you mean. I've known you for a long time—and anyway, I've never liked killing women."

"So you'll inform me before you betray me," she said.

His eyes crinkled slightly. "I will."

"Send Bunta and his son back," Miki said later, when they had arrived at Yamagata and were alone. Rather than stay in the Muto house with Yoshio, Shizuka had gone to the castle, where Kahei's wife made them welcome, tried to persuade them to stay longer, and when that failed offered to provide an escort as well as the extra horse.

"It's difficult to judge," Shizuka said to Miki. "If I send them back, I no longer have any contact with the Muto family on the road, and I'll drive Bunta further away from me. If I accept Lady Miyoshi's offer, we go openly—you as Lord Otori's daughter."

Miki made a face at this suggestion. Shizuka laughed. "Decisions are never as simple as you think."

"Why can't we go together, just the two of us?"

"Two women, traveling alone, with no servants or escort only attract attention—usually of the undesirable kind!"

"If only we had been born boys!" Miki said, and though she made an effort to speak lightly, Shizuka glimpsed the sadness behind the words. She thought of Kaede's adoration of her baby son, the intense love that she had never shown to her twin daughters, saw the loneliness of the girls, growing up in two worlds. If the Muto family turned against their father, they would reject the girls, too, would do their utmost to eliminate them along with Takeo.

"Bunta and his son will come with us to Hofu. When we get there, Taku will look after us; you will be with Maya, and we will all be safe!"

Miki nodded and forced a smile, but though she had spoken the words to comfort her, Shizuka found herself regretting them. They seemed to have fanned into flame some tiny spark of unease. She felt she had tempted the gods, and that they would turn and strike her.

There was a small earthquake that night, making buildings shake and causing fires in some parts of the city. The air was still filled with dust and smoke as they left with two extra horses, one ridden by a groom from the Miyoshi household. They met Bunta and his son as arranged, on the bank of the moat, just outside the castle gates.

"Do you have any word from Taku?" Shizuka asked Bunta, thinking her son might have made contact with the Muto family.

"Yoshio's heard nothing since the last new moon, and then only a report that he was still in Hofu." Bunta grinned suggestively as he said this, and winked at his son, who laughed.

Does everyone know of his infatuation with Sada? Shizuka asked herself, feeling a wave of irritation against her younger son.

However, on the first night of their journey, after Shizuka and Miki had gone to bed, Bunta came to the door, calling softly to her. He had been drinking with other travelers in a tavern in the small post town. She could smell the wine on his breath.

"Come outside. I've just heard some bad news."

He was not drunk, but the wine had dulled his sensibilities and loosened his tongue.

She took her knife from beneath the mattress and tucked it inside her night robe, pulling her cloak around her. She followed him to the end of the veranda. There was no moon; the town had fallen silent as travelers snatched a few hours' sleep before dawn saw them on the road again. It was too dark to make out any expression on his face.

"It may be just a rumor, but I thought you'd want to hear it." He paused and said clumsily, "It's not good news—you should prepare yourself."

"What?" she said, more loudly than she intended.

"Taku, your son, has been attacked on the road—by bandits, apparently. He and his woman, Sada, were both killed."

"It can't be true," she said. "What bandits are there in the Middle Country?"

"No one knows the details. But people were talking about it in the tavern."

"Tribe people? Muto?"

"Muto and Kuroda." He added awkwardly, "I'm sorry."

He knows it is true, she thought, and knew it herself. When she had felt such sadness on the way to Kagemura, when she had felt Kondo's spirit near her, the dead had been calling out to her, and now Taku was among them. *This will kill me,* was her next thought, for the pain was already so intense she did not see how she could survive it, how she could keep living in a world in which he did not exist. She felt inside her robe for the knife, meaning to plunge it into her throat, welcoming the physical pain that would put an end to her anguish. But something prevented her.

She lowered her voice, aware of Miki sleeping nearby. "Lord Otori's daughter Maya was in Taku's care. Is she also dead?"

"No one's mentioned her," Bunta said. "I don't think anyone knew she was with them, apart from the Muto family in Maruyama."

"Did you know?"

"I heard that the child they called the Kitten was with Taku. I worked out who it must be."

Shizuka did not reply. She was fighting for self-mastery. Into her mind came an image from the past, of her uncle, Kenji, on the day he heard the news of his daughter's death at the hands of the Kikuta. *Uncle,* she called to his spirit. *You know what I am suffering and now I feel your pain. Give me the strength to carry on living, as you did.*

Maya. I must think of Maya. I will not think of Taku, not yet. I must save Maya.

"Will we go on to Hofu?" Bunta said.

"Yes, I must find out the truth." She thought of all the rituals that would need to be performed for the dead, wondered where the bodies were buried, felt the anguish tighten its bands of steel around her chest at the thought of the corpse that had been her son, in the earth, in the dark. "Is Zenko in Hofu?" she said, amazed that the words emerged calm and intelligible.

"Yes, his wife left for Hagi by ship a week ago, but he is still there. He is overseeing the trade arrangements with the foreigners. He has become very close to them, it is reported."

"Zenko must know. If it was bandits, he is responsible for capturing and punishing them, and rescuing Maya if she is still alive."

But even as she spoke she knew her son had not been killed randomly by bandits. And no one from the Tribe would touch Taku—no one but the Kikuta. Akio had spent the winter in Kumamoto. Akio had been in touch with Zenko.

She could not believe Zenko was involved in his brother's murder. Were both her sons to be lost to her?

I must not condemn him before I speak to him.

Bunta touched her tentatively on the arm. "Is there anything I can do? Can I get you wine, or tea?"

She recoiled from him, reading something more than sympathy in the gesture, suddenly hating all men for their lust and their murderous violence. "I would like to be alone. We will leave at first light. Say nothing to Miki. I will decide when to tell her."

"I'm really very sorry," he said. "Everyone liked Taku. It's a terrible loss."

When his footsteps died away, she sank down on the veranda, pulling the cloak around her, still holding the knife in her hand, its familiar weight her only comfort, her means of escape from the world of pain.

She heard the lightest of footfalls on the boards. Miki crawled up against her and into her arms.

"I thought you were asleep." Shizuka held the girl close and stroked her hair.

"His footsteps woke me, and then I couldn't help listening." Her thin body was trembling. "Maya's not dead. I would know if she was."

"Where is she? Can you find her?" Shizuka thought if she concentrated on Maya, on the living, she would not break down. And Miki, with her acute sensitivity, seemed to be aware of this. She said nothing about Taku, but helped Shizuka to her feet.

"Come and lie down," she said, as if she were the adult and Shizuka the child. "Even if you don't sleep, you will be resting. I want to sleep, because Maya talks to me in dreams. Sooner or later she will tell me where she is, and then I'll go and find her."

"We should return to Hagi. I should take you to your mother."

"No, we must go to Hofu," Miki whispered. "Maya is still in Hofu. If one day you find I'm gone, don't worry about me. I'll be with Maya."

They lay down and Miki curled into Shizuka's side, her hand on her breast. She seemed to fall asleep, but Shizuka lay awake, thinking about her son's life. All women, among the Tribe and in the warrior class, had to accustom themselves to the likelihood of the early violent death of their male children. Boys were brought up to have no fear of death, and girls were trained not to show weakness or grief. To fear for someone else's life was to attempt to bind them to you in some way, and she had seen how a mother's overprotective love turned boys into cowards or drove them into recklessness. Taku was dead, she grieved for him, but she was sure his death meant he had not betrayed Takeo—he had been killed for his loyalty. His death had not been random or meaningless.

In this way she was able to comfort and strengthen herself over the next few days as they rode toward Hofu. She was determined she would go not as a distraught and grieving mother but as head of the Muto family; she would show no weakness, but she would find out how her son had died and bring his murderers to justice.

THE WEATHER BECAME hot and sultry—even the sea breezes did not cool the port city. The spring rains had been sparse, and people spoke apprehensively of an unusually hot summer, possibly even drought, for there had been no drought in sixteen years or more. The spring rains and the plum rains had arrived at the right time and fallen heavily for so many years, many young people had never experienced the hardships endured when the rains failed.

There was an air of unrest in the city, not only due to the oppressive weather. Various ominous signs were reported daily; faces speaking of doom were seen in lanterns outside Daifukuji temple; a flock of birds had traced characters of ill-luck in the sky. As soon as they arrived, Shizuka was aware of the real grief and anger of the townspeople at Taku's death. She did not go to the Arai mansion, but stayed in an inn not far from the Umedaya, overlooking the river. On the first night the innkeeper told her that Taku and Sada were buried at Daifukuji. She sent Bunta to inform Zenko of her arrival, and rose early the next morning, leaving Miki asleep, limbs twitching and lips moving in some vivid dream, to walk along the riverbank to where the vermilion temple stood among the sacred trees, facing out to sea to welcome sailors home to the Middle Country. The sound of chanting came from within, and she heard the sonorous and holy words of the sutra for the dead.

Two monks were scattering water on the boardwalks before sweeping them. One of them recognized Shizuka, and said to the other, "Take Lady Muto to the graveyard. I will inform the Abbot."

She saw their sympathy and was grateful for it.

Under the huge trees there was a hint of coolness. The monk led her to the newly dug graves. No stones yet covered them, lamps burned beside them, and someone had laid an offering of flowers—purple irises—before them. She forced herself to picture her son's ashes in the casket beneath the ground, his strong agile body stilled, his quick sardonic mind silenced.

His spirit must be wandering restlessly between the worlds, demanding justice.

The second monk returned with incense, and shortly afterward, as Shizuka knelt in silent prayer, the Abbot himself came and knelt beside her. They remained in silence for some time, then the man began to chant the same sutra for the dead.

Tears formed in her eyes and traced their way down her cheeks. The ancient words rose into the canopy of the trees, mingling with the morning song of sparrows and the gentle cooing of doves.

Later, the Abbot took her to his room and served her tea. "I have taken it upon myself to arrange for the stone to be carved. I thought it was what Lord Otori would have desired."

She stared at him. She had known him for some years, but had always seen him in a merry mood, as able to joke with the sailors in their rough dialect as to compose elegantly humorous verses with Takeo, Kaede, and Dr. Ishida. Now his face was drawn, his expression grave.

"Surely his brother, Lord Zenko, has dealt with all this?"

"I'm afraid Lord Zenko has become somewhat influenced by the foreigners—no formal announcement has been made, but everyone's talking about it. He has taken on their religion and now professes it as the one true faith. This renders him unable to enter our temples and shrines, and unable to perform the necessary ceremonies for his brother."

Shizuka stared at the priest, hardly able to believe what she heard.

"It's caused a great deal of unrest," he went on. "There have been signs and omens that the gods are offended. People fear they will be punished for their lord's actions. The foreigners insist, on the contrary, that their great god, Deus, will reward Zenko and anyone else who joins him.

"Which includes most of his personal retainers," he added, "who have been ordered to convert or die."

"What absolute madness," Shizuka said, resolving to speak to Zenko as soon as possible. She did not wait to be summoned to his presence, but on her return to the inn dressed with care and ordered a palanquin.

"Wait here for me," she told Miki. "If I don't return by evening, go to

Daifukuji, and they will look after you." The girl hugged her with unusual intensity.

Zenko came out to the veranda steps as soon as the palanquin was set down inside the gates, lightening her heart for a moment and making her think she had misjudged him. His first words were of sympathy, followed by expressions of pleasure at seeing her, surprise that she had not come directly to him.

Her eyes fell on the prayer beads he wore round his neck, the symbol of the foreigners' religion, the cross, hanging from his chest.

"This terrible news is such a shock to us all," he said, as he led her into his private room overlooking the garden.

A little child, his youngest son, was playing on the veranda, watched by his nurse.

"Come and say hello to your grandmother," Zenko called, and the boy obediently came into the room and knelt before her. It was the first time she had seen him—he was about two years old.

"My wife, as you know, has gone to Hagi to be with her sister. She was reluctant to leave little Hiromasa, but I thought it best to keep at least one of my sons with me."

"You recognize then that you are gambling with the lives of your other children?" she said quietly.

"Mother, Hana will be with them within two weeks. I don't think they are in any danger. Anyway, I have done nothing wrong. My hands are clean." He held them up to her and then took the child's hands. "Cleaner than Hiromasa's," he teased him.

"He has Kikuta palms." Shizuka exclaimed in astonishment. "Why did you not tell me?'

"Interesting, isn't it? Tribe blood is never completely eradicated." He smiled broadly at her, and gestured to the maid to take the child away.

"He reminds me of Taku," he said, wiping his eye with his sleeve. "It is some shred of comfort to me that my poor brother lives on in my son."

"Perhaps you will tell me who killed him," Shizuka said.

"Bandits, obviously. What other explanation can there be? I will pursue them and bring them to justice. Of course, with Takeo out of the country, desperate men grow bold and come out of hiding."

It was obvious that he did not care if she believed him or not.

"What if I order you to tell me the truth?"

His eyes flickered away from her, and he hid his face in his sleeve again, but she had the feeling he was not weeping but smiling, in surprise and glee at his own audacity.

"Let us not speak about ordering, Mother. I will observe all my filial duty toward you, but in all other terms I believe it is now appropriate for you to obey me, both as Muto and Arai."

"I serve the Otori," she replied. "So did Kenji, and so have you sworn to."

"Yes, you serve the Otori," he said, his anger showing. "That has been the problem for years. Wherever we look in the history of the Otori's rise, we see your hand—in Takeo's persecution of the Tribe, in my father's murder, even in Lord Fujiwara's death—what led you to betray the secrets of the Tribe to Shigeru?"

"I will tell you! I wanted a better world for you and Taku. I thought you should live in Shigeru's world, not the one of warlords and assassins that I saw around me. Takeo and Kaede created that world. We will not let you destroy it."

"Takeo is already finished. Do you think the Emperor will favor him? If he does return, we will kill him, and I will be confirmed as ruler of the Three Countries. It is my right, and I am ready for it."

"Are you prepared to fight Takeo, and Kahei, Sugita, Sonoda—most of the warriors of the Three Countries?"

"It will not be a battle but a rout. With Saga in the East and the additional support we have from the foreigners"—he tapped the cross on his chest—"their weapons, their ships, Takeo will be easily defeated. He is not really much of a warrior: All his famous battles were won more by luck than skill."

He lowered his voice. "Mother, I can protect you to a certain extent, but if you persist in defying me I shall not be able to hold the Kikuta family back. They demand your punishment, for your years of disobedience to the Tribe."

"I will take my own life first," she exclaimed.

"That may be the best thing," he replied, looking directly at her. "What if I order you to, now?"

"I carried you under my heart for nine months." She recalled suddenly the day she had gone to Kenji to seek the Tribe's permission to have this child. He had been her gift to her lover—how proud his father had been. Now both father and son had sought her death. Anger and sorrow filled her; weeping for a year would not assuage them. She could sense her reason tipping into madness. *I wish I could kill myself,* she thought, deeply tempted by the annihilation of death; only the fate of the twin girls prevented her. She wanted to ask after Maya, but was afraid to reveal something that Zenko might not have known. Better to keep silent, to do what she had done all her life, dissemble, while acting as she deemed best. She made a huge effort to put her emotion away and assumed the gentle demeanor she had used so often before.

"Zenko, you are my oldest son, and I want to be a good and dutiful mother to you. I will think about all you have said. Give me a day or two. Let me make the arrangements for your brother's memorial. I cannot come to a decision while my mind is clouded by grief."

For a moment she thought he would refuse her. She assessed the distance to the garden and over the wall, but in the silence she thought she heard men breathing—there were guards hidden behind the screens, in the garden. *Is he really afraid I came to kill him? With Taku hardly buried?* Her chances of escape were small. She would go invisible—if the guards came after her, she would disarm one, take his sword . . .

Some vestige of respect worked on him. "Very well," he conceded. "I will have my guards escort you. Do not attempt to escape them, and on no account leave Hofu. When your mourning period is over, you either join me or kill yourself."

"Will you come and offer prayers for your brother?"

He gave her a chilling look, followed by an impatient shake of the head. She did not want to press him, for she was afraid he would detain her there, using force if necessary. She bowed submissively, feeling fury burn impotently in her gut. As she left, she heard voices at the far end of the main veranda. She turned her head and saw Don João with his interpreter, Madaren, coming toward her. They were dressed in new, splendid clothes, even Madaren, and they walked with a new confidence.

Shizuka greeted Don João coldly and then spoke to Madaren, using no courtesies, voicing the anger it had cost her so much to contain. "What do you think you're doing here?"

Madaren flushed at her tone, but collected herself and replied, "I am doing God's will, as are we all."

Shizuka did not answer, but stepped into the palanquin. As it was borne away at a sharp trot followed by six of Zenko's men, she cursed the foreigners for intruding with their weapons and their God. She hardly knew what the words were that came pouring from her mouth—rage and grief made her incoherent; she could feel them tug her toward madness.

When the palanquin stopped and was lowered to the ground outside the inn, she did not descend immediately, wishing she could remain inside this tiny space, so like a coffin, and never engage with the living again. Finally the thought of Miki drove her to emerge into the bronze glare.

Bunta squatted on his heels on the veranda, just as when she had left him, but the room was empty.

"Where's Miki?" she demanded.

"She's inside," he replied, surprised. "No one's come past me, in or out."

"Who's taken her?" Shizuka's heart was beginning to stammer in dread.

"No one, I swear to you."

"You had better not be lying," she said, going back into the room again, searching vainly for the thin body that could fold itself up and hide in the tiniest of places. The room was empty, but in one corner she found a new scratching in the wooden beam. Two half circles facing away from each other, and below them a full circle.

"She has gone to find Maya."

Shizuka knelt on the floor, trying to still her heart. Miki had gone—taken on invisibility, slipped past Bunta and out into the city. It was what her years spent in the Tribe had trained her for. There was nothing Shizuka could do for her now.

She sat for a long time, feeling the heat of the day build around her and the sweat form between her breasts and in her armpits. She heard the guards call impatiently to each other, and realized her choices were dwindling. She could not vanish away and leave Taku unmourned, but was she to stay in Hofu until either her son or the Kikuta arranged her death? There was no time to reach the Muto family and call them to her aid—and anyway, would they respond to her, now Zenko had claimed the leadership of the family?

She called to the dead to counsel her: to Shigeru, Kenji, Kondo, and Taku. Grief and sleeplessness began to exact their toll. She felt their cold breath on her as they sighed to her, *Pray for us. Oh, pray for us.*

Her exhausted mind fastened on this. She would go to the temple and mourn the dead, until either she became one of them, or they told her what to do.

"Bunta," she called. "There is one last task I must ask of you. Go and find me sharp scissors and a white robe."

He appeared on the threshold, his face ashen with shock.

"What has happened? Don't tell me you are to kill yourself."

"Just do as I say. I must go to the temple and arrange for Taku's headstone and funeral rites. After you have brought me what I request, do as you please. I release you from my service."

When he returned, Shizuka told him to wait outside. She unwrapped the bundles and took out the scissors. She untied her hair, divided it into two strands and cut through each strand, laying the long tresses carefully on the matting, noticing with detached surprise how many threads were white. Then she clipped the rest of her hair short, feeling the pieces fall around her like dust. She brushed them away and dressed herself in the white robe. She took her weapons—sword, knife, garrote, and throwing knives—and placed them on the floor, between the two strands of her hair. She bowed her head to the ground, giving thanks for the weapons and for all her life till this point. Then she called for a bowl of tea, drank it, and broke the empty cup in two with a quick movement of her strong hands.

"I will not drink again," she said aloud.

"Shizuka!" Bunta protested from the threshold, but she ignored him.

"Have her senses deserted her?" she heard his son whisper. "Poor woman!"

Moving slowly and deliberately, she went to the front of the inn. News of her visit to Zenko had spread and a small crowd had gathered outside. When she stepped into the palanquin, they followed it down the road along the riverbank to Daifukuji. Zenko's guards were made uneasy by this procession, and several times tried to beat the crowd back, but it grew in size, and became more unruly and more hostile. Many ran down to the river, for it was low tide, and, prising stones from the silt, began to throw them at the guards, managing to draw them back from the temple gates. The porters set Shizuka down outside the gates, and she went slowly into the main courtyard, moving as if floating. The crowd milled in the entrance. She sat down on the ground, her legs folded like a divine being on a lotus flower, and finally she allowed herself to weep for one son's death and the other son's treachery.

The funeral rites were held while she sat there, and the stones carved and erected. The days passed and she did not move, neither eating nor drinking. On the third night it rained gently, and people said Heaven was nourishing her. It rained every night after that; during the day birds were often seen fluttering around her head.

"They are feeding her with grains of millet and honey," the monks reported.

The townspeople said Heaven itself wept for the bereaved mother, and they gave thanks that the danger of drought was averted. Zenko's popularity waned as the moon of the fifth month began to grow toward fullness.

or many days and nights, Maya mourned the loss of the horses, unable to look at the greater loss. Shigeko had told her to look after them, and she had let them go. She relived the moment when she had dropped the reins and the mares had run away, and regretted it bitterly, as she regretted her inexplicable inability to move or to defend herself. It was only the third time she had faced real danger—after the attack at Inuyama and the encounter with her father—and she felt that in the extreme moment she had failed, despite her years of Tribe training.

She had plenty of time to reflect on her failure. When she regained consciousness, her throat raw, her stomach queasy, she found herself in a small, dimly lit room, which she recognized as one of the concealed chambers of a Tribe house. Takeo had often told his daughters stories of the times the Tribe had held him in such rooms, and now the memory comforted and calmed her. She had thought Akio would kill her at once, but he had not—he was keeping her for some purpose. She knew she could escape at any time, for the cat was not confined by doors or walls, but she did not want to run away yet. She wanted to stay close to Akio and Hisao. She would never let them kill her father; she would kill them herself first. So she curbed first her anger and then her fear, and set herself to learn all she could about them.

At first she saw Akio only when he brought her food and water; the food was sparse, but she was not bothered by hunger. She had always found that the less she ate, the easier it was to take on invisibility and use the second self. She practiced this when she was alone, sometimes even deceiving herself and seeing Miki leaning against the opposite wall. She did not speak to Akio but studied him, as he studied her. She knew he did not have invisibility or the Kikuta gaze that induces sleep, but he could perceive the one and evade the other. He had fast reflexes—her father had often said the fastest he had ever known—and was immensely strong and completely lacking in pity or any of the other gentler human emotions.

Two or three times a day one of the household maids came to take her to the privy; otherwise she saw no one. Akio in his turn hardly spoke to her. But after she had been imprisoned for about a week, he came late one evening, knelt in front of her, and took her hands, turning them palm upward. She could smell the wine on his breath, and his speech was unnaturally deliberate.

"I expect you to answer me truthfully, since I am the head of your family. Do you have any of your father's skills?"

She shook her head, and before the movement was finished, felt her head snap back and her sight darken as he slapped her. She had not seen his hand move.

"You tried to trap my eyes before—you must have the Kikuta sleep. And I saw you use invisibility in the inn. Do you have far-hearing?"

She nodded, because she did not want him to kill her then, but she did not tell him about the cat.

"And where's your sister?"

"I don't know."

Even though she was expecting it this time, she could not move quickly enough to avoid the second blow. Akio was grinning, as if it was a game he was enjoying.

"She is in Kagemura, with the Muto family."

"Is she? But she is not Muto; she is Kikuta. I think she should be here with us too."

"The Muto family will never give her to you," Maya said.

"There've been some changes in the Muto family; I thought you'd have realized. The Tribe always stick together in the long run," Akio said. "That's how we survive."

He tapped his teeth with his fingernails. The back of his right hand was scarred from an old wound, running from the wrist to the base of the first finger.

"You saw me kill that Muto witch, Sada. I won't hesitate to do the same to you."

She did not make any response to this; she was more interested in her own reaction, surprised that she was not afraid of him. She had not realized till that moment that, like her father, she possessed the Kikuta gift of fearlessness.

"This is what I've heard," he said. "That your mother would do nothing to save you, but your father loves you."

"It's not true," Maya lied. "My father does not care deeply for my sister and me. The warrior class hate twins and see them as shameful. My father has a kind nature, that is all."

"He always was soft-hearted," Akio said, and she saw the weakness in him, the deep-seated hatred and envy of Takeo. "Perhaps you will bring him to me."

"Only if it is to kill you," she replied.

Akio laughed and got to his feet. "But he will never kill Hisao!"

She found herself thinking about Hisao. For the last half-year, she had had to face the fact that this was her father's son, her half-brother, about whom no one spoke, of whose existence, she was sure, her mother had never been told. And she was equally sure Hisao did not know who his true father was. He had called Akio *Father*; he had looked at her in incomprehension when she had told him she was his sister. She heard in her mind over and over again Sada's voice, *So the boy truly is Takeo's son?* And Taku's reply, *Yes, and according to the prophecy is the only person who can bring death to him.*

Her half-grown character had an implacability all its own, some Kikuta legacy that made her ruthlessly single-minded. The balance for her had become simple: If Hisao died, then Takeo would live forever.

Apart from the training exercises, which she carried out assiduously, she had nothing to occupy her, and she often drifted between waking and sleep, dreaming vividly. She dreamed of Miki, dreams that were so clear she could not believe Miki was not in the room with her, and from which she woke feeling renewed. She also dreamed of Hisao. She knelt beside him while he slept and whispered in his ear, "I am your sister," and once she dreamed that the cat lay down next to him, and felt the warmth of his body through its fur.

She became obsessed with Hisao, as though she needed to know everything about him. She began to experiment with assuming the cat form at night while the household slept, tentatively at first, for it was something she wanted to keep hidden from Akio, and then with increasing confidence. By day she was a prisoner, but at night she roamed freely through the house, observed its occupants, and entered their dreams. She saw with contempt their fears and hopes. The maids complained of ghosts, of feeling a breath on their face or warm fur lying beside them, of hearing some large creature padding softly over the floor. Strange things were happening throughout the city, signs and apparitions.

Akio and Hisao slept apart from the other men, in a room at the back of the house. Maya went in the darkest, quietest time of night, just before dawn, to watch Hisao sleep, sometimes in Akio's embrace, sometimes alone. He slept restlessly, tossing and muttering. His dreams were vicious and jagged, but they interested her. Sometimes he woke and could not get back to sleep again; then he went to a small outbuilding at the back of the house, on the other side of the yard, where there was a workshop for forging and repairing household utensils and weapons. Maya followed him and watched him, noting his careful, meticulous movements, his hands, precise and dexterous, his absorption in the processes of invention and experimentation.

She heard snatches of conversation from the maids, but they never spoke to her. Apart from trips to the privy, she hardly saw them until one day a young woman came in Akio's place to bring her meal.

She was about Shigeko's age, and she stared at Maya with undisguised curiosity.

Maya said, "Don't stare at me. You know I am very powerful."

The girl giggled but did not look away. "You look like a boy," she said.

"You know I'm a girl," Maya retorted. "Haven't you seen me pissing?" She used boys' language, and the girl laughed.

"What's your name?" Maya asked.

"Nori," she whispered.

"Nori, I'll prove to you how powerful I am. You dreamed about a wrapping cloth; you had folded some rice cakes in it, and when you unwrapped them, they were crawling with maggots."

"I told no one!" the girl gasped, but took a step closer. "How did you know?"

"I know a lot of things," Maya replied. "Look in my eyes." She held the girl's gaze for a moment, long enough to see that she was superstitious and credulous, and something else, something about Hisao . . .

The girl's head rolled forward as Maya withdrew the power of her gaze. Maya slapped her on both sides of her face to waken her. The maid looked at her dazed.

"You're a fool if you love Hisao," Maya said bluntly.

The girl flushed. "I feel sorry for him," she whispered. "His father is so harsh with him, and he is often unwell."

"In what way, unwell?"

"He gets terrible headaches. He vomits, and loses his sight. He is sick today. The Kikuta Master was angry, as they were to meet Lord Zenko—Akio has gone on his own."

"Maybe I can help him," Maya said. "Why don't you take me to him?"

"I cannot! Akio would kill me if he found out."

"Take me to the privy," Maya said. "Close this door, but don't fasten it. I'll go to Hisao's room. Don't worry; no one will see me. But you must look out for Akio. Warn me when he returns."

"You won't hurt Hisao?"

"He is a grown man. I'm only fourteen years old—hardly even a woman yet. I have no weapons. How can I hurt him? Anyway, I said I would help him."

Even as she spoke, she was recalling all the ways she had been taught to kill a man with her bare hands. She ran her tongue over her lips; her throat was dry, but otherwise she was calm. He was unwell, weakened, possibly blinded by illness. It would be easy to disable him with her gaze. She touched her neck, feeling her own pulse, imagining his under her hands. And if that failed, she would summon up the cat . . .

"Come, Nori, let's go to Hisao. He needs your help." When Nori still hesitated, Maya said quietly, "He loves you too."

"He does?" Nori's eyes brightened in her thin, pale face.

"He doesn't tell anyone, but he dreams about you. I've seen his dreams in the same way I've seen yours. He dreams he is holding you and he cries out in his sleep."

Maya watched Nori's face as it softened; she despised the girl for her infatuation. Nori slid the door open, looked outside, and beckoned to Maya. They went quickly to the rear of the house, and at the door of the privy Maya grasped her stomach and cried out as if in pain.

"Hurry up, and don't spend all day in there," Nori said, with sudden inventiveness.

"Can I help it if I'm sick?" Maya replied in the same vein. "It's the foul food you give me!"

She touched Nori on the shoulder as her shape faded. Nori, used to such strangeness, stared stolidly ahead. Maya went swiftly to the room where Hisao slept, slid the door open, and stepped in.

The bright sun outside had closed her pupils, and for a moment she could see nothing. The room smelled stale, the faint odor of vomit hanging in the air. Then she saw the boy curled on the mattress in the corner, one arm covering his face. From the even rhythm of his breathing he seemed to be sleeping. She would never get another chance like this. Holding her breath, she flexed her wrists, called up all her strength, crossed the room, knelt beside him, and seized him around the neck.

The effort weakened her concentration so that she lost invisibility. His eyes opened, and he stared at her for an instant before twisting underneath her in an attempt to break her grip. He was stronger than she had anticipated, but she directed her gaze into his eyes and for a moment made him dizzy. Her fingers tightened like tentacles as his back arched and his arms flailed in his struggle to break free. She clung to him like an animal as he rose on hands and knees. His skin was sweaty, and she felt her fingers lose their grip. He also sensed it, and shook his head backward away from her as he twisted again. He grasped her and slammed her into the wall. The fragile screens splintered and tore, and somewhere she heard Nori, she thought, call out. *I've failed*, she thought, as Hisao's hands closed round her throat, and she prepared to die.

Miki! she said silently, and as if Miki answered her, she felt her rage against Hisao possess her and the cat came into being, spitting and snarling. He screamed in surprise and let go; the cat backed away, ready to escape but not yet willing to give up.

The pause gave Maya a moment to regain her control and concentration. She saw that despite the swiftness of his immediate reaction, something was still disabling him. His eyes went out of focus; he staggered slightly. He seemed to be trying to look at something just behind her, and listening to a whispering voice.

She thought it was a trick to get her to look away, and she continued to stare fixedly at him. The smell of decay and mold increased. The room seemed unbearably hot—the cat's thick pelt was stifling her. She heard the voice whisper again to her right; though she could not make out the words, she heard enough to know it was not Nori. There was someone else in the room.

She glanced sideways and saw the woman. She was young, perhaps nineteen or twenty, her hair cut short, her face pallid. She wore a white robe, crossed on the opposite side to the living, and she floated above the ground. Her face was set in an expression of such anger and despair that even Maya's hard heart was touched. She saw that Hisao both longed to look at the ghost and feared to. The cat spirit that possessed her moved freely between the worlds and for the first time she sought its knowledge and wisdom.

So this is what Taku meant, she reflected as she recognized her debt to the cat and how it might be fulfilled, and, immediately after, the power it gave her and how she might use it.

The woman called to her, "Help me! Help me!"

"What is it that you want?" the cat said.

"I want my son to listen to me!"

Before she could respond to this, Hisao came closer to her.

"You came back!" he said. "You have forgiven me. Come here, let me touch you. Are you a ghost too? Can I hold you?"

He put out his hand, and she saw the change in it, how it had softened into a curved shape that longed to fit itself round the denseness of a cat's fur, and to her amazement and not altogether to her liking, the cat responded as if to its master, lowered its head and flattened its ears, and allowed him to caress it.

She obeyed the wisdom of the cat. His touch united something innate in both of them. Hisao gasped. Maya felt the pain as if inside her own head, then it receded. She saw through his eyes, the half-blindness, the spinning lights like cogwheels of some machine of torture, and then the world came into focus in a new way, and Hisao said, "Mother?"

The ghost woman spoke. "At last!" she said. "Now will you listen to me?"

His hand was still on the cat's head. Maya sensed his confusion—his relief that the pain had gone, his dread of entering the world of the dead, his fear of half-glimpsed powers awakening. At the edge of her own mind hung a similar terror, of a way forward that she did not wish to take, a path that she and Hisao had to tread together, though she hated him and wanted to kill him.

Nori called from outside. "Quick! The Master is returning!"

Hisao took his hand from her head. Maya returned with relief into her own girl's shape. She wanted to get away from him, but he caught her arm; she thought she could feel his grip all the way through to the inner marrow of her bones. He was gazing at her, his eyes amazed and hungry.

"Don't go," he said. "Tell me. Did you see her?"

Nori, on the threshold, gazed from one to the other. "You are better," she exclaimed. "She has cured you!"

They both ignored her.

"Of course I did," Maya said as she slipped past him. "She's your mother, and she wants you to listen to her."

· *43* ·

e will tell Akio, she thought, as Nori hurried her back to the concealed room. *He tells him everything. Akio will learn about the cat. Either he will kill me or they will use me in some way against Father. I should run away. Yes, I must go home; I will warn Mother about Zenko and Hana. I must go home.*

But the cat had felt its master's hand on its head, and it was reluctant to leave. And Maya wanted, against her better judgment, to feel that moment again when she walked between the worlds and talked to ghosts. She wanted to know what they knew, what it was like to die, and all the other secrets the dead keep from the living.

She had slept fitfully for weeks, but as soon as she got back to the small stuffy room, an irresistible lassitude came over her. Her eyelids grew heavy; her whole body ached with weariness. Without speaking to Nori she lay down on the floor and fell instantly into the deep river of sleep.

She was awakened, as if dragged up from underwater, by a command. *Come to me.*

It was the darkest time of night, the air still and humid. Her neck and hair were damp with sweat. She did not want to feel the cat's heavy fur, but its master was calling—it had to go to him.

The cat's ears pricked; its head swiveled. It flowed easily through the inner screens and the outer walls into the yard at the back of the house, across the yard toward the workshop where the fire of the forges burned all night. The household was used to Hisao being here in the early morning, before dawn. He had made the place his own and no one disturbed him.

He held out his hand and the cat went to him, as if longing for the touch, the caress. He rubbed its head, and it licked his cheek with its rough tongue. Neither of them spoke, but there flowed between them an animal need for affection, a yearning for closeness, for touch.

After a long time Hisao said, "Show your true shape."

Maya realized that she was pressed against the boy's body, his hand still on the nape of her neck. It was both exciting and repulsive to her. She broke free from his embrace. She could not see his expression in the half-light. The fire crackled and the smoke made her eyes sting.

He lifted the lamp and held it close, gazing at her face. She kept her eyes lowered, not wanting to challenge him. Neither of them spoke, as if they did not want to return to the human world of language.

Finally Hisao said, "Why do you come as a cat?"

"I killed a cat with the Kikuta gaze, and its spirit has possessed me," she replied. "No one among the Muto knows how to deal with it, but Taku had been helping me master it."

"I am its master, but I don't know why or how. It dispelled my sickness, being with me, and it quieted the spirit's voice so I could hear it. I like cats, but my father killed one in front of my eyes because I liked it—you are not that cat?"

She shook her head.

"I still like you," he said. "I must like you very much; I can't stop thinking about you. I need you with me. Promise you will stay with me."

He put the lamp back on the floor and tried to pull her close to him again. She resisted him.

"You know we are brother and sister?" she said.

He frowned. "She is your mother? The ghost woman? Is that why you can perceive her?"

"No, we do not share the same mother, but the same father."

She could see him more clearly now. He did not look like her father, or like herself and Miki, but his glossy hair with its birdwing sheen was like theirs, and his skin had a similar texture and color, with the same honey tone that had been such a trial to Kaede. Maya had a sudden memory of childhood—sunshades and lotions to lighten the skin. How stupid and frivolous all that seemed now.

"Your father is Otori Takeo, who we call the Dog." He laughed in the sneering way she loathed. Suddenly she hated him again, and despised herself for the eagerness and ease with which the cat surrendered to him. "My father and I are going to kill him."

He leaned away, out of the lamp's glow, and brought out a small firearm. The light glinted on the dark steel barrel. "He is a sorcerer, and no one has been able to get near him, but this weapon is stronger than sorcery." He glanced at her and said, with deliberate cruelty, "You saw how it dealt with Muto Taku."

Maya made no reply, but she looked clearly and with no sentimentality at Taku's death. He had been killed fighting, with a kind of honor; he had betrayed no one. He and Sada had died together. There was nothing to regret in his death. Hisao's baiting did not touch her or weaken her.

"Lord Otori is your father," she said. "That's why I tried to kill you, so you would not kill him."

"Akio is my father." Doubt and anger showed in his voice.

"Akio treats you with cruelty, abuses you, and lies to you. He is not your father. You do not know how a father should behave toward his children."

"He loves me," Hisao whispered. "He hides it from everyone, but I know it's true. He needs me."

"Ask your mother," Maya replied. "Didn't I tell you to listen to her? She will tell you the truth."

There was another long silence. It was hot; she could feel sweat on her forehead. She was thirsty.

"Be the cat again, and I will listen to her," he said so quietly she could barely hear him.

"Is she here?"

"She is always here," Hisao said. "She is tied to me by a cord, as I was once tied to her. I am never free from her. Sometimes she is silent. That's not so bad. It is when she wants to talk—then the sickness comes over me."

"Because you try to fight the spirit world," Maya said. "It was the same for me. When the cat wanted to appear and I resisted it, I was ill in the same way."

Hisao said, "I have never had any Tribe skills. I'm not like you. I don't have invisibility. I can't use the second self. Even witnessing these things makes me slightly sick. But the cat doesn't. The cat makes me feel good, powerful."

He seemed unaware that his voice had changed and taken on a hypnotic quality, laced with an appeal that she could not resist. Maya felt the cat stretch and flex with longing. Hisao drew the supple body close to him and ran his hands through the dense fur.

"Stay close to me," he whispered, and then, more loudly, "I'll listen, Mother, to what you have to say."

THE FLAMES OF the forge and the lamplight dimmed and flickered as a gust of warm, fetid air blew suddenly across the dirt floor, stirring up the dust and making the shutters rattle. Then the lamp flared up, burning more brightly, illuminating the spirit woman as she drew close, floating just above the ground. The boy sat without moving; the cat lay beside him, its head beneath his hand, its golden eyes unblinking.

"Child," the mother said, her voice trembling. "Let me feel you; let me hold you." Her thin fingers touched his forehead, stroked his hair, and he felt her form close to his, the faintest of pressure as she embraced him.

"I used to hold you like this when you were a baby."

"I remember," he whispered.

"I could not bear to leave you. They made me take poison, Kotaro and Akio, who wept with love for me while he obeyed the Master and forced the pellets into my mouth, and watched me die in agony of body and spirit. But they could not keep me from you. I was only twenty years old. I did not want to die. Akio killed me because he hated your father."

His hands worked in the cat's fur, making it show its claws.

"Who was my father?"

"The girl is right. She is your sister; Takeo is your father. I loved him. They ordered me to lie with him, to make you. I obeyed them in every-thing. But they did not realize I would love him, and that you would be born from a love of such sweet fierceness, so they tried to destroy us all. First me; now they will use you to kill your father, and then you, too, will die."

"You are lying," he said, his throat dry.

"I am dead," she replied. "Only the living lie."

"I have hated the Dog all my life; I cannot change now."

"You do not know what you are? There is no one left in the Tribe, in all the five families, who can recognize you. I will tell you what my father told me in the moment of his death. You are the ghostmaster."

MUCH LATER, when she had returned to her room and lay sleepless, watching the darkness pale slowly into dawn, Maya relived the moment when she had heard the spirit speak those words: Her spine had chilled; her fur had stood erect. Hisao's hand had gripped her neck. He had not fully understood what it meant, but Maya recalled Taku's words: The ghostmaster was the one who walked between the worlds, the shaman who had the power to placate or incite the dead. She remembered the voices of the phantoms that had pressed around her on the night of the Festival of the Dead, on the shore in front of Akane's house; she had felt their regret for their violent and untimely deaths and their demand for revenge. They sought Hisao, their master, and she, as the cat, gave him power over them. But how could Hisao, this cruel and crooked boy, have such power? And how would Akio use him if he discovered it?

Hisao had not wanted her to leave him. She felt the strength of his need for her, and found it both enticing and dangerous. But he did not seem to want Akio to know, not yet. . . . She did not fully understand what his real feelings were toward the man he had always believed to be his father—a mixture of love and hatred, contempt and pity, and fear.

She recognized the emotions, for she felt the same toward him.

She did not sleep, and when Nori brought her rice and soup for the morning meal, she had little appetite. Nori's eyes were red, as if she had been crying.

"You must eat," Nori said. "And then you are to get ready to travel."

"Travel? Where am I going?"

"Lord Arai is returning to Kumamoto. The town of Hofu is in ferment. Muto Shizuka is fasting in Daifukuji and being fed by birds." Nori was trembling. "I shouldn't tell you this. The Master is to accompany him, and Hisao too. They are taking you, of course." Her eyes filled with tears and she dabbed at them with the patched sleeve of her robe. "Hisao is well enough to travel. I should be happy."

Be thankful he is going away from you, Maya thought. She said, "Shizuka is in Hofu?"

"She came to bury her younger son, and they say she has lost her mind. People blame Lord Arai—and accuse him of being involved in Taku's death. He is furious, and is returning home to prepare his troops for war, before Lord Otori gets back from Miyako."

"What nonsense you talk! You don't know anything about these things!" Maya hid her alarm with anger.

"I'm only telling you because you helped Hisao," Nori replied. "I won't say another word." She pursed her lips, looking petulant and offended.

Maya picked up the soup bowl and drained it, her mind racing. She must not let them take her to Kumamoto. She knew Zenko's sons, Sunaomi and Chikara, had been sent to Hagi to guarantee their father's loyalty, and that Zenko would not hesitate to use her to put similar pressure on her father. Hofu was in the Middle Country and loyal to the Otori— she knew the city and the road home. Kumamoto was far away in the West; she had never been there. Once there she would have no chance of escape.

"When do we leave?" she said slowly.

"As soon as the Master and Hisao are ready. You will be on the road before noon. Lord Arai is to send guards, I heard." Nori picked up the bowls. "I have to take these back to the kitchen."

"I haven't finished."

"Is it my fault if you eat so slowly?"

"I'm not hungry anyway."

"It's a long way to Kumamoto," Nori said as she left the room.

Maya knew she had very little time to make up her mind. They would surely transport her hidden in some way, with hands tied, probably. She might outwit Zenko's guards, but she would never get away from Akio. She began to pace the room, tiny as it was. The heat was rising, and she was hungry and tired. As she walked without thinking, she fell into a waking dream, and saw Miki in the alley behind the house. She snapped awake. It was perfectly possible—Shizuka would have brought Miki with her. As soon as they heard of Taku's death, they had come to find her. Miki was outside. They would go to Hagi together; they would go home.

She did not pause to reflect a moment longer, but leaped into cat shape and through the walls.

A woman on the veranda tried to swat her with a broom as she raced past. She ran across the yard, not bothering to hide, but as she came to the outer walls, she passed the workshop building and felt Hisao's presence there.

He must not see me. He will never let me go.

The rear gates were open, and from the street beyond she heard the tramp of horses approaching. She looked back and saw Hisao run from the foundry, the weapon in his hand, his eyes searching the yard. He saw her and called, "Come back!"

She felt the strength of the command, and her resolve weakened. The cat heard its master—it would never leave him. She was outside, in the street, but the cat's paws were heavy. Hisao called again. She had to go back to him.

Maya was aware out of the corner of her eye of the vague shimmer of an invisible figure. As swift as a sword, from across the road something came darting between the cat and Hisao, and it possessed an indestructible sharpness that cut between them.

"Maya," she heard Miki call. "Maya!" and in that moment Maya found the strength to change. Miki, visible now, stood next to her. Her twin sister gripped her by the hand. Hisao was shouting from the gateway, but his voice was only a boy's. She no longer had to listen to him.

Both girls went invisible again, and as Lord Arai's guards came trotting round the corner, they ran unseen into the narrow tangled streets of the port city.

· 44 ·

akeo's departure from Miyako took place with even greater ceremony and more excitement than his arrival, though there was both surprise and disappointment that he was leaving so soon.

"Your appearance has been like a comet," Lord Kono said, when the nobleman came to make his farewells. "Blazing swiftly across the summer sky."

Takeo wondered how much of a true compliment this was, since the common people believed that the comet heralded disaster and famine.

"I am afraid I have compelling reasons to return," he replied, reflecting that Kono possibly already knew what they were; but the nobleman gave no such indication, nor did he mention Taku's death.

Saga Hideki was even more outspoken in his shock and displeasure at the sudden departure, pressing for them all to stay longer—or if Lord Otori was truly obliged to return to the Three Countries, to leave Lady Maruyama at least to enjoy the pleasures of summer in the capital.

"There is so much more that we need to discuss—I want to know the way you govern the Three Countries, what underpins your prosperity and success, how you deal with the barbarians."

"We call them foreigners," Takeo dared to correct him.

Saga raised his eyebrows. "Foreigners, barbarians, it's all the same."

"Lord Kono spent most of the last year with us. He has surely reported to you."

"Lord Otori." Saga leaned forward and spoke confidentially. "Lord Kono gained the greater part of his information from Arai. Circumstances have changed since then."

"Do I have Lord Saga's assurances on that?"

"Of course! We made a public and binding agreement. You need not concern yourself. We are allies, and will soon be relatives."

Takeo resisted his persuasiveness with firm politeness; from all accounts the pleasures they would forgo were not great, for the capital sweltered in its hill-rimmed bowl during the weeks of the greatest heat, and the plum rains that were due to begin at any time brought humidity and mildew. He did not want to subject Shigeko to this, any more than to Saga's increasingly persistent courtship. He himself longed to be home, to feel the cool sea breezes of Hagi, to see Kaede and their son, and then to deal decisively with Zenko.

Lord Saga paid them the great honor of accompanying them for the first week of their journey, as far as Sanda, where he arranged a farewell feast. Saga knew how to charm as well as how to bully, but once this was over and they had finally said their last good-byes, Takeo felt his spirits lighten a little. He had hardly expected to be returning in such triumph. He had the favor and recognition of the Emperor, and apparently sincere offers of alliance from Saga. The Eastern borders would be safe from attack. Surely without Saga's support Zenko would be cured of his ambitions and would submit, accepting the reality of Takeo's legitimacy.

If there is proof of his complicity in Taku's death, he will be punished. But if at all possible, for my wife's sake and Shizuka's, I will let him live.

He had traveled in the palanquin, with great formality, as far as Sanda. It was a relief once Saga had left them to put off his elegant robes and ride Tenba again. Hiroshi had been riding him thus far, for the horse became overexcited and hard to control if he was not ridden every day. Now Hiroshi was on his old horse, Keri, Raku's son.

"The girl, Mai, told me Ryume, Taku's horse, died at the same time as his master," he said to Takeo as they rode side by side. "But whether he, too, was shot is not clear."

The day was hot, without a cloud in the sky; the horses dripped sweat as the climb steepened toward the still-distant ranges.

"I remember so clearly when we first saw the colts," Takeo replied. "You recognized them at once as Raku's sons. They were the first sign to me of returning hope, of life springing always from death."

"I will miss Ryume almost as much as Taku," Hiroshi said quietly.

"Fortunately, the Otori horses show no sign of dying out. Indeed, under your skillful guidance I believe they are improving. I thought I would never have another horse like Shun, but I have to admit I am delighted with Tenba."

"He was a challenge to break in, but he's turned out well," Hiroshi said.

Tenba had been trotting calmly enough, but just as Hiroshi spoke, the horse threw his head up and spun round to face the direction from which they had come, giving a shrill neigh.

"You spoke too soon," Takeo said, bringing the horse back under control and urging him to move forward again. "He is still a challenge—you can never take him for granted."

Shigeko, who had been riding at the end of the procession with Gemba, came cantering toward them.

"Something has upset him," she said, and turned in the saddle to gaze back behind her.

"He misses the kirin," Hiroshi suggested.

"Perhaps we should have left him with her," Takeo said. "The idea occurred to me, but I did not want to part with him."

"He would have become wild and unmanageable in Miyako." Hiroshi glanced at Shigeko. "He was broken in with gentleness; he cannot be roughly handled now."

The horse continued to be unsettled, but Takeo enjoyed the daily challenge of persuading him to calm, and the bond between them strengthened. The full moon of the sixth month turned, but it did not bring the expected rains. Takeo had feared they would have to cross the highest pass in wet weather, and was relieved, but the heat grew more intense, and the waning moon had a reddish hue that made everyone uneasy. The horses grew thin; the grooms feared they had intestinal worms or had eaten sand. Sandflies and mosquitoes plagued humans and animals at night. By the time the new moon of the seventh month rose in the east, thunder rolled and lightning played in the sky every night, but no rain fell.

Gemba had become very silent; often Takeo woke during the night to see him sitting motionless in meditation or prayer, and once or twice he dreamed, or imagined, Makoto, far away in Terayama, doing the same thing. Takeo's dreams were of broken threads and empty caskets, mirrors that gave no reflection, men without shadows. *Something is amiss,* Gemba had said, and he felt it in the flow of his blood and the weight of his bones. The pain that had lessened during the outward journey now returned, seeming more intense than he remembered. With an urgency he only half understood, he ordered the pace of the journey to increase: They rose up before dawn and rode under the light of the moon.

Before the moon reached its first quarter, they were a short distance from Hawk Pass—less than half a day's journey, Sakai Masaki, who had gone ahead to scout, reported.

The forest grew closely around the path, live oak and hornbeam, with cedars and pines on the higher slopes. They made camp under the trees; a spring provided water, but they had to eat sparingly, for the food they had brought with them was all but exhausted. Takeo slept lightly, and was woken by one of the guards calling, "Lord Otori!"

It was barely dawn, the birds just beginning to sing. His eyes opened, but he thought he was still dreaming. He glanced, as always, first at the horse lines, and saw the kirin.

It stood beside Tenba, its long neck bent down, its legs splayed out, its head close to the horses, its white markings gleaming eerily in the gray light.

Takeo stood up, his limbs stiff and aching. Hiroshi, who had been sleeping not far from him, was already on his feet.

"The kirin is back!" Hiroshi cried.

His exclamation woke the others, and in moments the kirin was surrounded.

It showed every sign of being delighted to be among them: It nuzzled Shigeko, and licked Hiroshi's hand with its long gray tongue. Its coat was scratched in many places, its knees grazed and bleeding; it favored its left hind foot, and its neck was marked with rope burns, as if it had made many attempts to break loose.

"What does this mean?" Takeo said in consternation. He pictured the creature's flight across the unfamiliar countryside, its long awkward stride, its fear and loneliness. "How could it have escaped? Did they let it go?"

Shigeko replied, "It's what I was afraid of. We should have stayed longer, made sure it was happy. Father, let me take it back."

"It is too late for that" he replied. "Look at it; we cannot give it to the Emperor in this condition."

"It would not even survive the journey," Hiroshi agreed. He went to the spring, filled a bucket with water, and allowed the kirin to drink, and then began to wash the matted blood away from its wounds. Its skin flinched and shuddered, but it stood quite still. Tenba whickered gently to it.

"What does it mean?" Takeo said to Gemba after the creature had been fed and orders given for their journey to resume as soon as possible. "Should we press on to the Three Countries and take the kirin with us? Or should we send some restitution back to Miyako?" He paused for a moment, gazing at his daughter as she soothed and petted the animal. "The Emperor can only be insulted by its escape," he went on in a low voice.

"Yes, the kirin was greeted as a sign of Heaven's blessing." Gemba said. "Now it has shown it prefers you to His Divine Majesty. It will be taken as a terrible insult."

"What can I do?"

"Prepare for battle, I suppose," Gemba said calmly. "Or take your own life, if you think that's a better idea."

"You foresaw everything—the outcome of the contest, my surrender of Jato, my victory. Did you not foresee this?"

"Everything has a cause and an effect," Gemba replied. "A violent occurrence like Taku's death has unleashed a whole chain of events—this must be one of them. It's impossible to foresee—or forestall—them all." He reached out his hand and patted Takeo on the shoulder, in the same way as Shigeko patted the kirin. "I'm sorry. I told you earlier something was amiss. I have been trying to hold the balance together, but it has been broken."

Takeo stared at him, hardly comprehending. "Has something happened to my daughters?" He took a deep breath. "My wife?"

"I can't tell you that sort of detail. I'm not a sorcerer or a shaman. All I know is that something that held the delicate web together has been snapped."

Takeo's mouth had gone dry with dread. "Can it be mended?"

Gemba did not answer, and at that moment, above the bustle of preparation, Takeo heard the sound of horse's hooves in the distance.

"Someone is riding fast toward us," he said.

A few moments later, the horses on the lines raised their heads and whinnied, and the approaching horse neighed back as it cantered around the curve in the path and came into view.

It was one of the Maruyama horses that Shigeko had given to Lord Saga, and its rider was Lord Kono.

Hiroshi ran forward to take the reins as the nobleman came to a halt; Kono jumped from the horse's back. His languid appearance had quite gone; he looked strong and skillful, as he had during the contest.

"Lord Otori, I am glad to have caught up with you."

"Lord Kono," Takeo returned. "I am afraid I cannot offer you much in the way of refreshment. We are about to move on. We will be across the border by midday." He did not care if the nobleman was offended now. He did not believe anything could redeem his position.

"I must ask you to delay," Kono urged. "Let us talk in private."

"I cannot believe you have anything to say to me now." Unease had turned to rage. Takeo could feel it building up behind his eyes. He had acted for months with supreme patience and self-control. Now he saw all his efforts about to be destroyed by a random event, an animal's uncontrollable preference for its companions over strangers.

"Lord Otori, I know you look on me as an enemy, but believe me, I have your best interests at heart. Come, give me a little time to deliver Lord Saga's message to you."

Without waiting for Takeo to reply, he walked a short distance away to where a fallen cedar provided a natural seat. He sat and beckoned Takeo to join him. Takeo glanced toward the east. The edge of the mountain was stark black against the glowing sky, already limned with gold.

"I will give you until the sun clears the peaks," he said.

"Let me tell you what has happened. The triumph of your visit had already been dimmed a little by your early departure. The Emperor had hoped to get to know you better—you made a strong impression on him. Still, he was contented enough with your gifts, especially this creature. He was concerned when it became more and more restless after your departure. He himself went to visit it every day, but it fretted, and would not eat, for three days. Then it ran away. We pursued it, of course, but all attempts to catch it failed, and finally it eluded us altogether. The mood in the city changed from delight that our Emperor had been blessed by Heaven to derision, that Heaven's blessing had run away, that it was Lord Otori whom Heaven favored, not the Emperor and Lord Saga."

He paused. "Of course, such an insult cannot be overlooked. I met Lord Saga as he was leaving Sanda; he immediately turned around. He is barely a day's ride behind me. His forces were already mustered; his special troops are always prepared, and they have been waiting for just such an eventuality as this. You are completely outnumbered. I am instructed to tell you that if you do not return with me and submit to the natural outcome of the Emperor's displeasure, that is, you will take your own life—I'm afraid the alternative of exile no longer exists—Saga will pursue you with all these warriors, and take the Three Countries by force. You and your family will all be put to death—except Lady Maruyama, whom Lord Saga still hopes to marry."

"Is this not what he intended all along?" Takeo replied, making no attempt now to control his rage. "Let him come after me—he will find more than he expects."

"I cannot say I am surprised, but I am deeply sorry," Kono said. "You must know how much I have come to admire you . . ."

Takeo cut him off. "You have flattered me many times, but I believe you have always wished me ill and tried to undermine me. Perhaps you feel in some way that you are avenging your father's death. If you had any true honor or courage, you would challenge me to my face, instead of conspiring in secret with my vassal and brother-in-law. You have been an indispensable go-between. You have insulted me and wronged me."

Kono's pale face had gone even whiter. "We will meet in battle," he replied. "Your tricks and sorcery will not save you then!"

He rose, and without bowing, went to his horse, leaped onto its back, and pulled roughly on its reins to turn its head. It was reluctant to leave its fellows, and fought against the bit. Kono drove his heels into its flanks; the horse bucked and kicked in response, unseating the nobleman, who fell ignominiously to the ground.

There was a moment of silence. The two guards closest drew their swords, and Takeo knew everyone expected him to give the order to kill Kono. He himself thought he would, needing something to release his rage, wanting to punish the man on the ground at his feet for all the insults, the intrigue and treachery that had hemmed him in. But something restrained him.

"Hiroshi, fetch Lord Kono's horse and help him mount," he said, and turned away so as not to humiliate the nobleman further. The guards lowered their swords and returned them to their scabbards.

As he heard the hoofbeats fade away down the path, he turned to Hiroshi and said, "Send Sakai ahead to inform Kahei and tell him to prepare for battle. The rest of us must get across the pass as quickly as possible."

"Father, what about the kirin?" Shigeko said. "It is exhausted. It will not be able to keep up with us."

"It must keep up—otherwise it is kinder to kill it now," he replied, and saw the shock come into her face. The next day might see her fighting for her life, he realized, yet she had never killed anything.

"Shigeko," he said, "I can save your life and the kirin's by surrendering now to Saga. I will take my own life, you will marry him, and we will still avoid war."

"We cannot do that," she replied without hesitation. "He has deceived and threatened us, and broken all the promises he made to us. I will make sure the kirin does not lag behind."

"Then ride Tenba," Takeo said. "The two of them will encourage each other."

He took her horse, Ashige, in exchange, and sent her ahead with Gemba, thinking that she would be safer there than in the rear. Then there was the question of what to do with the packhorses, and the lavish gifts from the Emperor and Lord Saga that they carried. They could not keep up with the other horses. Reflecting that the Emperor was already irredeemably offended, Takeo ordered the bales and baskets to be left beside the path by the little rock shrine at the spring's edge. He regretted the loss of the beautiful objects, the silk robes, the bronze mirrors and lacquered bowls, thinking how much Kaede would have appreciated them, but could see no other solution. He also abandoned the palanquins, and even the ornamental suits of armor that had been Lord Saga's gift. They were heavy and impractical, and Takeo preferred his own armor, which had been left in Kahei's charge.

"They are an offering to the gods of the mountain," he said to Hiroshi, as they rode away. "Though I do not believe any gods will help us now. What does the blessing of Heaven mean? We know the kirin is just an animal, not a mythical creature. It ran away because it missed its companions."

"It has become a symbol now," Hiroshi replied. "That is the way human beings deal with the world."

"This is hardly the time for philosophical discussions! We would do better to discuss our battle plan."

"Yes, I have been thinking about it ever since we came this way. The pass is so narrow and difficult that, once we are through, it will be easy to defend our rear against Saga's men. But will it be undefended now? I keep thinking, if I were Saga, I would have closed off your escape route before you left the capital."

"The same thought had occurred to me," Takeo admitted, and their fears were confirmed within the next hour when Sakai returned to report that the pass was filled with Saga's men hidden among rocks and trees, armed with bows and firearms.

"I climbed a tree, and looked back toward the East," Sakai said. "Using the far-seer I could make out Saga's army in the distance, pursuing us. They are flying red war banners, and Saga's defense troops at the pass must have seen them too. I sent a scout around—Kitayama will get through if anyone can—but he has to climb the mountain and descend the other side before he reaches Lord Miyoshi."

"How long will that take him?" Takeo asked.

"If he gets there before nightfall, he'll be lucky."

"How many in the pass?"

"Fifty to a hundred. We did not have much time to count."

"Well, we are more or less equally matched," Hiroshi said. "But they have all the advantages of the terrain."

"It is too late to take them by surprise, but can we outflank them?" Takeo inquired.

"Our only hope is to bring them out into the open," Hiroshi replied. "We can then pick them off—you and Lady Shigeko must ride at full speed while we cover you."

Takeo brooded in silence for a while, then sent Sakai up ahead with the order for the guards to halt well before the pass, and to conceal themselves. He himself caught up with Shigeko and Gemba.

"I must ask for my horse back," he said. "I have a plan to bring them out of hiding."

"You will not go alone?" Shigeko questioned, as she dismounted from Tenba and took Ashige's reins from her father.

"I will go with Tenba and the kirin," he replied. "But no one will see me."

He rarely displayed his Tribe skills to Shigeko, or even spoke of them to her, and he did not want to explain them now. He saw her look of doubt, swiftly controlled.

"Don't worry," he said. "Nothing can harm me. But you must ready your bows and be prepared to shoot to kill."

"We will try to disable them rather than take their lives," she replied, glancing at Gemba, who sat silent and impassive on the black horse.

"This will be a true battle, not a friendly contest," Takeo said, wanting to prepare her in some way for what lay ahead, for the madness and blood-lust of war. "You may not have a choice."

"You must take Jato again, Father. You should not go without it."

He took it from her gratefully. A special mount had been made for the sword, for it was too heavy for Shigeko to carry. It was already on Tenba's back, just in front of the saddle. The sword was still in its ceremonial dress and looked magnificent. He tied the kirin's silken cord to the horse's neck-strap, and before remounting he embraced Shigeko, praying silently for her safety. It was about midday and very hot; even here in the mountains the air was still and heavy. As he took up Tenba's reins in his left hand, Takeo glanced upward and saw huge thunderhead clouds banking up in the West. The horse tossed his head against the clouds of biting midges.

As he rode away from the group with the kirin, he was aware that someone was following him on foot. He had given orders that he was to go alone, and he turned in the saddle to command whoever it was to stay behind.

"Lord Otori!" It was Mai, the Muto girl, Sada's sister.

He halted for a moment and she came to the horse's flank. Tenba swung his head toward her.

"Maybe I can help you," she said. "Let me go with you."

"Are you armed?"

She drew a dagger from inside her robe. "I also have throwing knives, and a garrote. Lord Otori plans to use invisibility?"

He nodded.

"I could also use it. The aim is to make them show themselves so the warriors can get them?"

"They will see a warhorse and the kirin, apparently alone. I am hoping curiosity and greed will make them approach. Do not attack them until they are in the open and Sugita has ordered the first shots. They must be lulled into carelessness. Take whichever side seems to have fewer men hidden and kill as many as you can. The more confused they are, the better for us."

She smiled slightly. "Thank you, Lord. Each one will be some consolation for my sister's murder."

Now I am committed to warfare, he thought with sorrow as he urged Tenba forward again, and let invisibility descend on him.

The path became steeper and rockier, but just before the pass itself it leveled a little and widened. The sun was still high in the sky, but had begun its descent into the west, and the shadows were beginning to lengthen. On either side the mountain ranges, emerging from the dense forest, stretched away; ahead of him lay the Three Countries, covered now in cloud. Lightning flashed in the distance, and he heard the roll of thunder. It made Tenba throw up his head and tremble; the kirin walked as calmly and gracefully as ever.

Takeo heard the distant mewing of kites and the flutter of birds' wings, the creaking of ancient trees, the faraway trickle of water. As he rode into the valley, he heard the whisper of voices, the slight rustle of men shifting position, the sigh of bowstrings drawn back, and even more ominously, the tap of a firearm being loaded with powder.

For a moment his blood chilled. He had no fear of death; he had brushed with it so many times it held no horrors for him. Moreover, he had convinced himself that no one would kill him until his son did, but now a barely realized dread surfaced, of the bullet that killed from afar, the iron ball that tore roughly through flesh and bone. *If I am to die, let it be by the sword,* he prayed, as the thunder rolled again, *though if I die by the firearm it is only justice, for I introduced them, and developed them.*

He could not remember ever using invisibility on horseback before, accustomed to keeping his warrior skills quite separate from those of the Tribe. He let the horse's reins fall on its neck and took his feet from the stirrups so no sign of a rider would be discernible. He wondered what the watching men were thinking as the horse and the kirin progressed through the valley. Did it look like something from a dream, or some old legend come to life? The black horse, mane and tail shining as brightly as the decorated saddle, the sword on its flank; and the kirin, tall and unfamiliar, its long neck, its strangely patterned skin.

He heard the thrum of an arrow. Tenba heard it, too, and started, Takeo keeping his balance as the sudden movement whipped him sideways. He did not want to fall like Kono; nor did he want to lose invisibility through lack of concentration. He slowed his breathing and let his body follow the horse's movements as though they were one creature.

The arrow thudded into the ground a few yards ahead of him. It had not been aimed directly at the animals, merely as a sort of exploration of their nature. Takeo let Tenba skitter a little, and then pressed his legs slightly into his sides, urging him forward, grateful to the horse for his responsiveness and for the bond between then. The kirin followed docilely.

A shout came from his right, from the northern side of the valley. Tenba pricked his ears and swiveled them toward the sound. Another man shouted in reply, from the southern side. Tenba broke into a trot, and the kirin began to lope in its up-and-down way beside him.

The soldiers began to show themselves one by one, emerging from their hiding places and running down onto the valley floor. They were lightly armored, favoring easy concealment and flexibility over full battle armor—they had hoped for a quick ambush. They were armed mostly with bows, and a few firearms, but they laid these aside.

Tenba snorted, alarmed by them as if by a pack of wolves, and quickened his pace until he was cantering. This made more of the men emerge and run faster, trying to cut the animals off before the end of the valley. Takeo felt the ground begin to slope away. They had crossed the highest point; in front of him the view opened out. He could see the plains below where Kahei's army waited.

Now there was shouting all around as the soldiers gave up any idea of concealing themselves, vying to be the first to grasp the warhorse's reins and claim him. Ahead, five or six horsemen appeared in the gap between the crags. Tenba was galloping now, snaking like a stallion herding mares, teeth bared, prepared to bite. The kirin's huge stride made it appear to float above the ground. Takeo heard another arrow come whistling past him, dropped flat on the horse's neck, clutching at the luxuriant mane, and saw the first soldier fall, the arrow through his chest. Behind him he could make out the drumming of hooves as his own troops swept into the valley.

The terrible sound of arrows filled the air, like the beating of wings. Too late, the soldiers realized their entrapment and began to run back to the cover of the rocks. One dropped immediately, a star-shaped knife in his eyes, making those behind him hesitate long enough to fall to the next volley of arrows. Either Tenba and the kirin were just out of range, or the marksmanship of his archers was superb, for though Takeo heard the clack of the shafts all around him, nothing hit the animals.

The horsemen loomed ahead of him, their swords drawn. He fumbled for the stirrups, secured his feet, braced himself, and drew Jato with his left hand, letting visibility return at the same moment as he swung the sword to his left, knocking the first horseman from the saddle with a blow that cut open neck and chest. He sat deep in the saddle, throwing his weight backward in an attempt to slow Tenba down, and at the same moment slashed the cord that tied the kirin to the horse. The kirin ran awkwardly onward while Tenba, remembering perhaps what he had been bred for, slowed and spun to face the other horsemen who now surrounded Takeo.

He had almost forgotten how it felt, but it all came rushing back to him: the single-minded madness that thought of nothing but the strength, skill, and resolve that would ensure its possessor's own survival. He forgot his age and his disabilities, the left hand taking over the crippled right hand's role, Jato leaping as it always had done, as if with its own will.

He was aware of Hiroshi joining him, Keri's pale gray coat reddened with blood, and then the galloping thrust of his own small group of warriors all around him, Shigeko, Gemba, their bows over their backs, swords in their hands.

"Ride on," he called to them, and smiled inwardly as they went past him and began to descend. Shigeko was safe, at least for today. The conflict slackened and he realized the last of the enemy horsemen were trying to escape, and the men on foot were also running away, seeking the shelter of rocks and trees.

"Do we go after them?" Hiroshi called, getting his breath, turning Keri back.

"No, let them go. Saga must be close behind. We cannot delay. We are in the Three Countries now. We will be with Kahei tonight."

This is just a skirmish, Takeo was thinking as he returned Jato to the mount and sanity began to return. *The main battle is still to come.*

"Gather up our dead and wounded," he told Hiroshi. "Leave no one behind." Then he shouted loudly, "Mai! Mai!"

He saw the flicker of invisibility on the northern flank, and rode Tenba toward her as she came into view. He reached down and swung her up behind him.

"Are you hurt?" he called over his shoulder.

"No," she shouted back. "I killed three men and wounded two."

He could feel her quickened heartbeat against his back; the smell of her sweat reminded him that it was months since he had lain with his wife. He longed for Kaede now—she filled his thoughts as he surveyed the valley for survivors and rounded up the last of his men. Five dead, it seemed, maybe six more wounded. He grieved for the dead, all men he had known for years, and determined to bury them with reverence in their homeland in the Three Countries. Saga's dead he left in the valley, not bothering to take their heads or to dispatch the wounded. Saga would be in this place the following day, and either that same day or the next they would be joined in battle.

His mood was grim as he greeted Kahei on the plain below. Relieved to see that Minoru was unhurt, he went with the scribe to Kahei's shelter, where he related to the commander all that had happened and discussed the plans for the next day. Hiroshi took the horses to the lines, where Takeo could see his daughter with the kirin. She was pale, and looked somehow diminished. His heart ached for her.

Sakai's scout, Kitayama, arrived, scratched and bruised but unwounded, full of apologies for his lateness.

"At least we know Saga cannot come round any other way," Takeo said. "He must come through the pass."

"We will send men at once to defend it," Kahei declared.

"No, we will leave it open. We want Saga to think we are in flight, demoralized and confused. And he must be seen to be the aggressor. We are defending the Three Countries, not defying him and the Emperor. We cannot stay here and hold him off indefinitely. We must defeat him decisively and take the army back to the West to face Zenko. You have heard of Taku's death?"

"I had heard rumors, but we have had no official correspondence from Hagi."

"Nothing from my wife?"

"Not since the third month, and then she did not mention this sad loss. It was too early for her to have heard, perhaps."

It depressed Takeo further, for he had expected to have letters from her, with news of the situation in the Middle Country and the West, as well as of her health and the child's.

"I have not heard from my wife either; we have had messages from Inuyama but nothing from the Middle Country."

Both men were silent for a moment, thinking of their distant homes and children.

"Well, bad news travels faster than good, they say," Kahei exclaimed, pushing aside his anxieties in the usual way, with physical activity. "Let me show you our army."

Kahei had already established his troops in battle formation: the main forces on the western side of the plain, and a flank along the northern edge shielded by a small spur of land. Here he had placed those soldiers with firearms, as well as an auxiliary force of archers.

"We face bad weather," he said. "If it is too wet to use firearms, we lose our major advantage."

Takeo went out with him in the light midsummer evening to inspect the positions, guards carrying smoldering grass torches. The white moon was approaching full, but dark clouds blew raggedly, and lightning flashed in the western sky. Gemba was seated beneath a small cypress tree, near the pool that supplied their water, eyes closed, apparently far removed from the bustle of the camp around him.

"Maybe your brother can continue to hold off the rain," Takeo said, as much to raise his own spirits as Kahei's.

"Rain or not, we must be prepared for them to attack at any time," Kahei replied. "You have already fought one battle today. I'll keep guard while you and your companions get some sleep."

Since he had been at the encampment since the fifth month, Kahei had set himself up in some comfort. Takeo washed in cold water, ate a little, and then stretched out under the silken folds of the shelter. He fell asleep at once, and dreamed of Kaede.

They were in the lodging house in Tsuwano, and it was the night of her betrothal to Shigeru. He saw her as she had been at fifteen, her face unlined, her neck unscarred, her hair a silky mass of black. He saw the lamplight flicker between them as she stared at his hands and then raised her eyes to his face. In the dream she was both Shigeru's betrothed and already his wife; he passed the betrothal gifts to her, and at the same moment reached for her and pulled her toward him.

As he felt her beloved form in his arms, he heard the crackling of fire and realized that in his haste he had knocked over the lamp. The room was erupting in flames; the fire swept over Shigeru, Naomi, Kenji . . .

He woke, the smell of burning in his nostrils, rain already splashing through the roof, lightning searing the encampment with its sudden, unearthly brilliance, thunder cracking the sky.

· 45 ·

fter Takeo had cut its silk cord, the kirin had continued to run blindly through the valley, but its feet were not suited to the rocky floor, and it soon slowed to a limping walk. The noise behind alarmed it, but ahead were the smells and shapes of strange men and horses. It was aware that the people and the horse that it was familiar with and cared for most were still behind it, and so it waited for them with its customary patience and docility.

Shigeko and Gemba had found it, and brought it to the encampment. Shigeko was subdued; she did not speak as she unsaddled Ashige herself, fastened the head ropes to the horse lines, and then set about tending to the kirin, while Gemba fetched dried grass and water.

They were surrounded by soldiers from the camp, eager for information, full of questions about the skirmish, Saga Hideki and his troops, and if they might expect a battle soon, but Gemba fended them off, saying that Kahei must be informed first, and that Lord Otori was right behind them.

Shigeko saw her father ride into the camp, the Muto girl, Mai, on the back of his horse and Hiroshi alongside him. For a moment they both looked like strangers to her, blood-stained, ferocious, their faces still set in the furious expression of battle. Mai had the same expression, turning her features masculine. Hiroshi dismounted first and held out his arms to lift the girl down from Tenba. After Takeo had dismounted and was greeting

Kahei, Hiroshi took the reins of both horses, but stood for a while talking to Mai.

Shigeko wished she had the sharp hearing to discern what they were saying to each other, then berated herself for what she suspected might be jealousy. She had even let it taint her relief that her father and Hiroshi were unhurt.

Tenba caught the kirin's scent and whinnied loudly. Hiroshi looked in her direction and she saw the expression that washed over his face, changing him instantly into the man she knew so well.

I love him, she thought. *I will marry no one but him.*

He said good-bye to Mai and brought both horses to the lines, tying his own, Keri, next to Ashige, and Tenba beside the kirin.

"They are all happy now," Shigeko said, as the animals ate and drank. "They have food, they have their companions, they have forgotten the horrors of today. . . . They don't know what awaits them tomorrow."

Gemba left them, saying he needed to spend some time alone.

"He has gone to strengthen himself in the Way of the Houou," Shigeko said. "I should do the same. But I feel I have betrayed everything the Masters have taught me." She turned away, tears suddenly pricking her eyelids.

"I don't know if I killed today," she said in a low voice. "But my arrows hit many men. My aim was true: Not one arrow missed its target. I did not want to hurt the dogs, yet I wanted to hurt these men. I was glad when their blood spurted. How many of them are now dead?"

"I also killed today," Hiroshi said. "I was trained throughout my childhood for this, and it came naturally to me, though now, afterward, I feel regret and sorrow. I do not know how else I could have stayed loyal to your father, to the Three Countries, or done my best to protect him and you."

After a pause he added, "Tomorrow will be worse. This skirmish was nothing compared with the battle to come. You should not take part in it. I cannot leave your father, but let me suggest that Gemba take you away. You can take the kirin with you. Go back to Inuyama; go to your aunt."

"I don't want to leave Father, either," Shigeko said and could not help adding, "Nor Lord Hiroshi." She felt the color rise in her cheeks and said, without really meaning to, "What were you saying to that girl?"

"The Muto girl? I thanked her for helping us again. I feel deep gratitude to her, for bringing us the news of Taku's death, for fighting alongside us today."

"Oh! Of course," Shigeko said, and turned her face toward the kirin to hide her confused feelings. She longed to be held by him. She feared they would both die without ever speaking of love, yet how could she speak of it now, surrounded by soldiers, grooms, horses, when she was filled with regret for having taken life, and when their future was so uncertain?

The horses were done; there was no reason for them to stand there any longer.

"Let's walk a little," she said. "We should look at the terrain, and then find my father."

It was still light; far in the west the sun's last rays spilled out from behind the massed clouds. The sky between their dark gray citadels was the color of cold ash. The moon was high in the eastern sky, slowly silvering.

Shigeko could think of nothing to say. Finally Hiroshi spoke. "Lady Shigeko," he said. "My only concern now is for your safety." He also seemed to be struggling for words. "You must live, for the sake of the whole country."

"You have been like a brother to me all my life," she said. "There is no one who means more to me than you."

"My feelings for you are far more than those of a brother. I would never mention this to you, but for the fact that one of us may die tomorrow. You are the most perfect woman I have ever known. I know your rank and position place you far beyond me, but I can never love, nor will I ever marry, anyone but you."

She could not prevent herself from smiling. His words dispelled her sadness, filling her with sudden delight and boldness.

"Hiroshi," she said. "Let us marry. I will persuade my parents. I do not feel obliged to become Lord Saga's wife now that he has treated my father so wrongly. All my life I have tried to obey my parents and act in the right way. But now I see that in the face of death there are other things that take on a new importance. My parents put love before their duty to their elders; why should I not do the same?"

"I cannot do anything against your father's wishes," Hiroshi replied, with intense emotion. "But to know that you feel the way you do satisfies all my longings."

Not all of them, I hope! Shigeko dared to think as they parted.

She wanted to go at once to her father, but restrained herself. By the time she had washed and eaten, she was told he was already sleeping. A separate hut had been erected for her, and she sat alone in it for a long time, trying to compose her thoughts and reignite the calm, strong flame of the Way of the Houou within her. But all her efforts were undermined by flashes of memory—the cries of battle, the smell of blood, the sound of arrows—and by Hiroshi's face and voice.

She slept lightly and was wakened by the crack of thunder and splashing rain. She heard the camp erupt into action around her, and leaped to her feet, dressing quickly in the riding clothes she had worn the day before. Everything was getting wet, her fingers more slippery.

"Lady Maruyama!" a woman's voice called from outside, and Mai came into the hut, bringing a pot for Shigeko to urinate in. She took this away and returned in a few moments with tea and cold rice. While Shigeko ate quickly, Mai disappeared again. When she came back, she was carrying a small leather and iron cuirass and a helmet. "Your father sent these for you," she said. "You are to prepare at once, yourself and your horse, and go to him. Here, I will help you."

Shigeko felt the unfamiliar weight of the armor. Her hair caught in the lacing. "Tie it back for me," she told Mai; then she took up her sword and fastened it to her belt. Mai put the helmet on Shigeko's head and tied its loops.

The rain lashed down, but the sky was paling. It was nearly dawn. She went swiftly to the horse lines, through the water like a gray steel veil. Takeo was already in armor, Jato at his side, waiting for Hiroshi and the grooms to finish saddling the horses.

"Shigeko," he said without smiling, "Hiroshi has pleaded with me to send you away, but the truth is I need every man I've got—and woman too. It is too wet to use firearms, and Saga knows this. I am sure he will not wait for the rain to cease before he attacks. I need you and Gemba, since you are both archers."

"I'm glad," she said. "I did not want to leave you. I want to fight alongside you."

"Stay with Gemba," he said. "If defeat seems inevitable, he will take you to safety."

"I will take my own life first," she retorted.

"No, daughter, you must live. If we lose, you must marry Saga, and preserve our country and people as his wife."

"And if we win?"

"Then you may marry whom you choose," he replied, his eyes crinkling as he glanced at Hiroshi.

"I shall keep you to your word, Father," she said lightly, as they both mounted their horses.

Takeo rode with Hiroshi to the center of the plain, where the horsemen were assembling, and she followed Gemba to the northern flank, where foot soldiers, archers, and men armed with pikes and halberds were taking up positions.

There were several thousand of them, the archers arranged in two ranks, for Kahei had drilled them in the art of alternating shots so that the hail of arrows was almost continuous. If it had not been wet, they would have done the same with their firearms.

"Saga expects us to concentrate only on firepower," Gemba said. "He does not expect us to be equally formidable with bows. He was surprised at the dog contest, but he learned nothing from it. He will be equally surprised now.

"We are to remain here," he added, "even when the troops move around and forward. Your father wants us to aim with care and take out their captains and other leaders. Make every arrow count."

Shigeko's mouth was dry. "Lord Gemba," she said, "How did it come to this? How did we fail to solve things peacefully?"

"When the balance is lost and the male force dominates, war is inevitable," Gemba replied. "Some wound has been dealt to the feminine force, but I don't know what it is. It is our fate to be here at this time, our fate to have to kill or be killed. We must embrace it with all our resolve, wholeheartedly, knowing that we did not desire it or seek it."

She heard his words but hardly took them in, her attention focused on the scene before her as the light strengthened—the scarlet and gold of armor and harness, the impatient horses tossing their heads, the banners of Otori, Maruyama, Miyoshi, and all the other clans of the Three Countries, the cascading rain, the darkened trees of the forest, the white splash of waterfalls against the mountain rocks.

Then, impossibly numerous, like ants disturbed from their nest, the first wave of Saga's army came pouring through the pass.

he battle of Takahara was fought over three days during severe thunderstorms. The fighting continued from dawn to sunset; at night the combatants tended their wounded and scoured the battlefield for spent arrows. Saga Hideki's forces outnumbered Otori Takeo's army three to one, but the Emperor's general was hampered by the narrow pass that gave onto the plain, and by the Otori command of the vantage points. As each wave of Saga's men thrust into the plain, they were assailed by the arrows from their right; those that survived the arrows were repelled by the main Otori army, fighting first on horseback with swords, and then on foot.

It was by far the most brutal battle Takeo had ever fought, the one he had done his utmost to avoid. Saga's troops were disciplined and superbly trained. They had already subdued vast areas to the north. They hoped to be rewarded with the spoils of the Three Countries, and they fought with the blessing of the Emperor. On the other hand, Takeo's men were not only fighting for their lives, they were fighting for their country, for their homes, their wives and children, their land.

Miyoshi Kahei had been with the Otori army at the battle of Yaega-hara when he was fourteen years old, nearly thirty years earlier. The Otori had suffered a crushing defeat, partly due to the treachery of their own vassals. Kahei never forgot the years that followed: the humiliation of the

warriors, the suffering of the people under Iida Sadamu. He was determined not to live through such a defeat again. His conviction that Saga
would never prevail strengthened the will of his men.

Equally important, his preparations had been meticulous and imagina-
tive. He had been planning this campaign since spring, and organizing the
transport of supplies and weapons from Inuyama. He had been impatient
for months, wanting to deal decisively with the threats to Takeo's rule, chafing
at the endless negotiations and delays. Now the battle had finally begun, his
mood was ebullient. The rain was unfortunate, as he would have liked to have
seen his troops use the firearms in action, but there was something magnificent
about the traditional weapons: bow and sword, pike and halberd, spears.

The banners of the clan were streaked with moisture; the ground underfoot was quickly churned to mud. Kahei watched from the slopes, his
chestnut horse ready beside him. Minoru, the scribe, sat near him under an
umbrella, trying in vain to keep his writing dry and to record the events.
When the first attack from Saga's men was repulsed and the men driven
back toward the pass, Kahei leaped on the horse's back and joined the pursuit, his sword hacking and slashing at the backs of the fleeing men.

ON THE MORNING of the second day, Saga's horsemen came back
through the pass before daylight, fanning out to try to outflank the archers
to their north and to come around the southern side of Kahei's main army.
Takeo had not slept but had kept watch all night, listening for the first
sound of activity from the enemy. He heard the pad of horses' hooves,
even though they were wrapped in straw, the creak and jingle of harness
and weaponry. The northern archers were shooting blind, and the rain of
arrows was less effective than the previous day. Everything was soaked—
food, weapons, clothes.

When day came, the battle was already an hour old, and the light
dawned on its pitiful spectacle. The easternmost of the archery divisions

were locked in hand-to-hand combat with Saga's men. Takeo could not make out any individuals in the fray, though the emblems of each group of foot soldiers could be seen dimly through the rain. He saw immediately that his own right-hand side was equally under threat, and unable to render any help. He himself rode at once to their aid, Jato in hand, Tenba quivering in excitement but steady beneath him. He thought he had ceased to feel any soul-searching or regret, that he had moved into the ruthlessness of battle madness, as all his old skills returned to him. He noted half-consciously the Okuda crest close on his right-hand side, remembered Saga's retainer who had come to meet him in Sanda, sent Tenba sideways to evade a sword thrust to his leg, turned the horse to face the attacker, and looked down into the eyes of Okuda's son, Tadayoshi.

The boy had fallen from his horse and lost his helmet, and, surrounded as he was, defended himself bravely. He recognized Takeo and called out to him. Takeo heard him clearly through the din of battle: "Lord Otori!"

He did not know if it was a challenge or a call for help, and would never find out, for Jato had already descended onto the skull and split it. Tadayoshi died at his feet.

Now Takeo heard a scream of rage and grief, and saw the boy's father riding toward him, sword in both hands. Takeo was unsettled by Tadayoshi's death, and unprepared. Tenba stumbled at that moment, and Takeo slipped slightly in the saddle, falling forward, grasping for the mane with his damaged right hand. The stumble deflected Okuda's blow slightly, but Takeo still felt the impact as the tip of the sword caught him on top of the arm and across the shoulder. Okuda's horse galloped on, giving Takeo and Tenba time to recover. He felt no pain and thought he had escaped injury. Okuda turned his horse and came back toward Takeo, his path impeded by the milling soldiers. He ignored them all, intent only on Takeo. His rage ignited a reciprocal primitive fury in Takeo, and he surrendered to it, for it obliterated regret. Jato responded, and found the unprotected point in Okuda's neck. The man's own impetus took the sword deep into his flesh and veins.

LATER ON THE second day, Hiroshi and his men were pushing Saga's troops back toward the pass in a counterattack. Kahei had initiated a pincer movement that would trap the retreating men, already exhausted after hours of hand-to-hand fighting. Hiroshi's cousin Sakai Masaki was close behind him, and in sudden flashes of memory Hiroshi recalled a mad journey, in rain like this, with Sakai, when he had been a boy of ten. At that age battle was what he longed for, yet the path he had followed had been one of peace, the Way of the Houou. Now he felt all the blood of his ancestors rise in his veins. He threw off all other thoughts and concentrated on fighting, on killing, on winning, for his whole future now depended on victory. If the battle was lost, he would either die in it or kill himself. He fought with a fury he did not know he possessed, inspiring the men around him, driving the opposing forces back toward the pass, where they were trapped in the bottleneck.

With nowhere to go, Saga's men defended themselves more desperately. In one of their counter-surges Keri went down, blood spurting from his neck and shoulder. Hiroshi found himself fighting two unhorsed warriors. He lost his footing in the mud and fell to one knee, turned as the sword came on him and thrust upward, parrying it. The second sword descended toward him. He saw Sakai throw himself beneath the blow— blood, his own or Sakai's, was blinding him. The weight of Sakai's body held him down in the mud as the fray trampled across them. For a moment he felt only disbelief that this was how it was to end, and then pain washed over him, drowning him.

Gemba found him at nightfall, near death from loss of blood from slashes to head and legs, the wounds already suppurating in the dirt and humidity. Gemba staunched and cleaned them as best he could, then carried Hiroshi back behind the lines to join the rest of the wounded. Takeo was among them, his shoulder and arm cut deeply but not dangerously, already washed and wrapped in paper bandages.

Shigeko was unhurt, pale with exhaustion.

Gemba said, "I found him. He is alive, but barely. Sakai lay dead on top of him. He must have saved his life."

He laid the wounded man down. Lamps had been lit, but they smoked and smoldered in the rain. Takeo knelt beside Hiroshi, taking his hand and calling to him. "Hiroshi! Dear friend! Do not leave us. Fight! Fight!"

Hiroshi's eyes flickered. His breath came in shallow panting; his skin held a damp sheen of sweat and rain.

Shigeko knelt next to her father. "He cannot be dying! He must not die!"

"He has survived this far," Gemba said. "You can see how strong he is."

"If he makes it through tonight, there is hope," Takeo agreed. "Don't despair yet."

"How terrible it all is," Shigeko whispered. "What an unforgivable thing it is to kill a man."

"It is the way of the warrior," Gemba said. "Warriors fight and they die."

Shigeko did not reply, but tears dripped steadily from her eyes.

"**HOW MUCH MORE** of this can Saga take?" Kahei said to Takeo later that night, before they snatched a short respite of sleep. "It is madness. He is sacrificing his men to no purpose."

"He is a man of immense pride," Takeo replied. "He has never been defeated. He will not acknowledge the idea of it."

"How can we persuade him? We can resist him indefinitely—I hope you are impressed by your soldiers; they are superb in my opinion—but we cannot avoid huge loss of life. The sooner we can put an end to the fighting, the more chance we have to save the wounded.

"Like poor Sugita," he added. "And yourself, of course. Wound fever is inevitable in these vile conditions, with no sunlight to dry and heal. You should rest tomorrow; stay out of the fray."

"It's not serious," Takeo replied, though the pain had been increasing steadily all day. "Luckily, I am accustomed to using my left hand now. I have no intention of staying out of the fight—not until Saga is dead, or in flight back to the capital!"

SHIGEKO STAYED WITH Hiroshi all night, bathing him with cold water to try to reduce the fever. He was still alive in the morning, but shivering violently, and she could find nothing dry with which to warm him. She brewed tea and tried to get him to drink. She was torn between staying with him and returning to her position alongside Gemba to counter Saga's next onslaught. The bark shelters that had been erected for the wounded dripped constantly; the ground beneath them was saturated. Mai had spent day and night here, and Shigeko called to her.

"What should I do?"

Mai squatted beside Hiroshi and felt his brow. "Ah, he's freezing," she said. "This is how we warm the sick in the Tribe." She lay down alongside him, pressing her body gently against him. "Lie down on the other side," she instructed Shigeko, and Shigeko did so, feeling her warmth spread into him. The girls held him between them without speaking until his temperature began to rise again.

"And this is how we heal wounds," Mai said quietly, and moving aside Gemba's bandages licked the raw edges of cut flesh with her tongue and spat saliva onto them. Shigeko copied her, tasting the man's blood, giving him moisture from her mouth as if exchanging kisses.

Mai said, "He is going to die."

"No!" Shigeko replied. "How dare you say it?"

"He needs looking after properly. We can't do that day and night. You should be fighting, and I've got others to look after who've got more chance."

"How can we bring the fighting to an end?"

"Men love to fight," Mai said. "But even the fiercest of them tire of it, especially if they're hurt." She looked across Hiroshi at Shigeko. "Hurt this Saga, and he'll lose his appetite. Hurt him as bad as Lord Hiroshi is hurt and he'll want to scurry back to the doctors in Miyako."

Shigeko said, "How do I get to him? He does not appear on the battlefield, but directs his men from afar."

"I'll find him for you," Mai said. "Put on some drab clothing and prepare your most powerful bow and arrows. There's not much you can do for Lord Hiroshi," she added when Shigeko hesitated. "He's in the hands of the gods now."

Shigeko followed these instructions, wrapping a length of cloth around her head and neck and smearing mud across brow and cheeks so that she was unrecognizable. She took up the bow she had been fighting with, restrung it, and found ten new arrows, iron-barbed with single points, fletched with eagles' feathers. These she placed in the quiver. While she waited for Mai to return she sat next to Hiroshi, and between bathing his face and giving him water, for he was now burning again, she tried to calm her thoughts as she had been taught at Terayama, by Hiroshi and the other Masters.

Dear teacher, dear friend, she called silently to him. *Don't leave me!*

The battle had resumed with even greater ferocity, bringing the noise of crazed shouts, the screams of the wounded, the clash of steel, the pounding of horses' hooves, but a kind of silence had descended on the two of them, and she felt their souls entwine.

He will not leave me, she thought, and on a sudden impulse went to her hut and unpacked the tiny bow and the houou-feather–fletched arrows. She tucked these inside her jacket, while she slung the larger bow on her left shoulder, the quiver of arrows on her right.

When she went back to the wounded, Mai had returned.

"Where were you?" the girl said. "I thought you'd gone back to the fighting. Come on, let's hurry."

Shigeko wondered if she should inform Gemba where she was going, but when she came over the top of the slope and saw the battle scene, she realized she would never find him in the confusion. Saga's strategy now seemed to be to overwhelm the Otori positions by ever greater force of numbers. His new troops were fresh and rested; the Otori army had been fighting for two days.

How long can they resist? she asked herself as she followed Mai around the southern side of the plain, her feelings already dulled by the sight of so many dead. The Otori had taken their dead and wounded behind the lines, but Saga's men lay where they had fallen, the corpses one more element in the horror and confusion. Wounded horses tried to struggle to their feet; a small bunch of them trotted, halting and lame, away to the southwest, their broken reins dangling in the mud. Looking briefly after them, Shigeko saw them come to a halt just before the Otori camp. They put their heads down and began to graze, as though they were in a meadow, removed and distant from the battlefield. A little beyond them was the kirin. She had hardly thought of it for two days. No one had had time to build an enclosure for it; it was tethered by neck ropes to the horse lines. It looked forlorn and diminished in the pouring rain. Could it survive this ordeal and then the long journey back to the Middle Country? She felt a pang of terrible pity for it, so alone and far from its home.

The two girls made their way behind the rocks and crags that surrounded the plain. Here the noise of battle abated a little. Around them in every direction rose the peaks of the High Cloud Range, disappearing into the mist that hung like hanks of unspun silk. The ground was stony and slippery; often they had to crawl on all fours over huge rocks. Sometimes Mai went ahead, making a sign to Shigeko to wait for her, and Shigeko crouched in the shelter of some dripping boulder for what seemed like half her lifetime, wondering if she had not perhaps died in battle and was now a ghost, hovering between the worlds.

Mai returned out of the mist like a wraith herself, completely silent, and led the way onward again. Finally they came to a huge rock, which they scaled, scrabbling like monkeys up its southern side. Two stunted pine trees clung to its top, their hooped, misshapen roots making a kind of natural railing.

"Keep down," Mai whispered. Shigeko wriggled into a position where she could see through the roots across to the east, and the entrance to the pass. She gasped and flattened herself against the rock. Saga was directly in front of them, perched on a similar crag, from which he had a hawk's-eye view of the battlefield beneath him. He sat beneath a large umbrella on an elegantly lacquered camp stool, fully armed in black and gold, his helmet decorated with twin gold peaks, like the mountains of his crest that fluttered beside him on black and white banners. Several of his officers, all equally resplendent, and clean despite the rain, stood around him, along with a conch shell player and runners ready to take messages. Just beyond him, a series of fallen boulders made natural steps down to the pass. She saw agile men leap up and down them, reporting on the progress of the battle. She could even hear Saga's voice, noted its timbre of fury; she peeped again and saw him stand, shouting and gesticulating with the iron war fan in his hand. His officers took a step back from the force of the rage, and several of them immediately rushed down the rocky stairway to hurl themselves into the battle.

Mai breathed in her ear, "Now, while he is standing. You will only have one chance."

Shigeko took a deep breath and thought through each movement. She would use the nearest pine tree to pull herself to her feet. She would step beneath the trunks. The rock's surface would be slippery, so she would need to maintain her balance as she pulled the bow from her shoulder and the arrow from the quiver. It was a move she had practiced a thousand times in the last two days, and had not missed her target yet.

She took another look and noted his vulnerable points. His face was exposed, his eyes fierce and brilliant, and she could see clearly the whiter skin of his throat.

She stood—the bow arched; the arrow thrummed; the rain splashed around her. Saga looked at her, sat heavily. The man behind him clutched his chest as the arrow pierced his armor. There were shouts of shock and surprise, and now they were shooting at her. One arrow flew past her, striking the pine tree and splintering the bark against her face; another struck the rock at her foot. She felt a sharp jab, as if she had stumbled against a stick, but felt no pain.

"Get down!" Mai was shouting, but Shigeko did not move; nor did Saga cease staring toward her. She drew the smaller bow from her jacket and set one of the tiny arrows to it. The houou feathers glinted dull gold. *I am about to die,* she thought, and let it fly like a dart toward his gaze.

There was a dazzling flash, as though lightning had struck, and the air between them seemed suddenly full of the beating of wings. Around Saga his men dropped their bows and covered their eyes; only Saga himself kept his eyes open, staring at the arrow until it pierced his left eye, and his own blood blinded him.

ALL THAT MORNING Kahei fought on the southern flank, where he had increased the number of his men, fearing Saga's forces might attempt to surround the camp from that side. Despite his confident words to Takeo the previous night, he was more worried now, wondering how long his sleep-deprived soldiers could withstand the seemingly endless onslaught, cursing the rain for depriving them of their superior weapons, recalling the last hours of Yaegahara, when the Otori army, realizing their betrayal and inevitable defeat, had fought with a desperate, mad ferocity, until hardly a man was left standing. His own father had been one of the few survivors. Was family history to repeat itself—was he, too, destined to return to Hagi with news of a total defeat?

His fears only fueled his determination to achieve victory.

TAKEO FOUGHT IN the center, calling up everything he had ever been taught by warrior Master and the Tribe alike to dominate fatigue and pain, marveling at the determination and discipline of those around him. In a sudden lull, when Saga's troops had been driven back, he looked down at Tenba's shoulder and saw the horse was bleeding from a deep slash across the chest, the redness dissolving into the rain-soaked hair. Now the fight had stopped momentarily, the horse seemed to become aware of the wound, and began to shudder in shock. Takeo slipped from his back, call-

ing to one of the foot soldiers to take the horse back to the camp, and prepared to face the next attack on foot.

A group of horsemen came galloping from the pass, the horses leaping
in the air in their efforts not to step on the fallen. The swords flashed, cutting down the foot soldiers, who retreated to the barriers they had erected
while the archers on the northern side let fly a volley of arrows. Many
found their mark, but Takeo could not help noticing that there were far
fewer than the day before, and that the attrition of battle was eroding his
forces. Like Kahei's, his confidence faltered. How many more men did Saga
have? The supply seemed endless, and they were all fresh and rested. . . .

Like the horsemen who were now nearly upon him. With a dull shock
he recognized their leader as Kono. He saw the Maruyama horse, his gift
now used against him, and felt the pure singe of fury. This man's father had
nearly wrecked his life; the son had intrigued against him, had lied to him,
had dared to suggest admiration while plotting his downfall. He took Jato
more firmly in his grip, ignoring the building shaft of pain that ran from
elbow to shoulder blade, and leaped nimbly sideways so the nobleman
would meet him on his left side.

His first swift stroke upward caught the nobleman's foot and almost
severed it. Kono gave a cry, turned the horse, and came back; now Takeo
was on his right-hand side. He ducked under the flailing sword, and would
have cut upward again, aiming for the wrist, but heard the next horseman's
sword descend toward his back, split himself, and rolled away from it, trying not to cut himself with his own sword. Now the horses' hooves were
trampling around him. He struggled to find his footing in the mud. His
own foot soldiers had rushed forward with spears and pikes; a horse came
down heavily next to him, its rider pitching headfirst, already dead, into
the mire.

There was a sudden flash of lightning directly overhead, and the rain
fell even more heavily. Through its relentless drumming, Takeo heard another sound, a thin and ghostly music that echoed across the plain. For a
moment he could not comprehend what it meant. Then the crush around

him thinned. He stood, wiping the rain and the mud from his eyes with
his right hand.

The Maruyama horse passed him, Kono clinging to its mane with
both hands; his leg was still spurting blood. He did not seem to notice
Takeo; his eyes were fixed on the safety of the pass.

They are retreating, Takeo thought in disbelief, as the sound of the conch
shell was drowned by a roar of triumph and the men around him surged
forward to pursue the fleeing enemy.

he former outcastes, from their village in Maruyama, moved across the battlefield to deal with the injured horses and bury the dead. When the corpses of the fallen were laid out in rows, Kahei, Gemba, and Takeo walked along them, identifying all those they could, while Minoru recorded their names. As for Saga's men, there were too many to identify; they were buried quickly in one huge pit in the center of the plain. The taking of heads had been forbidden. The soil was stony; the graves were shallow. Crows were already gathering, looming through the rain on huge black wings and cawing to one another from the crags. At night foxes prowled, and Takeo knew once the humans had departed the foxes would be joined by the shyer wolves, who would feast all summer.

The stakes of the palisades were pulled out and litters constructed from some of them to carry the wounded back to Inuyama. The rest were used to erect a barrier across the pass, and Sonoda Mitsuru and two hundred of his men remained to guard it. By the evening of the following day, when the dead were buried, the defenses were in place, and there had been no sign of Saga returning, it seemed as if the battle was truly over. Kahei gave the order to rest; men took off their armor, laid down their weapons, and fell instantly asleep.

The rain had slackened to a drizzle after the sudden downpour at the moment when Saga Hideki had been wounded and had ordered the retreat. Takeo walked among the sleeping men as he had walked earlier among the dead, hearing the soft hiss of the drops on leaves and rocks, the distant splash of the waterfall, the evening birdsong, feeling the moisture bead his face and hair. The entire right side of his body from shoulder to heel ached fiercely, and relief at victory was tempered by sorrow at its cost. He also knew that the exhausted soldiers could sleep only till dawn, and must then be mustered for the march back to Inuyama, and then on into the Middle Country to prevent Zenko rising in the West. He himself was deeply anxious to return as soon as possible; Gemba's warning of some unknown event that had upset the harmony of his rule now returned to torment him. It could only mean something had happened to Kaede . . .

Hiroshi had been moved into Kahei's shelter, which offered the greatest comfort and the most protection from the rain. Takeo found his daughter there, barely recognizable, still in her fighting garb, her face still covered in mud, her foot roughly bandaged.

"How is he?" he asked, kneeling beside Hiroshi, noting the pale face and shallow breath.

"He is still alive," Shigeko replied in a low voice. "I think he is a little better."

"We will transport him to Inuyama tomorrow. Sonoda's physicians will take care of him."

He spoke with confidence, though privately he did not think Hiroshi would last the journey. Shigeko nodded without speaking.

"Were you wounded?" Takeo said.

"An arrow struck me in the foot. It's not serious. I didn't realize till afterward. I could hardly walk back. Mai almost had to carry me."

He did not understand what she was saying.

"Where did you and Mai go? I thought you were with Gemba."

Shigeko looked at him and said quickly, "She took me to where Lord Saga was. I shot him in the eye." Tears suddenly filled her eyes. "He will never want to marry me now!" The tears turned to a kind of shocked laughter.

"So we have you to thank for his sudden retreat?" Takeo was overwhelmed by a sense of the justice of this outcome. Saga had not accepted his defeat in the peaceful contest, but had sought conflict—now Shigeko had dealt him a serious, possibly fatal wound, and had ensured their victory.

"I tried not to kill him, only to wound him," she said. "Just as I tried all the time, all through the battle, to disable but not to kill."

"You have acquitted yourself marvelously," he replied, masking his emotion with formal language. "You are a true heir to the Otori and to the Maruyama."

His praise brought the tears again.

"You are exhausted," he said.

"No more than anyone else; no more than you. You must sleep, Father."

"I will, as soon as I have checked on Tenba. I want to ride on ahead to Inuyama. Kahei will bring the men. You and Gemba must escort Hiroshi and the other wounded. I hope Tenba is fit—if not I will leave him with you."

"And the kirin," Shigeko said.

"Yes, and the poor kirin. It did not know what a journey it was coming on, or what impact it would have in this strange land."

"You cannot ride alone, Father. Take someone with you. Take Gemba. And you can ride Ashige; I do not need a horse."

The clouds were breaking up slightly, and there was a faint glow in the west as the sun set, the hint of a rainbow in the opposite sky. He hoped it would mean a drier day tomorrow, though now the rains had begun they were likely to continue for weeks.

Tenba stood next to the kirin, back to the drizzle, head lowered. He gave a small whicker of greeting as Takeo approached. The wound on his chest had already closed over, and seemed clean, but when Takeo led him out he was lame on the right side, though his feet seemed unharmed. Takeo concluded the shoulder muscles were inflamed, took the horse to the pool, and spent some time applying cold water, but Tenba still favored the right foreleg, and could probably not be ridden. Takeo then recalled Hiroshi's horse, Keri. He could not find it among the living horses. The black-maned, pale gray horse, Raku's son, must have been killed in the battle, just a few weeks after its half-brother, Taku's horse Ryume. The horses had reached seventeen years, a fine age, yet their death saddened him. Taku was gone, Hiroshi near death. His mood was somber as he returned to the shelter. It was dim inside, the light pallid. Shigeko had fallen asleep next to Hiroshi, her face close to his. *Like a married couple.*

Takeo looked at them with deep affection. "Now you may marry as you desire," he said aloud.

He knelt beside Hiroshi and placed his hand on his brow. The young man felt cooler; his breathing had slowed and deepened. Takeo had thought he was unconscious, but Hiroshi suddenly opened his eyes and smiled.

"Lord Takeo . . ." he whispered.

"Don't try to talk. You are going to be all right."

"The battle?"

"It's over. Saga is in retreat."

Hiroshi closed his eyes again, but the smile did not leave his lips.

Takeo lay down, his spirits a little lightened. Despite the pain sleep fell on him at once, like a dark, obliterating cloud.

HE LEFT FOR Inuyama the following morning, with Gemba, as Shigeko had suggested, and Minoru, who rode on his own placid mare. Both the mare and Gemba's black were as fresh as Ashige, and their passage was swift. By the third day a mild wound fever had hit Takeo, and the hours passed in slow agony as his body fought its effects. He was plagued by dreams and hallucinations; he alternately burned and shivered, but refused to abandon the journey. At each stopping place they spread the word of the battle and its outcome, and soon a stream of people began to make their way up into the High Cloud Range to take food to the warriors and help bring the wounded home.

The rain had fallen heavily throughout the Three Countries, making the rice grow and swell, but it had come late and the harvest would suffer because of it. The roads were muddy and frequently flooded. Often Takeo forgot where he was, and thought he was back in the past, riding Aoi alongside Makoto toward a flooded river and a broken bridge.

Kaede must be cold, he thought. *She has not been well. I must get to her and warm her.*

But he was shivering himself, and suddenly Yuki was beside him. "You look cold," she said. "Shall I bring tea?"

"Yes," he said. "But I must not lie with you, because I am married."

Then he remembered Yuki was dead and would never lie with him or anyone else again, and felt piercing regret for her fate and the part he had played in it.

By the time they reached Inuyama the fever had abated and he was lucid again, but his anxieties remained. They were not even dispelled by the heartfelt welcome he received from the townspeople, who celebrated his return and the news of victory with dancing in the streets. Kaede's sister, Ai, came out to greet him in the castle bailey, where he was helped down from the horse by Minoru and Gemba.

"Your husband is safe," he told her at once, and saw her face lighten with relief.

"Heaven be thanked," she replied. "But you are wounded?"

"I believe I am over the worst of it. Do you have news from my wife? I have heard nothing since we left in the fourth month."

"Lord Takeo," she began, and his heart fell in dread. It had begun to rain again, and servants ran forward with umbrellas, gleaming in the gray air.

"Dr. Ishida is here," she went on. "I will send for him at once. He will take care of you."

"Ishida is here? Why?"

"He will tell you everything," Ai said, her gentleness terrifying him. "Come inside. Will you bathe first? And we will prepare food for you all."

"Yes, I will bathe," he replied, wanting both to delay the news and to face it prepared and strengthened. The recent fever and pain had left him light-headed—his hearing seemed more than usually acute, each sound ringing painfully distinct in his ears.

He and Gemba went to the hot spring pools and stripped off their filthy robes. Gemba carefully took away the bandage from Takeo's shoulder and arm and washed the wound with scalding water, turning him even more faint.

"It's healing well," Gemba said, but Takeo made no reply beyond nodding in assent; nor did they speak as they washed and rinsed themselves and entered the bubbling, sulfurous water. The rain fell gently on their faces and shoulders, surrounding them as if they had been transported to another world.

"I cannot stay here forever," Takeo said finally. "Will you come with me to hear what has brought Ishida to Inuyama?"

"Of course," Gemba said. "To know the worst is to know how to go forward."

Ai brought soup and grilled fish, rice and summer vegetables, and served them herself. They ate quickly; she told the maids to remove the trays and bring tea. When they returned, Dr. Ishida was with them.

Ai poured the tea into the dark-blue glazed bowls. "I will leave you now." As she knelt to slide open the door, Takeo saw her put her sleeve to her eyes to wipe away tears.

"Not another wound?" Ishida said, after they had exchanged greetings. "Let me look at it."

"Later," Takeo said. "It is healing now."

He took a sip of tea, barely tasting it. "You have not come all this way with good news, I imagine."

"I thought you should know as soon as possible," Ishida replied. "Forgive me, I feel it is all my fault. You left your wife and son in my care. These things happen; infants have a precarious grip on life. They slip away from us." He stopped and stared helplessly at Takeo, his mouth working in grief, tears on his cheeks.

Takeo's blood was pounding in his ears. "Are you telling me my son is dead?" The rush of grief took him by surprise, and tears immediately burst from his eyes. The tiny creature, whom he had hardly known, he was now never to know.

I cannot bear this new blow, he thought, and then, *If I cannot bear it, how can Kaede?*

"I must go to my wife at once," he said. "How has she taken it? Was it some illness? Is she sick as well?"

"It was one of those inexplicable childhood deaths," Ishida said, his voice breaking. "The boy was perfectly healthy the night before, fed well, smiled and laughed, and fell asleep without fussing, but never woke again."

"How can that be?" Takeo said, almost angrily. "It was not witchcraft? What about poison?" Hana was in Hagi, he remembered; could she have brought about his son's death?

He wept, making no attempt to hide it.

"There was no sign of poison," Ishida said. "As for witchcraft—I really have no idea. These deaths are not uncommon, but I know nothing about their cause."

"And my wife—how is her state? She must be half-mad with grief. Is Shizuka with her?"

"Many terrible things have happened since you went away," Ishida whispered. "My wife has also recently lost a son. She has gone mad with grief, it seems. She sits without eating in front of Daifukuji, in Hofu, and calls for her other son to act with justice. In response, Zenko has retired in rage to Kumamoto, where he is raising an army."

"Zenko's wife and sons are in Hagi," Takeo said. "Surely he will not throw away their lives."

"Hana and the boys are no longer in Hagi," Ishida said.

"What? Kaede let them go?"

"Lord Takeo," Ishida said miserably. "She has gone with them. They are all on their way back to Kumamoto."

"Ah!" Gemba said quietly. "Now we know what went wrong." He did not weep, but an expression of sorrow and compassion came into his face. He moved a little closer to Takeo, as if he would physically hold him up.

Takeo sat as if frozen into ice. His ears had heard the words, but his mind could not comprehend them. Kaede had left Hagi? She had gone to Kumamoto, put herself into the hands of the man who was conspiring against him? Why would she do such a thing? Leave him to ally herself with her sister's husband? He could not believe it of her.

446

But some part of his body felt riven, as if his entire arm had been wrenched off. He felt his spirit teeter toward darkness, and saw the darkness about to swallow the whole country.

"I must go to her," he said. "Gemba, prepare horses. Where will they be by now? When did they leave?"

"I left about two weeks ago," Ishida replied. "They were to go a few days later, by way of Tsuwano and Yamagata."

"Can I intercept them at Yamagata?" Takeo asked Gemba.

"It is a week's ride away."

"I will get there in three days."

"They are traveling slowly," Ishida said. "Their departure was delayed because Lady Kaede is taking as many men with her as possible."

"But why? Is it grief at the child's death? Has it truly driven her out of her mind?"

"I can think of no other reason," Ishida said. "Nothing I said would comfort her or dissuade her. I could only think of seeking Ai's help, so I left Hagi secretly, hoping also to meet you on your way home."

He did not look at Takeo; his manner was both guilty and confused. "Lord Takeo," he went on, but Takeo did not allow him to continue. His mind had suddenly started racing, looking for answers, arguing and pleading, promising anything to any god, if only she had not left him.

"Hiroshi is badly wounded, Shigeko slightly," Takeo said. "The kirin also probably needs your attention. Tend them as best you can, and as soon as they are able to travel, bring them to Yamagata. I will go there immediately and find out for myself what has happened. Minoru, send messages at once to Miyoshi Kahei; inform him of my departure." He broke off and stared at Gemba, desolate.

"I must prepare to fight Zenko. But how can I fight against my wife?"

· 48 ·

n Hofu, high tide at the start of the fifth month, the opening of summer, came after noon, in the Hour of the Horse. The port was at its most active, with ships leaving and arriving in a steady flow, taking advantage of the mild west wind that would drive them to Akashi, laden with the produce of the Three Countries. Eating houses and inns were crammed with the newly disembarked, drinking, exchanging news and travelers' tales, voicing their shock and regret at Muto Taku's death and marveling at the miracle of his mother, who was fed by birds in Daifukuji, resentful of Arai Zenko, who showed such a lack of filial duty and such contempt for the gods and would surely be punished for it. The townspeople of Hofu were bold and opinionated. They had loathed their enslavement under the Tohan and the Noguchi; they had no desire to return to those days under the Arai. Zenko's departure from the town was accompanied by jeers and other manifestations of ill-will; his guards at the end of his long train were even pelted with refuse, and in some cases stones.

Miki and Maya saw little of this; they ran blindly and unseen through the narrow streets, intent only on distancing themselves from Hisao and Akio. It was stiflingly hot away from the sea; the town smelled of fish and rotting seaweed, and the dark shadows alternating with brilliant sunshine disoriented them. Maya was already exhausted from the sleepless night, the encounter with Hisao, the conversation with the ghost woman. She kept looking nervously behind her as they ran, sure that Hisao would pursue her; he would never let her go. And Akio would have learned by now about the cat. *Hisao will be punished,* she thought, but did not know if the idea pleased or pained her.

She felt invisibility leave her as she tired; she slowed to catch her breath, and saw Miki reappear beside her. The street here was quiet; most people were indoors eating the midday meal. Immediately next to them, outside a small shop, a man was squatting on the ground, sharpening knives with a grindstone, using water from the little canal that ran past each house. He jumped in surprise at their sudden appearance and dropped the knife he was holding. Maya felt frantic, defenseless. Almost without thinking she seized the knife and jabbed it into the man's hand.

"What are you doing?" Miki cried.

"We need weapons, and food, and money," Maya answered. "He will give them to us."

The man was staring in disbelief at his own blood. Maya split herself and came behind him, cutting him again, this time on the neck.

"Get us food and money, or you die," she said. "Sister, get a knife too."

Miki picked up a small knife from where it lay on a cloth spread out on the ground. She seized the man by the unwounded hand and led him into the shop. His eyes bulging with terror, he showed them where he kept a few coins, and pressed the rice cakes his wife had prepared for him into Maya's hand.

"Don't kill me," he pleaded. "I hate Lord Arai's wickedness. I know he has stirred up the gods against him, but I had no part in it. I'm just a poor craftsman."

"The gods punish the people for the wickedness of the ruler," Maya intoned. If this fool thought they were demons or ghosts, she would make the most of it.

"What was all that about?" Miki asked when they had left the shop, now both armed with knives hidden inside their clothes.

"I'll tell you later. Let's find somewhere to hide for a bit, somewhere where there's water."

They followed the canal until, on the road leading out of town toward the north, they came upon a roadside shrine, a small grove of trees around a spring-fed pool. Here they drank deeply, and found a secluded spot behind bushes, where they sat down and shared the rice cakes. Crows were cawing high in the cedars, and cicadas were rasping monotonously. Sweat trickled down the girls' faces, and under their clothes their bodies, on the cusp between child and woman, were damp and itchy.

Maya said, "Our uncle is preparing an army against Father. We have to go to Hagi and warn Mother. Aunt Hana is on her way there. Mother must not trust her."

"But Maya, you used your Tribe skills against an innocent man. Father's told us we must never do that."

"Listen, Miki, you don't know what I've been through. I saw Taku and Sada murdered in front of my eyes. I've been kept prisoner by Kikuta Akio." For a moment she thought she was going to cry, but the feeling passed. "And that boy, who was calling out to me, is Kikuta Hisao; he's Kenji's grandson. You must have heard about him in Kagemura. His mother, Yuki, was married to Akio, but after the boy was born the Kikuta made her kill herself. It's the reason why Kenji brought the Tribe back to Father."

Miki nodded. She had heard all these Tribe stories since childhood.

"Anyway, no one's innocent in the long run," Maya said. "It was that man's fate to be there when he was." She was staring moodily at the surface of the pool. The branches of the cedars and the clouds behind them were reflected in its still surface. "Hisao is our brother," she said abruptly. "Everyone thinks he's Akio's son, but he's not. He's Father's."

"It cannot be true," Miki said in a faint voice.

"It is true. And there was some prophecy that said Father would only be killed by his own son. So Hisao is going to kill Father, unless we stop him."

"What about our baby brother?" Miki whispered.

Maya stared at her. She had almost forgotten the existence of the new child, as if by not recognizing his birth she could make him unreal. She had never seen him; nor had she even thought about him. A mosquito settled on her arm and she slapped it.

Miki said, "Father must know all this too."

"If he does, why has he done nothing about it?" Maya replied, wondering why this made her so angry.

"If he chooses to do nothing, we should too. Anyway, what can he do?"

"He should have Hisao put to death. Hisao deserves it anyway. He is evil, the most evil person I've ever met, worse than Akio."

"But what about our little brother?" Miki said again.

"Stop making it all so complicated, Miki." Maya stood and brushed the dust off her clothes. "I need to piss," she said, using men's language, and went a little farther into the grove. Here there were tombstones, mossy and neglected. Maya thought she should not defile them, so she climbed the side wall and relieved herself in its shelter. As she clambered back over the wall, the earth shook, and she felt the stones slide sideways beneath her hands. She half-fell onto the ground, made dizzy for a moment. The tops of the cedars were still quivering. At that moment she felt an intense longing to be the cat, along with an emotion she did not recognize, but which unsettled her and nagged at her.

When she saw Miki still sitting by the pool, she was struck by how thin her sister had become. This also irritated her. She did not want to have to worry about Miki—she wanted things to be as they always had been, when the twins seemed to share one mind. She did not want Miki disagreeing with her.

"Come on," she said. "We have to get going."

"What's our plan?" Miki said as she stood up.

"To go home, of course."

"Are we going to walk all the way?"

"Do you have any better ideas?"

"We could get help from someone. A man called Bunta came with Shizuka and me. He would help us."

"Is he Muto?"

"Imai."

"None of them can be trusted anymore," Maya said in disgust. "We've got to go alone."

"It's a long way," Miki said. "It took us a week from Yamagata on horseback, riding openly with two men to help us. From Yamagata to Hagi is ten days, by the road. If we're on foot, and hiding, it will take three times as long. And how will we get food?"

"Like we did before," Maya said, touching the hidden knife. "We'll steal it."

"All right," Miki said, not looking happy about it. "Are we to follow the high road?" She gestured at the dusty road that wound through the rice fields, still bright green, toward the forest-covered mountains. Maya peered at the usual travelers moving along it in both directions: warriors on horseback, women wearing large hats and veils against the sun, monks walking with staffs and begging bowls, peddlers, merchants, pilgrims. Any one of them might try to detain them, at worst, at best ask difficult questions. Or they might be members of the Tribe, already warned to look out for them. She looked back toward the city, half-expecting to see Hisao and Akio pursuing them. Her heart lurched and she realized she missed Hisao and longed to see him again.

But I hate him! How can I want to see him?

Trying to hide this from Miki, she said, "Even though I'm in boy's clothes, anyone can see we're twins. We don't want people looking at us, gossiping about us. We'll go through the mountains."

"We'll starve," Miki protested, "or get lost. Let's go back to the town. Let's go and find Shizuka."

"She's in Daifukuji," Maya said, recalling the servant girl's words. "Fasting and praying. We can't go back. Akio is probably there waiting for us."

The tension within her was growing by the moment; she could feel the pull on her, feel him looking for her. She jumped suddenly, hearing his voice.

Come to me.

It echoed like a whisper through the shadowy grove.

"Did you hear that?" She grabbed Miki by the arm.

"What?"

"That voice. It's him."

Miki stood, listened intently. "I can't hear anyone."

"Let's go," Maya said. She looked up at the sky. The sun had moved from its zenith toward the west. The high road was almost due north, through some of the most fertile land in the Three Countries, following the bed of the river all the way to Tsuwano. Rice fields lay on either side of the valley, farmhouses and huts dotted here and there among them. The road ran along the western side until the bridge at Kibi. There was also a new bridge, just before the confluence of the Yamagata River. The river often flooded over the coastal plain, but a day's journey north of Hofu it became shallow, white water rushing in rapids over a rocky bed.

Both girls had traveled this road frequently; Miki the most recently, just a few days before, Maya the previous autumn with Taku and Sada.

"I wonder where the mares are," she said to Miki as they left the shelter of the trees and stepped out into the afternoon heat. "I lost them, you know."

"What mares?"

"The ones Shigeko gave us to ride from Maruyama."

As they began to climb up the slope into the bamboo groves, Maya told her sister briefly about the attack, and the deaths of Taku and Sada. By the time she was finished, Miki was crying silently, but Maya's eyes were dry.

"I dreamed about you," Miki said, wiping her eyes with her hand. "I dreamed you were the cat, and I was its shadow. I knew something terrible was happening to you."

She was silent for a while, and then said, "Did Akio hurt you?"

"He nearly throttled me to shut me up, and then he hit me a couple of times, that's all."

"What about Hisao?"

Maya began to walk faster, until she was almost jogging through the silver-green trunks. An adder slid across the path in front of them, disappearing into the tangled undergrowth, and somewhere to their left a small bird was piping. The relentless droning of cicadas seemed to intensify.

Miki was running too. They slipped easily between the shafts of bamboo, as surefooted as deer, and more silent.

"Hisao is a ghostmaster," Maya said, when finally the steepening slope forced her to slow down.

"A Tribe ghostmaster?"

"Yes. He could be terribly powerful, except he doesn't know how to deal with it. No one's ever taught him anything much, other than how to be cruel. And he knows how to make firearms. I suppose someone taught him that."

The sun had slipped behind the high peaks of the mountains on their left. There would be no moon, and already low clouds were spreading across the sky from the south; there would be no starlight either. It seemed a long time since they had eaten the rice cakes at the shrine. As they walked, the girls now began instinctively to look for food—early mushrooms beneath pine trees, wineberries, the tender shoots of bamboo, the last of the fern heads, though these were becoming hard to find. Since childhood they had been taught by the Tribe to live off the land, to gather its leaves, roots, and fruits as both sustenance and poison. They followed the sound of trickling water and drank from a small stream, where they also found small crabs, which they ate raw and living, sucking the muddy flesh from the fragile shells. So they went through the long twilight until it was too dark to see. They were now in the deep forest, and there were many craggy outcrops and fallen trees to provide shelter.

They came upon a huge beech that had been half uprooted by an earth tremor or a storm. Its leaves had fallen year after year to provide a soft bed, and its massive trunk and roots formed a cave. There was even some mast still edible among the leaves. The girls lay down, curled together like animals. In her sister's embrace Maya felt her body at last begin to relax, as if she were becoming whole again.

She was not sure if she spoke the words or only thought them.

Hisao loves the cat and is its master.

Miki stirred slightly against her. "I think I knew that. I felt it outside the house in Hofu. I cut through the bond between the boy who was calling to you and the cat, and you changed into your real self."

"Moreover, his mother is always with him. When Hisao is with the cat, he can talk to her spirit."

A small shiver ran through Miki's thin frame. "Have you seen her?"

"Yes."

An owl hooted in the trees above them, making them both jump, and in the distance a vixen screamed.

"Were you afraid?" Miki whispered.

"No." Maya thought about it. "No," she repeated. "I feel sorry for her. She was made to die before her time, and she's had to watch her son being turned into someone evil."

"It's so easy to become evil," Miki said in a small voice.

There was a slight cool change in the quality of the air, and a light pattering on the ground.

"It's raining," Maya said. Under the first drops, a moist smell began to rise from the earth. It filled her nostrils with both life and decay.

"Are you running away from him? As well as going home, I mean."

"He is looking for me, calling to me."

"He's following us?"

Maya did not answer directly. Her limbs twitched restlessly. "I know Father and Shigeko will still be away, but Mother will protect us, won't she? Once we are in Hagi, I will feel safe from him."

But even as the words left her lips, she was not sure they were true. Part of her feared him and wanted to flee. Part of her was drawn back to him, longing to be with him and to walk with him between the worlds.

Am I becoming evil? Maya recalled the knife grinder, whom she had wounded and robbed without thinking twice. *Father would be angry with me,* she thought. She felt guilty and did not like it, so she poured her own anger over it to extinguish it. *Father made me; it is his fault I am how I am. He should not have sent me away. He should not have left me so much when I was little. He should have told me he had a son. He should not have had a son!*

Miki seemed to have fallen asleep. Her breathing was quiet and even. Her elbow was digging into Maya, and Maya shifted slightly. The owl hooted again. Mosquitoes had scented their sweat and were whining in Maya's ear. The rain was making her cold. Almost without thinking, she let the cat come, with its thick warm pelt.

Immediately she heard his voice. *Come to me.*

And she felt his gaze turn toward her, as though he could see across the tracts of forest and through the darkness, right into the cat's golden eyes, as its head swiveled in his direction. The cat stretched, flattened its ears, and purred.

Maya struggled to change back. She opened her mouth, trying to call to Miki.

Miki sat up. "What's happening?"

Maya felt again the swordlike strength of Miki's spirit that came between the cat and its master.

"You were yowling!" Miki said.

"I changed into the cat without meaning to, and Hisao saw me."

"Is he close?"

"I don't know, but he knows where we are. We must leave at once."

Miki knelt at the edge of the tree-cave and peered out into the night. "I can't see a thing. It's all completely black. It's raining too. We can't go on now."

"Will you stay awake?" Maya said, shivering with cold and emotion. "There's something you can do that comes between him and me and frees me from him."

"I don't know what it is," Miki said. Her voice sounded frail and tired. "Or how I do it. The cat takes so much from me; what is left is sharp and hard."

Pure was the word that came to Maya, like the purity of steel after it

has been heated, folded, and hammered so many times. She put her arms
round Miki and drew her close. Huddled together, the girls waited for
dawn as it crept slowly toward them.

THE RAIN STOPPED at daybreak, and the sun rose, making the
ground steam and turning the dripping branches and leaves into frames of
gold and fractured rainbows. Spiders' webs, bamboo grass, ferns: Everything glittered and shone. Keeping the sun on their right they continued
northward, on the eastern flank of the mountains, struggling up and down
deep gullies, often having to retrace their steps. Occasionally they caught
sight of the high road below, and the river beyond it. It was never empty,
and though they longed to walk for a while on its easy surface, they did not
dare to.

Around midday they both stopped at the same time, but without
speaking, in a small clearing. Ahead of them there seemed to be a rough
path that promised to make the next part of the day's journey a little easier. They had not eaten all morning, and they began to search now in the
grass, silently, finding a little more beech mast, moss, last autumn's sweet
chestnuts already sprouting new shoots, a few berries, barely ripe. It was
hot, even under the canopy of the forest.

"Let's rest for a while," Miki said, taking off her sandals and rubbing
the soles of her feet in the damp grass. Her legs were scratched and bleeding, her skin turning dark copper.

Maya was already lying on her back, gazing upward into the green and
gold pattern of the shifting leaves, her face dappled with round shadows.

"I'm starving," she said. "We've got to get some real food. I wonder if
that path leads to a village."

The girls dozed for a while, but hunger woke them. Again, hardly
needing to speak to each other, they refastened their sandals and began to
follow the path as it wound along the side of the mountains. Now and
then they caught sight of a farmhouse roof far below them, and thought

the path would lead them there, but they came to no habitation, no village, not even a remote mountain hut or shrine, and the cultivated fields remained out of reach below them. They walked in silence, pausing only to grab at the sparse mountain food that offered itself, their stomachs growling and complaining. The sun passed behind the mountain; the clouds gathered again in the south. Neither of them wanted to spend another night in the wild—and all the nights that stretched ahead of them daunted them—but they did not know what else to do, other than walk on.

The forest and the mountain were wrapped in twilight; birds were singing the last songs of dusk. Maya, who was in front on the narrow path, came to a sudden halt.

"Smoke," Miki whispered.

Maya nodded, and they went on more cautiously. The smell became stronger, now mixed in painfully with the odor of roasting meat, a pheasant or a hare, Maya thought, for she had tasted both in the mountains around Kagemura. The saliva rushed into her mouth. Through the trees she could make out the shape of a small hut. The fire was lit in front of it, and a slight figure knelt by it, tending the cooking meat.

Maya could tell from the outline and the movements that it was a woman, and something about her seemed very familiar.

Miki breathed in her ear. "It looks like Shizuka!"

Maya caught her sister's arm as she was about to run forward. "It can't be. How could she get here? I'll go and look."

Taking on invisibility, she slipped through the trees and behind the hut. The smell of the food was so intense she thought she would lose all concentration. She felt for her knife. There seemed to be no one else around, just the woman, her head covered in a hood, which she held away from her face with one hand while she turned the meat on its makeshift spit with the other.

A slight breeze came through the clearing and sent brown and green feathers swirling in its eddy. The woman said, without turning her head, "You don't have to use the knife. I'll feed you, and your sister."

The voice was like Shizuka's, and yet unlike. Maya thought, *If she can see me, she must be from the Tribe.*

"Are you Muto?" she said, and relaxed into visibility.

"Yes, I am Muto," the woman replied. "You can call me Yusetsu."

It was a name Maya had never heard before, with a cold and mysterious sound, like the last lingering traces of snow on the north side of the mountain in spring.

"What are you doing here? Did my father send you?"

"Your father? Takeo." She spoke his name with a kind of profound yearning regret, both sweet and bitter, that sent a shiver down Maya's spine. She looked at Maya now, but the hood covered her face, and even in the firelight Maya could not make out her features.

"It's nearly ready," Yusetsu said. "Call your sister and wash."

There was a pitcher of water on the step of the hut. The girls took it in turns to pour it over each other's hands and feet. Yusetsu put the charred pheasant on a slab of bark covered with leaves, placed it on the step and, kneeling beside them, cut it into pieces with a small knife. The girls ate without speaking, bolting the meat like animals; it burned lips and tongue. Yusetsu did not eat, but watched every bite they took, studying their faces and their hands.

When they had sucked the last bone, she poured water onto a cloth and wiped their hands, holding them upward and tracing the Kikuta mark with her fingers.

Then she showed them where to go to relieve themselves, and gave them moss to wipe afterward; her manner was attentive and matter of fact, as if she were their mother. Later she lit a lamp from a spill taken from the last of the fire, and they lay down on the floor of the hut while she continued to stare at them with hungry eyes.

"So you are Takeo's daughters," she said quietly. "You resemble him. You should have been mine."

And both the girls, warm and fed, felt that it would have been better if they had been, though they still did not know who she was.

She extinguished the lamp and spread her cloak over them. "Sleep," she said. "Nothing will harm you while I am here."

They slept without dreaming and woke at daybreak, the rain falling on their faces, the ground damp beneath them. There was no trace of the hut, or the pitcher, or the woman. Only the bird's feathers in the mud and the cold embers of the fire gave any proof that she had been there.

Miki said, "It was a ghost woman."

"Mmm," Maya replied, agreeing.

"Is it Hisao's mother? Yuki?"

"Who else could it be?" Maya began to walk toward the north. Neither of them spoke anymore about her, but the taste of the pheasant lay on their tongues and in their throats.

"There's a sort of path," Miki said, catching up with her. "Like yesterday."

A rough track, like a fox's road, led away through the undergrowth. They padded along it all day, resting in the heat of noon in a tangle of hazelnut bushes, walking again until nightfall as the new moon rose, a slender sickle in the eastern sky.

There was the same sudden smell of smoke, the mouthwatering fragrance of cooking meat, the woman tending the fire, her face hidden by her hooded cloak. Behind her was the hut, the pitcher of water.

"We're home," Maya said in the familiar greeting.

"Welcome home," she replied. "Wash your hands; the food is ready."

"Is it ghost food?" Miki asked when the woman brought the meat—it was hare, this time—and cut it for them.

Yusetsu, whose name in the world had been Yuki, laughed. "All food is ghost food. All food has already died and gives you its spirit so that you may live.

"Don't be afraid," she added, when Miki hesitated; Maya was already cramming the meat into her mouth. "I am here to help you."

"But what do you want in return?" Miki said, still not eating.

"I am paying back a favor. I am in your debt. For you cut the bond that tied me to my child."

"I did?"

"You set the cat free, and at the same time freed me."

"If you are freed, you should move on," Miki said in a calm, stern voice that Maya had never heard before. "Your time is over in this world. You must let go, and allow your spirit to go forward to its next rebirth."

"You are wise," Yuki replied. "Wiser now, and more powerful, than you will be once you become a woman. Within a month or two, you and your sister will start bleeding. Being a woman makes you weak, falling in love destroys you, and having a child puts a knife against your throat. Never lie with a man; if you never start, you will not miss it. I loved the act of love; when I took your father as my lover, I felt I had entered Heaven. I let him possess me completely. I longed for him day and night. And I was doing what I was told to do: You are children of the Tribe; you must know about obedience."

The girls nodded, but did not speak.

"I was obedient to the Kikuta Master and to Akio, whom I knew I was supposed to marry one day. But I thought I would marry Takeo and have his children. We were perfectly matched in Tribe skills, and I assumed he had fallen in love with me. He seemed as obsessed with me as I was with him. Then I discovered that it was Shirakawa Kaede whom he loved, a stupid infatuation that led him to abscond from the Tribe and signed my death warrant."

Yuki fell silent. The girls also said nothing. They had never heard this version of their parents' history, told by the woman who had suffered so much because of her love for their father. Finally Maya said, "Hisao fights against listening to you."

Miki leaned forward and took a piece of meat, chewing it carefully, tasting the grease and the blood.

"He does not want to know who he is," Yuki replied. "He is split against his own nature, and so feels terrible pain."

"He cannot be redeemed," Maya said, the anger returning. "He has become evil through and through."

Night had fallen; the moon had passed behind the mountains. The fire crackled quietly.

"You are his sisters," Yuki said. "One of you becomes the cat, whom he loves; the other has some spiritual quality that resists his power. If he ever realizes that power completely, then he will become truly evil. But until then he can be saved." She leaned forward, and let the hood fall away from her face. "When he is saved, I will move on. I cannot let my child kill his true father. But his false father must pay for his brutal murder of me."

She is beautiful, Maya thought, *not like Mother but in a way I would like to be, strong and vital. I wish she had been my mother. I wish she had not died.*

"Now you must sleep. Keep walking north. I will feed you and guide you back to Hagi. We will find your father and warn him, while we are free, and then we will save Hisao."

Yuki washed their hands as she had the previous night, but this time she caressed them more intimately, like a mother. Her touch was firm and real—she did not feel like a spirit. But in the morning the girls woke in the empty forest. The ghost woman had gone.

Miki was even more silent than the previous day. Maya's mood was volatile, swinging between excitement at the prospect of seeing Yuki again that night, fear that Akio and Hisao were already close behind them, and a deeper unease. She tried to get Miki to talk, but Miki's replies were short and unsatisfactory.

"Do you think we did the wrong thing?" Maya said.

"It's too late now," Miki snapped, and then relented a little. "We've eaten her food and accepted her help. There's nothing we can do about it; we just have to get home and hope Father returns soon."

"How do you know so much about it?" Maya said, irritated by Miki's bad temper. "You're not a ghostmaster, too, are you?"

"No, of course I'm not," Miki cried. "I don't even know what that is. I'd never heard of it until you said Hisao was one."

They were making their way down a steep slope. The path wound between huge boulders. It seemed to be a favorite basking spot for snakes, and as the sinuous bodies whisked out of sight beneath the rocks, Maya couldn't help shuddering. She remembered all the stories she'd heard about ghosts, and thought of Akane's spirit, and how she had teased Sunaomi about the dead courtesan without believing her own words.

"What do you think Yuki really wants?" she asked.

"All ghosts seek revenge," Miki answered. "She wants revenge."

"On Akio?"

"On everyone who has hurt her."

"You see, you do know all about it," Maya said.

"Why is she guiding us to Hagi?" Miki said.

"To find Father; she said so."

"But Father will not be back all summer," Miki went on, as if carrying out an argument with herself.

SO THEIR JOURNEY continued as the moon grew toward full and waned again. The sixth month came and summer moved toward the solstice. Yuki met them every night; they became accustomed to her, and then, without their noticing it, came to love her as if she truly were their mother. She stayed with them only between sunset and sunrise, but each day's walk seemed easier now that they knew she would be waiting for them at its end. Her desires became theirs. Every night she told them stories from her past. Her childhood in the Tribe, in many ways so like theirs; the first great sorrow of her life, when her friend from Yamagata burned to death with all her family the night Otori Takeshi was murdered by the Tohan warriors; how she had brought Lord Shigeru's sword, Jato, and put it in Takeo's hands before they had rescued Shigeru together from Inuyama castle; and how Yuki had taken the lord's head back to Terayama, alone, through hostile country. They were full of admiration for her courage and her loyalty, shocked and outraged at her cruel death, moved with grief and pity for her son.

· 49 ·

he girls came to Hagi late one afternoon just before the solstice. The sun was still high in the western sky, turning the sea brassy. They crouched in the bamboo grove just on the edge of the cultivated fields, the rice a brilliant luxuriant green, just tinged with a hint of gold. The vegetable fields were a mass of leaves, beans, carrots, and onions.

"We won't need Yuki tonight," Miki said. "We can sleep at home."

But the thought saddened Maya. She would miss Yuki, and she suddenly and perversely wanted to go wherever Yuki went.

The tide was ebbing and the mud banks were exposed along the twin rivers. Maya could see the arches of the stone bridge, the shrine to the river god where she had killed Mori Hiroki's cat with the Kikuta gaze and its spirit had possessed her, the wooden piles of the fish weir, and the boats lying on their sides, like corpses waiting for the water to bring them back to life. Beyond them were the trees and garden of the old family house. Farther to the west, above the low tiled and shingled roofs of the town, rose her other home, the castle, the golden dolphins on its topmost roof glinting in the sun, its walls brilliant white, the Otori banners fluttering in the slight breeze from the sea. The water in the cup of the bay was a deep indigo blue, hardly ruffled by white. In the gardens opposite the castle, around the volcano crater, the last azaleas glowed against the lush, golden-tipped summer foliage.

Maya squinted against the sun. She could make out the Otori heron on the banners, but alongside them were others, the black bear's foot on a red background: the Arai.

"Aunt Hana is here," she whispered to Miki. "I don't want her to see me."

"She must be at the castle," Miki said, and they smiled at each other, thinking of Hana's love of luxury and importance. "I suppose Mother is there too."

"Let's go to the house first," Maya suggested. "See Haruka and Chiyo. They'll send word to Mother."

She realized she was not sure what her mother's reaction would be. She recalled suddenly their last meeting, Kaede's anger, the slaps. She had heard nothing from her since, no letters, no messages. Even the news of the birth of the little boy had only come to her through Shigeko in Hofu. *I could have been killed with Sada and Taku*, she thought. *Mother does not care.* The emotions were deep and troubled: She had longed to come home, but now she feared her reception. *If only it were Yuki*, she thought. *I could run to her and tell her everything, and she would believe me.*

A terrible grief washed through her—that Yuki was dead and had never known her child's love. That Kaede lived . . .

"I'll go," she said. "I'll see who's there, if Father is back."

"He won't be," Miki said. "He has gone all the way to Miyako."

"Well, he is safer away than at home," Maya replied. "But we must tell Mother about Uncle Zenko, how he had Taku killed and is raising an army."

"How does he dare when Hana and his sons are here in Hagi?"

"Hana's probably planning to spirit them away; that's why she's come. You wait here. I'll be back as soon as possible."

Maya was still in boy's clothes and she did not think anyone would take any notice of her. Lots of boys her age played on the riverbank and used the fish weir to cross the river. She ran lightly over it as she had many times before. The tops of the piles were damp and slippery, and green weed hung lankly from them. The river smelled familiarly of salt and mud. At the farther side she paused in front of the opening in the garden wall, where the stream flowed out into the river. The bamboo grill was not in place. Taking on invisibility, she stepped into the garden.

A large gray heron was fishing in the stream. It sensed her movement, swung its beak toward her, and launched itself into flight, its wings making a sudden sharp clack like the sound of a fan.

In the waters of the stream, a gold carp leaped. The fish splashed, the bird flew on silent wings overhead, the water trickled: It was just like it always was.

She set her ears to listen to the sounds of the house, longing now to see Haruka and Chiyo. *They will be surprised,* she thought. *And happy. Chiyo will cry for joy like she always does.* She thought she heard their voices from the kitchen.

But above the murmur she heard other voices, coming from outside the wall, from the riverbank. Boys' voices, chattering, laughing.

She shrank down behind the largest rock as Sunaomi and Chikara came splashing through the stream. At the same moment there were footsteps from inside the house, and Kaede and Hana came out onto the veranda. They were not at the castle after all. They were here.

Kaede was carrying the baby. He was about eight weeks old, already active and alert, smiling and trying to grasp his mother's robe. She held him up so he could watch the boys approach.

"Look, my treasure, my little man. Look at your cousins. You will grow up to be as fine a boy as they are!"

The baby smiled and smiled. He was already trying to use his feet and stand.

"How dirty you are, my sons," Hana scolded them, her face glowing with pride. "Wash your feet and hands. Haruka! Bring water for the young lords!"

Young lords! Maya watched as Haruka came and washed the boys' feet. She saw their confidence and arrogance, saw the love and respect they commanded effortlessly from all the women surrounding them.

Hana tickled the baby and made him giggle and squirm. A look of complicit affection passed between her mother and her aunt.

"Didn't I tell you," Hana said. "There is nothing like having a son."

"It's true," Kaede replied. "I did not know I could feel like this." She hugged the baby to her, her face rapt with love.

Maya felt a pure hatred like nothing she had felt in her life, as if her heart had cracked and its blood washed through her, molten steel. *What will I do?* she thought. *I must try to see Mother alone. Will she listen to me? Should I go back to Miki? Go to the castle to Lord Endo? No, I must see Mother first. But Hana must not suspect I am here.*

She waited silently in the garden as dusk fell. Fireflies danced above the stream, and the house glowed from the lamps lit within. She smelled the food being taken to the upstairs room, heard the boys talking, boasting while they ate. Then the young maids took the trays back to the kitchen, and the beds were spread out.

The boys slept at the back of the house, where the maids would also go when their last tasks were done. Hana and Kaede would sleep in the upstairs room with the baby.

As the house fell silent, Maya dared to go inside. She crossed the nightingale floor without conscious effort, having been familiar with it all her life. She tiptoed up the stairs and watched her mother feed the child, saw him suck hungrily and strongly until his eyelids began to flicker and close. Maya felt an intimation of some presence beside her. She glanced sideways and saw the ghost woman, Yusetsu, who had once been Muto Yuki. She no longer wore the hooded cloak but was dressed as she had been when Maya first saw her, in the white garments of the dead, as white as her flesh. Her breath was cold and smelled of earth, and she stared at the mother and child with an expression of naked jealousy.

Kaede wrapped the baby tightly and laid him down.

"I must write to my husband," she said to Hana. "Fetch me if the baby wakes."

She went downstairs to Ichiro's old room, where the records and writing materials were kept, calling to Haruka to bring lamps.

Now I must go to her, Maya thought.

Hana sat by the open window, running a comb through her long hair; she was humming a lullaby to herself. A lamp burned in an iron stand.

Hana sang:

Write to your husband,
My poor sister.
He will never get your letters.
He does not deserve your love.
You will soon find out
What kind of a man he is.

How dare she sing so, in my father's house! Maya thought. She was torn between conflicting desires to throw herself at Hana and to run downstairs to her mother.

Hana lay down, her head on the pillow block. *I could kill her now!* Maya thought, feeling for the knife. *She deserves it!* But then she reflected that she should leave such punishment to her father. She was about to go out of the room when the baby stirred. She knelt beside him and looked at him. He gave a little cry. His eyes opened and he gazed back at her.

He can see me! she thought in surprise. She did not want him to wake properly. And then she found she could not stop looking. She had no control over what she was doing. She had become a channel for the conflicting emotions that raged within and around her. She gazed at her brother with her Kikuta eyes, and he smiled once at her and fell asleep, never to wake again.

Yuki said beside her, *Come, we can leave now.*

Maya knew suddenly that this was part of the ghost woman's revenge, revenge on her mother, a terrible payment of an old score of jealousy. And she realized that she had committed an act for which there was no forgiveness, that there was no place for her anywhere anymore except in the realm between the worlds where spirits walked. Not even Miki could save her now. She summoned the cat and let it take her over, and then leaped through the walls, running across the river, into the forest, tireless and unthinking, back to Hisao.

Yuki followed her, floating above the ground, the ghost child in her arms.

· *50* ·

aede's son died on the night before the full moon of midsummer. Infants often passed away—no one was particularly astonished—in summer from illness or plague, in winter from cold or croup. Generally it was thought wise not to become too attached to young children, since so few survived infancy. Kaede tried to control and contain her grief accordingly, aware that as the ruler of the country in her husband's absence she could not allow herself to break down. Yet privately she wanted simply to die. She went over and over in her mind what failing of hers had brought about this unbearable loss: She had fed him too much or too little; she should not have left him; she had been cursed, first with twins, then with this death. In vain Dr. Ishida tried to convince her that there might be no reason, that it was a common thing for infants to die for no apparent cause.

She longed for Takeo's return, yet she dreaded telling him. She longed to lie with him and feel the familiar consolation of their love, yet she also thought that she could never bear to take him inside her again, for the idea of conceiving another child only to lose it was unendurable.

He must be told, yet how was it to be done? She did not even know where he was. It would take weeks for letters to reach him. She had heard nothing from him since he had sent letters from Inuyama, which she had received at the beginning of the fifth month. Every day she determined to write to him, yet each day she could not bring herself to do so. All day she longed for night to come so she could give rein to her grief, and all night lay sleepless, longing for dawn, so she might lay the pain aside temporarily.

Her only comfort was the company of her sister and the boys, whom she loved as if they were her own children. They distracted her, and she spent much time with them, overseeing their studies and watching their military training. The baby was buried at Daishoin; the moon had waned to a tiny sliver above his grave when messengers came finally with letters from Takeo. When she unrolled the scroll, the sketches he had done of birds observed on the journey fell out. She smoothed them out and gazed on them, the quick black strokes catching perfectly the crow on a craggy rock, the flycatcher and the bellflower.

"He writes from a place called Sanda," she said to Hana. "He is not yet even at the capital." She looked at the letter without really reading it; she recognized Minoru's hand, but the birds Takeo had drawn himself—she could see the power of the stroke, saw him supporting the right hand with the left, forcing skill from disability. She was alone with Hana; the boys were at the riding ground, the maids occupied in the kitchen. She let the tears flow. "He does not know his son is dead!"

Hana said, "His grief will be nothing compared to yours. Do not torment yourself on his behalf."

"He has lost his only son." Kaede could hardly speak.

Hana held Kaede and spoke into her ear. Her voice was very quiet. "He will not be sad. I promise you. He will be relieved."

"What do you mean?" Kaede pulled away slightly and stared at her sister. She saw dully how beautiful Hana still was, and regretted her own scars, the loss of her hair. Yet none of this mattered. She would have plunged into the fire again, torn out her own eyes to bring her child back. Since his death, she had come to rely completely on Hana, had put aside her suspicions and lack of trust, had almost forgotten that Hana and her sons were in Hagi as hostages.

"I was thinking about the prophecy."

"What prophecy?" Kaede recalled with almost physical pain the afternoon of the last day of the year at Inuyama, when she and Takeo had lain together, and they had talked afterward of the words that had ruled their lives. "The Five Battles? What has that go to do with it?" She did not want to talk about this now, but something in Hana's voice had alerted her. Hana knew something that she did not. Despite the heat, her skin was cold, and she was trembling.

"There were other words spoken then," Hana said. "Did Takeo never tell you?"

Kaede shook her head, hating to admit it. "How do you know?"

"Takeo confided in Muto Kenji, and now it is common knowledge among the Tribe."

Kaede felt the first flash of anger. She had always hated and feared Takeo's secret life: He had left her to go with the Tribe, left her with his child, which she had lost, almost dying. She thought she had understood his choice, made in the face of death when he was half out of his mind with grief, had forgiven and forgotten, but now the old resentment stirred within her. She welcomed it, for it was an antidote to grief.

"You had better tell me exactly what was said."

"That Takeo is safe from death, except at the hands of his own son."

For a few moments Kaede did not respond. She knew Hana was not lying to her. She saw at once how Takeo's life had been shaped by this, his fearlessness, his resolve. So many things he had said in the past made sense to her now. And she understood his relief when all their children had been girls.

"He should have told me, but he was protecting me," she said. "I cannot believe he will be happy that our child died. I know him better than that." Relief swept over her—she had feared something far worse from Hana. "Prophecies are dangerous things," she said. "Now this one cannot possibly come true. His son has died before him, and there will be no more children."

He will come back to me, she was thinking, *as he always has. He will not die in the East. Even now he is probably on his way home.*

"Everyone hopes Lord Takeo will have a long and happy life," Hana said. "Let us pray that this prophecy does not refer to his other son."

When Kaede stared at her without speaking, she went on, "Forgive me, older sister, I assumed you knew."

"Tell me," Kaede said with no emotion.

"I cannot. If it is something your husband has kept from you . . ."

"Tell me," Kaede repeated, and heard her voice crack.

"I dread causing you more pain. Let Takeo tell you when he returns."

"He has a son?" Kaede said.

"Yes." Hana sighed. "The boy is seventeen years old. His mother was Muto Yuki."

"Kenji's daughter?" Kaede said faintly. "So Kenji had known all along?"

"I suppose so. Again, it was no secret among the Tribe."

Shizuka, Zenko, Taku? They had all been aware of this, had known it for years when she had known nothing? She began to shiver.

"You are not well," Hana said solicitously. "Let me get you some tea. Shall I send for Ishida?"

"Why did he never tell me?" Kaede said. She was not so much angry at the infidelity—she felt little jealousy for a woman who had been dead for years—it was the deception that shattered her. "If he had only told me."

"I suppose he wanted to protect you," Hana said.

"It is just a rumor," Kaede said.

"No, I have met the boy. I saw him a couple of times in Kumamoto. He is like most of the Tribe, devious and cruel. You would never believe he is half-brother to Shigeko."

Hana's words stabbed her afresh. She recalled all the things that had troubled her about Takeo throughout their life together: the strange powers, the mixed blood, the unnatural inheritance embodied in the twins. Her mind was already unbalanced by grief, and her shock at this revelation distorted everything she had lived by. She hated him; she loathed herself for devoting her life to him; she blamed him for everything she had suffered, the birth of the accursed twin girls, the death of her adored son. She wanted to wound him, to take everything from him.

She realized she was still holding the sketches. The birds had made her think of freedom, as always, but that was an illusion. Birds were no more free than humans, bound equally by hunger, desire, and death. She had been bound for over half her life to a man who had betrayed her, who had never been worthy of her. She ripped the sketches into pieces and trampled them beneath her feet.

"I cannot stay here. What shall I do?"

"Come with me to Kumamoto," Hana said. "My husband will take care of you."

Kaede remembered Zenko's father, who had saved her life and been her champion, whom she had defied and turned into an enemy, all for Takeo's sake.

"What a fool I have been," she cried.

A febrile energy seized her. "Send for the boys and get them ready to travel," she told Hana. "How many men came with you?"

"Thirty or forty," Hana replied. "They are lodged in the castle."

"My own men are also there," Kaede said. "Those that did not go with him to the East." She could not bring herself to say *my husband* or to speak his name. "We will take them all with us, but let ten of your men come here. I have a task for them. We will leave before the end of the week."

"Whatever you say, sister," Hana agreed.

iki had waited all night on the riverbank for Maya to return. By dawn she realized that her sister had fled into the world of the spirits, where she could not follow her. She wanted to go home above all; she was exhausted and hungry, and she could feel the power of the cat, unleashed and all-demanding, drawing her energy from her. But when she came to the gate of the house by the river, she heard the screams of grief; she realized that the baby had died in the night, and a terrible suspicion grew in her, filling her with dread. She crouched down outside the wall, her head in her hands, afraid to go inside but not knowing where else to go.

One of the maids rushed past her without noticing her, and returned within the hour with Dr. Ishida, who looked shocked and pale. Neither of them spoke to Miki, but they must have seen her, for not long afterward Haruka came out and crouched beside her.

"Maya? Miki?"

Miki looked at her, the tears beginning to trickle from her eyes. She wanted to say something, but she did not dare speak, in case she voiced what she suspected.

"What in Heaven's name are you doing here? It is Miki, isn't it?"

She nodded.

"This is a terrible time," Haruka said, weeping herself. "Come inside, child. Look at you, the state you're in. Have you been living in the forest like a wild animal?"

Haruka led her quickly into the back of the house, where Chiyo, her face also wet with tears, was tending the fire. Chiyo shrieked in surprise, and started muttering about bad luck, and curses.

"Don't carry on so," Haruka said. "It's hardly the child's fault!"

The iron kettle hanging above the fire made a soft hissing sound, and steam and smoke filled the air. Haruka brought a bowl of water and washed Miki's face, hands, and legs. The hot water made all the cuts and scratches sting.

"We'll prepare a bath for you," Haruka said. "But eat something first." She put rice in a bowl and poured broth over it. "How thin she is!" she said aside to Chiyo. "Shall I tell her mother she is here?"

"Better not," Chiyo replied. "Not yet, anyway. It might upset her further."

Miki was crying too much to eat, her breath coming in sobs.

"Talk to us, Miki," Haruka urged her. "You'll feel better for it. Nothing's so bad it can't be shared."

When Miki shook her head dumbly, Haruka said, "She's like her father when he first came to this house. He didn't speak for weeks."

"His speech came back in the end," Chiyo murmured. "Shock took it away, and shock brought it back."

Some time later, Dr. Ishida came to talk to Chiyo about brewing a special tea to help Kaede sleep.

"Doctor, look who is here," Haruka said, indicating Miki, who was still huddled in one corner of the kitchen, pale and shivering.

"Yes, I saw her earlier," Ishida replied distractedly. "Don't let her near her mother. Lady Otori is overcome by grief. Any further stress could push her into madness. You will see your mother when she is better," he told Miki somewhat sternly. "In the meantime you must not be a nuisance to anyone. You can give her some of the same tea, Haruka; it will calm her down."

Miki was confined to a solitary storeroom for the next few days. She heard the sounds of the household around her as her Kikuta hearing increased in intensity. She heard Sunaomi and Chikara whisper to each other, subdued yet somehow excited by the death of their little cousin. She heard the terrible conversation between her mother and Hana and longed to run to them and intervene, yet she did not dare open her mouth. She heard Dr. Ishida remonstrate with her mother in vain, and then tell Haruka that he would go himself to Inuyama to meet her father.

Take me with you, she wanted to call out to him, but he was impatient to be on his way, wrapped up in many concerns, for Kaede, for his own wife, Shizuka, for Takeo. He did not want to be saddled with a child, dumb and unwell.

She had plenty of time in the long hours of silence and solitude to go over, in remorse, the journey with Yuki and the revenge the ghost woman had exacted on her mother. She felt she had known all along what Yuki's purpose was, and that she should have prevented it. Now everything was lost to her—her sister, her mother—and she dreamed every night of her father and feared she would never see him again.

Two days after Ishida left, Miki heard the sound of men and horses in the street. Her mother, Hana, and the boys were leaving.

Haruka and Chiyo had a brief, fierce argument about her, Haruka saying Miki should see her mother before she left, Chiyo replying that Kaede's mood was very fragile; there was no telling how she would react.

"This is her daughter!" Haruka said in exasperation.

"What is a daughter to her? She has lost her son; she is on the verge of madness," Chiyo replied.

Miki stole into the kitchen and Haruka took her hand. "We will watch your mother's departure," she whispered. "But stay out of sight."

The streets were full of people, milling in vague alarm. Miki's sharp ears caught fragments of what they were saying. Lady Otori was leaving the city with Lady Arai. Lord Otori had been killed in the East. No, not killed but defeated in battle. He was to be exiled, his daughter with him . . .

Miki watched as her mother and Hana came from the house and mounted the horses that were waiting outside the gates. Sunaomi and

Chikara were lifted onto their ponies. Men bearing the emblems of Shirakawa and Arai closed around them. As the group rode away, Miki tried
to catch her mother's eye, but Kaede stared straight ahead, unseeing. She
spoke once, giving some prearranged order. Ten or more foot soldiers ran
into the garden; some had blazing torches, others armfuls of straw and
dried kindling. With swift efficiency they set fire to the house.

Chiyo ran out to try to stop them, beating at them with feeble fists.
They pushed her roughly away. She threw herself on the veranda, wrap-
ping her arms around one of the posts, crying, "It is Lord Shigeru's house.
He will never forgive you."

They did not bother to try to remove her, but simply piled the straw
around her. Haruka was screaming beside her. Miki stared in horror, the
smoke bringing tears to her eyes as the nightingale floor sang for the last
time, the red and gold carp boiled to death in the pools, the art treasures
and the household records melted and shriveled. The house that had survived earthquake, flood, and war burned to the ground, along with Chiyo,
who refused to leave it.

Kaede rode to the castle without looking back. The crowd swept after
her, carrying Haruka and Miki with them. Here Hana's men were waiting,
armed and also carrying straw and torches. The captain of the guard,
Endo Teruo, whose father had surrendered the castle to Takeo and had
been killed on the stone bridge by Arai Daiichi's men, came to the gate.

"Lady Otori," he said. "What's happening? I beg you to listen to me.
Come inside. Let us reason."

"I am no longer Lady Otori," she replied. "I am Shirakawa Kaede. I am
of the Seishuu and I am returning to my clan. But before I go, I command
you to surrender the castle to these men."

"I don't know what has happened to you," he replied. "But I will die
before I surrender Hagi castle while Lord Otori is away."

He drew his sword. Kaede looked at him with scorn. "I know how few
men you have left," she said. "Only the old and the very young remain.
And I curse you, the city of Hagi, and the entire Otori clan."

"Lady Arai," Endo called to Hana. "I brought your husband up in my household with my own sons. Do not allow your men to commit this crime!"

"Kill him," Hana said, and her men surged forward. Endo wore no armor, and the guards were unprepared. Kaede was right—they were mostly boys. Their sudden deaths horrified the crowd; people began to throw stones at the Arai soldiers and were beaten back with drawn swords and spears. Kaede and Hana turned their horses and galloped away with their escort while the remaining men set fire to the castle.

There was some random fighting in the street as the Arai men escaped, and a halfhearted attempt to put out or contain the blaze with buckets of water, but a stiff breeze had sprung up; sparks blew onto roofs as dry as tinder and the fire soon took hold inexorably. The townspeople gathered in the streets, on the beach, and along the riverbank, silent in shock, unable to comprehend what had happened, how disaster had struck in the heart of Hagi, sensing that some harmony had been lost and that peace was at an end.

Haruka and Miki spent the night on the riverbank with thousands of others, and the next day joined the streams of people fleeing from the burning city. They crossed the stone bridge, walking slowly so Miki had plenty of time to read the inscription on the stonemason's grave.

The Otori clan welcomes the just and the loyal.
Let the unjust and disloyal beware.

It was the ninth day of the seventh month.

et me go with Lord Otori," Minoru begged as Takeo pre-
pared to leave for Yamagata.

"I would prefer you to stay here," Takeo replied.
"The families of the dead must be informed, and provisions arranged for the next long march. Kahei must take
our main army back toward the West. And besides, I have a special task for
you," he added, aware of the young man's disappointment.

"Certainly, Lord Otori," the scribe said, forcing a smile. "I have one request, though. Kuroda Junpei has been awaiting your return. Will you allow him to accompany you? I promised I would ask you."

"Jun and Shin are still here?" Takeo asked in surprise. "I had expected
them to return to the West."

"It seems the Tribe are not altogether happy about Zenko," Minoru
murmured. "You will find many of them still loyal to you, I suspect."

Is it a risk I can take? Takeo wondered, and realized that he cared little
about the answer. He was half-numb with grief and exhaustion, anxiety
and pain. Many times in the hours since Ishida had brought the terrible
news, he felt he was hallucinating, and Minoru's next words added to his
sense of unreality.

"It is only Jun; Shin is in Hofu."

"They have fallen out? I would not have thought it possible."

"No, they decided one should go and one should stay. They drew lots. Shin went to Hofu to protect Muto Shizuka; Jun stayed here to protect you."

"I see." Ishida had told Takeo briefly about Shizuka: how rumors spread that she had lost her mind after her son's death and sat in the courtyard of the temple of Daifukuji, sustained by Heaven. The idea of the stolid, silent Shin watching over her moved him.

"Then Jun may ride with me," he said. "Now, Minoru—I depend on you to present a faithful record of our journey to Miyako, Lord Saga's promises, the provocation that led to the battle, our victory. My daughter, Lady Maruyama, will be here soon. I charge you to serve her as faithfully as you have served me. I am going to dictate my will to you. I don't know what lies ahead of me, but I expect the worst: It will be either death or exile. I am relinquishing all power and authority over the Three Countries to my daughter. I will tell you whom she is to marry and what the conditions must be."

The document was swiftly dictated and written. When it was finished and Takeo had affixed his seal, he said, "You must put it into Lady Shigeko's hands. You may tell her I am sorry. I wish things could have been otherwise, but I am entrusting the Three Countries to her."

Minoru had rarely showed his emotions in all his years with Takeo. He had faced the splendor of the Emperor's court and the savagery of battle with the same apparent indifference. Now his face was contorted as he struggled to hold back tears.

"Tell Lord Gemba I am ready to leave," Takeo said. "Farewell."

THE RAINS HAD come late and were not as heavy as usual; a brief storm occurred each afternoon and often the sky was overcast, but the road was not flooded. Takeo gave thanks now for the years of careful development of the highways of the Three Countries and the speed with which he was able to travel, though, he reflected, the same roads were open to Zenko and his army, and he wondered how far they had advanced from the southwest.

On the evening of the third day, they crossed the pass at Kushimoto and stopped to eat and rest briefly at the inn at the head of the valley. It was barely a day's ride from Yamagata. The inn was full of travelers; the local landowner learned of Takeo's arrival and came rushing to greet him, and while he ate, this man, Yamada, and the innkeeper told him what news they had heard.

Zenko was reported to be at Kibi, just across the river.

"He has at least ten thousand men," Yamada said gloomily. "Many of them have firearms."

"Is there any news from Terada?" Takeo asked, hoping the ships might launch a counterattack on Zenko's castle town, Kumamoto, and force him to withdraw.

"It's said that Zenko has been given ships by the barbarians," the innkeeper reported, "and they are protecting the port and the coastline."

Takeo was thinking of his exhausted army, still ten days' march away.

"Lady Miyoshi is preparing Yamagata for a siege," Yamada said. "I have already sent two hundred men there, but it leaves no one here; the harvest is nearly due, and most of the Yamagata warriors are in the East with Lord Kahei. The city will be defended by farmers, children, and women."

"But now Lord Otori is here," the innkeeper said, trying to raise everyone's spirits. "The Middle Country is safe while he is with us!"

Takeo thanked him with a smile that hid his growing sense of despair. Exhaustion brought a few hours' sleep; then he waited restless and impatient until dawn. It was the beginning of the month, too dark to ride at night with no moon.

They were barely on the road, a little after daybreak, going at the fast lope that was easiest on the horses, when hoofbeats sounded in the distance. It was gray and still, the mountain slopes sporting their great banners of mist. Two horsemen were approaching at a gallop from the direction of Yamagata. He recognized one of them as Kahei's youngest son, a boy of about thirteen years old; the other was an old retainer of the Miyoshi clan.

"Kintomo! What news?"

"Lord Otori!" the boy gasped. His face was white with shock, and his eyes bewildered under the helmet. Both helmet and armor looked too large for him, for he was yet to fill out to his adult stature. "Your wife, Lady Otori . . ."

"Go on," Takeo ordered as the boy faltered.

"She came to the city two days ago, has taken command of it, and intends to surrender it to Zenko. He is marching from Kibi now."

Kintomo's gaze turned to Gemba and he said in relief, "My uncle is here!" Only then did the tears spring to his eyes.

"What about your mother?" Gemba said.

"She tried to resist with such men as we have. When it became hopeless, she told me to leave while I could, to tell my father and my brothers. I believe she will take her own life, and my sisters'."

Takeo turned his horse away slightly, unable to hide his shock and confusion. Kahei's wife and daughters dead, while their husband and father had been fighting to defend the Three Countries? Yamagata, the jewel of the Middle Countries, about to be handed to Zenko by Kaede?

Gemba drew up alongside him and waited for Takeo to speak.

"I must talk to my wife," Takeo said. "There must be some explanation. The grief, her loneliness, have driven her mad. But once I am with her, she will see reason. I will not be refused entry to Yamagata. We will all go there—in time to save your mother, I hope," he added to Kintomo.

The road became thronged with people, fleeing from the city to escape the fighting, slowing their progress, adding to Takeo's anger and despair, and when they came to Yamagata in the evening, the city was closed against them, the gates barred. The first messenger they sent was refused entry; the second was shot through by an arrow as soon as he came within range.

"There is nothing we can do now," the Miyoshi retainer said as they drew back into the shelter of the forest. "Let me take my young lord to his father. Zenko will be here on the morrow. Lord Otori should also retreat with us. He must not risk capture."

"You may leave," Takeo said. "I will stay a little longer."

"Then I will stay with you," Gemba said. He embraced his nephew. Takeo called to Jun, and told him to accompany Kintomo and see him safely reunited with Kahei.

"Let me stay with you," Jun said awkwardly. "I could get inside the walls after dark and take your message to . . ."

Takeo cut him off. "I thank you, but it is a message only I can take. Now I am ordering you to leave me."

"I will obey you, but once this task is complete, I will rejoin you—in life, if possible; if not, in death!"

"Till then," Takeo replied. He commended Kintomo for his courage and loyalty, and watched for a moment as he joined the crowds fleeing toward the east.

Then he turned his attention back to the city. He and Gemba rode a little way around its eastern side, halting beneath a small grove of trees. Takeo dismounted from Ashige and gave the reins to Gemba.

"Wait for me here. If I do not return, either later tonight, or if I am successful in the morning through the open gate, you may assume I am dead. If it is possible, bury me at Terayama, next to Shigeru. And keep my sword there for my daughter!"

Before he turned away, he added, "And you may do that prayer thing for me if you wish."

"I never cease doing it," Gemba said.

AS NIGHT FELL, Takeo crouched beneath the trees and gazed for a long time at the walls that encircled the town. He was recalling an afternoon in spring, many years before, when Matsuda Shingen had set him a theoretical problem: how to take the city of Yamagata by siege. He had thought then that the best way would be to infiltrate the castle and assassinate the commanders. He had already climbed into Yamagata castle as a Tribe assassin, to see if he could do it, to learn if he could kill. He had taken a man's life—several men's—for the first time, and still recalled the sense of power and guilt, the responsibility and the regret. He would put his detailed knowledge of the city and the castle to good use, for one last time.

Behind him he could hear the horses tearing at the grass with their strong teeth, and Gemba humming in his bearlike way. A nightjar thrummed in the trees. The wind soughed briefly and then was still.

The new moon of the eighth month hung above the mountains on his right. He could just make out the dark mass of the castle directly to the north. Above it the stars of the Bear were appearing in the soft summer sky.

From the walls that surrounded the city, and the gates, he could hear the guards: Shirakawa men, and Arai, their accents from the West.

Under cover of darkness he sprang for the top of the wall, misjudged it slightly, grabbed at the tiles, forgot for a moment the half-healed wound on his right shoulder, and gasped with pain as the scab parted. He made more noise than he had intended, and flattened himself, invisible, on the roof. He guessed the guards were jumpy and alert, barely in control of the city, expecting a counterattack at any time, and indeed two men immediately appeared below him with flaming torches. They walked the length of the street and back again, while he held his breath and tried to ignore the pain, crooking his elbow over the top of the tiles, pressing his right shoulder with his left hand, feeling a slight dampness as the wound oozed blood, not enough, luckily, to drip and give him away.

The guards retreated; he dropped to the ground, silently this time, and began to work his way through the streets to the castle. It was growing late, but the town was far from quiet. People were milling about anxiously, many planning to leave as soon as the gates were opened. He heard young men and women declaring they would fight Arai's men with their bare hands, that Yamagata would never be lost from the Otori again; he heard merchants bewailing the end of peace and prosperity, and women cursing

Lady Otori for bringing war to them. His heart twisted with pain for Kaede, even as he searched for some understanding of why she had acted as she did. And then he heard people whisper, "She brings death to all who desire her, and now she will bring death to her own husband, as well as to our husbands and sons."

No, he wanted to cry out. *Not to me. She cannot bring death to me.* But he feared she already had.

He passed among them unseen. At the edge of the moat he crouched beneath the clump of willow trees that had spread along the riverbank. They had never been cut. Yamagata had been unthreatened for over sixteen years; the willows had become a symbol of the peacefulness and beauty of the city. He waited for a long time in the way of the Tribe, slowing his breathing and his heartbeat. The moon set; the town quieted. Finally he took one huge breath and slipped, concealed by the willow's fronds, into the river, swimming beneath the surface of the water.

He followed the same path he had taken half a lifetime ago, when his aim had been to put an end to the suffering of the tortured Hidden. It was years since prisoners had been suspended in baskets from this keep; surely those grim days would not return. But he had been young then, and he had had grapples to help him ascend the walls. Now, crippled, wounded, exhausted, he felt like some maimed insect, crawling awkwardly up the face of the castle.

He crossed the gate of the second bailey; here, too, the guards were nervous and uneasy, both confused and excited by their unexpected possession of the castle. He heard them discuss the swift and bloody skirmish that had secured it, their surprise tinged with admiration at Kaede's ruthlessness, their pleasure at the rise of the Seishuu at the expense of the Otori. Their fickleness and narrow-mindedness enraged him. By the time he had climbed down into the bailey and run lightly through the narrow stone passage into the garden of the residence, his mood was fierce and desperate.

Two more guards sat by a small brazier at one end of the veranda, lamps burning on either side of them. He passed by so close he saw the flames bend and the smoke eddy. The men, startled, gazed out into the darkness of the garden. An owl drifted past on silent wings, and they laughed at their own fears.

"A night for ghosts," one said mockingly.

All the doors were open, and small lights glimmered in the corner of each room. He could hear the breath of sleepers within. *I must know hers,* he thought. *She has slept beside me for so many nights.*

He thought he had found her in the largest room, but when he knelt beside the sleeping woman, he realized it was Hana. He was amazed at the hatred he felt for Kaede's sister, but he left her and went on.

The air was stifling inside the residence; he was still wet from the river, but he did not feel cold. He bent over several sleeping women and listened to their breathing. None of them was Kaede.

It was high summer, barely six weeks since the solstice. Dawn would come soon. He could not stay here. His one aim had been to see her: Now that he could not find her, he did not know what to do. He returned to the garden; it was then that he noticed the dim shape of a separate building that he had not seen before. He made his way toward it, realized it was a little pavilion built above a tinkling stream, and through the sound of the water recognized her breath.

Here, too, there was a lamp burning, very faint as though it was about to consume the last of its oil. Kaede sat, legs folded beneath her, staring into the darkness. He could not make out her face.

His heart was pounding far more than before any battle. He let visibility return as he stepped up onto the wooden floor, and whispered, "Kaede. It is Takeo."

Her hand went immediately to her side, and she brought out a small knife.

"I have not come to harm you," he said. "How can you think that?"

"You cannot hurt me any more than you already have," she replied. "I would kill you, except I believe only your son can do that!"

He was silent for a moment, at once understanding what had happened.

"Who told you this?" he said finally.

"What does it matter? It seems everyone knew except me."

"It was a long time ago. I thought . . ."

She did not let him go on. "The act may have been a long time ago. The deception has been constant. You have lied to me throughout our years together. That is what I will never forgive."

"I did not want to hurt you," he said.

"How could you watch me swell with your child, always fearing I might bear the son who would grow up to kill you? While I was longing for boy children, you were praying to avoid them. You preferred to see me cursed with twin girls, and when our son was born, you hoped he would die. Maybe you even arranged his death."

"No," he said angrily. "I would never kill any child, least of all my own blood." He tried to speak more calmly, to reason with her. "His death was a terrible loss—it has driven you to this."

"It opened my eyes to what you really are."

Takeo saw the full extent of her rage and grief and was helpless before it.

"It is one more deception in a life that has been full of deceit," she went on. "You did not kill Iida; you were not raised as a warrior. Your blood is tainted. I have given my whole life to what I see now was a delusion."

"I have never pretended to you to be anything other than I am," he replied. "I know all my failings: I have shared them with you often enough."

"You have pretended openness while hiding many worse secrets. What else are you keeping from me? How many other women were there? How many other sons?"

"None. I swear to you. . . . There was only Muto Yuki, when I thought you and I were separated forever."

"Separated?" she repeated. "No one separated us, save you. You chose to go: to abandon me, because you did not want to die."

There was enough truth in this to shame him deeply.

"You are right," he said. "I was stupid and cowardly. I can only ask for your forgiveness. For the sake of the whole country. I beg you not to destroy everything we have built up together."

He wanted to explain to her how they had held the country together in harmony, how that balance must not be broken, but no words would repair what had been shattered.

"You yourself destroyed it," she replied. "I can never forgive you. The only thing that will relieve my pain is to see you dead." She added bitterly, "The honorable thing would be to take your own life, but you are not a warrior and would never do that, would you?"

"I promised you I would not," he said in a low voice.

"I release you from that promise. Here, take this knife! Cut open your belly, and then I will forgive you!"

She held it out to him, gazing directly at him. He did not want to look at her, lest the Kikuta sleep should fall on her. He stared at the knife, tempted to take it and slash into his own flesh. No physical pain could be greater than the anguish within his soul.

He said, trying to control himself, hearing his own stilted words as though they were a stranger's, "There are arrangements to be made first. Shigeko's future must be ensured. The Emperor himself has recognized her. Well, there are many things I wanted to tell you, but probably I will never have the chance to. I am prepared to abdicate in our daughter's favor. I trust you to come to some suitable agreement with Zenko."

"You will not fight like a warrior; you will not die like a warrior. How deeply I despise you! I suppose you will sneak away now, like the sorcerer you are."

She leaped to her feet, shouting, "Guards! Help me! There is an intruder!"

Her sudden movement made the lamp expire. Complete darkness fell on the pavilion. The guards' torches glimmered through the trees. In the distance Takeo could hear the first cocks crowing. Kaede's words struck him like Kotaro's poisoned knife blade. He did not want to be discovered here like a thief or a fugitive. He could not bear the idea of further humiliation.

He had never found it so hard to take on invisibility. His concentration had been fragmented; he felt as if he had been torn into pieces. He ran to the garden wall and clambered over it, crossed the courtyard to the outer wall, and inched his way up. When he reached the top, he could see all the way down to where the surface of the moat gleamed an ink black. The sky was paling in the east.

Behind him he could hear the pounding of feet. He lost invisibility, heard the creak of the bowstring, the thrum of the arrow, and half-dived, half-fell into the water; the impact knocked the breath from his body and made his ears ring. He surfaced, gulped air, saw the arrow next to him, heard others splash around him, dived again and swam to the bank, pulling himself into the shelter of the willows.

He took several deep breaths, shook the water from him like a dog, went invisible again, and ran through the streets to the town gate. It was already open, and people who had been waiting all night to leave the city were passing through it, their possessions wrapped up in bundles on shoulder poles or stuffed into small handcarts, their children solemn-eyed and bewildered.

Takeo was filled with pity for them, once again at the mercy of the warlords. Through his own grief he tried to fathom some way to help them, but there was nothing within him. All he could think was *It is finished.*

In his mind he saw the gardens at Terayama and the incomparable paintings, heard Matsuda's words echo down the years. *Come back to us when all this is over.*

Will it ever be over? he had asked then.

Everything that has a beginning has an ending, Matsuda had replied.

Now the ending had come suddenly but inevitably; the fine mesh of Heaven's net had closed around him, as in the end it closes around all living beings. It was all over. He would go back to Terayama.

He found Gemba still sitting in meditation on the edge of the forest, the horses grazing beside him, their manes beaded with dew. They lifted their heads and whickered at his approach.

Gemba did not speak, simply gazed on Takeo with his shrewd, compassionate eyes, then got to his feet and saddled the horses, humming all the while under his breath. Takeo's shoulder and arm were aching again and he felt the fever trying to take hold. He was briefly grateful that he was riding the gentle Ashige, and thought of Tenba far away with Shigeko in Inuyama.

The sun was rising, burning off the mist as they rode along the narrow path toward the temple, deep in the mountains. A kind of lightness came over him. Everything fell away beneath the rhythm of the horses' feet and the heat of the sun. Grief, regret, shame all dissolved. He recalled the dreamlike state that had descended on him in Mino when he had come face to face for the first time with the bloody violence of warriors. Now it seemed to him that he had indeed died that day and that his life since had been as insubstantial as the mist, a dream of passion and striving that was burning away in the clear, dazzling light.

higeko had made the slow journey back to Inuyama with the many wounded, including the horse, Tenba, the kirin, and the man she loved. Despite the desperate state of many of the men, Kahei had ordered them to wait on the plain while the main army returned to Inuyama, for the road was steep and narrow, and the need for haste was pressing. When the way was finally clear, she had thought the horse and the kirin would recover and Hiroshi would die. She spent the long day tending the wounded with Mai, and at night she gave way to the weakness of making impossible bargains in her mind, for Heaven and all the gods to take whatever they wanted but to spare him. Her own wound healed quickly. She walked for the first few days; it did not matter that she limped as their progress down the mountain track was so slow. The wounded moaned or babbled in fever, and every morning they had to dispose of the corpses of those who had died in the night. *How terrible even victory in war is,* she thought.

Hiroshi lay uncomplaining on the litter, drifting in and out of consciousness. Every morning she expected to find his limbs still and his skin cold, but though he did not seem to be getting better, he did not die. On the third day the road improved, the slope became less steep, and they began to cover more distance between dawn and dusk. That night they rested at the first proper village. An ox and cart were available, and Hiroshi was transferred onto it in the morning. Shigeko climbed up and sat next to him, holding water to his lips and keeping the sun off his face. Tenba and the kirin walked alongside, both limping.

Just before Inuyama they were met by Dr. Ishida, who had brought with him a train of packhorses, fresh supplies of soft paper and silk wadding, as well as herbs and salves. Under his care many men who would otherwise have died recovered, and though Ishida would make no promises to Shigeko, she began to have a faint seed of hope that Hiroshi might be among them.

Ishida's mood was grim, his thoughts obviously elsewhere. When he was not occupied with the wounded, he liked to walk next to the kirin. Its progress was slow. It was obviously ailing—its dung was almost liquid and its bones stood out like knobs. It was as gentle as ever, and it seemed to enjoy Ishida's company.

Shigeko learned of her little brother's death and her mother apparently driven out of her mind by grief; she longed to return to the Middle Country to be with her father. She was also profoundly concerned for the twins. Ishida said he had seen Miki in Hagi, but no one knew where Maya was. After a week in Inuyama, Ishida also declared that he had to go to Hofu, for he could not rest for thinking about his wife, Shizuka.

Yet they had no news, and without news it seemed foolish to risk traveling on. They did not know who held the port of Hofu, where Zenko was with his forces, or how far Kahei had advanced on his journey home.

The kirin, anyway, could travel no farther, and Hiroshi could only benefit from remaining in the city while he grew stronger. Shigeko resigned herself to staying in Inuyama until some word came from her father. She begged Ishida to remain with her and help her care for the wounded and the kirin, and he reluctantly agreed. Shigeko was grateful, for his company as much as anything. She made him relate all he knew to Minoru and made sure all the events, somber as they were, were recorded.

The moon of the eighth month was in its first quarter when messengers finally came, but neither they nor their letters were what she had expected.

They came by ship from Akashi and bore the crest of Saga Hideki on their robes, acted with great deference and humility, and asked to speak to Lady Maruyama herself. Shigeko was astonished—she had last seen their lord blinded by her arrow. If she had expected anything from him, it would have been a warship. She became aware of her looks for the first time in weeks, bathed and had her long hair washed, and borrowed elegant robes from her aunt Ai, for all her finery had been abandoned on the way back from the capital. She received the men in the audience room of the castle residence; they had brought many gifts, and letters written by Saga Hideki himself.

Shigeko welcomed them gracefully, hiding her embarrassment. "I trust Lord Saga is in good health," she inquired. They assured her that he had recovered from his battle wound; the sight of his left eye was gone, but otherwise his health was as good as ever.

She gave orders that the men should be entertained with as much lavish ceremony as possible. Then she retired to read what Lord Saga had written to her. *He must be making some threat,* she thought, *or seeking retribution.* However, the tone of the letter was quite different, warm and respectful.

He wrote that he deeply regretted his attack on Lord Otori. He felt the only strategy for a satisfactory outcome was for the threats to the Otori from the Arai to be eliminated; marriage between himself and Lady Maruyama would ensure that. If she agreed to a betrothal, he would dispatch his forces immediately to fight alongside Lord Otori and his great commander Miyoshi Kahei. He made no mention of his wounds. When she had finished the letter, she felt, along with her astonishment and her anger, something akin to admiration. He had hoped to gain control of the Three Countries first by threats, then by subterfuge, and finally by force, she realized. He had been defeated in one battle, but he had not given up. Far from it—he was preparing for another attack, but he had changed tactics.

She returned to the audience room and told the visitors that she would write a reply to Lord Saga the following day. After they had retired, she went to the room where Hiroshi lay near the open doors, looking out onto the garden. The scents and sounds of the summer night filled the air. She knelt beside him. He was awake.

"Are you in pain?" she said quietly.

He made a slight sideways movement of his head, but she knew he was lying—she could see how thin he had become, his skin taut and yellow over his bones.

"Ishida tells me I will not die, this time," Hiroshi said. "But he cannot promise that I will ever have full use of my legs again. I doubt I will ever ride a horse, or be much use in battle."

"I hope we never have to fight such a battle again," Shigeko said. She took his hand; it lay between hers, as frail and dry as an autumn leaf. "You are still feverish."

"Only slightly. It is a hot night."

Her eyes filled with tears suddenly.

"I am not going to die," he said again. "Don't weep for me. I will return to Terayama and devote myself truly to the Way of the Houou. I cannot believe that we failed—we must have made some mistake, overlooked something."

His voice trailed away, and she could see that he had slipped into some other world. His eyes closed.

"Hiroshi," she said in alarm.

His hand moved and closed over hers. She felt the pressure of his fingers; his pulse was beating, faint but regular. She said, not knowing if he heard or not, "Lord Saga has written, suggesting again that I should marry him."

Hiroshi smiled very slightly. "Of course you will marry him."

"I have not yet decided," she replied. She sat holding his hand all night, while he drifted in and out of sleep. They talked from time to time, about horses and their childhood in Hagi. She felt she was saying good-bye to him, that they would never be this close again. They were like the wandering stars in the sky that seemed to approach each other and then were swung apart by the inexorable movement of heaven. From this night on, their trajectories would take them away from each other, though they would never cease to feel the invisible attraction.

AS IF IN answer to her unspoken bargain, it was the kirin that died. Ishida, utterly distraught, came to tell Shigeko the following afternoon.

"It had been improving," he said. "I thought it had turned the corner. But it lay down in the night and could not get up again. The poor, poor creature. I wish I had never brought it here."

"I must go to it," Shigeko said, and went with Ishida to the stables by the water meadow, where an enclosure had been constructed. She, too, felt an overwhelming grief at the death of the beautiful, gentle animal. When she saw it, huge and ungainly in death, its long-lashed eyes dulled and filled with dust, she was seized by a terrible sense of premonition.

"It is the end of everything," she said to Ishida. "The kirin appears when the ruler is just and the realm peaceful; its death must mean all that is gone."

"It was only an animal," Ishida replied. "Unusual and marvelous, but not mythical."

Yet Shigeko could not rid herself of the conviction that her father was dead.

She touched the soft coat, which had regained some of its sheen, and remembered Saga's words.

"He will get what he wanted," she said aloud. She gave orders for the animal to be skinned, and for its hide to be cured. She would send it, along with her answer, to Lord Saga.

She went to her apartment and asked for writing materials. When the servants returned, Minoru accompanied them. For the last few days she had felt he wanted to speak to her in private, but there had been no opportunity. Now he knelt before her and held out a scroll.

"Lady Maruyama's father commanded me to put this into her hands," he said quietly. When she had taken it, he bowed to the ground before her, the first person to honor her as ruler of the Three Countries.

· 54 ·

From Kuba Makoto, to Lady Otori.

I wanted to tell you myself about the last days of your husband's life.

It is nearly autumn here in the mountains. The nights are cool. Two nights ago I heard the hawk owl in the graveyard, but last night it had gone. It has flown south. The leaves are beginning to turn; soon we will have the first frosts, and then the snow.

Takeo came to the temple with Miyoshi Gemba at the beginning of the eighth month; I was relieved to see him alive, for we had heard of the destruction of Hagi and Zenko's advance on Yamagata. It seemed obvious to me that no attack on the Middle Country could succeed while Takeo lived, and I knew Zenko would try to have him murdered as soon as possible.

It was in the middle of the day. He and Gemba had ridden from Yamagata. It was a very hot day; they had not come in haste, but in a rather leisurely fashion, like pilgrims. They were tired, obviously, and Takeo was a little feverish, but they were not desperate and exhausted as fugitives might be. He told me little about his meeting with you, the previous night. These matters lie between husband and wife, and outsiders cannot interfere. All I can say is that I am truly sorry, but not surprised. Passionate love does not die away, but turns to other passions, hatred, jealousy, disappointment. Between man and wife it can only be dangerous. I had made my feelings on this clear to Takeo many times.

Later I realized that what you had been told had been part of a long intrigue to isolate Takeo at the temple, where we have all sworn a vow to take no life, and where we are unarmed.

Indeed, the first thing Takeo did was to remove Jato from his belt.

"I've come to do some painting," he said as he gave the sword to me. "You looked after this for me once before. Now I will leave it here until my daughter Shigeko comes for it. It was placed in her hands by the Emperor himself."

And then he said, "I will never kill again. Nothing in my life should gladden me right now, but this does."

We went together to Lord Shigeru's grave. Takeo spent the rest of the day there. Usually there are many pilgrims, but because of the rumors of war it was deserted. He told me afterward he was concerned that people would think he had abandoned them, but it was impossible for him to fight against you. I myself was undergoing the greatest conflict I had ever experienced since I first made the vow never to kill again. I could not bear his serene acceptance of death. All my human emotions made me want to urge him to defend himself, to destroy Zenko, and you, too, I must confess. I struggled with this night and day.

Takeo himself seemed to have no conflict. He was almost lighthearted, though I knew he also experienced great sorrow. He was grieving for the loss of his baby son, and, of course, the rupture with you, but he had relinquished power to Lady Shigeko and he had put aside all desires. Gradually this heightened mixture of emotions overtook all of us at the temple. Everything we did, from the mundane chores of everyday life to the sacred moments of chanting and meditation, seemed touched by an awareness of the divine.

Takeo devoted himself to painting; he made many studies and sketches of birds, and the day before his death he completed the missing panel on our screens. I hope you will see it one day. The sparrows are so lifelike that the temple cats are deceived, and are often seen stalking them. Every day I half expect to see them flown.

He was also greatly comforted by the presence of his daughter, Miki. Haruka brought her from Hagi.

"I could think of nowhere else to go," Haruka told me. We had come to know each other well, years ago when Takeo was fighting for his life after the earthquake and the fight with Kotaro. I liked her very much. She was resourceful and intelligent, and we were all deeply grateful to her for bringing Miki.

Miki had been struck dumb by the terrible things she had seen. She followed her father like his shadow. Takeo questioned her about her sister, but Miki did not know where she was; she could not speak to him other than by gestures.

At this point Makoto laid down the brush for a while, flexing his fingers and gazing out onto the beauty and tranquility of the gardens. Should he tell Lady Otori what Miki had written down for her father and all that she had revealed to him about Maya and the baby's death? Or should the truth remain hidden with the dead? He took up the brush again; the new ink making the characters dark.

On the morning of his death, Takeo and Miki were in the garden. Takeo had started a new painting—of his horse, Tenba. Gemba and I had just come out to join them. It was around the first half of the hour of the Horse in the second quarter of the eighth month, very hot. The showers of noise of the cicadas seemed even more intense than usual. There are two paths leading up to the temple: the main one from the inn to the temple gates, and the one that follows the course of the stream, more overgrown and narrow, leading straight into the garden. It was up this path that the Kikuta came.

Takeo heard them before anyone else, of course, and seemed to know who they were immediately. I had never seen Akio, though I knew all about him, and I had known about the boy for years, and about the prophecy. I am sorry that I knew and you did not. If your husband had told you years ago, no doubt everything would have turned out differently, but he chose not to; in this way we build our own fate.

I saw two men come swiftly into the garden; beside the younger one loped a huge cat, black, white, and gold, the largest one I have ever seen. For a moment I thought it was a lion.

Takeo said quietly, "It is Akio; take Miki away."

None of us moved, except Miki, who stood and came closer to her father.

The young man was holding a weapon. I recognized it as a firearm, though it was much smaller than the weapons the Otori use, and Akio held a pan full of smoldering charcoal. I remember the smell of the smoke and the way it went straight upward in the still air.

Takeo was staring at the younger man. I realized this was his son—it was the first time father and son had set eyes on each other. They were not really alike, yet there was a similarity, in the texture of the hair, the color of the skin.

Takeo was completely calm, and this seemed to unnerve the young man— Hisao, he was called, though we will change his name, I think. Akio was shouting at him. "Do it! Do it!" But Hisao seemed frozen. He slowly put his hand on the cat's head, and looked upward as if someone was speaking to him. The hairs stood up on the back of my neck. I couldn't see anything, but Gemba whispered, "I can sense spirits of the departed here."

Hisao said to Takeo, "My mother says you are my father."

Takeo said, "I am."

Akio was shouting, "He's lying. I am your father. Kill him. Kill him!"

Takeo said, "I ask your mother to forgive me, and you too."

Hisao laughed incredulously. "I have hated you all my life!"

Akio shrieked, "He is the Dog—he must pay for the death of Kikuta Kotaro and so many of the Tribe."

Hisao raised the firearm. Takeo said clearly, "Don't try to stop him; don't harm him."

Suddenly the garden was full of birds, golden-plumed. The light was dazzling. Hisao cried, "I can't do it. She won't let me."

Several things happened at once. Gemba and I have tried to piece it all together, but we both saw slightly different things. Akio seized the firearm from Hisao, and pushed him aside. The cat leaped at Akio, fastening its claws on his face. Miki screamed, "Maya!" There was a flash and an explosion that deafened us, the smell of burned flesh, and fur.

The weapon had misfired in some way, had exploded. Akio's hands were blown off, and he bled to death within moments. Hisao was stunned, and had burn marks on his face, but otherwise seemed unharmed. The cat was dying. Miki ran to it, calling her sister's name. I have never seen a more awe-inspiring sight: Miki seemed to become a sword. The light blinded our eyes as it reflected from her. Gemba *and I both had a sense of something being severed. The cat dissolved as Miki threw herself on it, and when we could see again, Miki was holding her dead sister in her arms. We believe Miki saved Maya from being a cat spirit forever, and we pray for her rebirth in a better life, where twins are not hated and feared.*

Takeo ran straight to them, and embraced the dead girl and the living. His eyes were bright, like jewels. Then he went to Hisao and lifted him from the ground and embraced him, or so we thought. In fact he was reaching inside the boy's jacket for the hidden weapons of the Tribe. He found what he was looking for, drew it out and closed his son's hands over the handle. He did not stop looking at him as he drove the knife into his own belly, cutting and turning it. Hisao's eyes were glazing, and when Takeo released his hands and began to stagger, Hisao's legs also buckled as he fell into the Kikuta sleep.

Takeo dropped to his knees, next to his sleeping son.

Death from a belly wound is inevitable, hideous, and lingering. I said to Gemba, "Bring Jato," and when he returned with the sword, I put it to its last act of service to its master. I was afraid I would fail him, but the sword knew its purpose and leaped in my hand.

The air was full of birds calling in alarm, and white and gold feathers fluttered to the ground, covering the pool of blood that flowed from him.

It was the last time we saw the houou. They have deserted the forest. Who knows when they will return?

At this point the Abbot felt grief overwhelm him again. He gave way to it briefly, honoring his dead friend with tears. But there was one more matter to write about. He lifted the brush again.

Two of Takeo's children remain with us. We will keep Hisao here. Gemba believes that out of such great evil a great spirit can be born. We will see. Gemba takes him into the forest; he has an affinity with its wild animals and a deep understanding of them. He has begun to make small carvings of them, which we see as a good sign. We feel Miki needs to be with her mother if she is to recover, and I ask you to send for her. Haruka can bring her to you. She is already a great spirit, but she is very fragile. She needs you.

He looked out into the garden again and saw the girl about whom he was writing, silent, so thin she looked like a ghost herself. She spent many hours there, in the place where her father and sister had died.

He rolled the letter and put it with all the others he had written to Kaede. He had repeated the story many times, in many variations, sometimes revealing Maya's secret, sometimes putting noble words of farewell, to Kaede, to himself, into Takeo's mouth. This stark unembellished version he felt came closest to the truth. However, he could not send it, for he did not know where Kaede was, or even if she was still alive.

he leaves had fallen; the trees were bare. The last of the migrating birds had crossed the sky in long skeins like brushstrokes when Kaede came to Terayama at the full moon of the eleventh month.

She brought the two young boys with her, Sunaomi and Chikara.

"I am glad to see Sunaomi here," Gemba said when he came to welcome them. He had met Sunaomi the previous year, when the boy had seen the houou. "It was your husband's wish that he should come to us."

"There is nowhere else for them to go," Kaede replied. She did not want to say more in front of the children. "Go with Lord Gemba," she urged them. "He will show you where you are to live."

"Your daughter has gone into the forest with Haruka," Gemba said.

"My daughter is here?" Kaede said. She felt faint, and continued with difficulty, "Which daughter?"

"Miki," Gemba replied. "Lady Otori, come and sit down. You have made a long journey; the day is cold. I will fetch Makoto and he will tell you everything."

Kaede realized she was on the verge of breaking down. For weeks she had been numb with grief and despair. She had retreated into the icelike state that had sustained her when she was young and alone. Here in this place everything recalled Takeo with fresh clarity. She had, unconsciously, held the illusion that he would be here, even though she had heard the news of his death. Now she saw how foolish that illusion was. He was not here: He was dead and she would never see him again.

The temple bell sounded, and she was aware of the tread of feet across wooden floors. Gemba said, "Let us go to the hall. I will send for a brazier, and some tea. You look frozen."

His kindness undid her completely. The tears poured from her eyes. Chikara began to sob too.

Sunaomi said, fighting back his own tears, "Don't cry, brother. We have to be brave."

"Come," Gemba said. "We will get you something to eat, and our Abbot will talk to Lady Otori."

They were standing in the cloister of the main courtyard. Kaede saw Makoto come from the opposite side, almost running across the gravel path between the leafless cherry trees. The expression on his face was more than she could bear. She covered her face with her sleeve.

Makoto took her other arm and supported her, as he led her with great gentleness into the hall where the Sesshu paintings were kept.

"Let us sit here for a few moments," he said. Their breath was white. A monk came with a brazier, and shortly afterward returned with tea, but neither of them drank.

Struggling to speak, Kaede said, "I must tell you first about the boys. Zenko was surrounded and defeated by Saga Hideki and Miyoshi Kahei a month ago. My oldest daughter, Shigeko, is betrothed to Lord Saga. They will marry at the New Year. The whole of the Three Countries passes to Lord Saga, and will be united with the rest of the Eight Islands under the Emperor. Takeo left a will stating his conditions and Saga has agreed to everything. Shigeko will rule the Three Countries equally with him. Maruyama will be inherited by her female heirs, and Saga has promised nothing will change in the way we have governed."

She fell silent for a moment.

"It is a good outcome," Makoto said gently. "Takeo's vision will be preserved and it must mean the end of warlords fighting among themselves."

"Zenko and Hana were ordered to take their own lives," Kaede continued. Speaking of these matters had helped her regain her self-control a little. "Before her death, my sister killed their youngest son rather than leave
him. But I was able to persuade Lord Saga through my daughter to spare
Sunaomi and Chikara, on condition they be brought up here. Saga is ruthless and pragmatic: They will be safe as long as no one tries to use them as
figureheads. He will have them killed if there is any sign of that. They will
lose their name, of course—the Arai are to be destroyed. Foreigners are to
be expelled and their religion crushed. I suppose the Hidden will go un-
derground again."

She was thinking of Madaren, Takeo's sister. *What will become of her? Will
Don João take her with him? Or will she be abandoned again?*

"Of course the boys are welcome here," Makoto said. After that, neither of them spoke.

Finally Kaede said, "Lord Makoto, I want to apologize to you. I have
always felt dislike, even hostility toward you, but now, of all the people in
the world, you are the only person I want to be with. May I also stay here
for a while?"

"You must stay for as long as you wish. Your presence is a comfort to
me," he replied. "We both loved him."

She saw the tears spring into his eyes. He reached behind him and took
out a scroll from a box on the floor. "I have tried to write down truthfully
what happened. Read it when you feel able."

"I must read it now," Kaede said, her heart pounding. "Will you sit
with me while I do so?"

WHEN SHE HAD finished, she laid the scroll down and looked out
toward the garden.

"He was sitting there?"

Makoto nodded.

"And this is the screen?" Kaede rose and stepped toward it. The sparrows looked at her with their bright eyes. She put out her hand and touched the painted surface.

"I cannot live without him," she said abruptly. "I am filled with regrets and remorse. I drove him away into the arms of his assassins. I can never forgive myself."

"No one escapes his fate," Makoto whispered. He stood and came to face her. "I, too, feel as if I will never recover from my grief, but I try to comfort myself with the knowledge that Takeo died in the same way he lived, fearlessly and with compassion. He accepted that it was his time, and died in complete serenity. He is buried as he wanted to be, next to Shigeru. And like Shigeru, he will never be forgotten. Moreover, he leaves children behind, two daughters and a son."

Kaede thought, *I am not ready to accept his son yet. Will I ever be? All I feel in my heart is hatred toward him and jealousy of his mother. Takeo is with her now. Will they be together in all their future lives, will I ever see him again? Are our spirits separated forever?*

"His son tells me all the spirits are at rest now," Makoto continued. "His mother's ghost has haunted him all his life, but he is now free of her. He is a shaman, we believe. If his crookedness can be straightened, he will be the source of wisdom and blessing."

"Will you show me the place where my husband died?" Kaede whispered.

Makoto nodded and stepped out onto the veranda. Kaede slipped into her sandals. The light was fading; the garden was stripped of all color, but on the rocks next to where Takeo had died there were splashes of blood, dried to a rusty brown. She pictured the scene, his hands around the knife, its blade entering his beloved body, the blood leaping from him.

She sank to the ground, sobbing convulsively.

I will do the same, she thought. *I cannot stand the pain.*

She felt for her own knife, the one she always carried inside her robe. How many times had she planned to kill herself? In Inuyama, in her own home at Shirakawa, and then she had promised Takeo not to take her own life until after his death. She recalled in agony her words to him. She had urged him to cut open his own belly, and he had done so. Now she would do the same. She felt a rush of joy. Her blood and her spirit would follow his.

I must be quick, she thought. *Makoto must not stop me.*

But it was not Makoto who made the knife fall from her hands; it was a girl's voice crying from the hall, "Mother!"

Miki ran into the garden, barefoot, her hair loose. "Mother! You have come!"

Kaede saw with shock how like Takeo Miki had become, and then she saw herself in her daughter, at that age, on the brink of womanhood. She had been a hostage, alone and unprotected; she had been without a mother throughout her girlhood. She saw her daughter's grief and thought, *I cannot add to that.* She remembered that Miki had lost her twin sister and her tears flowed anew for Maya, for her child. *I must live for Miki's sake, and Sunaomi's, and Chikara. And of course Shigeko, and even Hisao, or whatever he is to be called—for all Takeo's children, for all our children.*

She lifted the knife and threw it from her, then opened her arms to her daughter.

A flock of sparrows alighted on the rocks and grass around them, filling the air with their cheeping. Then as if at some distant signal they rose as one and flew away into the forest.

ACKNOWLEDGMENTS

I would like to thank:

Asialink, for the fellowship that enabled me to go to Japan for twelve weeks in 1999/2000;

The Australia Council and the Department of Trade and Foreign Affairs, for supporting the Asialink program;

The Australian Embassy in Tokyo;

Akiyoshidai International Arts Village, Yamaguchi Prefecture, for sponsoring me for that time;

Shuho-cho International Cultural Exchange House program, for inviting me for a further three months in 2002;

ArtsSA, the South Australian Department for the Arts, for a mid-career fellowship that gave me time to write;

Urinko Gekidan in Nagoya, for inviting me to work with them in 2003;

My husband and children, who have supported and encouraged me in so many ways;

In Japan, Kimura Miyo, Mogi Masaru, Mogi Akiko, Tokuriki Masako, Tokuriki Miki, Santo Yuko, Mark Brachmann, Maxine McArthur,

ACKNOWLEDGMENTS

Kori Manami, Yamaguchi Hiroi, Hosokawa Fumimasa, Imahori Goro, Imahori Yoko, and all the other people who have helped me with research and travel;

Christopher E. West and Forest W. Seal at www. samurai-archives.com;

All the publishers and agents who are now part of the Otori clan around the world, especially Jenny Darling, Donica Bettanin, Sarah Lutyens, and Joe Regal;

My editors, Bernadette Foley (Hachette Livre) and Harriet Wilson (Pan Macmillan), and Christine Baker from Gallimard;

Sugiyama Kazuko, calligrapher, who passed away early in 2006.